Rebuilding Friendship Inn

ROMANTIC WOMEN'S FICTION

FIVE ISLAND COVE
BOOK EIGHT

JESSIE NEWTON

ISBN-13: 978-1-63876-153-2

Chapter One

Clara Tanner knelt in front of her daughter, pressing the busyness of the airport out of her peripheral vision. "Lena," she said. "Look at Mom."

The twenty-year-old clutched her stuffed elephant, her eyes blitzing all over the place. This man. That woman. The television screen with the news playing on silent, the captions running along the bottom.

Everywhere but at Clara.

"Lena."

Her daughter had been born with Down Syndrome. She possessed the chubbier cheeks classic of those with the mutated gene, and she was lovable, bright, and still very much a child. So much of her world had been upended in the past couple of weeks, and Clara reached way down deep for her extra reserve of patience.

"Lena, we have to get on the plane soon. I need you to look at me."

Lena finally brought her hazel eyes to meet Clara's dark brown ones. She gave her daughter a kind smile and reached up to brush her bangs back off her forehead. "It's like going to see Grandma. Uncle Reuben and Aunt Jean will be at the airport to meet us."

"Dad's coming," Lena said, and Clara nodded encouragingly.

She refused to make her voice higher pitched. She'd never talked to Lena like she was an infant. She had a disability; she wasn't stupid. "Yes," she said. "Dad's getting the pretzels you asked for. He's coming this time too."

Their whole family was making the move from Montpelier to Five Island Cove. Clara had arranged with Jennifer Golden to rent a house on the island. It waited in a sleepy, old neighborhood that Clara told herself would be perfect for all of them. It would be away from the news crews, the cameras, and the rumors. The house would offer them far more than protection; the new location, with a new address, would give them anonymity.

Neither she nor Scott would be looking for a new job. They'd managed to get the sale of Friendship Inn to go through with her mother's generous donation for the down payment. Scott's only remaining friend in Vermont had financed the loan. Otherwise, they never would've been able to do it.

As it was, he was probably putting their soft pretzels on a credit card right now. She'd have to figure out how to pay them off later.

Later.

The word ran through Clara's mind, as it had been one she'd been seizing onto for a while now. She'd be able to pick up the pieces of her life *later*, once she figured out where she'd be living.

She'd be able to provide a sense of safety and normalcy for Lena *later*, once they'd left Vermont and settled in the cove.

She'd be able to find a way to forgive her husband *later*, once all the dust had finally settled from the indictments, the bankruptcy, and the nervous looks from friends and neighbors.

"Here you go, Lena-Lou," Scott said.

Clara looked up at her husband and got to her feet, a pinch in her back telling her she was getting too old to crouch down. Her knees testified of it too.

Scott still made her world light up, and Clara turned away from him physically, almost wishing he didn't. His light hair made her think of California, and his blue eyes had spoken to her soul the first time she'd met him.

She clenched her arms across her midsection, feeling how much weight she'd lost recently. Only fifteen pounds or so, but it was enough to make her clothes baggy and her ribs a bit more pronounced.

Since she didn't have money to buy new blouses and shorts, she wore her old ones, the belt loop just one or two tighter than before.

Clara was a master at cinching everything tight. Life hadn't been horrible to her; she felt like she'd taken the good with the bad, rolled with the punches, and survived some of the worst storms. She'd been able to do so, because of the man at her side.

Scott Tanner had always given Clara strength. He was rational when she was emotional, and when he needed to vent, their roles reversed. He'd been kind and attentive to both Clara and Lena as the girl grew up, and heaven knew how many challenges the three of them had faced as they dealt with counselors, therapists, and doctors.

Lena's disability would challenge anyone, but when Clara had found out about the Down Syndrome, her first reaction had been peace. It would be okay. She and Scott could dedicate their lives to their daughter—who'd turned out to be their only child.

She'd felt like that *because* of Scott. The man had a larger-than-life personality, which had attracted Clara as well. From small-town Five Island Cove, where everyone knew everyone else, she'd been looking for excitement and adventure once she'd finally gotten out from underneath her father's thumb.

Scott had provided that. She'd fallen in love with him so fast, and she still loved him now, as she sat down in a hard airport seat a couple away from Lena. Their carryon luggage took up the space between them, and Scott sat to her immediate right, holding the cup of soft pretzel bites for their daughter.

Clara's thumb moved to her ring finger, where her wedding band should be sitting. She still hadn't put it back on. She wondered how she could learn to forgive faster. She puzzled through how to feel betrayed and broken and still in love with the man who'd done that to her.

She riddled through when she'd put the band back on, and how she'd feel when she finally did.

A few hours later, Clara's well of patience had dried up. They couldn't fly a car over from Montpelier. Couches and beds, all the Christmas decorations, the treadmill, even dishes had remained in Vermont.

Clara had the clothes, toiletries, and essential papers in her carryon, with more shoes, clothing, and other necessities in her checked bag.

Times three, that's what the Tanner family currently possessed. The rest of their stuff would arrive on a ship in four to six weeks, and that was only if Clara managed to find the funds to pay for it.

She couldn't look through couch cushions or strategically move money from one account to another. Not anymore. She had no couch, and the federal government had seized and frozen all of their bank accounts.

They'd gotten one back after the first couple of months, and without the help of a few kind souls in Montpelier who'd been Clara and Scott's closest friends, along with Scott's father, they'd survived.

Her phone chimed several times as Reuben maneuvered the SUV into the parking lot at the beachside condo where their mother lived.

The house which Scott and Clara had rented wouldn't be ready for another three weeks, and they'd been forced to ask for more help. A weight of exhaustion pressed against the back of Clara's skull, sending shockwaves of pain through her brain to her eyes.

She told herself over and over that it was okay. Everyone needed help at some point in their lives. She'd been there with meals, babysitting, and money for others over the years. Service brought her joy, and she needed to seize onto that word instead of the one that had been rotating through her mind lately.

"All right," Reuben said, pulling into an uncovered parking space. "This is as close as I can get you." He smiled at Scott in the front seat, his eyes moving to the rearview mirror to flash a grin in Clara's direction too.

She didn't want to seem ungrateful for the free ride, so she quickly curved her lips up. The cost to do so took the minute amount of energy she had left, so she moved just as rapidly to open the back door.

"Lena," she said across Jean, who sat in the middle. "Please come to the back and help with your bag."

The girl wouldn't, and Scott would have to ask her again. Jean would probably be the one to get Lena to do what she'd been asked to do, because Jean was gentle and powerful at the same time.

Clara glanced at her before she slid out, and she found the stress around her sister-in-law's eyes. Compassion filled her, making tears flood her eyes.

She couldn't hide them, so she simply let them fall down her face as she stood and faced her brother.

"Oh, come on," he said, his voice infused with kindness. He took her into a hug, and Clara clung to her big brother now as a forty-two-year-old the same way she had as a child. "It's not so bad here. Especially in the summer."

They shifted out of the way as Jean exited the car, and Clara nodded as she stepped away from Reuben. "It's not that." She grabbed onto Jean and hugged her too. "Thank you guys for helping us. It means so much to me. To all of us."

She couldn't see what was happening on the other side of the SUV, and it didn't matter. Clara didn't say thank you enough, and she needed to do better at that. Heck, simply the fact that Reuben thought she'd been crying about being back in the cove told her what her brother thought of her.

She told herself it wasn't a crime to be strong. She was allowed to have her own opinions, *and* to voice them. It wasn't her job to make anyone else feel good about their choices, though she could lend a listening ear.

"You're welcome," Jean said. "If you're dying here, come to the lighthouse."

"Or we'll help pay for a hotel room," Reuben said, his dark eyes filled with concern. He flicked a glance toward the back of the vehicle as the hatch opened.

"Mom," Lena said at the same time Clara wiped her face.

"Thank you," she said again. "We'll be okay. I'm okay." She took a deep breath, willing the oxygen to make the okay-ness she wanted to simply appear.

She wasn't sure if it did or not, but she was able to step to the back of the car to help Lena and Scott with the bags. Reuben and Jean came too, and the five of them towed their six pieces of luggage across the lot and down the sidewalk.

"I'm sure Kristen will have coffee waiting," Jean said.

"She's been cooking for a couple of days, I know that," Reuben added.

A hot meal sounded like a slice of heaven to Clara, but she said nothing. What she really wanted was a room where she could be alone. Where she could cry as much as she wanted. Where she could scream until her throat ripped and all of the negativity inside her fled.

Then, she'd be able to rejoin her family with a better attitude and without tears.

They went past the dog park, where a couple of pooches played with one another while a man watched, and on to her mom's building.

She wasn't sure she could take another step, and then she did. One after the other, she did.

Reuben reached the door first, and he twisted the knob. Or tried to. "Huh." He looked down and then over to Clara. "It's locked."

He reached to ring the doorbell, and the *cling-clang-clong* of it reverberated through the condo, loud enough for everyone to hear outside on her porch.

She didn't come to the door. No one called from inside.

Reuben's eyebrows furrowed at the same time Clara's panic rose. "Where is she? She knew we were coming. I texted her."

Clara leaned closer to the door, trying to edge past a huge bag they'd checked. "Mom?" she called.

No answer.

Frustration piled on top of Clara's already frayed nerves, and the scream she needed to let loose migrated up her throat.

"I'll check the patio," Jean said, leaving behind the luggage she'd been carrying.

Reuben leaned toward the door too. "Mom?" He tried

the doorknob again. "It's Reuben and Clara. Are you okay? We can't get in."

Clara dropped her carryon, her shoulder aching. Tears slipped down her face again, the thought of not having her mother for support as she transitioned her family from life in Vermont to life in Five Island Cove completely overwhelming.

And also selfish, she thought. But that didn't erase the fact that they couldn't get in the condo.

There was no relief from the heavy baggage and hot sun.

Her mother wasn't there, so that only left one question in her mind—and which she found in Reuben's eyes—where was their mom?

Chapter Two

Kristen Shields pressed the square of tissue she'd found in her pocket to the scrape on her knee. She hissed through her teeth, angry at herself for not watching the ground as intently as she should've.

Her and her bleeding heart—and now her knee. She'd just finished the appetizer tray for her children's arrival that evening when she'd seen the feral cat she'd been slowly taming over the past couple of months.

She'd grabbed the chicken cubes she'd cut up for her and dashed outside. Cats could move like ninjas, but with a little persistence and a lot of chicken, she'd managed to find the gray and white cat hiding out in the bushes lining the picnic area of the condo association, where Kristen lived.

She'd lured the cat down the decorative rocks to the beach and fed her the rest of the chicken. She'd even managed to give the cat a stroke or two before the feline had gotten startled and scampered off.

She hadn't been able to go through with getting the puppy she'd once said she'd take. She really was more of a cat person, and she'd been leaning feline for the past few months.

"Are you okay?" The male voice startled Kristen, and she very nearly stumbled again.

She looked up and away from her simple scrape—right into the navy eyes of Theodore Sands.

He lived in her community, and she'd seen him at a couple of the activities she'd managed to attend. She'd never spoken to him much, though sometimes their morning walks had her going out to the beach as he came in.

A nod. A hello. She knew him.

"Yes," she said with a sigh. "I was just feeding this cat, and my foot got caught in the rocks." As if a testament to what had happened, Kristen's ankle sent a spike of pain up her calf.

"I twisted my ankle and just went down on the one knee." She'd gotten up by herself too. No one had seen her, she was fairly certain of that.

Her chest heated, and she certainly hoped Theo had not seen.

Why? she asked herself. *Why does it matter if he saw you fall?*

Confused, she looked up at him. He was a handsome

man, Kristen could admit that. The moment she did, her heartbeat stuttered in her chest.

"Let me help you back to your place," he said, extending his hand toward her. Feeling dumb, Kristen put her hand out too. That was what one did when offered help, wasn't it?

His fingers slid along hers, and he froze. She did too, not sure why her blood had started popping and fizzing and bubbling.

She quickly pulled her hand away. "I'm okay," she said. "My kids will be here any minute. I was just trying to stop the bleeding, so I didn't have it dripping down my leg while I walked."

Theo's eyes slipped down to her knee. "I think it looks okay now."

"Yes," Kristen said. "I'm okay." She straightened and wadded up the bloody tissue, quickly stuffing it back into her pocket. She offered Theo a wide smile, hoping that would let him know he could move along.

He gestured for her to go first up the steps that led back to the picnic area. Kristen couldn't think of a reason why she wouldn't go that way, so she went. His footsteps came behind her, a fact that sent her pulse into a whirlwind.

"It's Kristen, right?" he asked once they'd both reached the top of the steps. He gave her a smile that seemed genuine and kind.

"Yes," she said. "And you're Theo." She glanced over at

him, finding him ducking his head as he smiled.

"Yes." They walked down the sidewalk together, and Kristen found herself taking in the glorious June evening. Somewhere in the distance, a dog barked, probably at the dog park on the other side of her building.

"Listen," Theo said. "I notice you go walking on the beach, same as me."

"Sometimes," Kristen said. Sometimes she went walking with AJ in the morning. Jean had been joining them this summer, as had Alice. Robin punished herself by running, and far too early for Kristen's liking. The older she'd gotten, the more sleep she'd needed. Especially since Joel's death, Kristen felt far older than she ever had previously.

"Maybe we could synchronize our walking schedule," he said, his silver eyebrows going up.

Kristen's mind screamed at her to say yes. Of course she wanted to go walking with Theo. He seemed interesting, and he was handsome, and she hadn't reacted to a man like this in a long, long time.

"There you are," someone said, and Kristen turned away from Theo, realizing she'd stopped walking. So had he.

Her son rushed toward her, pure panic on his face. He scooped her right into his arms, saying, "The door is locked, and we thought maybe you'd fallen inside." He stepped back and held onto Kristen's upper arms, his eyes searching for injuries. "Are you okay?"

"Yes," Kristen said, somewhat surprised at his worry.

Clara, Scott, and Jean came around the corner too, and Kristen's embarrassment doubled. "I just...saw that feral cat." She threw a look at Theo. "I'm fine."

He smiled, and his teeth certainly looked real. He ticked all the boxes for Kristen, especially as he kept her secret about twisting her ankle and scraping her knee. It was what toddlers did, and she really was fine.

"Clara's exhausted," Reuben said. "Do you have the key? I'll get the house unlocked and everyone settled." He focused on Theo for longer this time, his eyes harboring questions when he looked at Kristen again. "Then you can finish your conversation."

"We're finished," Theo said. "No intrusion." He waved his hand like Kristen's children's worry over her was nothing, but it sent a hot poker of embarrassment through her once again.

"I don't have my key," Kristen said slowly. Theo paused in his exit, and Reuben's eyebrows bushed over his eyes again.

"The door's locked," her son said. "The sliding door too."

"We'll have to call the front office," Kristen said. "I must've hit the lock in my haste to find the cat."

Reuben looked like he had something to say about her chasing down feral cats, but he held his tongue. Thankfully. Kristen didn't want to get into anything with him in front of Theo, and she had no idea what that meant.

"I've got a key," Theo said, sending shock through her.

"You do?"

He started walking again, and she practically leapt to get to his side again. "Yeah," he said. "I work in the front office sometimes. I can get in and get you a spare." He gifted her with another brilliant smile, and Kristen swore her muscles melted right off her bones.

"Mom?" Clara asked as they approached one another.

"Hello, dear." Kristen set aside her hormones, a bit surprised they worked after all these years. "I'm sorry about this. How was the flight?" She put one hand on Clara's shoulder while the other brushed the hair off her daughter's forehead. She looked one breath away from a complete break-down, and Kristen found Scott hovering back near the corner.

"It went well enough," Clara said.

"I'll only be a few minutes, Kristen," Theo said, touching her forearm. "Be right back."

"Thank you, Theo," Kristen said, and she watched him walk away for a few steps before she looked at her daughter again.

Everyone had gone silent, and a charge rode in the air she hadn't felt in a while. Her gaze moved from Clara's narrowed eyes to Reuben's, which held a calculating look. Jean wore a bright smile on her face, and it looked like she might start laughing at any moment.

"What?" she asked just as Clara opened her mouth.

She stopped, breathed again, and asked, "Who was that, Mother?"

"Theo," she said.

"He's running off to get your spare key." Clara made it sound like a scandalous thing to do.

"He said he works in the front office," Kristen said, stepping past her. She couldn't look at Reuben, so she focused on Scott and Lena. "Hello, my family. Sorry I locked us out."

"The door is locked," Lena said, her voice loud and blunt.

Kristen grinned at her. "Yes," she said. "It sure is. Is that a new backpack?"

"Mom bought it for the plane." Lena looked down at the bright purple straps. She adored anything with purple and glitter, and Kristen wished she hadn't locked the sticker book she'd bought for her granddaughter in the condo.

"Are you dating him?" Clara demanded, to which Jean burst out laughing.

Kristen almost twisted her compromised ankle, but thankfully, it held her. She gave Clara the best withering look she could. "No," she said. "Of course not."

"Grandma," Lena said, whose attention had wandered somewhere else. "Come look at this gray cat."

Later that night, Kristen finally entered her bedroom, the light off. She didn't reach to flip it on, because she needed the dark, quiet space. She closed the door behind her, glad everyone had found an acceptable place to sleep.

Scott had ended up going to the lighthouse with Reuben and Jean. They had an extra room on the second floor, and everyone could feel and see that Clara and Scott weren't really getting along.

That wasn't right. It wasn't that they argued or fought. They simply didn't speak to one another at all. Clara spoke *about* Scott, never truly looking him in the eye. Scott would say, "Clara has all of our important documents," and smile at her while she refused to look at him.

Kristen didn't know all the details and having Reuben and Jean living in the cove had taught her a boundary she couldn't cross when it came to her children's relationships. Scott and Clara got to decide how things functioned inside their marriage, and Kristen wasn't going to say anything about it.

Lena had taken the second bedroom, just on the other side of the wall from Kristen's, and Clara was once again sleeping on an air mattress in the formal dining room. Kristen had commissioned a barn door to section that room off from the rest of the condo to give her daughter some privacy, and it would be here in a couple of days.

Clara said she didn't mind. Kristen had seen so many

changes in her already, and while she'd thoroughly enjoyed this evening, their dinner, the conversations, and presenting Lena with the sticker book, her emotions had been through a garbage disposal.

She sighed as she sank onto the bed and removed her shoes. Theo had been fairly quick in getting the spare key to her condo, and she'd thanked him. He'd left without another word about synchronizing their walking schedules, but the thought hadn't left Kristen's mind, not even for a minute.

Her phone lit up the room, and Kristen looked at it. She'd put it on silent a while ago, and she hadn't bothered to check it. The only people who texted her were her Seafaring Girls—and any others they'd adopted into the group.

Jean was on the string, and Kristen had it on her list of things to do to ask the girls if she could add Clara. Her daughter would need the support this summer, and so many of Kristen's girls had been through hard things in the past several years.

Marriages, babies, divorces, new relationships, children graduating. The list went on and on.

She found over one hundred messages in the group thread from her girls, and she sighed as she tapped to read them. The arrow shot her back up to the last unread message, and she sucked in a breath as the words entered her brain.

Kristen was seen flirting with a very handsome older man outside her condo.

"Jean," Kristen murmured, stunned her daughter-in-law had tattled on her.

The thread had exploded from there, with everyone chiming in to know who it was, what was said, done, the whole nine yards.

"My goodness," she said, reading something she wished she could scrub from her eyeballs. "Alice."

Her thumbs started flying across her screen. *None of this is true. Yes, a man helped me after I twisted my ankle on the beach. It was and remains nothing.*

She sent the message and pressed her fingers against the corner of her phone to take off the case. There, a slip of paper fluttered to her thigh, and she shined her phone on it, the blue light illuminating the numbers there.

The name.

Theo.

She'd spoken true—she had twisted her ankle on the beach. A man had helped her. It was nothing, and it remained nothing.

At least until she got up the nerve to text him to let him know what time she liked to go walking on the beach.

Another message came in, and Kristen started typing again. This text would settle things once and for all, and nervous excitement fluttered through her stomach.

Chapter Three

Kelli Webb hated packing up her son and shipping him across the water to the mainland. Her ex-husband, Julian, would meet him in the airport, but her son had never made the trip alone. Last year, Julian had flown to Five Island Cove to get him, but this year, they'd agreed that Parker could fly by himself.

It was an hour at most, and the airline provided a flight attendant to watch over him. Still, Kelli sniffled as she folded one of her ten-year-old's T-shirts, rolled it, and stuffed it in his suitcase. She could go in and help him through security, so she could get the bag checked. Julian would be there to make sure they picked up the right bag.

Parker would be eleven soon, and he had grown about four inches this year alone. He acted more and more grown up all the time, and Kelli suspected he was secretly thrilled to be able to fly by himself.

She couldn't help worrying about him. He was her only child, and she'd been incredibly lucky to get him. She hadn't been able to get pregnant again, and in a lot of ways, Parker was her whole life. In others, he was only a small part of it.

She owned a yoga and nutrition bar in her childhood home on Bell Island, and she had plenty to do there this summer. She'd "barely miss him," as Julian had texted when Kelli had said she didn't know how to fill the hours without Parker.

Sending him to New Jersey every summer felt unfair, but she'd done it because she had to follow the custody agreement. It just felt like it would be nice to share the splendor of the cove with Parker during the best months of the year. When the skies were blue for endless days, and it felt like she could tip her head back and disappear into it simply by closing her eyes.

Right now, she wasn't doing any disappearing nor relaxing. She folded a pair of shorts she'd just taken from the dryer and crammed them into the suitcase too.

"Here are the socks," Parker said as he brought in an armful of balled socks. "Dad said he'd buy me new shoes, so I'm not going to take any."

Kelli looked down to his feet, but he wasn't currently wearing shoes. "What are you going to wear on the plane?"

"My tennis shoes." He dropped the socks on top of the

suitcase, letting them bounce and scatter wherever they may.

Irritation hinted through Kelli's bloodstream, but she said nothing. She'd rearrange everything anyway, probably twice, before she deemed the packing done. Then, they had to take the ferry to Diamond Island, where they'd meet Shad for lunch at a new restaurant that had just come to the cove, and then Parker had a late afternoon flight to the mainland.

"You don't want to take any flip flops?" she asked. "It's summertime."

"He said he'd buy me new shoes."

"Yes, but are they going to be flip flops? Or something you can wear to the pool?"

Her son looked at her, and she didn't have to look as far down. He wore the same frustration in his expression that she felt firing through her. "Do you want me to take flip flops?"

"Yes," she said. "You have no idea what or when your father will do something."

Parker rolled his eyes, but he left her bedroom to go retrieve his flip flops from the room next door. Kelli pressed her lips together and kept folding laundry. She'd much rather be sitting on the patio out front, smelling the sweet fragrance of the flowers as they grew and listening to the dull roar of the waves in the distance. Since the townhome where she and Shad and Parker lived sat up on one of the highest points of Pearl Island, she could see the ocean from her front patio.

She liked looking at the water but not so much going near it or in it. Her memories flashed to only a couple of weeks ago, when she'd gone out purposefully into a bad storm to rescue Jean and her Seafaring girls. She'd gone over a railing she would've never even approached as a teenager, and a new sense of strength filled Kelli.

Yes, sending Parker to New Jersey for the summer wasn't her favorite thing to do. But he was safe and cared for there, and she wouldn't have to worry about trying to fill the long summer hours with activities the way other moms did.

Her son returned with a pair of flip flops, and Kelli said, "Thank you, baby."

"Is Jean going to be at lunch?"

Kelli shook her head. "Nope. She and Reuben have a meeting today."

"About a baby?"

"I'm not sure," Kelli said, giving her son a glance out of the corner of her eye. "She didn't say. She just said she couldn't make it." She tossed a pair of folded shorts on top of the pile in the suitcase and turned away from the laundry. "She gave me this to give to you."

She moved over to her dresser and pulled a slim, blue-paper-wrapped package from the top of her dresser. "She said you could open it on the day you left." Kelli handed him the package and sat on the end of her bed.

He joined her and started peeling back the tape. "What is it?"

"I don't know. She didn't tell me." Kelli had gotten the gift a few days ago, when she'd gone to Diamond Island to visit Jean. She always took the ferry from Pearl to Bell to work, and more days than she didn't, Kelli then continued to Diamond Island to pick up her son from school. They'd stop by Shad's office in the city buildings, and sometimes Kelli would take Parker to the lighthouse.

He loved the lighthouse, but most of all, he loved Jean. Kelli found the world so unfair sometimes, and the fact that Jean couldn't have a baby was one of those wholly unjust things. She'd be such a great mother, and Kelli's heart beat out a thump of sadness for her.

Parker got the paper off the box, but it was plain brown without any markings. He looked up at Kelli, who gave him a smile of encouragement to keep going. He slipped his fingers under the edge of the box and lifted the lid. He sucked in a breath while Kelli was still trying to figure out what she was looking at.

"It's a pen." He jumped to his feet. "For my tablet. She got me that pen so I can draw on the plane." He grinned like he'd won a multi-million dollar lottery, and he ran from the room. "I'll show you!"

Kelli laughed quietly while she picked up the wrapping paper he'd left behind. She could always tell where Parker had been. Lights got left on, shoes and clothes and backpacks discarded, dishes left out, and apparently, wrapping paper floating to the floor. She also plucked a small card from the box, and when Parker returned to the room, she held it out to him.

"You should write her a thank you card too, bud."

"Okay," he said, and he wouldn't unless Kelli reminded him ten times and then sat down with him to do it. He held up the tablet. "Look. It pairs with it with just a press of a button. Then, I can write with it or draw with it." He showed her how the pen worked with his tablet, and Kelli wasn't a genius, but she knew that electronic pen wouldn't have been cheap.

She'd need to write Jean a thank you card too.

Her stomach bubbled, and Kelli said, "Read the card, baby. I have to go to the bathroom, and then we better get going." She hurried into the bathroom, but she barely had to go. She told herself over and over that it was just her nerves making her nauseous, and once Parker touched down in Newark and she got a text from him and Julian, she'd be fine.

The trip to Diamond Island was easy. Shad met them at the pier and he had a car waiting to take them to The Glass Dolphin. The restaurant was a little more upscale than where they usually ate as a family. It was more of a place where Shad would take Kelli for their anniversary.

The interior of the building held cozy booths that barely fit two people, as well as some bigger accommodations for groups. The lunch crowd was lively, and waiters and waitresses moved back and forth through the open, airy space. The building overlooked the water, so one entire side of it was built of only windows, and just like most restaurants in nautical locations, The Glass Dolphin had a gigantic fish tank with tropical fish motoring around inside it.

Kelli wouldn't want to be the one in charge of feeding those fish or cleaning the tank. She'd once thought having a pet fish was easy, but she knew better now.

"How did the packing go?" Shad slipped his arm around her, and she leaned into his strength and comfort. She hadn't expected to find another chance at love here in Five Island Cove, but she had. She and Shad had been married since late last summer, when she'd tied the knot with him in a near-impromptu wedding where Alice had married Arthur on the same day.

"It's done," she said while Parker ran off to look at the fish. She turned fully into her husband and wrapped her arms around him. "We're going to have a great summer, aren't we, Shad?"

He smiled down at her softly. "I don't see why not. Just me and you, the sun, the sky, the sand." He leaned down and kissed her. "I'll take a ton of time off work, and we can go do something. Travel. Go to Belize. I don't care."

She smiled at him too. "Belize. I've never been there." Kelli had never been outside of the US, in fact. Going to the Canadian side of Niagara Falls didn't count, at least in her book.

"We can kiss in every room in the house," he whispered. "I'll make love to you in the kitchen if I want." He grinned at her, and Kelli's blood heated at the very thought. "I'll help you finish up the back room at Whole Soul, and yeah, Kel. It's going to be a great summer."

"Mm." She ran her hands up the back of his neck, her fingertips lightly scratching the short hair there. "Will you make love to me on the beach?" she whispered.

"Anywhere you want," he murmured, kissing her again.

"We're ready for you," someone said, and embarrassment shot through Kelli. She'd never really been the type to kiss in public, and she disentangled herself from her husband and faced the hostess.

"Parker," she called, and her son turned back to her. She waved at him to come as Shad started to follow the woman with their menus. She put her arm around her boy and they went after them. "Be sure to text me when you get to Newark," she said.

"I will, Mom." He squirmed out from under her arm and jogged to catch up to Shad. He looked at the boy with a smile, and Kelli felt a bit removed from the two of them. Several paces behind, able to see them from a distance. Shad loved Parker, and Parker loved Shad. That had never been in question for her. Her heart sang at the sight of them, and Shad turned toward her once they reached the table.

He pulled out her seat for her, waiting for her to get adjusted before he sat down. "Thank you," he said to the hostess. They buried themselves in the menu, as they'd not been here before. The Glass Dolphin had only been open for two months, but the online reviews were great, and Kelli had heard from a lot of her clients at the yoga studio about how much they liked the salads here.

"Mango raspberry salad," she read, her mouth already rejoicing. She scanned the other ingredients—spring greens, lemon-cured green beans, a citrus vinaigrette, and dried apricots. "That sounds good."

"Can I get a grilled cheese?" Parker asked.

Kelli almost told him no. They could get one of those from a food truck outside the airport for far cheaper than here. She already felt out of patience though, so she simply nodded. "Get what you want," she said.

"I'm thinking short ribs," Shad said. "Did you see those?"

Kelli hadn't, because she hadn't made it out of the impressive salad section yet. Her phone buzzed on the table, and her eyes moved over to it automatically. Robin had texted, and Kelli abandoned the menu in favor of her phone.

There'd been some really juicy gossip about Kristen starting to date a man in her fifty-five-plus community.

Kristen had denied the allegations wholeheartedly, but Kelli had been messaging with Jean, AJ, and the others off the main thread.

However, this message had come to the main group feed, and Robin had said, *Who can come to my house for lunch tomorrow? I have a proposition for all of you...*

More messages had started to come in already, as Alice had said, *Proposition? This sounds scandalous. Need more details.*

No more details, Robin said. *I'll feed you for free, tell you about it, and you can decide.*

Sounds like you're going to sell me a timeshare, AJ joked. *But Asher and I are in.*

I'll be there, dear, Kristen said. *Can I bring Clara and Lena?*

Bring them, Robin said just as Jean confirmed she'd be there.

Kelli could definitely go if she rearranged a class at Whole Soul. She sometimes held herself back from her friends, but this time, she tapped out, *I can be there, but I'm voting with Alice. We need more details.*

All of my cop alarms are going off, Laurel said. *But I'm always down for a free lunch, so I'll be there.*

Only Eloise hadn't responded yet, and Alice had never truly said if she'd be there or not, but Kelli looked up as Shad said, "They're taking our order, hon. Do you know what you want?"

She glanced at him and then the menu she'd set down. "I'll have the mango raspberry salad, please," she said. Then she set her phone aside so she could enjoy her last lunch with Parker before he left for the summer.

Whatever Robin had up her sleeve could wait for a few hours.

Chapter Four

"I'm going to ask them tomorrow," Robin Grover said as she entered the kitchen. Her oldest daughter, Mandie, sat at the bar, writing something in a notebook. She didn't look up, and Robin would have to take a sneak peek at her daughter's musings later.

Duke, her husband, turned to her from the fridge. "That's great, babe. They'll say yes, right?"

"I think so," she said, stepping into his arms. "But it would be better if you could get all your fishing buddies to come help us move. These are my *girl*friends."

He wrapped her in his arms, and Robin counted herself lucky to be there. Not only that, but Duke would be home for the next two and a half weeks while they packed up everything they owned in the house they'd lived in for twenty years and then moved it into their new house. She'd once taken a lot of weddings to be able to make their ends meet, but she'd only scheduled a few events this summer. Duke had been to Alaska and back on his fishing boat once already this year, and he'd return the moment they were moved into their new house. Then, Robin would be a single parent for the rest of the summer, and Duke would return right before Mandie had to pack everything she owned and move it to New York City.

She was starting at NYU in the fall, and if Robin didn't think about it for longer than three seconds, she was fine. If she even allowed that fourth second to drag on, she got a little teary. She didn't want to act like that in front of Mandie, because she wanted her to think Robin believed in her. She did, of course. She was just going to miss her daughter a lot.

"I got the schedule worked out," Mandie said, and Robin turned out of her husband's arms to find her daughter holding up the notebook. "If we can get the bride out of the dressing room by four o'clock for the first wedding, then the second bride can take it at that time so she can be ready for her wedding at five."

Robin smiled at her daughter and rounded the island to see the schedule more clearly. "Have you called Tina to talk to her about this?"

"It shouldn't even be me doing this," Mandie said, her eyes shooting daggers at Robin as if it were her fault the wedding venue had double-booked. They'd called Robin yesterday to tell her the wedding she had booked there in only two more weeks wouldn't actually be able to be held there.

Mandie had taken the call, as she was working for Robin this summer. She also worked at the grocery store, and Robin was proud of her daughter for how responsible and hardworking she was. She'd argued back with Tina and said she'd make it work.

"The first wedding only has the building until four. That's why Tina booked us in the first place. We agreed to have the four to ten slot."

"We could call Laney and see if she'll move the wedding back a half-hour."

"All the printed materials have gone out," Mandie said with a shake of her head. "No. I'll call Tina in the morning." She snapped the notebook closed and got to her feet. "I found this new recipe in the produce section today, and I want to try it tonight. Is that okay?"

"Someone else cooking for me?" Robin asked. "That's always okay with me."

"Yeah," Duke said. "Me and your mom will go sit outside." He grinned at Mandie, took Robin's hand, and led her toward the sliding glass door that opened to their backyard. They sat in the swing, and Duke rocked them back and forth with a push of his toe.

"I am going to miss this backyard," Robin leaned her head against his bicep.

"Hon, our other place has a backyard nicer than this one."

"Yeah," she said. "But this one is full of memories." She could see all the birthday parties she'd hosted here for the girls. Mandie's graduation party. Anniversaries. Backyard barbecues before Fourth of July fireworks.

Jamie had loved it when Robin would stake down a long piece of plastic and spray it with the ice-cold water from the hose while she slid down it. She could hear the giggles, see the joy in their eyes, and feel herself wrapping them up in towels when they got too cold.

She smiled to herself, grateful for such a thing as her memories. They weren't all good, but she'd rather have the good with the bad than not be able to remember anything at all.

A sigh slipped from her lips. "I should tell my mom we're moving a few days early, right?"

"If you want," Duke said. "Clara would probably like to move in. Kristen, I know, would like her to be out of that condo."

Robin nodded. "I agree." She did, but she hadn't told anyone that Duke had come back from Alaska, and that they could honestly move into the house much earlier than she'd said. She wasn't sure why she'd withheld the information, but Kristen was bringing Clara to lunch tomorrow. They'd all know then.

She hadn't invited her mother to the luncheon tomorrow either, and she should probably do that too.

Her phone rang, and Robin took if from her pocket and glanced at it. The number on the screen was her business number, so she knew someone had called her secondary number, and it was being forwarded to this phone. She didn't want to answer it, because that meant a new client.

She was already fully booked for the summer, what with her move and trying to get Mandie ready to live in a big city —a huge city—alone in only a couple of months.

"You're not going to answer?" Duke asked, his voice soft and tender. She loved moments like this between the two of them.

"It'll be a new client." Robin lowered her phone to her thigh. "I don't have room for new clients."

"Mandie does," he reminded her. "I heard you guys talking about your schedule the other day. She wants to take on more clients."

"She can't take on clients of her own," Robin said. "I have to help her." Not only that, but Robin wanted her daughter to leave Five Island Cove. Yes, she was sad her daughter and good friend would be off experiencing life without her. At the same time, Robin didn't want Mandie to stay here for her entire life, the way Robin had.

She wanted more for her daughter, and if Mandie could take on clients of her own, and Robin taught her everything she knew, then what? Mandie would work with her or start her own arm of the event planning and never leave?

No, Robin told herself. She loved her life on Five Island Cove. It had been perfect for her. Mandie was destined for *more*, though. Robin wanted her to experience that more, and in the end, if she decided to come back to the cove, fine.

Her phone rang again, this time from a number she didn't know. She watched the number, trying to place it. The area code wasn't local, but it wasn't far either. "Nantucket," she said. "Or maybe New York."

"Answer it," Duke said. "It won't be a client."

Robin touched and swiped and then tapped the speaker. "Hello?"

"Hello, yes," a woman said, her voice rushed. "Is this Robin Grover?"

She looked at Duke and rolled her eyes. This was totally a new client. "Yes," she said wearily.

Duke's arm along her shoulders tightened, and she leaned further into him. That was his way of saying he'd help her, but she'd like to know how he could do that from a fishing boat off the coast of Alaska.

"Yes, hello," the woman said. She'd calmed already, and Robin could appreciate that. "My name is Madeline Lancaster, and I know this is a huge long shot. My son and future daughter-in-law have been engaged for almost a year, and they just found out that the venue they booked in New

York City can't accommodate their wedding. So I'm in a bit of a bind trying to find another venue."

"It's June on Five Island Cove," Robin said. "Places book up here too."

"I'm aware of that," she said. "That's why I asked Theresa Travis for your number."

Robin pulled in a breath and held it. "Theresa Travis gave you my number." She wasn't asking, and she silently prayed Madeline would say no.

"Yes," Madeline said.

Robin sighed and pressed her eyes closed. "Fine," she said as she exhaled heavily. "When is the date?"

"Next, uh, Friday night."

"Next Friday night." Robin's eyes came open. "You have to be joking."

The woman laughed, but it sounded a touch manic. "I wish I was, trust me. My daughter-in-law is in tears; my son is raving and ranting. I'm the new manager at The Glass Dolphin, and I've already gotten permission to be able to cater the wedding. Not all of their guests will be able to come now, what with the location change, but if you could get us a venue, some flowers, some decent décor... They'll take anything at this point. A beach, if possible, with some dressing rooms, even if they're tents. I have some friends who are coming to help, and we can tie bows, make table centerpieces, anything you need."

Someone else spoke on Madeline's end of the line, so

Robin didn't launch right into her spiel about setting up an appointment to meet and go over everything. She'd have to get on the phone the moment she hung with Madeline to find a venue that wasn't being used in only eight days, on the weekend, in the evening.

She honestly wasn't a miracle worker, but if she could pull this off, she'd be as close as anyone ever had.

"Theresa says she can mobilize some women too," Madeline said. "We just need your genius and the supplies. You tell us what to do, and we'll do it."

"You're with Theresa right now?"

"Yes," Madeline said.

Robin sat up, away from Duke's body. "Okay, number one, Madeline, I need to see you and if at all possible, your son and daughter-in-law first thing in the morning. Number two, you tell Theresa this squares us. I don't owe her anything after this."

"If you can pull it off!" Theresa yelled, and Robin heard her loud and clear.

"Oh, I'll pull it off," she said. "Madeline, can you come by around eight? I have another client call at nine, and then a luncheon I'm doing."

"I'll be there when you tell me to be there," Madeline said. "And yes, my son and daughter-in-law will be with me."

"Great," Robin said. She recited her address, and then

said, “I’ll start pulling some strings, and hopefully I’ll have good news for you in the morning.”

The call ended, and Robin wanted to chuck her phone toward the dormant firepit. “Theresa Travis,” she muttered.

“Hey,” Duke said. “Look at it this way. She’s been holding that favor over your head for five years. Now, it’ll be done.”

“Done?” Robin practically screeched. “Where am I going to find a wedding venue that will allow dinner, dancing, and have dressing rooms—oh, oh the beach—for next Friday night?” She shook her head, because she knew every venue in the cove. They weren’t all on Diamond Island either, and Robin’s mind buzzed and boiled.

Then she picked up her phone and started texting. A challenge had just been thrown down, and Robin had never shied away from one of those. She wasn’t going to start now.

Chapter Five

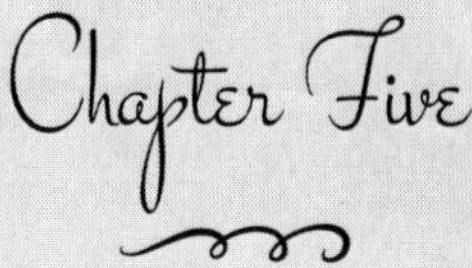

Alice Rice glared as Charlie reached over to adjust the volume on the radio. “I said—leave it.”

“I love this song,” he said.

Part of her wanted to tattle on him to her husband, who rode in the back seat with Ginny. Turned out, Arthur didn’t super-love road trips, and his motion sickness had reared its ugly head several times on the trip out west.

“It’s too loud,” Alice said, using the buttons on the steering wheel to lower the volume again. “We’re trying to talk.”

“There’s an elk!” Ginny yelled. Alice startled, the adrenaline in her spiking and causing her to stomp on the brake pedal.

“Where?” Charlie asked, his attention now out his window.

"It's a moose," Ginny said. "Mom, a *moose.*" She carried wonder in her voice, and Alice grinned at her daughter in the rearview mirror. Ginny wasn't looking at her, of course. Her eyes were glued to the wildlife beyond the rented SUV, and Charlie practically leaned out the window.

"I'll pull over," she said, maneuvering the vehicle off the narrow, winding road in Yellowstone National Park. When she'd first suggested the trip to the twins, neither of them had seemed terribly excited about it. She'd kept bringing it up, and since the twins had lived on the East Coast for their whole lives, they had never seen mountains like the Rockies or the Grand Tetons.

Ginny had been especially touched by the wide open sky and the big spaces in Utah, Wyoming, and Montana. They'd been on the road for four days now, with four more to go before they returned to Five Island Cove and real life.

Alice had a case to settle then, and she'd agreed to help Robin move into her house literally three days after her return to the cove. Not only that, but Clara would be moving on the very same day, and Alice's back and shoulders already ached from phantom boxes she hadn't carried yet.

"I've never seen a moose before," Charlie said as they all got out of the car.

"You have to be quiet," Ginny said. She threw him a dirty look, to which he gave her a glare back.

"I'm quiet."

"I'm pretty sure you singlehandedly scared away those deer."

To Charlie's credit, he didn't respond. Alice gave Ginny a look too, but she was already focused on the moose.

"Mama," she whispered. "There's two of them." They joined the crowd of onlookers already assembled, and Alice could plainly see the two moose down in the stream. The bigger of the two moved as if in slow motion, and Alice herself was mesmerized by them.

Arthur came up beside her and took her hand in his. "They're magnificent," she said, plenty of awe in her voice. "Have you ever seen anything like this?"

They'd said that a lot in the past four days, but Alice truly hadn't. She hadn't traveled growing up, and then she'd been so focused on keeping up with everyone in the Hamptons that she hadn't had time to experience the wilderness. She wasn't even sure places like this existed on the Eastern Seaboard.

"No," Arthur said. "This is amazing." His fingers around hers tightened, and Alice squeezed back. She'd booked two rooms for them everywhere they'd been. They'd spent two days in Jackson Hole, but they now had a couple of cabins just outside the west entrance to the National Park.

They stood there for a long time watching the moose. People came and went, and a couple of park rangers came to make sure the people and the animals stayed safe. Eventually

Alice realized the time, and she reached over to touch Ginny's arm.

"If you want to be at the hot pots when they boil, we need to go."

She nodded and turned away from the moose. Alice looked over to Charlie, who seemed as equally awed and peaceful. "Charlie," she said. "We're leaving."

He came toward her too, and he hugged her arm in both of his hands. "This is incredible, Mom. Thanks for bringing us on this trip."

"You're welcome." She leaned her head against his shoulder briefly. "You're getting along with Ginny, aren't you?"

"For the most part," he said, and they both watched the girl walking several paces ahead of them. "She stays up all night talking to Ray. It annoyed me last night, so we're not on the best of terms today."

Alice said nothing, but a frown came to her face. "I'll talk to her."

"Let me," Arthur said, and Alice looked over to him. Their eyes met, and she nodded. Arthur had a way of saying things that Ginny heard far more clearly than when Alice said them. She'd told him about her choice in colleges and that she'd accepted her place at NYU before she'd told Alice.

Her ribs seemed to cave in around her heart, but Alice drew a deep breath and pushed them back out. She'd loved having her twins. Two babies at the same time had been difficult, but they'd always had each other growing up. They'd never been alone, and Alice had enjoyed raising them, connecting to them in different ways, and being their mother.

It hadn't occurred to her until this year that she'd lose them both at the same time too. She wasn't as emotional as Robin was about Mandie going off to college, but she did worry about Ginny and Charlie. For very different reasons, but she worried nonetheless.

They were both going to NYU. They both had dorms with people they'd never met before. Ginny would thrive on the responsibility of getting herself to class. She'd keep her space clean. If anything, she'd be the one driving her roommate nuts about how much trash she'd allow in the tiny dorms, and she'd be the one down the hall in the community kitchen making lunch and dinner while everyone else went out to eat.

Charlie on the other hand... Alice worried he wouldn't be happy in a university setting. He'd never really liked school that much, outside of chemistry classes. He liked to sleep late, but Alice reminded herself every time she started to list some of Charlie's lazier qualities of just how good her son was.

He'd told his friends they couldn't come to the house if they brought pot. He'd broken up with his girlfriend instead of sleeping with her. He'd talked to Alice about everything, and he'd said some things against his father that had been extremely difficult for him to admit.

He held a lot of strength inside him, and Alice told herself not to doubt him.

"All right," she said once they were all buckled back into the car. "Hot pots, and then to the lodge for our chuck-wagon dinner."

"Is it by Old Faithful?" Charlie asked. "I want to see that go off again."

"Can we hike out to Swan Lake tomorrow?" Ginny asked.

Alice barley knew which twin to answer. "Yes," she said to Charlie. "Dinner is near Old Faithful. I'm sure we'll get to see it." She looked over her shoulder to check for traffic. Transportation around this park was no joke, and they'd already been caught in a herd of buffalo, two traffic jams, and plenty of slow-downs.

"I'm not sure what we're doing tomorrow," she said to Ginny. "We'll decide when we get back to the cabins tonight."

"It's card game night," Arthur added, to which both twins groaned. They talked over one another about how tired they were, and they couldn't possibly play card games after the hot pots, the dinner, and the drive.

"Oh, we're playing," Arthur said, undeterred. His grin filled the car with sunshine and love. "Charlie has to defend his win, or maybe a new leader will arise."

Alice giggled, and she wished Arthur rode up front with her so she could hold his hand. She absolutely adored him, and she was so glad her life had taken such a sharp turn a few years ago when Joel Shields had died and she'd come back to the cove.

LATER THAT NIGHT, WHILE ARTHUR AND THE twins yelled and laughed over cards, Alice made hot chocolate and coffee to take outside to the picnic tables behind the cabins. The sun had started to set, and the sound of crickets filled the air. She set mugs on the table and dang near got elbowed by Charlie as he slapped a card onto the table.

"I'm never fast enough," Ginny complained, but she wore a smile on her face. Arthur just laughed and laughed as Charlie pushed all the cards toward his sister.

"Hot drinks," she warned, and then she sat on the end of the bench on Arthur's side and looked at her phone.

I found the perfect place for that last-minute wedding, Robin had texted. Alice smiled, because she loved Robin to the core. No, they didn't always get along. If there was anyone who rubbed Alice the complete wrong way sometimes, it was Robin. At the same time, Alice could simply look at Robin and have a complete conversation without a single word being spoken.

They worried in similar ways, and they had children the

same age, which had bonded them further since Alice had moved to the cove.

Several of the other women chimed in to congratulate Robin, and Kristen asked her where the wedding would take place.

Tower Heights Beach, Robin said. *On Pearl Island. I know it's a lot to ask, but Mandie and I would love some help with the decorations on Thursday night and Friday morning.*

Alice was returning from her trip out west on Tuesday night, and she quickly thumbed out that she'd be there to help. *I can maybe bring the twins too*, she said. Both Charlie and Ginny had jobs, and Alice didn't have their schedules memorized. If they were available, she'd somehow get them to come help.

She realized the card game had quieted, and she glanced down the table. Only Ginny sat there, and she asked, "Where did Arthur and Charlie go?"

"Charlie heard an ice cream truck." Ginny rolled her eyes and went right back to her phone. Her fingers flew over the screen, and she wore a small smile that told Alice she was texting Ray.

"Ginny," she said. She placed her own phone face-down on the picnic table. She took a deep breath of the clear, pine-scented air and looked at her daughter. It took Ginny several seconds to finish her conversation and focus on Alice. "You're not staying up too late talking to him, are you?"

Ginny blinked. "Charlie tattled on me."

"He couldn't sleep last night."

Ginny practically growled. "Yeah, well, he's talking to Mandie day and night."

Alice wanted to roll her eyes, but she didn't. Charlie and Mandie had dated for a while, and yes, Alice knew he still liked her. They talked a lot, and Robin and Alice had decided their children were adults, and they could figure things out on their own.

"Besides," Ginny said. "It's not Ray anyway. I was actually texting Emily."

Alice could find out simply by holding out her hand. That would be a silent request for Ginny to put the phone in her palm so Alice could see. Instead, she said, "How's she doing?" Ginny's best friend had been living with them for the past few months, and Alice had seriously considered bringing her on this trip. In the end, it hadn't felt right, and since Emily didn't want to be alone in the house, she'd gone to stay with Laurel.

"Okay," Ginny said with a sigh. Something troubled her, but Alice didn't ask. Ginny would usually volunteer the information when she was ready. Almost a full minute passed in silence, the two of them looking out toward the woods that bordered the cabins. "Mom?"

"Yeah?" She looked over to Ginny, who continued to gaze at tree trunks and who knew what else.

"Were you scared to go to college?"

"Terrified," Alice said with a smile. "Excited too. But yeah, scared. Everyone is. It's normal."

"Charlie doesn't seem to be."

"Charlie shows his nerves in different ways," Alice said. "That's all."

"Dad asked us if he could help us move in," Ginny said next.

That brought Alice's attention away from the forest. "Oh?" She'd tried to be as neutral as possible when it came to her ex-husband. "He asked both of you?"

She nodded. "In our twin text thread."

"You don't talk to him a lot, do you?"

Ginny shook her head. "Not really. He seems to be texting more lately, though."

Alice didn't like that, because Frank didn't do much without some sort of motive. Something in it for him. "He can come help you move in," she said. "He's your father, and he probably wants to see where you'll be living."

Knowing him, he'd probably leave with a college-age date. Alice pushed the poisonous thoughts from her head. After all, she didn't have to deal with Frank Kelton on a daily basis anymore, and she had a wonderful, loving husband who didn't cheat on her.

"Okay," Ginny said, "I'll tell him."

Alice's phone chimed and Arthur said, "We got you pineapple sherbet," at the same time. She took the frozen treat from him, gave him a smile, and then looked down at her phone, expecting to see more of the conversation about the wedding.

Robin had sent a few more pictures of the centerpieces and décor for the wedding, but this message wasn't about the wedding.

It had come from Kristen and she'd said, *I went walking with Theodore Sands this morning, and...he held my hand.*

Alice gasped, her fingers dropping the popsicle in favor of her phone. She needed to be in the cove right now for an emergency meeting of the Seafaring Girls and all the women they'd added to their fold over the past few years.

This was *huge* news.

I wasn't going to tell anyone, Kristen said to the empty chat. Alice couldn't believe no one had responded in the time it had taken her between messages. Perhaps they were all as stunned as she was.

At least not for a while. But I don't know what I'm doing.

I need help.

Alice stared at the words, wondering if she should be the first to respond. If so, what would she say? She certainly had no advice for Kristen as to how to proceed with Theodore Sands.

That's great, Kristen, Eloise said. *Maybe when Alice gets back, we can all go to lunch and talk about what you're unsure of. Brainstorm some things.*

Alice loved Eloise so much in that moment. If she'd been in the cove, she'd have suggested they get together for breakfast the very next day. She didn't want to be left out of this very important conversation, but she was on vacation with her family.

I'm shocked, Robin said. *Not about Theo, but that you lied to us. Not a week ago, you said this was nothing.*

It was nothing a week ago, Kristen said.

Sure, AJ sent. *I believe her. (Not.)* She added a smiley face, and Alice simply watched the conversation as it continued.

In a lull, she typed out, *I think this is great, Kristen. I'd love to be there for the brainstorming, but I get it if you guys want to talk before I get back.*

I can wait, Kristen said. *He's going to Nantucket to visit his son tomorrow, and he won't be back until after the wedding.*

So we've got time, Robin said.

Yes, Kristen said. *Plenty of time.*

We haven't gotten any pictures from Yellowstone today, Kelli said, and again, Alice's heart warmed with love for her friends.

We saw two moose today, Alice tapped out and sent. *You guys simply have to come to Yellowstone. There's nothing like it.*

She sent the pictures, and the conversation wove and meandered, eventually dying out as she was two hours behind them and their bedtimes had come and gone.

She sent Kristen a text just for her eyes, and she said, *I'm excited for you, Kristen. Love can be found at any stage of life, and yeah. I'm excited for you.*

Thank you, dear, Kristen responded. *I'll be excited when Clara gets into her own house. Haha.*

She'd added the laughing, but Alice knew she wasn't really enjoying having her daughter staying with her. *Tell me more about Theo,* Alice said. *Do I need to do a background check on him?*

She smiled at her phone while the twins and Arthur started another rowdy game of cards, and while Alice really loved being there with them, she also couldn't wait to get back to Five Island Cove and all the drama unfolding there.

Chapter Six

Clara stepped off the ferry first and turned back to help Lena. It wasn't really a ferry, but a semi-tugboat that seemed one or two chugs away from dying. She, Scott, and Lena loaded up every morning and met the boat captain, a man by the name of Ryan Balincia, at the Sanctuary Island pier.

That did require an actual ferry ride from Diamond Island, and Clara had to grit her teeth against the long travel times around the cove every single day. She'd forgotten that everything took so long here, because cars couldn't swim.

Scott always brought up the rear, because he spent the fifteen-minute boat ride from Sanctuary Island to Friendship Island jawing with the captain. Clara spent it centering herself, listening to the wind, and going through her to-do list for the day.

Every day, the tasks she needed to accomplish went on and on, and she simply did the best she could. Today, she was expecting to find the general contractor on-site, as he'd promised her he'd be there that day. She'd been hounding him via text for a week now, ever since the first day her little family of three had started here on the inn.

They couldn't do much if they couldn't get the building to pass safety inspections. She'd hired Lance Amentrout to do exactly that, and he'd condemned half of the inn—the part that sat on the northern end of the island.

Clara couldn't say she was upset about it. That half of Friendship Inn hadn't been remodeled or converted in the early two-thousands, when the last major effort to fix up the inn had been.

Lance had said he'd bring his construction equipment and crews, and they'd knock down that part of the inn, clean it all up, cart it all away. Clara had no idea what that meant, but as a tremendous, thundering sound filled the air, she spun toward the building that was literally her last lifeline to a real life.

Lena shrieked and scampered behind the nearby lamppost, as if that skinny pole would be able to save her from a monster. Even Scott yelped, and Clara alone had been able to remain silent. Her heart pounded like the jackhammer that now filled the air, and she could only stand and watch as a significant plume of white dust rose into the summer sky.

Well, Lance had come today, and Clara supposed she couldn't be too upset by that. There was quite a bit of construction happening in Five Island Cove right now, mostly on Diamond Island, as more and more businesses came to the cove. Restaurants, a new specialty mall, and three housing developments would take Diamond Island from a thriving small town into a near metropolis.

Clara didn't want to live on Diamond for long, but her housing options at the moment were quite limited. The caretakers' apartment here on Friendship Island, inside the inn, on the first floor behind the lobby and check-in desk, were actually in decent condition. The very first thing they'd done when they'd purchased the inn a month ago was to have it assessed by a restoration company.

They'd come in and fixed the leaking pipes and then applied mold treatments, blown dried walls, and gotten everything as safe as possible.

Now, it was just a matter of making sure the structure was sound, and then Clara could turn her attention to cleaning and decorating.

It sounded so simple in her head. Like she just needed to sweep out the kitchen, put new bedding in the master suite, and settle down in her reading nook as guests flocked to the inn. She'd been coming here every day for a solid week, and she knew better.

Her determination had her marching across the weed-filled parking lot—which made no sense to her. There would be no cars coming here—and toward the construction workers on the north side of the island. The lot wasn't big, and Clara could see them eventually repaving it, repainting the lines in bright pink, and having a fleet of golf carts.

On this north side of the island, they'd have sand volleyball courts, swimming pools, and playgrounds. At least three on-site restaurants would be needed, as well as a little market, all housed within the inn.

Clara had no idea how to staff something like that, but with just over sixty-five rooms, no regular services, and people coming to stay for a while, they'd need food, amenities, and activities.

You need regular ferry services, she thought, and she needed to talk to people who'd lived here and came here while Friendship Inn had been open.

She immediately thought of her mother's Seafaring Girls. They were all several years older than her, and she knew they'd once rowed out here, gotten stuck, and had to spend the night in the nearly condemned inn.

Clara's fingers fisted, and she told herself she'd have to get past her stubborn streak. She'd been added to the group text with all the women her mother communicated with all day long. All—day—long. Sometimes at the end of the day, Clara had over two hundred messages to scroll through on the boat ride back to Sanctuary Island. Sometimes, there were only fifty, but she hadn't seen less than that yet.

"Lance," she called, catching sight of the tall, dark-haired man. He turned toward her and raised one hand. He said something to the man next to him, and then he came toward her. "What on earth?" she asked. "It sounded like the whole building was going to come down."

He grinned like a little boy on Christmas morning. "We blew the wall between the old and the new," he said. "We're sifting through anything we need to, and then we'll have the debris gone in a bit."

"Gone?"

"Yes," he said.

She glanced around, but she didn't see any trucks. Of course she wouldn't. How this place had been built, Clara had no idea. "How are you going to do that?"

"Put it in the ocean," he said.

Her mouth dropped open. Her eyelids fluttered as she tried to keep them open for too long. "You can't do that," she said. She wasn't exactly sure what he could and couldn't do, but she knew there were regulations for what a person could dump into the ocean.

"We have a permit," he said. "We have a list. We're sifting through things, and then whatever we can put in the ocean, we will."

Clara didn't know what to say. She surveyed the mess of walls and floors and windows. Friendship Inn only stood three stories tall, so it wasn't one of those big Los Angeles building blow-ups. Still, it felt like a lot to sift through. "How long will this take?" she asked.

"Couple of weeks," he said, and she instantly felt better for some reason. He'd made it sound like they'd sift through a few pieces of rebar and start splashing by lunchtime.

"Okay." Clara looked over to Scott as he arrived.

"Morning, Lance," he said. His grin was too wide for Clara's liking, and she barely caught herself before she frown-glared at him. The two of them shook hands, and Lance proceeded to repeat himself.

Clara turned away, collected Lena by the hand, and led her toward the main entrance of the inn. The doors didn't lock, and Clara wasn't sure what she'd be trying to protect inside if they did. "All right, Lena-Lou," she said to her daughter. "Today, we're going to clean out all of section D, okay?"

She'd sectioned off the remaining half of the inn into quadrants. Each one had between five and eight rooms in it, and by breaking down the huge chunks into manageable pieces, she could keep Lena motivated and see real progress on the inn.

"What floor?" Lena asked. "I don't want to do anything on the second or third floors."

Clara smiled at her daughter. "I know, sweetie. It's on the first floor, section D." She had no idea what she'd do once this section was cleared. It was the last one on the first floor, and it sat on the west side of the inn, overlooking the ocean. It only had five suites in it, the rooms larger and intended for higher-end clients or families. The windows took up whole walls, and Clara had discovered that her mother's concoction of vinegar, CLR, and hot water could get them clean enough to call new.

That would save them a lot of money, and Clara had vowed to scrub every pane of glass herself if that was what it took.

Inside the inn, the lobby took up two floors and spread to her right, with vaulted ceilings and a grand staircase that Lance had said only needed minor repairs. He hadn't done those yet, and a sense of impatience brewed inside Clara.

She swallowed it back, because she'd given herself and her family a year to get this inn open. Nothing here happened quickly or all that efficiently, as neither she nor Scott really knew what they were doing.

To her left would be two of the on-site restaurants. One space was in decent condition and needed a lot of cleaning to be functional. All new appliances were required too, as laws had changed over the years. The other space... Well, Clara was considering using it for more of a deli-type restaurant, or a grab-and-go option.

Go where? she asked herself, but she squashed the thought. She planned to have kayak rentals, boat rentals, jet skis, and more. Families would definitely need a grab-and-go option.

She envisioned senior parties here, and weekends with

the inn full of teenagers. They didn't want to sit down in fussy restaurants. They wanted cups of pretzel bites, cold sodas, cheese fries, and to get back out to the beach.

Clara had walked the perimeter of the entire island, and it had taken her about three hours. She'd noted places that needed to be cleaned up, and drawn a map of where they could put picnic tables. The west side of the island was rocky, very much resembling Rocky Ridge's cliffs, but there were paths down to the sand there.

Black sand.

Clara could only hope that black sand could turn into gold for her, Lena, and Scott.

"Get your cleaning bucket," she said to Lena. Her daughter actually did a pretty good job on the rooms. She could pull out anything inside them and stack it in the halls. One of her greatest strengths was cleaning a bathroom until it sparkled, and then Clara would go behind her the next day and really make everything shine.

Lena went into the office behind the lobby, where they mostly spent their days. Her cleaning cart was there, and she dutifully pushed it through the doorway and down the hall, moving further into the inn. At least once a day, she'd come running back to the lobby, calling for Clara or Scott and claiming she'd heard something scary.

They definitely weren't in Montpelier anymore, and Lena's comfortable, predictable life had been tipped over, tossed out, and trampled on. She'd coped much better than

Clara had thought she would, actually, and a rush of love for her daughter filled her.

Scott came inside, and Clara looked over to him. They hadn't been talking much, and Clara knew all of that stemmed from her. He spoke about her, and Clara let him though it did set her blood to boiling sometimes, depending on what he said.

In general, he was trying very hard, and Clara suddenly felt the weight of that. Tears pressed behind her eyes as he neared, and she opened her arms and took him into a hug as the first drops of wetness tracked down her face.

She didn't know what to say. She didn't know why she'd instantly started crying. She hadn't touched Scott in a while, but she found absolute comfort in his arms now.

"Hey," he whispered, his voice throaty and pinched too. "What is it? Lance says they'll have that part of the island scraped bare for me. I'll get it looking so good, Clara. I promise."

He'd taken over the landscaping and outdoor appearance of the inn. She'd shown him her map, and he'd said, "I can do that."

Everything in his life had started with those four words, and Clara had once loved that about him. If there was something Scott didn't know, he learned it. If he failed, he tried again.

He stepped back now, and foolishness filled Clara. She was so used to being strong; it had been a long time since she'd broken down like this, especially in front of him. "I'm sorry," she whispered.

"Don't be," he said. "This is a lot, every single day, it's a lot."

She looked up, tears clinging to her lashes. "No, I meant I'm sorry for what's going on between us." The inn was a mess, and Clara honestly thought it always would be. But her and Scott? She didn't want them to be a mess for much longer.

She ran the tip of her thumb down her ring finger, expecting to feel the cool touch of metal. A bump as she went over her wedding band.

It wasn't there. She needed it to be there.

"I know I've put you through a lot," he said. "Too much." He didn't drop his chin this time, as he had in previous talks they'd had about things. She'd never seen a man as broken as Scott had been when he'd come home in the middle of the day and told her what was happening at work.

What he'd done. What he'd allowed to happen. What he could've said and didn't.

Clara had held him then. She'd told him it would be okay. She'd said they'd work through everything together. It was only later that the anger and betrayal snuck up on her, infiltrating everything from the way Scott never put his deodorant away, to how he got to leave the house every day without dealing with Lena, their dog, or anything. He got up when he wanted. He came home when he wanted. He didn't do much of anything around the house.

He loved Lena, and he loved Clara, and he'd supported them. That had always been enough.

Until it wasn't; until he couldn't support them.

"I love you," she said, and his face brightened with hope. "I love you, Scott, but I'm still so angry at you."

"I know that." He nodded. "You have the right to be." Instead of backing up the way he had in the past, he moved into her, easily taking her into his arms again. "I love you too, Clara, and I *promise* you I'm going to make this work for us."

He pulled away slightly and leaned his forehead against hers. "Okay? I'm going to be the man you've stood by for all these years. I am."

She nodded and closed her eyes. He wisely didn't kiss her, because she didn't want to be kissed right now. The only thing in her mind was the word, *How?*

How was Scott going to make it work?

How? How? How?

Chapter Seven

Eloise Sherman's hands stilled around the fake flowers she was arranging in a glass vase. Her phone had chimed, and she'd glanced down at the notification of a new message on their group text.

Almost everyone on that string was already here, and she'd found it odd that someone would be texting when they'd all gathered in the same room.

"Holy mother of pearl," Robin said from two spots over. Her voice held awe and wind, the same kind Eloise felt moving through her soul.

She looked up from her phone, her hands dropping to her sides. "Clara finally texted," she said.

Between her and Robin, AJ continued to twist stems, perhaps a little too violently. Her normally sleek, straight hair had been pulled messily into a ponytail, with plenty of haphazard strands that hadn't cooperated. She honestly looked a little unkempt, but Eloise would never say so.

"Is someone going to respond to her?" AJ asked. She finally looked away from her throttled arrangement. She blew out her breath and pushed some errant locks back. "I need a haircut."

Of course, AJ was still stunningly beautiful. She had been for her entire life, and that didn't go away because her hair needed to be trimmed.

"I don't know what to say," Robin admitted.

"Dibs on telling her about the night we stayed in the inn," Alice called from the next table over. She sounded gleeful, and Eloise didn't think she got how big of a moment this was. Eloise looked over to Robin, who had likewise stopped working.

Clara hadn't participated or responded to anyone, about anything, since the day Kristen had added her to the group chat. Eloise had messaged and spoken with Kristen privately, and Kristen was almost desperate for her daughter to find a place to belong here on Five Island Cove.

She'd hoped it would be with everyone there, twisting wired flower stems and filling tall, cylindrical vases with colored stones.

Kristen and Clara hadn't arrived yet, but Kristen had alerted them of their late departure, but that she, Clara, and Lena would be there soon.

"I'm going to respond," Kelli said. She came over to Eloise's table, her phone in her hands. "Okay?"

Eloise nodded, because Kelli would say something kind and pleasant. She'd grown quite the backbone in recent years, and Eloise loved her dearly.

"I will right after you," Jean said. She hadn't stopped her work at Alice's table, and Robin's daughter Mandie kept on putting things where they needed to be as well. Jamie worked in the back room at the venue where a fabulous beach wedding that had been put together in only eight days would take place.

The Tower Plaza had the perfect building for staging a wedding, and the narrow strip of beach beyond it had not been reserved for tomorrow night. Robin had even convinced them to let her into the building in the morning to finish all their prep, and then she'd get access to the beach an hour before the ceremony began.

Eloise's phone chimed again, and her attention flew to it. *Of course we'll talk to you about Friendship Island and the inn*, Kelli said. *AJ in particular has some great stories about it.*

I do not, AJ said. *Besides, our stories are the same, Kel.*

Kelli giggled, and Eloise found herself smiling too. *Not true*, Kelli said. *I'm pretty sure I didn't sneak out of any rooms to meet boys.*

"Hey," AJ said out loud. "That was Matt."

"Still happened," Kelli said. "To you, not me."

I can come help any day at the inn, Jean said. *Didn't you hire someone too? Do they work every day, or no?*

"She did hire someone," Robin said.

Before anyone could say anything else, and before Eloise could chime in that she'd help too if she could, the door to the small space opened and no less than six women entered.

They chattered the way Eloise imagined she did with her friends when they went to lunch, and she was instantly intimidated by them.

One woman emerged as the leader, and Robin put down her wire cutters to go greet her. Robin was personable and fun, especially with clients, and she stepped right into the tall, lithe blonde and hugged her.

"Come meet my friends," she said, and Robin brought the whole group of them over. "Guys, let's pow-wow."

"I hate it when she says that," Alice muttered as she stepped to Eloise's side.

"Would you rather she say, 'huddle up'?" Eloise grinned as Alice rolled her eyes. "Because I hate that." Robin had said it that morning, and Eloise had wanted to ask her if they were about to play football.

Robin waited for everyone to finish up their tasks, and then she nodded to Mandie. "Oh," the young woman said. "So this is Madeline Lancaster. Her son is the one getting married. Beside her—"

Robin cleared her throat, and Mandie stared blankly at

her for a moment. "I mean, did your son and his fiancée get in all right?"

Madeline smiled, and she was a natural beauty the way AJ was. "Yes, they did," she said. "They've been here for a couple of hours. Bea should be here in a few minutes to help."

"The bride doesn't need to help." Robin looked aghast at such a thing. In Eloise's opinion, the more hands they had, the better.

"She's going to wear gloves so she doesn't scratch herself." Madeline exchanged a glance with a dark-haired woman who reminded Eloise more of herself than the other women. "This is Julia Harper. We used to run the Lighthouse Inn together."

Julia waved her hand, and Laurel's chair scraped as she said. "I know you guys. I thought I did." Her whole face beamed with light. "One of you has a sister named Annie."

"That's me," Julia said, her head tilting to the side. "How do you know Annie?"

"We met her at The Holiday House." She gestured to her and Robin. "When we went last year with Heidi. Remember, Robin?"

"I remember Annie," Robin said slowly. "She's a nurse, right?"

Julia smiled. "Yep. In Chatham." She said the last two words with Robin.

Eloise marveled at how small the world could be sometimes. She smiled at the women there, another couple of them brunettes like her. "I'm Eloise," she said, stepping forward to shake hands with one nearest to her.

"Tessa," the woman said. "I think I know one of you too. I'm going to be working with her at Friendship Inn."

"Clara," several people said together, including Eloise.

"Yes." Tessa smiled and glanced to the woman beside her. "Clara Tanner."

As if on cue, the door opened again, and Clara entered first, then held the door for her daughter and her mother. They approached the group, and Jean went right over to Lena, took her hand, and helped her blend easily into the group.

"Tessa," Clara said with surprise. "What are you doing here?" She surveyed the group as if something nefarious was going down, but Eloise had learned that that was simply how Clara operated—at least in the beginning.

She'd thaw and open up as time went on, but she actually liked to keep people at arm's length.

"Maddy is one of my best friends," Tessa said. "We're here to curb the wedding emergency."

"So are we," Alice said. She smiled at the group too and shook a few hands as she added, "I'm Alice Rice. Welcome to the cove."

"I live here now," Tessa said. "On Sanctuary." She smiled around and then finally indicated the woman at her side. "This is my sister, Janey Forsythe."

"And we brought an excellent baker, Helen Ivy," Julia said. "She's going to finish up the wedding cake tonight and in the morning."

The older woman—maybe even more aged than Kristen, who was nearly seventy-nine-years-old—beamed sun rays out of her bright blue eyes. "How early can I get into this building?"

"We can be here from eight to eleven," Robin said. "Then we have to leave until six. The wedding is at seven, and we have the beach until ten." She exchanged a glanced with Maddy, who was smiling with what felt like everything she had.

Eloise could feel her gratitude streaming into the air, and she wasn't surprised when Maddy stepped into Robin and hugged her again. "Thank you so much." She stepped back and cleared her throat, nodding to everyone gathered round. "To all of you. It really does take a village to pull off a wedding in only eight days."

"That it does," Robin said with a laugh. "All right, everyone. Pick a buddy and show them what we're doing with the vases. I'll take Maddy and put her on wreaths. Okay?" She clapped her hands, which reminded Eloise of a football coach, and turned into Maddy. They started talking, and Eloise met Tessa's eyes.

"Want to be my buddy?" she asked.

Tessa grinned and nodded. "Yes, I do."

Eloise started showing her how to group the flowers.

"It's not rocket science," she said. "Robin and Mandie couldn't get anything shorter than these, though, so we have to clip all the stems. Some of them are a little bent and they don't like being un-bent." Eloise manhandled the bouquet she'd been working on. "So we kind of stab them into the stones until they sit right and look good."

Tessa nodded, and Eloise went with her to get more supplies. "We have to make corsages from these too, but Alice is the master at that." Eloise gave Alice a smile as she went by. "Or Laurel. They're more delicate with their hands."

With more women in the room, the talking increased, but Eloise didn't mind. Tessa wasn't terribly talkative, and Eloise asked, "How long have you lived here?"

"Six months," Tessa said.

"Do you like Sanctuary?" Eloise cut a flower stem and put it in the vase. Too short. She set it aside to give to Laurel to make a corsage with.

"Yes," Tessa said. "I love it."

"Where do you live?"

"On Beachfront Row?" Her eyebrows went up. "There's a row of cottages there, right on the beach."

"Yeah, of course," Eloise said. "Kelli over there lived there for a little bit when she first moved back to the cove."

"Back?" Tessa watched Kelli, who stood with Helen, Jean, and Lena, none of them doing much of anything.

"Yeah," Eloise said. "We're all from here originally." She

looked around, realizing she hadn't said that right. "Some of us, at least. Laurel grew up on Nantucket. Jean's from Long Island. Clara grew up here, but she's lived in Vermont for a long time now." Eloise couldn't explain their whole history, so she just shrugged. "Robin never left, but the rest of us did. But now we've all moved back here. Kelli lives here on Pearl now, after she got remarried, but she lived in one of those beach cottages when she first came back to the cove."

"Interesting," Tessa said, but Eloise didn't see what was interesting about it. "What do you do, Eloise?"

"I own the Cliffside Inn." She tried to keep the pride out of her voice, and she hoped the little that had bled in hadn't been heard by Tessa.

"Oh, I love that place." She came alive and added, "I haven't stayed there or anything, but I drove up to it, and you can see the whole world on top of those cliffs."

Eloise nodded, the view there in her mind's eye. "Yes," she murmured. "Yes, you can."

The whirring of a sewing machine joined the fray in the room, and that meant Jean had gone back to stitching together the napkins they'd use for dinner. "These can be folded," Mandie yelled, and Eloise watched as Kristen and Clara went to learn how to properly fold hand-made napkins for a beach wedding.

"Did you say you own the Cliffside Inn?"

Eloise looked up from her flowers to meet Julia's eyes. "Yes," she said. "I own it and run it. It's only six rooms, but it keeps me on my toes. We serve two meals a day, and I have a ton of day-events, deliveries, staffing issues, and more." She shook her head. "I'm married to the Chief of Police here in the cove too, and we have two teenagers. So my life is a little crazy sometimes."

She caught the look Tessa and Julia exchanged, and an older version of Eloise wouldn't have said anything. The version of herself she was now, however, asked, "What was that look for?"

Neither of them said anything. Finally, Tessa said, "Tell her."

"You tell her," Julia said.

Tessa gave her a look under drawn-down eyebrows. "Julia runs the Lighthouse Inn on Nantucket. It only has five rooms, and she's drowning—and that's *with* a co-manager."

Eloise had no idea what it would be like to have a co-manager. "I have a night manager," she said. "She lives on-site and handles everything so I can be home with my family in the evenings." She didn't mention that she still had to answer texts constantly and deal with things mentally.

"She's looking for a job here in the cove." Tessa stabbed her iris down into the stones, and her vase slipped. She tried to catch it, but Eloise knew it was going to fall before it did.

She jumped back as Tessa still fumbled with it. In the end, it did topple to the floor—a very cement floor—where it shattered.

The conversations came to a halt as blue, green, and white seaglass went skidding along the floor and the sound of breaking glass filled the air. It only lasted for three seconds, and then the silence took over.

"Okay," Mandie said. "It's okay. It's just one vase. We bought extras." She sounded and acted so much like Robin that Eloise had a moment of thinking she *was* Robin. Then Robin appeared with a broom, and several others dropped to pick up the scattered stones.

"I'm so sorry," Tessa said, her face full of shock. "It just got away from me."

"It's fine," Eloise said. She stepped back to the table and her own arrangement. "I think mine just needs one...more." She picked up another flower, clipped the stem, and put it in the blank spot in the bouquet.

She met Julia's eyes. "How long will you be here?"

"Through Sunday evening," she said. "I have to get back to Nantucket."

Eloise nodded. "Come by the inn on Saturday or Sunday before you go. We can talk."

"Really?"

"Absolutely." She glanced over to Clara, who wore a happy smile. That caused Eloise to smile too. "And you know what else? Clara over there just bought Friendship Inn, and I'm pretty sure she'd love someone with experience in the inn industry."

Julia spun toward Clara and Kristen, and Eloise felt like

she'd done her one good deed for the day.

Her phone rang, and she stepped away from the bouquets and blooms and booming voices to take Billie's call. "Hey, sweetie," she said. "Did you and Grace make it home?" They'd gone to the lighthouse that afternoon with several of Billie's friends from school. From there, they could walk down a path and along the cliffs to a secluded beach with a calm cove of water.

"No," Billie said, her voice panicked. "El, I need you here right now."

"Okay," Eloise said, alarm pulling through her. "Why?" She glanced over her shoulder to the other women in the room. She could easily slip out and no one would know. She headed for the door as Billie's stressed breathing came through the line. "Take a breath, Billie. What's going on?"

"I can't breathe," Billie said, her voice pitching up. "I just kissed Cameron Gillman, El. In this super-cute cave." She squealed, and Eloise very nearly went deaf.

Eloise's heartbeat had started to sprint in her chest, and as she went outside into the heat and humidity, she slowed. "You called me in a panic because you kissed a boy?"

"Not just *a boy*, El," Billie said in the special voice she used to let everyone else know how stupid they were. "Cam Gillman."

She grinned into the blue sky. "Wow, Billie. I guess he really did like you all this time."

Billie squealed again, and Eloise laughed with her. She'd

gone to Sweethearts with a boy named Luke Howard, and Eloise knew Billie had liked him too. He'd cooled off after the dance, and Billie wasn't sure why.

Eloise didn't know how to explain boys to Billie, and she still talked to Luke and hung out with him sometimes. "I hate to bring this up during such an exciting time," she said. "But what are you going to tell your dad?"

Billie's giggles dried right up too. "Now you know why I called in a panic. I need a plan, El. Cam asked me if I could go over to his house this weekend. He has a pool and a theater in one of those huge houses on Rocky Ridge."

"Just the two of you?"

"He said it could be a date. He'd take me to lunch, and we could swim and watch movies..." She let the words dry there, hanging on the line, and Eloise knew how teen boys would finish that sentence.

"Oh, honey, I don't know if that's a good idea," she said. Aaron would flip his lid, because he knew what Cam had really invited Billie to do.

"Why not?" Billie asked, always so innocent. Always trying to be more grown up than she really was, though she was extraordinarily mature for her age.

Eloise exhaled. She loved Aaron's girls as if they were her own, but she was ill-prepared to talk about a lot of the challenges teenagers had to face these days. "Billie, he wants to have sex with you," she said as quietly and as gently as she could. "That's why he invited you to his house."

Billie said nothing, and Eloise hated that she had to be the one to make something she was excited about into this. "He said his parents will be there."

"I think this one goes to your dad," she said. "And we both know what he's going to say."

Billie exhaled too. "He'll want to come with me to the house, interview the boy, meet the parents."

"Yes." Eloise couldn't deny it, and truth be told, she wanted to do all of those things too. She certainly wasn't going to put Billie on the ferry by herself to get to Rocky Ridge, to go to some boy's house whom she'd never met before. "Billie, are you—do you want to sleep with him?"

"No," Billie said instantly. She exhaled right after. "I'm so stupid."

"No, you're not," Eloise said quickly. "He's a popular, good-looking boy. All the girls love him, including you. It doesn't make you stupid."

Billie sniffled, and Eloise wished she wasn't two islands away, having this conversation. "What do I tell him?"

"First, it's not your job to make sure he doesn't feel bad," Eloise said. "Second, this is where having a Chief-of-Police-father comes in really handy. I think you can come up with some reason why you don't want your dad coming along on your 'date' at Cam's house..."

Billie actually giggled again, but Eloise still wanted to wrap her in a hug and hold on tight. Tell her to hold onto her youth and her innocence for as long as she could. "Thanks, El."

"I love you, Bills," she said.

"Love you too."

The call ended, and Eloise drew in a deep breath. She then let her fingers fly across the screen, first texting Billie. *You should tell your dad about this tonight.*

Then she texted her mother. *I love you so much, Mom. I don't know how you raised teenagers, and I apologize for any worry and grief I caused you.*

Neither of them answered her right away, and Eloise went back inside to the air conditioning, the long list of tasks to be done for the wedding, and all of her biggest supporters. If she needed help with Billie or Grace, she didn't have to look any further. Both Robin and Alice had raised their kids to adulthood. Kelli, Kristen, Laurel, and Jean would listen to anything Eloise wanted to vent about.

AJ would remind her that no one could be worse than she'd been as a teen. Eloise rejoined the people at the table she'd been at, flashing a smile at Tessa, and then listening to AJ talk to Matt about something their baby was doing at home.

She was right where she wanted to be. Life wasn't perfect, but Eloise wanted to live it anyway—right here on Five Island Cove. She looked over to Clara, standing there with her mother, and Eloise hoped she'd find the perfect place for her too—right here on Five Island Cove.

Chapter Eight

Madeline Lancaster stood very still while Ben slid up the zipper on her dress. He touched his lips to the back of her neck and said, "Done, gorgeous."

She turned into his arms, beyond grateful he'd gotten the weekend off to attend this wedding with her. Originally, she thought she'd attend the wedding from the balcony of the church in New York City, watching her only son get married from afar.

Now, she got to sit on the front row, only an arm's length from Kyle and Bea. They'd been on Five Island Cove for ten days, and Maddy was so excited for them. The trip from Rocky Ridge to Pearl Island had taken over an hour, but they'd all made it.

Her parents. Chelsea. Ben. Julia and Annie had come from Nantucket and Chatham. Tessa and Janey had been here for a few days as well, and Maddy had put her big house on the northernmost island to good use, sheltering them all.

They'd talked and laughed for too long last night, but Maddy didn't care. Her motto right now was she'd sleep when she was dead.

Or at least, after her son got married.

The only person who wasn't here that Maddy had thought would be for sure was Chris. Her ex-husband. The politician both of her children had chosen over her in the divorce. Apparently, new things had come to light, but neither Kyle nor Chelsea would talk about them.

Maddy hadn't pressured her children; she was just glad to have them close to her again.

Kyle had apologized profusely, and Maddy had been talking to Chelsea for months previous to this.

"Thank you for being here," she whispered against his lips. "I needed you here, and you're here."

"I'll always be where you need me," he said. He matched his mouth to hers and deepened their kiss. The man knew how to make her feel like a much younger woman, and Maddy had to sternly tell herself not to get too carried away with him.

The wedding was set to begin in only fifteen minutes, and though he could be and had been quick with her in the past, she didn't want that right now. She wanted love, not just sex. She wanted understanding and passion, not just physical touch. She wanted to create memories, not just give in to lust.

"Maddy." Ben pulled away and stroked his rough hand down the side of her face. "I'm in love with you."

She looked at him, searching for any hint of deception in those glorious blue eyes. He was a much younger man than her—eleven years younger. She couldn't give him children, and he said he didn't care. He only wanted her.

"What do you think of us?" He cleared his throat and dropped his chin. He rarely did that. The strong, sometimes a bit tactless, Coast Guard Captain didn't mince words. He looked up, a storm in his expression now. 'What do you think of us doing what Kyle and Bea are doing?"

"Getting married?" she asked, though she knew exactly what he was saying.

"Yeah," he said.

Maddy grinned up at him and leaned her full weight into his chest. "You want to marry me."

He barely twitched his lips into a smile. "Yeah," he said. "I do."

Maddy giggled and stretched up to kiss him again. Maybe she rushed it a little this time. Maybe she did like giving into the lust and physicality of her relationship with Ben. She slowed her stroke and pulled away gently. "I think if you ask me properly, Captain, I'd say yes."

"Yes, ma'am," he whispered. "My mother wants to meet you. She won't stop hounding me about it, especially now that I've—and I quote—'rearranged my whole life to be near you.'" He stepped away and straightened his tie. He wasn't wearing his uniform. If he had been, Maddy might not have been able to control herself.

"Let's go on your next vacation," she said.

Ben turned toward her. "That's not until August."

"Then tell her it's your work schedule preventing us from coming, and that of course, I want to meet her too."

"You need a passport to go to Canada, you know." He took her into his arms again and swayed with her.

"I'll get the application filled out the moment this wedding done." She smiled up at him. "I can't believe this is happening like this."

"Are you happy?" he asked.

"Yes," she murmured.

A knock sounded on the door, and Maddy barely had time to step out of his arms before Robin poked her head into the room. Her angel from on-high. Without Robin Glover, Maddy was quite sure she'd be hosing Kyle and Bea's wedding in her backyard on Ricky Ridge.

"We need you out here," Robin said, her gaze flicking over to Ben. "Both of you."

"Coming." Maddy took Ben's hand in hers and led him into the hall. Only a few steps separated them from the beach through the glass doors in front of her, and Maddy knew once they stepped outside, the heat would assault them.

She'd chosen the lightest fabric she could that wasn't see-through, and she didn't even want to think about Ben in his suit and tie, the latter of which was done up all the way to his throat.

She went outside to find almost every chair filled. Her chest expanded with a breath, as Kyle's best friends had made the trip here, and everyone who really mattered to Bea had too.

Maddy padded through the sand, nodding to her friends, as well as Bea's mother. She sat beside her and reached over to hold the woman's hand. "Is she ready?"

"She was when I left the room," Susan said with a smile.

The pastor came down the aisle and took his place behind the altar, then Kyle exited the building and came toward her. Everyone rose to their feet, and Maddy clutched her hands together in front of her breastbone as her son approached.

He came to her and gripped her in a hug. "I love you, Mom."

"I love you too," she whispered, clutching his broad shoulders. "I'm sorry your father isn't here."

Kyle pulled away, a moment of hardness entering his eyes. "It's fine, Mom." He moved over to the altar and turned to face the way he'd come.

Maddy did too, her heart still worrying over what had happened between Chris and the kids. Chelsea exited the building, and she carried an enormous bouquet of flowers in front of her pale pink dress. She led Bea's sisters and her best friend down the aisle, and then Bea appeared.

Her dress had come straight from a historical fairy tale, with layer upon layer of white fabric. Lace, ruffles, and fluff made her seem like a princess about to claim her prince.

She was almost due with their baby, but her dress flowed out so much in all directions, and she held her bouquet strategically to disguise a lot of her belly.

Behind her, Kyle sighed, and Maddy adored the sound of it. She wanted her son to be blissfully in love with his wife, and he sure seemed to love Bea.

Her father escorted her down the aisle, and they had to carry the bouquet together. When she reached the first row, she handed the flowers to her mother, who moved around the altar and arranged them there. They perfectly complimented the modern altar Robin had managed to procure for them.

Susan returned to her spot but didn't sit until Bea had kissed her father and he'd moved to the first row too. Only then did everyone take their seats, and this time, Ben took her right hand while Susan took her left.

Maddy's heart had never felt so full. She knew the food would be perfect after the ceremony, as she'd had a hand in almost all of it. Bea had selected the music, and they'd tested the speakers this morning. Everything was set.

All they had to do now was get through the vows and say I-do.

Maddy sighed and wiped her eyes through the things they said to one another, and she was sure she was the first to burst to her feet once Kyle dipped Bea and kissed her.

The crowd started to cheer, but Maddy's voice was tied in a knot in the back of her throat. She applauded as hard as she could, and she stepped forward to hug Bea and Kyle simultaneously before anyone else could claim them.

"I love you two," she said. "Thank you for letting me be part of this."

"Are you kidding?" Bea asked. "Without you, this wouldn't have happened at all." She smiled at Maddy, and the feeling of forgiveness permeated the air.

Maddy was glad for such a thing in her life, because she'd been on the other side of the aisle, and it wasn't a pleasant place to be. She felt so free, and she returned to Ben's side while Bea's mother and father went to hug the newly married couple.

They edged out of the way, and Maddy started thinking about dinner. Then she saw Robin, and she knew the woman would have everything perfectly ready at the precise time it needed to be ready.

"I don't want something big for our wedding," she said to him. "Very close friends. Family. Something simple."

Ben grinned down at her, a flirtatious twinkle in his eyes. "Maddy, baby, you know I love you. But you don't do anything simply."

A few defenses flew into place. "Yes, I do."

"You'll cater with fancy food."

"That's simple," she said. "I could make it all."

"You'll want a fancy dress."

"Every bride needs a fancy dress," she said. "And it'll be a simple kind of fancy."

He put his arm around her waist, and she cuddled into him again as Kyle and Bea moved down the aisle to chat with everyone.

Robin caught her attention and motioned that they could move from the tent where the ceremony had taken place to the dinner tent. Maddy stepped over to Susan and told her, and Bea's mother did a stand-up job of mobilizing the guests.

Maddy and Ben joined the flow of people now moving to the dinner tent, and she took him to the head table.

"Do we have to have a formal dinner like this?" he asked. He shifted in his seat, because he didn't like being the center of attention. Maybe hers, but that was all. He'd barely tolerated coming to dinner at the inn, and that had been a small affair with people he knew. Usually.

Now that they both lived in Five Island Cove, she saw him every day, sometimes in the morning, sometimes at night. They both lived on Rocky Ridge, and he slept at the Coast Guard station a lot. When he wasn't there, he stayed with Maddy, and joining their lives in holy matrimony would be easy.

"No," she said. "No stuffy dinner. No head table."

"Praise the heavens," he muttered.

"Where do you want to get married?" she asked. "What will your mother want?"

"She won't care," he said. "She just wants me to settle down and be an 'honest man.'" He rolled his eyes, but Maddy knew Ben loved his mother very much. He talked to her almost every day, and when he had time off, he usually went to Toronto to visit her.

"So maybe my backyard," she said. "My house could host the dinner. And we can stay the first night in the Cliffside Inn and then jet across the ocean for an amazing European honeymoon." She lifted her eyebrows, expecting Ben to scoff and say they wouldn't be going to Europe on their honeymoon.

He scoffed. He said, "Europe? No. We need to go somewhere like Iceland or Belize."

Maddy giggled as the guests continued to file into the tent and take seats at the tables set up there. Each boasted a large flower arrangement, with tall glass vases and blue, green, and white stones in them. All the chairs had been draped in bows, and the napkins matched them here as well as the ones they'd used for the ceremony.

Lights hung in the rafters of the tent, and flowers hung from every pole as well. With all of Robin's friends and all of Maddy's, the job hadn't been too big or taken too long.

She reached for her goblet of water and took a small sip. "You realize Iceland and Belize are in opposite directions."

"Depending on when we get married, we might want to go north or south," Ben said.

"When do you want to get married?"

"Tomorrow?" he guessed, that bad-boy edge in his eyes again.

Maddy smiled, shook her head, and gave him a playful shove against his heartbeat. "Not tomorrow."

He took her hand and lifted it to his lips. "Soon, though, Mads. Right?" His gaze burned now, the way it did when he made love to her. "Soon."

She wasn't going to argue with him when he spoke in that voice and looked at her with those eyes. She nodded. "Yes, Ben. Soon." She leaned closer to him, and he bent his head down so she could whisper in his ear. "I'm just waiting for that proper proposal, Captain Gorgeous."

Chapter Nine

Jean Shields bent over the sewing machine, the tiny T-shirt she'd been working on for Asher nearly finished. The baby monitor sat nearby, and she'd thought she'd heard him fuss. She glanced over to it, and the lights would vibrate and move across the walkie-talkie if he did.

They stayed still, and if he had made a noise, it was isolated; he hadn't woken yet. She glanced at her phone, realizing that he shouldn't be waking up from his nap yet. She finished the T-shirt, and she'd dress him in it before his mother came to pick him up.

Jean loved babysitting, and she'd considered putting her name out there to get more jobs. She tended to Asher for AJ and Matt when they needed her, and she often had Parker at the lighthouse too. He'd gone to New Jersey for the summer, and Jean already missed him. Sometimes Eloise would bring her girls or text to let Jean know Billie was coming to the lighthouse to go down to Seal Harbor with some friends.

That didn't require Jean to babysit, and she dismissed the idea of taking on other jobs. She had her sewing lessons, and her Seafaring Girls lessons would start up again in July. She'd been planning those with Kristen, and she'd been perfecting a few new cookie recipes to try with the girls who came to the lighthouse for lessons in boat care, ocean navigation, water safety, and more.

"Babe," Reuben called, and Jean looked up, startled. He rarely came back downstairs during the day, and he'd practically bellowed.

She got to her feet and went down the short hall to the kitchen. "Asher's asleep." She put her forefinger over her lips, noting how brightly he glowed. "What's going on?"

"You've been sewing," he said, the words rushing out of him. He held up his phone. "We got an email from Miranda. She said a birth mother has selected our adoption profile and wants to know more."

Jean's heart fell all the way to her stomach. "Are you kidding?" Her husband would never joke about this. He'd found her on the bathroom floor. He'd sobbed with her when they'd lost their baby. He'd been at her side for years as they'd tried to get pregnant.

She rushed over to him, her joy competing with her adrenaline as both soared through her. "What does it say?

What do we need to do?" Jean grabbed onto his forearm so he'd lower the phone. He did and she peered at it.

Jean and Reuben,

I hope this email finds you well. I have a bit of good news! A sweet birth mother has selected a few couple profiles to go over, and yours was one of them. She'd like a bit more information, and I've attached a list of her questions below. Please fill them out and get them back to me at your earliest convenience.

Yours,

Miranda

Jean looked up at Reuben. "What kind of questions?"

"I don't know," Reuben said. "She said she selected a few profiles." He lowered his phone, his expression turning serious. "This could be nothing, Jean."

"I know," she said, though her pulse and her hopes had soared into the atmosphere at the reading of the email. "But it's an email we haven't gotten before. She's never told us anyone has selected our profile." That was something, and Jean had decided at the beginning of the year to count her blessings instead of worrying about things she couldn't control.

This email was a blessing, even if it caused her hopes to skyrocket. They might come crashing back to earth, which would hurt, yes. But they could also be satisfied, and Jean could potentially have a baby of her own soon enough.

"I can answer the questions right now." She turned

toward the tiny built-in desk on the cusp of the kitchen. She sat in the chair, glad when Reuben didn't immediately go back upstairs. She clicked a few times, and it seemed to take an hour for the computer to come to life and connect to the internet.

She checked her email, and she had the same email from their adoption case worker. She opened the document in the attachments, and the page filled the screen. Everything rushed at her then, and Jean closed her eyes tightly. "I can't read it, Reuben. You do it."

"The first question is where are you from?" he read. "How many brothers and sisters do you have? How many kids do you want? Your profile says you live in a lighthouse. Can I see some pictures of it?"

Jean opened her eyes and read the questions. Reuben had read almost all of them, and she quickly scanned the last two.

Would one baby be enough for you? Or will you try to adopt again?

Do you want a boy or a girl? And don't tell me any baby that's healthy. I really want to know.

She looked up to Reuben. "The last one's the hardest."

He nodded. "What are you going to put?"

Timber barked, and Jean startled in her seat. Her heartbeat got jumpstarted for the second time in the past five minutes, and she scolded the canine for scaring her. He simply barked again, and Jean looked toward the stairs that led into the bottom floor of the lighthouse.

"It's just me," a woman called, and Jean hurried to darken the screen.

"AJ's here," she said. "She's early." She got to her feet as AJ entered the doorway. "Hey." She moved toward her, her nerves off the chart for some reason. She loved AJ; she adored all of the women who had become her friends. They'd been there for her when she'd miscarried, and all of them had rushed to her aid when she and her Seafaring Girls had been adrift at sea.

She and AJ were close, but Jean didn't want to tell anyone about the email yet.

"You've done early," she said as she hugged AJ. "I didn't have time to put his new shirt on."

AJ grinned at her and tucked her long, straight hair. "Lisa got a little seasick, so we came in sooner than we thought." She glanced over to Reuben. "Hey, Reuben."

"Hello, AJ. He's still asleep." He gestured over his shoulder to the hall behind them. Two bedrooms sat that way, and Jean used one for her sewing studio. Asher slept in a bassinet in the master bedroom.

"I'll get him," Jean said. "You have to see his shirt. You're going to love it." The pull to the computer nearly smashed her, but Jean went by it and down the hall as Reuben said something else to AJ. She grabbed the tiny tee off the sewing machine and ducked into the main bedroom.

The walls curved around, and Jean hadn't loved living underground at first. She did now—she loved everything about Five Island Cove—and she peered over the edge of the bassinet.

Asher was wide awake, silently laying there. He screeched and kicked his legs and wagged his arms when he saw her. "Ma-ma-ma-ma," he babbled. Jean giggled and reached in to pick him up.

"You didn't call for me, you silly boy." She sank onto the bed and held the chunky baby in her lap. "Let's get you changed for your mama." She had to manhandle him, as Asher didn't help at all to get his current T-shirt off and the new one on.

Jean tugged it down and stood him on his feet on her knees. "Oh, so handsome," she cooed at him. He grinned at her, the tiniest bit of slobber in the corner of his mouth. She stood and put him on her hip before going down the hall.

She stopped at the end of it and turned him so AJ could see the T-shirt from the front. "Look."

AJ was already looking, her face growing brighter with every second that passed. She laughed, and Jean sure did love causing that joy in people. "I love this," she said, sweeping over to Jean in the sophisticated, elegant way she had.

Asher squealed again, clearly excited to see his true mama. AJ tickled him and said, "Look at you in that T-shirt, buddy. It's got a great big crab on it. Are you crabby?" She took him from Jean, his little legs still going.

The T-shirt did have a big cartoon crab on the front of it, and Jean had applied that with sure stitches. The saying she'd stitched on said *I'm not crabby. I'm teething.*

And he was. His fist went in his mouth, and Jean turned to the fridge, where she'd put his teething ring. "Here you go, baby." She handed him the toy, taking an extra couple of moments for Asher to get his chubby fingers around it.

That too went straight into his mouth, and AJ smiled at Jean. "Thank you, Jean."

"Anytime." She followed AJ all the way up two flights of stairs to the exit, and she held the door with her foot as the other woman left. She went outside and waved to Matt and Lisa, who'd stayed in the car.

Lisa actually got out and cooed at Asher too. "Look at your shirt, you lucky baby." She took him from AJ to put him in the car seat in the back, and Jean stood strong against the wind and watched them until they left.

Then she went back downstairs to the computer. Reuben had started to make coffee, and he put a mug on the desk as she finished the last question. "Coconut cream in that, my love," he said softly.

She stood and indicated that he should take the chair. "Read them."

He sat, and Jean perched herself in his lap. He held her around the waist, and she read over the questions and answers again.

"It's good, Jean," he said. "We are who we are."

"Do you want me to change the last one?"

"No," he said. His arms around her tightened, and she loved how completely he held her. How much he loved her. "I want to see all the dresses and shirts and tops you make for our daughter."

Happiness filled her, and Jean leaned her head against Reuben's shoulder. "All right. I'll send them back then." She got off his lap.

He stood and took his coffee with him. "I'm going back up."

She didn't say anything, because she was already back at the monitor. She sipped her coffee, read through the answers again, and waited in pure silence for someone or something to tell her to change one of them.

She heard nothing, so she saved the file, attached it to the email, and sent it back to Miranda. All she could do now was what she'd been doing all along.

Pray.

"THAT GOES IN THE DEN," ROBIN SAID AS JEAN went by with a bright green tote. "It's labeled!"

Jean wouldn't expect anything less from Robin, and she found the den easily. The bright blue sticky note with the three letters in a very wide-tipped marker helped a lot.

Robin's diligence didn't stop there. She'd actually taped

off places on the floor for the furniture, so Jean didn't set the tote there. She put it with a few identical bins and turned to go get more.

The weather had cooperated beautifully for today's double-move. Of course, it was barely eight in the morning, and in a few hours, when they moved over to Kristen's to get Clara and Scott's stuff out of the condo and over to their new house, Jean might be saying something different.

Jean loved the dawn of a new day, and she smiled into the still slightly chilled sky. It had been a week since she'd sent in the additional questions, and she'd labored over pictures of the lighthouse and its surroundings that night. Those hadn't been sent until the next day, but Miranda had confirmed it all. She said she'd pass it all along to the birth mother, and she hoped to have more news soon.

With every day that passed without any communication, Jean wanted to know what else she could do. Send more pictures? Give better details? Their profile had already been quite detailed as it was, and Jean would be overwhelmed looking through it.

Of course, if she was considering giving up her baby, she'd want to know every little detail about the people taking her.

She turned with another box in her hands, her thoughts far away. Therefore, she didn't see Alice until she'd knocked into her, and then Jean blinked her way back to the present. Alice stood in front of her, doubled-over.

"Alice." She dropped the box, and the clunking, then shattering, noise inside didn't soothe her. "I'm so sorry."

"I'm okay," Alice said, but it was almost a wheeze. She held her midsection, her eyes rimmed in pain. "It just knocked the wind out of me."

Jean kept her hand on Alice's elbow until she straightened. Her son came up behind her and asked, "Mom?"

"I'm fine." Alice moved out of the way as boxes and items kept getting placed on the lip of the truck for someone to take. Duke had loaded the truck last night with the help of some of his and Robin's friends, and they wanted this morning to go quickly.

Robin had ordered breakfast for everyone, and another round of guilt hit Jean that she'd slowed things down.

Charlie looked at Jean with his eyebrows sky-high.

"I hit her with a box," Jean said. She bent and picked it up. "She doesn't seem okay. I'll go get Arthur."

Charlie moved over to his mother, who'd leaned against the hood of a car parked in the driveway. Jean took the box inside, and it had been labeled kitchen.

She found Robin there, and she slid the box onto a patch of available countertop. "I think I may have broken something in here," she said. She gestured back the way she'd come. "I hit Alice with the box, and she seems...off. She said she's okay, but she's not."

Robin looked over to her, alarm on her face. "She's not?"

"Have you seen Arthur?"

"Yeah, he's with Shad in Jamie's room, putting the dresser back together."

Jean nodded and went to find him. Shad knelt on the floor in the first bedroom Jean came to, and she leaned halfway into the room. "Arthur."

He looked over from the corner of the dresser. "Yeah?"

"I hit Alice with a box, and she seems really hurt."

He waved his hand at her. "Come hold this for Shad."

Fear bolted through Jean. She couldn't help put together a dresser. She barely stood over five feet tall, and a stiff wind could whisk her feet off solid ground. Still, she did walk over to where he stood.

"Put your hand here," he said. "I'm holding that in place while he bolts it together."

"I don't think I can." Jean reached out hesitantly, and Arthur guided her hand to where it needed to go.

"Just stand here, Jean. You've got it." He left in a hurry then, and Jean watched as Shad worked with nuts, bolts, and tools.

A few minutes later, he got to his feet. "We're good now, Jean." He gave her a smile, but Jean could barely return it. Accidents happened, she knew. She just wished she'd kept a clear head instead of letting her hopes and dreams cloud her reality.

She'd lived in that land before, and coming back to

reality was too painful. She had to stay here all the time, or she never wanted to come back.

She left the bedroom with Shad, and she took a right and went out the front door. Alice now stood near the corner of the moving truck, drinking a bottle of water. Charlie, Ginny, and Arthur all crowded in around her, and she shook her head as she lowered the water bottle.

Jean approached, and she asked, "How are you, Alice?" when she got near enough for her voice to be heard.

Alice turned toward her. "I'm fine. Honestly."

Jean took her into a hug. "I'm sorry. I was just inside my own head and I didn't hear anyone come up behind me." She pulled away and couldn't meet Alice's eyes. The woman was a lawyer, and Jean already felt inferior to her in so many ways. She'd be able to see the turmoil in Jean, and she disliked that something amazing and joyous had caused turmoil at all.

"Are *you* okay?" Alice asked.

"Yes." Jean forced a smile to her face. "I was just up late last night practicing a gluten-free recipe. One of the girls texted last night that she was just diagnosed with a gluten allergy." That wasn't a lie, but it also wasn't the reason Jean had been caught in an alternate reality.

As the moving in continued, Jean kept her focus on the tasks at hand. She laughed and chatted with the people there to help Robin and Duke, and she could feel the impact they'd had on the lives of the people there. They were well-loved, and Jean counted herself lucky to know them.

Now, if she and Reuben could just get lucky enough to be chosen as adoptive parents, all of Jean's hopes and dreams would come true.

Chapter Ten

AJ Hymas helped in Robin's old kitchen, where she'd been all morning long. When she'd first arrived, she'd put Asher in a bouncy seat, plenty of toys attached to a bar in front of him. When he'd tired of that, she'd moved him to a swing.

He'd slept there for a while as she'd helped Eloise clean the entire first floor of the house. Robin and her girls had moved everything off the second floor days ago and cleaned that.

At the moment, they were waiting for Kristen, Clara, and Scott to arrive with the first load of items. AJ wouldn't leave the kitchen. She'd been assigned to be one of the unpackers here in the house. Matt couldn't come help as Saturday in the summertime was the busiest day at the golf course.

She currently wore Asher in a sling, the baby secure against the front of her body. "I'm guessing Aaron said no to that," she said.

"Billie said no," Eloise said. She'd just finished telling AJ and Laurel, who'd also been in the house for most of the morning, about Billie's first kiss—and the subsequent invitation to a boy's house on Rocky Ridge.

"You never want to go out to Rocky Ridge to meet a boy," AJ said. "Trust me on that."

Laurel looked at her with somber yet sparkling eyes. "Why's that, AJ?'

"Yes," Eloise said dryly. "Why's that?"

"They're all uppity out there," she said.

"Maddy's living out there," Eloise said.

"And that proves my point." AJ's eyebrows rose as she surveyed the other two women. "What? I'm right. She's a nice lady, but she's wealthy. She comes from money. She was married to a *congressman*, for crying out loud."

"Yeah, and you used to interview *professional athletes* while they wore *nothing but a towel*," El shot back. "Maddy is not uppity."

Sometimes those athletes wore nothing at all, but AJ kept that to herself.

"I broke up the biggest, longest drug ring in the cove," Laurel said. "No one's worshipping me."

Eloise burst out laughing, and AJ joined in. Laurel grinned widely, and then she straightened from where she'd been leaning over the island to get more pita and hummus. Robin had provided food at both houses for everyone coming to help that day, despite multiple protests. She simply didn't know how to let people do things for her without repayment, and food was the least she could do.

In a lot of ways, AJ admired Robin. If it had been her, she'd have been so frazzled with having to move out and clean her house so the next person could move in on the same day, she wouldn't have even remembered to feed herself. Robin had done that, and fed a dozen others as well.

"Hellllooo," a woman called, and the three of them turned toward the long hallway that led past the stairs to the front door.

"Who's that?" Laurel asked.

"Robin's mother," El muttered, and AJ was glad she recognized the voice for she hadn't.

Sure enough, Jennifer Golden breezed into the room, a designer handbag hanging off her forearm. "Wow." She looked around the room, barely acknowledging the women there. "This place looks good."

"We've got it all clean," El said. She moved over to Jennifer and gave her a quick hug. "Clara should be here any minute."

"I'm going to take some pictures first," Jennifer said. "Don't mind me."

AJ didn't know how to not mind Jennifer. She seemed to be judging everyone she came in contact with, and AJ didn't deal well with women her age. Her own mother had walked out on her as a teen, and AJ had done her best to reconcile that and move forward. She was still in therapy for a lot of things, and her mother came up every once in a while.

Jennifer began snapping photos of everything, and the conversation between Laurel, AJ, and Eloise didn't continue until she'd clicked her way down the hall. Then, they all seemed to take a big breath in together.

AJ blew hers out and smiled at the others. "She just radiates tension, you know?"

"Have you been around Clara lately?" Eloise asked. She shook her head and went back to wiping the counter she'd already wiped ten times. "I went over to Kristen's to talk to her about some booking systems for hotels and stuff, and we got nothing done. Absolutely nothing." She shook her head. "I hope I wasn't like that when I was getting Cliffside up and running."

AJ said, "Of course not, El. Things were stressful, but you never acted like we owed you."

"Clara doesn't do that either," El said. "It's...different. It's like she has a one-track mind. She has a question, and until it's satisfied, she can't think of anything else."

The rumble of the garage door going up met AJ's ears, and she turned again. "They're here." She threaded her finger through Asher's chubby ones and bounced his arm as she walked down the hall to the garage entrance. She opened it, and yes, Kristen had just pulled into the garage in her minivan.

A man rode in the passenger seat, and AJ's heartbeat sounded like a jackhammer in her ears. "Guys," she called over her shoulder without removing her eyes from the older gentleman. "You're gonna want to come here right now."

"What is it?" El asked. She and Laurel bustled up beside AJ, who simply waited for them to spot Kristen's new boyfriend.

She'd been very vehement about him *not* being her boyfriend. With the wedding last week, and everyone preparing to move this week, they hadn't had any of their weekly luncheons. AJ walked with Kristen and Lisa a couple of times a week, and she'd asked her about Theo.

Kristen had assured her over and over that she still wanted to do their walks together, and she'd walk with Theo on other days.

He emerged from the minivan, Kristen right behind him. She hurried around the front of the vehicle, and AJ didn't see Clara or Scott. They didn't have a car here on the island, but right now, AJ didn't much care where they were.

She wondered how she'd feel if her father ever started dating someone seriously. Or at all. After her mom had left, he'd gone through a lot of women, but none of them had been real relationships. It had been a way for him to blow off his steam and deaden himself to what his wife had done to him.

AJ understood that. She'd been using sex that way for a long time—until she'd met up with Matt again a couple of years ago.

"Girls." Kristen practically leapt in front of Theo. "This is Theodore Sands." She indicated him as if the three of them had gone blind in the past five seconds. "Theo, these are some of my girls."

"I'm not," Laurel said automatically.

Her voice almost sounded robotic, and Kristen chastised her and said, "Of course you are, Laurel. You may not have done the Seafaring program, but you are mine."

AJ loved Kristen with her whole heart in that moment. She stepped forward and out onto the squat, square cement block in the garage. "Hello, Theo. I'm AJ Hymas."

He pumped her hand as his gravelly voice said, "It's my pleasure to meet you."

No wonder Kristen was currently braiding her fingers together and pulling them apart. With his salt and pepper hair, that voice, and his height, even AJ would be attracted to him...in twenty years or so.

"Wow," she said. "I hope my husband ages as well as you, Theo."

"AJ," El said, pulling her back into the house. She stumbled over the lip, and everyone reached to steady her, what with Asher strapped to the front of her and making her weight unbalanced.

"Who's this little guy?" Theo extended his hand as if to tickle the baby, but AJ stood out of his reach now.

"Oh," AJ said. "My son, Asher."

"He's adorable." Theo's smile filled the garage with light, and he looked to El.

"Eloise Sherman," Kristen said. "Married to the Police Chief."

"Yes, you mentioned her." He shook El's hand too. "She came to help Clara the other day."

"Were you there?" El asked.

"No, no." Theo chuckled. "Kristen just told me about it." He looked at her with those blue eyes, and they sure seemed to say how much he liked her. AJ didn't know what to make of it, but it was just about the cutest thing she'd ever seen.

"And Laurel," Kristen said. "She's a cop and married to a cop. Due with their first baby in October."

"September," Laurel said. She wore a smile that said she didn't care which month Kristen said. "Nice to meet you, Theo. You said your last name is Sands?"

"That's right."

She exchanged a glance with Kristen, who cocked one hip. "You're not going to run a check on him."

"Of course not," Laurel said as she turned back to the house. "Aaron already did." She giggled as she retreated into the house.

AJ's smile filled her whole face when El said, "You knew

he would, Kristen. I'm happy to report you came back clean, Mister Sands."

"That's a relief," Theo joked. They all came into the house, and the garage door had just slammed when the front one opened.

Clara led the way inside, and AJ had a feeling Clara led the way in everything she did. Her daughter came after her, clutching a big brown stuffed monkey, followed by Scott in the rear.

"Hello, dear," Kristen said to Clara, and she quickly swept a kiss across her cheek.

"Jennifer said she'd be here," Clara said. "Her car is out front."

"She's here," AJ said. They all moved past the steps leading up and into the back of the house, which held the kitchen, dining room, and a decently-sized living room. It had a fireplace and a mantle, and the backyard was huge and well-maintained. If it wasn't on the opposite side of the island from the golf course, AJ would covet it.

She didn't have much of a yard for Asher to grow up in, and her house was so old, it was segmented into a lot of tiny little rooms. Still, she and Matt lived there for a nominal amount of rent, as his father owned the house. She couldn't complain, so she didn't.

Asher started to fuss, and AJ started to remove him from the sling. "You'll have to go back in the seat, buddy." He wore another of Jean's one-of-a-kind tees today, this one with a big sailboat on the front of it. It read "Mommy's best sailor" across the top, and she'd had a woman in the grocery store ask where she'd gotten it the first time he'd worn it.

"Can I hold him?" Lena asked, and AJ looked over to the woman. She sat on the couch, the monkey in her lap. He was probably half the size of Asher, and a stuffed animal didn't move or wiggle or cry.

AJ didn't know what to say, so she glanced over to Clara. Clara was talking to Laurel about something, but AJ caught Scott's eye. He raised his eyebrows and came over to her. "What's up?"

"Lena asked to hold Asher. Can she...do that?"

He glanced over to Lena, his smile coming quickly. "Yeah, she can." He went to sit beside her. "You have to hold him, Lena. He's a person. He doesn't just sit. You have to make sure he doesn't fall off your lap."

"Okay."

He stayed close, and once AJ had Asher unslung, she took him over to the couch too. She sat on Lena's other side, real close. She held her ten-month-old on her lap and said, "See? You tuck him right into you. Keep your arm wrapped around him."

She took a breath and passed the boy to Lena. She did exactly what AJ told her to do, just a little too tight.

"Don't crush him," Scott said with a laugh. "Lean back, Lena-Lou."

She did, and Asher, the bag of sand he was, sank into

her too. He looked over to AJ, who smiled at him. He kicked his legs, and babbled to himself, his fist going into his mouth.

AJ stood. "I'll get you a toy. He's teething so much right now, he'll chew on anything he can get in his mouth." She plucked a toy from the swing and turned back to Lena and Scott.

Lena leaned down and oh-so-softly placed a kiss on Asher's head. She looked at her dad, and pure love and joy radiated from her. Tears sprang to AJ's eyes, and her heart filled with love for Lena, her son, and Scott.

They'd been through hell and back, and AJ knew that journey by heart. She felt like she'd done it a few times in her life, and she never wanted to tread that path again. If holding a baby for a few minutes could bring such peace and joy to those doing it, AJ would let anyone hold Asher.

He squabbled, and the moment broke. AJ crouched in front of Lena and held the toy out for Asher. It took him a moment to latch onto it, but once he did, he brought it straight to his mouth. "See? He can gnaw on that while I help your mom unpack the kitchen."

She grinned at Lena, who smiled back.

"You have to help too," Scott said. "Remember, Mom wanted you to pick a room and then help carry in anything you carried out."

Lena said nothing, and AJ couldn't stay crouched with her knees bent the way she was. She groaned as she straightened, and she left Scott to watch over his daughter while she went to see what needed to be done to get Clara moved in quicker.

Then maybe they could do a late luncheon with everyone, and AJ pulled out her phone to send the text.

Chapter Eleven

Laurel Lehye missed sleeping on her back. With only a little over three months until her first baby was due, the weight of her belly exceeded what she could handle while lying flat. With the morning light coming in through the blinded windows, she finally opened her eyes.

Her husband Paul lay facing her, his eyes closed as he slept. He breathed in deeply, and Laurel matched her inhale to his. How she loved him. He'd always been so calm and steady with her. He loved her in word and deed, and Laurel hadn't had any idea of the kind of love two people could experience until she'd met him.

Her previous relationships had been so different than what she'd built with Paul. All of it came from him, she was sure, because she was still figuring out how to show her love in word and deed. He was much more vocal than she was, and every touch he gave her indicated how he felt.

Laurel had tried to do her best, and Paul said he'd never doubted her feelings for him.

She reached out and stroked her fingers down the side of his face. He started to wake, his hands moving toward her body too. He put one on their baby and one slid under her chin, cradling her face.

"What time is it?" he whispered.

"I don't know," she said back. She didn't have to go to work today, and he was only going into the station after they went to the doctor together that morning. "We're not late yet, I know that."

Paul opened his eyes, and Laurel smiled at him. "I love you."

"If you loved me, you'd have let me sleep until the very last minute." He teased her with a smile on his face. He did look exhausted, as he'd been assisting the Chief on hiring new officers for the past couple of weeks. With summer season in full swing, and more tourists on the island than ever before, Aaron didn't have the manpower to keep up.

That meant extra shifts for everyone, Paul included. Heck, Aaron himself had been out on a beat last week, and Laurel had never known the Chief of Police to get in a car and go out patrolling. At least not since she'd been employed by the Five Island Cove Police Department.

"Sorry," she said. "You looked so peaceful and handsome, I wanted to touch that." She pulled her hand away and covered his over her belly. "The baby is moving. Can you feel it?"

He looked down, but she wore a pair of pink pajamas. His face lit up. "Yeah," he said, his eyes coming back to hers as he pressed his palm more firmly against her body. "Does it hurt?"

"No," she said. "It's a little strange. A weird sensation. Sometimes it gets a little tight. But not really painful."

"He's squirming around."

"Yeah." Laurel felt the same squirming feeling in her chest. "Paul?"

"Mm?" He gazed evenly at her, fully alert now. She loved his dark eyes, and she hoped their baby inherited those. "What about Royce if it's a boy?"

"Royce." He tried the name out in his voice, and he didn't make a face. So, some improvement over the last name she'd suggested. The more she thought about it, the more she didn't like Carter either. Carter Lehye just didn't sound right.

With their last name, they really had to choose something carefully. If the doctor told them this morning that they were having a little girl, Laurel was fairly sure they'd name her Lucy. They both loved the name, and it sounded like angelic music when paired with Lehye.

"Royce Lehye," Paul said. "I don't hate it."

"I don't either." Laurel started to roll over, because she

had to in order to get out of bed on her side. She groaned as Paul pushed on her hip and then her back to help her, disliking that she even needed help. She felt like a giant beach ball, getting rolled around in her own bed, and she still had a third of her pregnancy to go.

"Paul?" she asked again.

"Yeah, sweetheart?"

She took a deep breath. She needed to get the snakes out of her stomach, and the best way to do that was to have a conversation. Even if it was hard. Even if she didn't know the outcome of it. "I've been thinking about...not going back to work after the baby is born." She twisted to look over her shoulder, needing to see his reaction.

She couldn't quite see him, but the mood in the bedroom shifted. "Yeah?" he asked, the bed moving as he did.

"Yeah," she said. Her hands worried around one another, and she looked at her fingers. "I don't know who we'd have watch the baby. My parents are in Nantucket, and your dad is in *Ohio*. Julie is busy with her own family, and she doesn't live here besides. We'd have to find a daycare, and I haven't even started looking."

Those were just the external reasons, and Laurel reminded herself that she loved and trusted Paul explicitly. "Plus, I sort of don't want to. I want to raise our child. Me and you. I don't want to give him to someone else during the day. The hours are crazy as it is, and I don't know. I've been thinking I'll take my maternity leave, but then that I should maybe...quit."

He knelt behind her, his hands on her shoulders now. He massaged and said nothing, and Laurel let her head roll left and right as he worked the tension from her muscles. He placed a kiss on the sensitive skin on the back of her neck, and she leaned back into the touch.

"It's fine with me, hon," he said. "I'd love to have you home with the baby."

"Can we afford it?"

"I'm sure we'll work it out," he said. "People do."

"Maybe we can sit down and look at the finances this weekend," she said. She didn't do a lot of that; Paul did. He paid the bills, and they didn't overspend. They should have money in savings, but Laurel didn't know how much.

She felt out of control because of it, and she didn't like it. Paul trailed kisses down both sides of her neck, his hands sliding down her arms. She sighed as he touched her in such an intimate way, and it was like he could take all of her cares and worries and make them disappear.

He held them inside himself so she didn't have to concern herself with them, and she appreciated that so much.

He got out of bed and knelt in front of her now, still carefully touching her with his big, Deputy hands. He looked right into her eyes as he said, "I don't want you to worry about the money, Laurel. I make a good salary. We've got savings."

Her chin shook as her emotions overcame her. She wrapped her arms around him and he leaned his face against her chest. "I love you," she whispered.

"Mm, I love you too." He pulled back and grinned at her. "Since you got us up early, can we shower together?"

Laurel smiled at him and took his face in her hands. She kissed him, so glad she'd taken another chance on being with a man. "Yes," she whispered.

A few hours later, Laurel once again lay in bed, this one completely different than hers at home. The doctor's office was cold, and her shirt had been pushed clear up under her chest.

Their doctor, a woman named Elizabeth Ellison, smiled at Laurel. "Are you ready to see how your baby is doing?"

Laurel nodded, and Paul's hand in hers tightened as he said, "Yes."

Cold gel got squirted onto her belly, and Dr. Ellison sat down on her rolling stool. "All right." She lubricated the wand too and pressed it to Laurel's body. "Last time, she was looking good. Nothing to be concerned about. She's big enough now for us to see the gender."

An infant heartbeat echoed through the room, and Laurel grinned at the black and white screen at her eye-level.

"Are you still wanting to know the gender?" Dr. Ellison asked.

Laurel looked away from the monitor to Paul, but he kept his gaze on the screen. "Yes," he murmured again. She forgot sometimes that he wasn't as connected to the baby. Laurel felt her every move, and she weighed on her physically and mentally and emotionally twenty-four seven.

But for Paul, he didn't get to experience any of that. Laurel had him feel the baby move whenever she did and he was home, but it was different.

"Yes," Laurel said, and Dr. Ellison looked back and the screen.

"She's on her back," she said. "Being shy, but her spine looks great." She continued to detail the lines and parts of the baby. "Good, strong heartbeat. Let's see...if we can't get her to turn..." She pressed a little harder on Laurel's belly, and she automatically tensed against it.

The baby did indeed roll, and Dr. Ellison said, "There you go, baby."

Laurel had such an odd sensation of feeling the baby move inside her and seeing it on the screen too. Paul chuckled and leaned down to kiss her forehead.

"Oh, there we see it," Dr. Ellison said. "See this right here?" She indicated a body part protruding from the baby's body. "That's your son's penis."

A sense of relief Laurel hadn't anticipated filled her. She'd told Paul numerous times she didn't care if their baby was a boy or a girl, and she didn't. At the same time, she wasn't sure how to deal with girls and all of their feminine issues. She herself didn't feel very feminine, and as her eyes filled with tears, she realized she'd been secretly hoping for a boy.

The problem now would be the name. They still didn't have a male name they both liked, but Laurel couldn't keep the smile from her face.

Dr. Ellison said everything looked great with the baby, and she wiped the gel from Laurel's belly. She and Paul pulled down her shirt together, and he offered her a hand to help her sit up. She couldn't have done it herself, so she appreciated the help, and she got to her feet as the baby—her son—settled on her sciatic nerve and pain shot down to her ankle.

She hissed out a slow breath as Paul put his hand on her lower back and Dr. Ellison said she should come back in a month to see how things were going. "Vitamins okay?" she asked.

"I need more," Laurel said.

The doctor nodded and started writing a scrip. "What else, Laurel? Are you sleeping?"

"Okay," she said at the same time Paul said, "No, she doesn't."

Their eyes met, and his eyebrows raised. "You don't," he said. He faced the doctor again. "She tosses and turns a lot. Sometimes she gets up and can sleep for an hour or so on the couch. She's tired all the time."

Dr. Ellison wore concern in her eyes. "I can give you a light sleeping aid," she said.

"No," Laurel said, firm on this. "I don't want to take anything." She shook her head. "I'm trying to do some meditation and calming mind methods before I go to bed. I ordered one of those massage guns. But I don't need any medication."

"Partner massage is a good idea too," Dr. Ellison said. "Paul seems very attentive." She gave him a smile, because he was one of the most personable people in the world, and everyone loved him. "I'm sure he'll rub your feet or back."

"He does," Laurel said, tucking herself into his side.

"Eat earlier in the day," Dr. Ellison said. "Reduce naps."

"She doesn't nap," Paul said. "I keep telling her to."

"I'm going to today," Laurel said, hipping him. She didn't like talking about herself like this, as if she could change everything wrong with herself while she stood here in the doctor's office, the scent of machines and gel hanging in the air.

"Other than being tired, you're doing okay?" Dr. Ellison asked.

"The heartburn chews have helped a lot," Laurel said. She'd also been avoiding spicy foods, and that had helped too. Sometimes, nothing helped, but the image of Laurel's son streamed through her mind, and she knew any amount of heartburn was worth the little boy growing inside her.

"All right," Dr. Ellison said. "Call me with anything."

She handed the prescription for the prenatal vitamins to Paul and opened the door. She held it for them while they left, and Laurel rested one hand protectively on her belly as she walked out of the building.

In the car, Paul started the ignition and the air conditioning started to blast into the vehicle. "A boy," he said with wonder. A huge smile filled his face. "I can't believe it."

"I've been pregnant for six months," Laurel said dryly. "You knew we were having a baby."

"It's just so...real now." He looked at her, and Laurel loved the light in his eyes. "Are you going to call your mom?"

"Yes," she said.

"Then we'll call Julie," he said. "And you can text all your girlfriends."

Laurel nodded and tapped to dial her mother. She put the phone on speaker so Paul could hear too, and they were both smiling when her mom said, "Laurel, dear, how are you?"

"Good," she said.

"Hello, Fae," Paul said.

"Oh, I get both of you," her mom said. "This must be something big."

"We went to the doctor today," Laurel said. She hadn't told anyone about today's appointment. She wasn't sure why she still had such a hard time sharing things. She'd existed for so long in a state of shame and secrets, and she was still trying to overcome that.

"Everything's okay with the baby?" her mom asked.

"Yes." Laurel smiled out the windshield. "Paul's excited about something. He wanted to call you."

He chuckled, and Laurel watched as he shook his head. "I am excited, but we both wanted to call," he said. "We're having a boy."

"A boy!" Her mom laughed, and Laurel joined her. She wasn't sure what was so magical about babies, only that there was something. Perhaps it was that they were touched by heaven, even before they were born. Perhaps it was because they came into the world so helpless and needed someone to take care of them for a long time before they could walk, talk, get their own food, or even use the bathroom by themselves.

No matter what, Laurel loved the magical feeling surrounding babies, and as Paul joked with her mom about the terrible boy names they'd discarded, Laurel had a thought that she'd like to have as many babies as she could.

She hardly recognized herself and her thoughts, as she'd once vowed to never get married again and to never, ever become a mother. Only five years ago, she wouldn't have been able to fathom wanting a baby. A helpless, tiny waif of a human who couldn't do anything for itself.

Now, she wanted a whole bunch of them?

She smiled to herself and closed her eyes. The car

moved, and Laurel let her body flow with it. "I love you, Mom," she said as the conversation wrapped up. "We'll come up to Nantucket soon, okay?"

"Yep, see you soon." The call ended, and Laurel positioned her phone right in front of her face.

Paul and I went to the doctor today, she tapped out as Paul started to dial his sister. *We're having a boy!*

She sent the text to her friends, expecting to get a flurry of responses. Boy, did she get them. Everything from, *I'm so excited for you, Laurel*, from Kristen to *Our boys will grow up together!* from AJ and then *!!!!!!!!!!!!!* from Robin, and then the sweetest note from Jean imaginable.

Oh, Laurel, how exciting. You and Paul must be thrilled. I'll start on the blue sailor outfit right away.

Laurel's eyes filled with tears. She had no idea how she would feel if she were Jean. If she wanted a baby more than anything—and had just lost a baby a few months ago—to be celebrating with another pregnant woman.

To be making clothes for that woman's baby instead of her own. Laurel couldn't even fathom it, and she sniffled and wiped her eyes, her love for Jean growing exponentially with how tender and graceful she was about everything.

"Laurel has something she wants to tell you," Paul said, and she looked up from her phone. He grinned at her, noticed the tears, and lifted his eyebrows.

She leaned toward the radio, as he'd called Julie through the Bluetooth in the car. "We're having a baby boy!"

His sister screamed, as she tended to be a bit over-dramatic. Laurel laughed, because she was having a baby boy, and she was excited about it too.

Paul talked to Julie as he drove them over to the west side of the island and into the parking lot at Chips. "All right, Jules," he said, starting to get a little frustration in his tone. "We just got to our lunch spot, so I have to go."

"Just think about Chester," Julie said. "It's a good name, Paul, and I never could use it."

Laurel shook her head and Paul said, "We'll think about it, sis. Love you. Bye." He jabbed at the screen to end the call, and silence settled over them.

She reached for his hand and said, "We have to find a name that starts with L that isn't Larry."

Paul chuckled and lifted her hand to his lips. He kissed the back of it, then flipped her arm and touched his mouth to the inside of her wrist. Shivers shot through her. When he looked up, his eyes meeting hers, he said, "I dunno. I kinda like Larry Lehye."

"No." She shook her head emphatically, though she knew he was kidding. "Absolutely not, Paul." She wouldn't be calling down the beach, "Larry! Larry, come back!" Nope. Never.

"Liam?" he said, and Laurel perked up.

"I actually like Liam," she said. "It's kind of a pretty-boy name, though. You think?"

He shrugged and said, "I have no idea. What I do know

is all this talk about babies and names and you quitting your job has me starving." He grinned and got out of the car. He jogged around to help her, and since she was big and slow and cumbersome, she'd only opened the door and gotten her legs out before he arrived.

He helped her up and kept her hands in his. Laurel faced Chips, which was one of their favorite fast-casual fish shops here on Diamond Island. "You're really okay with me not going back to work?" she asked.

"Yes, Laurel," he said, and she knew he was serious when he used her name. He usually called her "hon," or "sweetheart" or "baby" or even "my love." When he used her name, she never doubted him.

"I haven't decided for sure," she said. "I just wanted to talk to you about it."

"I think you're right." He reached to open the door to Chips, and he held it as she went into the blessed air conditioning first. "If you're going back, we better figure out child care."

"Yeah." She didn't want to do that, and deep down, she'd already decided. Now, she just needed to talk to Aaron and go over the finances with Paul so she could sleep better at night.

Chapter Twelve

Clara looked up from the newly installed countertop as the door to Friendship Inn opened. She expected to see Tessa Simmons enter, and she did. The woman had shoulder-length, dark brown hair, a quick smile, and a good, hardworking spirit.

She came to the inn a few mornings each week, and she worked incredibly hard. With her help, over the past few weeks, Clara and Scott had managed to clean out the administrative offices, get the new furniture and fixtures installed, and have a functional office space in the inn.

Outside, Scott had been working with the construction crews to get the debris off the property. They still had a long way to go, but every day the piles got a little smaller. The inn was structurally sound now, at least on the north side. It would need to be refinished once all the debris was gone, and Scott had been working with a landscape architect friend back in Montpelier to design the green space they'd put where that half of the inn had been.

"Good morning," she said to Tessa. She straightened from the counter, where she'd been leaning over, studying the list of things that needed to be done next.

It felt like the list would never be finished, and after she'd spoken to Eloise for only a few minutes, Clara had realized it wouldn't be. Ever. Eloise had opened the Cliffside Inn a couple of years ago, and she still had a monster-long to-do list every single day.

It'll consume you, Eloise said. *You have to find a way for it not to do that.*

Clara didn't know how to do that, at least right now.

She didn't know how to get a restaurant to come into the spaces she had. All the emails and phone calls she'd put out had either gone unanswered or the answer had been no, thanks.

Friendship Island was hard to get to, they said.

The space doesn't fit our needs, she'd heard.

We're not looking to expand to such a small market, one manager had told her.

Her spirits existed about an inch off the floor, especially when Tessa said, "They didn't come fix the stairs," her eyes stuck on the huge, could-be-beautiful staircase that led up to the second floor from the back of the lobby.

Clara followed her gaze. "No," she said, sudden tension

in her jaw. "I got the same thing as yesterday. 'We'll be there tomorrow.'"

Tessa looked at her. "Maybe you need to find someone else."

"Maybe." Clara didn't know *who.* She hadn't lived in Five Island Cove for decades, and she didn't have the connections other business owners may have had. She'd talked to Eloise for a few minutes, but she didn't want to bother the woman. She'd asked for stories about Friendship Inn and Island, and lots of her mother's girls had said they'd talk to her.

She hadn't followed up. That had never happened.

She wasn't sure why she was sabotaging herself, but it sure felt like she was. Clara instantly pushed against that idea, because why would someone make their own life harder?

"Are we going up to the second level?" Tessa asked. She gathered her hair into a blunt ponytail at the nape of her neck and secured it with a black elastic band.

"No," Clara said. "The stairs are unsafe, and there's no working elevator." She didn't even want to talk about how much an elevator cost. Not only that, but in order to get a grant to pay for it, she had to request and receive and turn in three current bids. With all the construction happening on Five Island Cove right now, bids changed every day, it seemed, and Clara had started to think perhaps she should just pay for the elevator instead of trying to get the grant.

"So the second café space today," Tessa said. She turned toward the left corner of the space, and Clara watched the disappointment roll across her face. To her credit, Tessa wiped it away before she looked at Clara again. "I'll get the cart. Is Lena here today?"

"I left her with my mother," Clara said. "They went walking with AJ and Jean, and then Jean is going to do some private sewing lessons with Lena."

"Oh, that's fantastic." Tessa seemed like she really thought so too. She was warm and genuine, if a bit distant sometimes too. She definitely got in a groove of working, and she didn't need to talk to anyone while she did.

She went into the back room to get the cleaning cart, and a few moments later, she pushed it toward the kitchen space they'd been working to clean up. Clara had looked once at replacement commercial kitchen appliances, and the price tags had been enough to make her cry.

She'd shut the laptop and gone to bed in pure darkness, after checking on Lena in her new bedroom. Her daughter had settled reasonably well in Five Island Cove, and Clara knew a large part of that came from her mother. Lena loved her grandmother, and Clara's mother adored Lena.

She told her about the stray cats at her condo, and spun tales of her Seafaring Girls from decades ago. They laughed together, and her mother knew all of Lena's favorite things. A sense of regret and wistfulness filled Clara.

She wished her summer days were filled with morning

walks with friends, sewing lessons, lunches at beachside cafés, and lazy afternoons with her family. Her life had never quite been that, as Clara had always denied herself the opportunity to really let people in.

She had Scott, and once Lena had come along, the girl had required so much attention. Clara loved her dearly, but she hadn't had time for lunches with friends, to sew clothes, or to perpetuate deep familial relationships.

She'd spent more than her fair share of her time fixing things Lena had broken or consoling the girl before, during, and after school. She had worked part-time for a few years while Lena was in junior high, but it had become hard again with a new school and more challenging curriculum.

Now that Lena was an adult, Clara had a bit more freedom. Now, however, she had no money and still no time to do any of the glorious things she saw her mother doing with her Seafaring Girls and their friends.

She was on their group text, and she didn't mind getting the messages. She never quite knew how to respond or fit into the conversation, so she rarely contributed. Her mom had asked her if she wanted to be removed, and Clara had said no.

Why, she wasn't sure. She felt some sort of lifeline to those women, and it made absolutely no sense.

She looked down at her list again, her thoughts scattered and lost now. "Where was I?" Outside, a machine beeped and growled, but in here, Clara had some semblance of air conditioning. It didn't work great, especially in this large, open room, but it was enough to ward off the worst of the heat.

After tucking her hair behind her ear, she focused on her list. "Ferry service," she said. She'd gone to a City Council meeting, intending to ask how she could get the ferry service to Friendship Island restored. They'd been so busy talking about zoning and new businesses coming to the island that she hadn't had the opportunity.

Helplessness filled her now too. She needed it to be easier to get to the island. If she couldn't do that, everything else she and Scott were doing here would be useless. For naught.

She picked up her phone, the blue light at the top indicating she'd received a text. It had come from Kelli Webb to the group, and it said, *Shad's on lockdown in the government building. Anyone know what's up?*

As Clara watched, texts rolled in. Robin, Alice, and AJ hadn't heard anything. No one in her family responded, which meant Jean, Lena, and Mom were probably in the lighthouse, sewing already.

Eloise didn't respond either, but Clara hadn't expected her to. She usually only did if something was a major event, or during set hours—when she rode the ferry to and from Sanctuary Island. She lived on Diamond with her husband and two girls, and her only downtime came on the ferry ride.

Laurel would have the most information, and she said nothing. If there was a situation, she'd probably be called to it, and since Clara had no TV or radio service out here, she had no clue why Kelli's husband would be locked down in the government buildings.

Her mind niggled at her, telling her to ask Kelli what her husband did. If he worked in the government here on Five Island Cove, would he know the right people Clara needed to talk to in order to get the ferry service to run to this island?

Even if there was one ferry that only went back and forth from the Sanctuary port to Friendship Island, it would be enough. It was a fifteen-minute boat ride. Leaves every half-hour, during regular ferry hours.

She knew Five Island Cove housed ferries at all the ports, so people wouldn't be stranded on any one island. Sanctuary could house one more ferry.

"You've got to get over yourself," she muttered to herself. The words drifted up into the air, getting lost among all the space above her.

She needed to talk to Kelli. And Alice. And AJ. All of them. She didn't have any more time to waste. Instead of sending a message to them, she called the manager at Boyd's Home Repair.

"Hello, Boyd's," their receptionist, Nancy, said.

"Yes, hello," Clara said crisply. "This is Clara Tanner,

and I'm still waiting for someone to come fix my staircase out at Friendship Inn?"

"Oh, Clara," the woman said. "I was going to call you this morning. Devon tried to get out there yesterday, but there's no ferry."

Clara ground her teeth together. "He has to come in the morning. Nine o'clock. We have a boat we charter out on every day."

"Oh, well, let me check his schedule..." That was the same run-around Clara had gotten last time. She'd told Nancy all of this already. "Looks like next Wednesday." She positively chirped the words, like she was doing Clara a grand favor.

"Fine," Clara said. "I won't let the boat captain leave without him. Nine o'clock. Sanctuary port."

"Yes, ma'am," Nancy said.

Clara ended the call and lowered the phone, something barbed and sticky in the back of her throat. She could barely swallow past it, and she hated the panic building in her chest.

On the group text, Kelli had texted to say it was a fire drill, and everything was fine. *Haha.*

Clara fingers hovered over the phone. She had to send this text now, or she'd lose all of her nerve and never do it.

Who can meet for lunch this week sometime? she typed out. *I'd love to hear the stories of Friendship Inn and Island,*

and Kelli, I'd love to know if your husband can help me get ferry service out here.

She read over the words again, fixed a couple, and sent the message. Her pulse sprinted in her chest, and she threw her phone away from her. It skidded across the new countertops and onto the floor. A loud *crack!* echoed up toward the ceiling, and Clara groaned as she hustled after her device.

"You don't have money to replace this," she scolded herself. She picked up the phone and checked it. Only a spider-web crack in the top left corner. Still usable.

No one had responded to her text, and her phone rang while she held it in her hand. She didn't know the number, but it had a local Five Island Cove area code. With a ball of nerves in her throat, she tapped to answer it.

"Hello?"

"Is this Clara Tanner?" a woman asked.

"Yes," she said.

"You're restoring Friendship Inn, correct?"

"Yes, ma'am." Clara turned toward the door, but no one came inside. What if no one came to the inn? What if she couldn't achieve all of the things that needed to be achieved to get the doors open? What would she and Scott and Lena do then?

"I'd like to meet with you," she said.

"About?" Clara came to her senses and pushed the panic out of her head. It had no place there, and she couldn't think around it. "And to whom am I talking to?"

"I'd like to propose the idea of being a silent partner," the woman said. "I'd love to see your business plans. Your sketches and ideas. All of it. If there's a way I can help from the sidelines, I'd be interested in seeing if we can work out a deal."

Clara's throat had gone dry. "You want to fund us," she said. She'd been married to a financial investor for over twenty years. She knew how people could talk in circles sometimes. "And be part-owner."

"In name only," the woman said. "I have several business ventures around the cove. This would just be another one."

"In exchange for...?" Clara prompted.

"Those details would be worked out in the future," she said. "Right now, I'm just asking if you'd like to sit down with me, have some lunch, and go over a few things. I want to see if *you're* the type of businesswoman *I* want to work with."

Clara suddenly felt completely out of her element. She was no businesswoman, she knew that. Her chest pinched; she closed her eyes and tried to think.

"I could always use a good meal," Clara said. "But I'm not agreeing to meet someone whose name I don't know."

The woman chuckled—not a giggle. Not a laugh. Something deeper and less feminine. "I wouldn't expect anything less from a potential partner, at least a smart one." Another light chuckle. "You already know me, Clara. It's Jennifer Golden."

"Jennifer Golden?" Her landlord? The woman whose house she and Scott lived in? Robin's mother.

"Yes," Jennifer said. "And there is a condition of our meeting and potential partnership."

Clara swallowed. "What is it?"

"You can't tell my daughter about it. Ever."

An hour later, Clara signaled to Scott. He left the construction site and came toward her. She met him, Tessa at her side. She gestured between them. "We're going to Diamond for lunch. I'm meeting with all of the girls there to talk about Friendship Inn and Island."

Scott beamed at her, and thankfully, he didn't embarrass her in front of Tessa. Of course he wouldn't. He'd never done that to her. "That's great, hon," he said. "Have fun."

"Did you want to stay? Ryan said he can come back and get you at the normal time." She hoped Scott would stay. He had nothing to do at the house on Diamond Island and plenty to get done here.

"Yeah, I'll stay," he said, and relief poured through Clara. "Have fun."

"You too." She wasn't sure why she'd said that. She turned with Tessa, and they walked toward the dock. "Now, remember," she said to Tessa. "Not a word to anyone during lunch today about Jennifer Golden."

Tessa nodded, her mouth pressed into a tight line. Clara had managed to get Jennifer to agree to lunch with her and Tessa, because she needed an outside opinion. She barely trusted herself anymore, and she wouldn't go into an agreement with Jennifer without a second opinion. She didn't know Tessa extremely well, but well enough to trust her. After all, she had no vested interest in the inn. She came and worked a few hours for a few days each week. Nothing more. Nothing less.

Clara would tell Scott about it after the meeting, and her gut writhed as she stepped onto the boat. The thought of sitting across from Robin at lunch in only another hour, this secret right beneath her tongue, absolutely terrifying.

She told herself to be brave. She needed the information these women had. She needed more money than she currently had. If she wanted to get this inn off the ground, she had to do something more than she'd been doing.

She had to do something drastic—and she was running out of time.

Chapter Thirteen

Tessa Simmons walked one step behind Clara at all times. She wasn't sure why. She knew where she was going just as well as the other woman did. She'd met all the women they were currently going to see for lunch.

Her breath felt labored, like it was hard to inhale all the way, and she knew it was because she'd come up against an opportunity—and she hadn't taken it.

She'd been chartering her own boat out to Friendship Island for a few weeks now. She'd seen what kind of shape the inn was in. She knew Clara and Scott were up to their eyeballs in garbage. Bad staircases. Mold. Mildew. Broken windows. No ferry services. No food on the island.

To be honest, she had no clue how Clara thought she could achieve anything with that inn. She'd seen the work Julia and Maddy had put in at The Lighthouse Inn, and it had been one-twentieth of the size. They'd done it by sheer will and hard work—and a nearly unlimited budget from the Nantucket Historical Society.

Tessa wasn't sure what Clara was dealing with, but the desperation reeked off of her. Tessa could feel it the moment she stepped onto the island until the second she got back on the boat. Even now, her shoulders stayed tense, and all Clara was doing was smiling and hugging Robin Grover.

Tessa took her turn doing that too, her friendship and admiration for the woman genuine. She cut a look over to Clara, who wasn't being genuine. Her gut ached, and she didn't want to be there. Tessa scented the same vibe coming from Clara too, and she realized she needed to be at the meeting with Jennifer Golden—Robin's mother—so she'd know what she was dealing with at Friendship Inn too.

Her bleeding heart had gotten the idea of helping Clara and Scott with the inn in a more formal and more pronounced role. That of an investor.

She and Janey had inherited a lot of money from their mother's estate after her death, and Tessa didn't need any of it. She got an alimony from her first husband. Her only child was grown and out of the house. What else did she have to do, really?

She thought of Abe, and she couldn't wait to text him about the developments in the past couple of hours.

"Tessa," Alice Rice said, and Tessa gave her a hug too. She liked all of the women here in this group on Five Island

Cove, but she was slow to trust. Her past experiences had made that difficult for her, and she looked around for Eloise Sherman.

She didn't see the woman, and Clara said, "No, no, Eloise can't come. She said she'd bring dinner to my house and meet with me one night this week." She wore a bejeweled smile that Tessa saw right past and led the way to a large table in the corner of the restaurant.

It was peak summer season, but after prime lunchtime. The restaurant still bustled with patrons and activity, and Tessa thankfully got a seat beside Jean on her left and Kelli on her right. They'd definitely been two of the quieter women during the wedding preparations two weeks ago, and Tessa gave them each a smile.

"How's the inn, Tessa?" Jean asked as she lifted her menu.

"It's..." Tessa threw a glance over to Clara, but she'd immediately gone into a near-huddle conversation with Robin, Alice, and AJ. Kristen sat beside them, looking rather lost until the hostess handed her a menu. "Okay," she said. "The work is fine. I honestly don't know how Clara and Scott are going to get it open, though. There's a *lot* that needs to be done."

"I had to remodel and renovate my childhood home," Kelli said. "I turned it into a health and wellness studio. It was one house and took forever."

"A lot of what they do is cookie-cutter," Jean said.

"They get one room done, and the others should go quickly."

If they have the budget, Tessa thought but kept to herself. There was a lot she needed to keep under her tongue, and so she buried herself in her menu too. A couple of waiters came and took drink orders, and then Alice said, "All right. I'm going to tell the story of our disastrous night on Friendship Island."

"Oh, come on," AJ said. "It wasn't that disastrous."

"That's because you and Kelli went up on the roof," Alice said. "Some of us had to stay in the room."

"You didn't have to do anything," AJ shot back. They both wore smiles, and Tessa sensed a deep history between these people.

Laurel said nothing, her attention still on her menu, and Tessa likewise watched Jean, who hadn't been part of the Seafaring Girls either.

Only five of them had been—Robin, Alice, AJ, Kelli, and Eloise—and they'd added others to their group over time. Laurel was a cop who'd come into their lives at some point, and Jean was Kristen's daughter-in-law. Clara was Kristen's daughter, and in that moment, Tessa realized everything and everyone at the table revolved around her.

Kristen Shields. She smiled at AJ and said something that didn't carry to Tessa further down the table. She was kind and wise, probably close to eighty years old, and to Tessa, reminded her of Helen Ivy.

Alice told the story of the five of them rowing out to the island. Losing sight of it. Finally getting there, and then getting stranded. "The island used to be a bustling place," Robin said. "Anyone who was anyone went there in the summer. We had school dances there, and all the cool kids had big parties there."

"How'd they get there?" Clara asked. Tessa watched as she clicked a pen into action, a small notebook on the table in front of her. She carried an enormous bag with her everywhere she went, so the notebook wasn't surprising. For all Tessa knew, she could have a desktop computer in that bright green-apple bag.

"There was a ferry service," Alice said. "Lots of boat rentals too. Canoes, kayaks, all of it. We rented kayaks and rowed. Lots of people did."

Clara's pen scratched over the paper. "Who do I talk to about resuming the ferry service, do you think?" Her eyes sought out Kelli, and the woman cleared her throat.

"I did text Shad," she said. "He said you should go talk to him. He's not over the ferry system, but he knows who is."

Alice raised her hand. "I know who is. The ferry service isn't run by the city or the township. It's a private company." She shifted in her seat.

"Yeah," Robin said with a grin. "One of Alice's ex-boyfriends—from high school and what? Last year?"

"No," Alice bit out. "Not last year."

Robin grinned like she'd won a million dollars in the lottery, and Tessa liked the banter between these women. She found herself smiling too, and appreciated the way Alice shot daggers at Robin and then cheered right back up.

"His name is Will Bridge," Alice said. "I have his number somewhere." She looked at her phone, but she didn't pick it up. Tessa didn't want to imagine the riot that might have started if she had.

"Great," Clara said. "I'd love to get that from you." She looked down the table to Kelli. "I'd still love to talk to Shad. Maybe I need permits or something."

"I'll text you his number." Kelli set about doing that, and Clara continued to ask questions. Everyone contributed something except Tessa. She sat and listened, laughed when the others did, and just enjoyed herself among these people.

She'd had no idea she'd find this many women to be friends with here in Five Island Cove. She'd had no idea that taking a job close to her beachfront cottage would yield such a thing. Once the lunch ended, she and Clara got in the RideShare to get back to the ferry station.

"That was amazing," Clara said. "I've been so nervous about doing that."

"Really?" Tessa asked. "I really like them. They all seem really nice and normal." Normal. That was all Tessa wanted after everything she'd been through in the past year.

"Yes," Clara said. "I don't know why I was nervous. I haven't had many female friends in my life." She looked over to Tessa, who nodded. "Lena and Scott have been everything for me for so long." She almost looked worried admitting that.

"You didn't like living here either, right?" Tessa asked. She felt like she'd stepped out onto ice when she wasn't sure if it was frozen all the way through.

Clara looked out her window. "Right."

"So you're being brave," Tessa said. "Coming back here and taking on such a big project." She folded her hands in her lap. The urge to tell Clara about her inheritance and offer help once again flew to the forefront of her mind. Tessa bit back the words. She didn't want to say anything until they'd met with Jennifer.

Clara turned toward her, a new light of hope in her eyes. "Yes," she said slowly. "I'm trying to be brave."

"I honestly don't know if you can get that inn open," Tessa said. "I'm willing to work with you and help as much as I can, but we're..." She trailed off, what they were obvious.

Middle-aged women.

They couldn't fix stairs or inspect buildings. Tessa couldn't drive a ferry or pour a new dock.

"It's a long shot," Clara admitted. "I did have Julia Harper talk to me about coming to help. She runs The Lighthouse Inn, I guess?" Her eyebrows went up.

Tessa nodded, her smile widening. "You'd be lucky to have Julia. She and Maddy fixed up and opened The Lighthouse Inn just last fall. And I heard her talking to Eloise, who obviously knows what she's doing too. She said the Cliffside Inn is booked through the end of the year."

Clara nodded and looked back out the window. "I need to talk to both of them."

"And now that you've talked to all of those ladies," Tessa said. "You won't be nervous to talk to them." She gave Clara an encouraging smile the other woman didn't see.

When they got back to Sanctuary Island, Tessa waved to Clara. "See you Thursday."

"On Diamond," Clara said, tapping and looking at her phone. "The Glass Dolphin. Eleven-thirty." She looked up. "Let's dress up. Look professional."

Tessa didn't need to look down at what she had on today to know it wouldn't pass muster. She rarely wore jeans, but a pair of black cotton shorts wasn't professional enough to meet with a potential investor.

"It is if the investor is you," she muttered to herself as she headed down the sidewalk. Her house sat about a mile from the ferry station, and rather than wait for a ride, she could walk. About halfway there, she regretted her decision.

There wasn't a breeze to be felt on the island and sweat ran down her face. By the time she made it home, her hair was soaking wet all along her hairline. Inside the house, Tessa washed her hands and plugged in her phone.

The sun beat down outside, and she changed into her

swimming suit, stocked up her beach bag with bottled water and red licorice, stepped outside, and sprayed herself with fifty SPF sunscreen. Then, only a few steps past her back deck, her sandaled feet met sand, and she sighed as she continued toward a lounger she'd put beneath a tree a month ago.

She settled into it, the breeze out here closer to the water finally kissing her skin. With her snacks and a drink nearby, she sighed. She'd brought out a book, but right now, she just wanted to drift.

Drift, and let her mind go wherever it wanted.

She must've fallen asleep, because the next thing she knew, someone said, "Tess, honey," and touched her shoulder.

She jerked away from the sound and the pressure, her adrenaline spiking. In a moment, she was back on the boat where she'd been drugged, tied, and kidnapped. She had to get off. Now. Swim to shore.

She blinked, and Abe's handsome face came into view. He sat on the end of her lounger, his eyes concerned even as his lips started to turn upward into a smile. "Sorry, I startled you."

She'd not told him about everything that had happened to her in Nantucket Point last year. Something told her to do so now.

He nodded back to her house. "I brought ribs. Did you still want me to smoke them for dinner?"

"Yes," she said. Her adrenaline faded, and she sat up. "Sorry. I…you scared me."

He nodded and looked at his hands. He knew there was something between them, and Tessa had told him she'd confide in him when the time was right.

"I was kidnapped last year," she said. She drew in a big breath, ready to expel this part of her life. It didn't get to control her anymore.

Abe's eyes flew to hers. "You were?"

She nodded. "By my mother's neighbor. It was all over the news."

"I didn't realize it was you," he said softly. He didn't try to touch her again, but Tessa wanted him to. She wanted him to know she wasn't broken.

She reached for his hand and knitted their fingers together. "I feel safe with you."

He lit up, the kindness in his face almost more than Tessa could bear. "Thanks, Tess." He leaned forward and kissed her. "Do you want to talk more about it?"

She took a moment to think about it as she gathered her wrappers and water bottle. Tucking them into her bag, she said, "I don't think so. It's not going to define me anymore." She stood, and Abe took her into an embrace. She did feel strong and safe in his arms—and out of them.

Leaving Nantucket had been the right thing for her, and true happiness filled her. They started back toward her beach cottage, and she said, "How was the shop today?"

"Good," Abe said. "I got the contracts for my son to sign." He smiled at the sand, and Tessa found him so adorable. "We're meeting with Sean in the morning."

"That's exciting." Tessa couldn't believe she'd found a man willing to relocate for her. For *her*. She hadn't realized how she'd followed her family around for her whole life, and it felt good to be the sun for once. To be the center of the universe and have everyone else circle her—even if it was only Abe.

Because "only Abe" was all she needed, and the moment they made it back inside her house, she turned toward him and kissed him. "How long do the ribs need to smoke?" she asked before pressing her lips to his again.

He kissed her back, his hands sliding along her hips and up her back. When he broke their connection, he looked hungry...for her. "At least an hour," he said. "After I get them on the grill."

She smiled at him and stepped back. "You do that then. I'll shower and...maybe you can come see my new air plant. It's in the bedroom."

He swallowed and licked his lips. "Yeah, all right." He spun toward the kitchen and jogged into it. Tessa grinned and then giggled as she entered her bedroom on the other side of the cottage. Yes, being in Five Island Cove had been good for her soul.

Chapter Fourteen

Kristen swiped one more errant piece of hair out of her face as the doorbell rang. "Coming!" she called out of pure habit. She'd lived in the lighthouse for five decades, and she could never get to the door very fast. Once Joel had installed the intercom, she could take a few steps and let her guests know she'd heard them, and she was on her way.

She still called almost every time someone knocked or rang, and she hustled as quickly as her seventy-eight-year-old legs would carry her toward the front door. Theo should be on the other side of it, and Kristen indeed opened the door to see his handsome face.

"Morning," he said, though they'd already seen each other that day. Kristen's fingers tingled up and down their lengths, as she'd held his hand twenty minutes ago as they'd come in from their beachly walk.

"Good morning." She twisted and bent to pick up her bag, which she'd placed by the door last night. "I just need to grab my water bottle and we can go."

She turned her back on him, and he said, "I like your sweater."

Kristen glanced down at it, though she knew what she wore. A navy blue sweater with red and white stripes and white stars. "Thanks," she said. "AJ found it at a boutique a couple of days ago." It had short sleeves, and Kristen had paired it with a pair of white shorts. Alice and Robin had come over the previous afternoon to help her with her outfit, and Kristen would die before she'd tell anyone she'd used that word.

She couldn't quite believe she was dating someone at all, and she hadn't given much thought to her clothes in a while. She thought she always looked nice, but she'd found herself wanting more than that since she and Theo had started walking together a few weeks ago.

He'd taken her to dinner a few times now too, and sometimes they met at the activities here at the condo that were happening for people their age.

He was six feet tall, a widower with three children who all lived off-island, and retired from a career in engineering. He and his wife had lived in Maryland for a lot of their marriage, but they'd started vacationing in Five Island Cove about a decade ago. When she'd died six years ago, Theo had moved here permanently.

Kristen retrieved a bottle of water from her fridge. "Do you want one?"

"It's pretty warm out there."

She grabbed another one and turned to face him. He wore a pair of blue shorts that hung to his knee, and his white polo had an American flag stitched into it right above his heart. It couldn't be more than an inch tall, and Kristen liked the understated nature of his patriotism.

"Ready for the balloon festival?" she asked, handing him the water.

He uncapped it, his dark blue eyes sparkling like fireworks themselves. "I suppose," he said. "I'm more excited for the funnel cakes."

She laughed with him, thinking that he was just like a little boy—always wanting the sweets. "I can't believe you've never been," she said.

"Not a people person," he said. He'd told her that before, but Kristen didn't really believe him. He'd charmed all of her girls. He showed up to every activity here in their community. He worked in the office sometimes, and that ensured he'd see and talk to people.

She gave him a side-eyed look and stepped outside. He pulled the door closed behind them. "How's the inn coming?"

Kristen exhaled, trying to find the words. "It's...not

going as well as Clara would like." That about summed it up. Kristen didn't like talking ill of her daughter, though sometimes her thoughts wandered that way. Clara had a tendency to jump into things with both feet before testing the waters.

Not only that, but she was just as stubborn as Joel, and it would take an act of God before she'd admit defeat. In Kristen's opinion, Friendship Inn couldn't be restored, not to the level it had been previously, at least.

"She's trying hard."

"Did she get Will to agree to do the ferry service?" He opened the passenger door for her, and Kristen put one palm against his chest as she slid by. She did like talking to Theo. She enjoyed having a friend and partner to attend activities with. She loved walking the beach in the morning with him.

They didn't go everyday, but often enough for her to feel connected to him. They'd be gone all day today, first to Bell Island for their balloon festival and fair at the Kaleidoscope Café, and then to Robin's for a backyard barbecue and fireworks. The girls had gone in together on a huge bin of fireworks, and Kristen didn't expect to be home until nearly midnight.

Theo pressed in closer to her, and Kristen looked up at him. He hadn't kissed her yet, and she honestly felt too old to be kissing at all. He smiled at her. "I ran and got you some breakfast."

Her heart pounded, and it took a moment for her ears to register and make sense of what he'd said. "You did?"

"It's one of those sausage and egg rolls you were talking about."

"Wonderful." She sat in the passenger seat and let him close the door behind her. She watched him round the SUV, wondering why she thought he'd kiss her in broad daylight, in the parking lot. That wasn't terribly romantic, was it?

"You don't need romantic at all," she muttered under her breath. Eloise, Kelli, and Jean had taken her to lunch a few days ago, and they'd put the idea in her head about how "romantic" it was for Kristen to be dating Theo. There had been sighing, along with laughter, good conversation, and excellent food.

Some of the new restaurants going in on Five Island Cove were fantastic, but they'd gone back to Mort's, one of their oldest, most favorite joints. Nothing could beat good soft-shell crab and good friends, and Kristen was lucky enough to have access to both.

Theo got behind the wheel, and the trip to Bell Island was easy and quick. A ferry ride. A quick RideShare to the festival, and before Kristen knew it, he'd taken her hand again, mostly to keep from getting separated.

She'd lived in Five Island Cove for her entire life, and it had been a quiet affair. Everyone knew the Shields ran the lighthouse, as they had for decades. Generations. She felt eyes landing on her and Theo, and she kept tilting her head left and right to avoid eye contact.

She could look at the balloons that had lifted into the sky that way, and she pointed to one and said, "There's the watermelon I told you about."

Theo chuckled, the sound deep and warm. "I like that one." He pointed out a beehive, which she'd never seen before, and they wandered around what was usually a sandy area. Booths had been set up, and plenty of people had gotten up early to watch the balloon launch and then spend the day at the festival.

Since they'd gone walking first, they'd missed the launch. Kristen didn't care. She wasn't hungry, thanks to the delicious breakfast roll Theo had gotten her, but when the bands started playing at noon, Theo leaned closer to her and asked, "Can we get that funnel cake now?"

"Yes, sir," she said. They had to walk the length of the beach again to do so, and they'd just reached the stand when someone called her name.

She recognized the voice and turned toward it. "AJ," she said. She came closer with her step-daughter, Lisa, at her side. On Lisa's other side walked her dad, Matt Hymas. Kristen didn't see him often, because he ran the golf course on Diamond Island. They had an extension on Rocky Ridge too, and the job definitely kept him busy.

He carried Asher in his arms, and the baby flailed as

Kristen smiled at him and said, “Hello, baby. Did you see the balloons?”

The little boy—who would turn one in another month—practically dove for her. She caught him at the last moment, but she had to bend deeply to do it. She went down on her knees to keep him from splatting against the sand, and everyone’s voices rose in a cry.

In a split second, Theo was there, kneeling at her side and helping her support Asher. Her breath whooshed out of her body as she took in the child. “Is he okay?”

“He’s fine,” Theo said. He looked only at her, and Kristen finally stopped examining Asher, who giggled in her arms, and met his gaze.

“I’m okay.” The moment solidified between them, and Kristen wasn’t sure what ran through her head. Maybe nothing. Maybe a future with the handsome older gentleman she’d been spending more and more of her time with.

“You can’t do that, Asher,” AJ said, and the moment broke. She took Asher from Kristen, and the boy fussed.

Matt dropped to his knees too, and he put both hands on Kristen’s elbows. He wore only concern in his eyes. “Are you all right?”

“I’m fine,” she said.

“I didn’t know he was going to do that. He just... jumped.” He steadied her while she got to her feet, and Kristen’s embarrassment streamed through her.

"You were like a ninja," Lisa said with a smile. "You caught him so fast." She was a lovely woman, on her way to medical school in another couple of months. She was living with Matt and AvaJane in the meantime, and she adored her half-brother.

Kristen smiled at her and said, "I love what you did with your hair, dear." She reached up and touched hers almost subconsciously. "I should cut mine short like that."

"You should." Lisa's face grew more animated. "I went to this woman named Sherri. She's fantastic with short hair." She threw a look at Matt. "She could color it too, if you want the gray taken out."

Kristen brushed at her strands again. Theo's hair was completely white now, and she adored it. "I rather like the gray," she said. "I think I've earned every one of them, and I don't want to cover them up."

She grinned at Lisa, who giggled. "I bet you have." She looked past Kristen to the funnel cakes. "Are we eating dessert first?"

"Is there a better time?" Theo asked. Kristen smiled at him and slipped her hand back into his. They moved forward in line again, and with their shoulders pressing together, almost hiding their hands from the trio behind them, he lifted her hand to his lips and kissed it.

It was so sweet and so simple, and Kristen missed the days where love and romance could bloom through letters. Telephone calls once a week had been expensive and oh-so-special. Old, yellow-and-brown photographs that had been exchanged. All of the simplicity of earlier times, without so much digital content and immediate access to everything.

She gave him a soft smile, and then it was their turn to order. "I want one with strawberries, please," he told the girl who stood a few steps above them. "Kristen?"

"I just want one with honey, please," she said.

"Matt?"

"We can get our own," he said.

"And whatever they want," Theo said. He stepped to the side slightly as he dug out his wallet. Kristen looked at Matt, Lisa, and AJ. She nodded toward the girl, and AJ looked like she'd been yanked forward by a rope.

"I'll have a strawberry one too."

"AvaJane," Matt said.

"Let him pay," Kristen said. "Lord knows he has a lot of money."

"Well, then." Lisa put in her order for a powdered sugar funnel cake, and Matt added on a third strawberry one.

"Are you headed over to the mayor's stage?" AJ asked.

"Yes," Kristen said. "We haven't missed it, have we?"

"It's not until one," AJ said. She wore big, movie-star sunglasses, and she'd put Asher back in the pack on Matt's back while they waited for their treats.

Kristen thought about Eloise at Aaron Sherman's side. Their wedding last year had been the single most beautiful event Kristen had attended in the past decade, but Eloise did not like the spotlight. Being married to the Chief of Police, whose father was the mayor, had effectively thrust her into such a light.

By some miracle, they found a table in the produced shade of an umbrella, and Kristen could sit there for a good, long while and watch the waves come ashore. "Remember when you girls came to the lighthouse on Halloween?"

AJ looked up from her cake and strawberries. Her face slowly settled into a smile. "Vaguely." She looked over to Lisa and Matt. "She forgets that I went to therapy for a lot of years to forget my childhood."

Kristen watched her smile and laugh, but she noticed that Matt didn't join in for as long. Kristen smiled too, but it wasn't super happy or supportive. She covered AvaJane's hand and said, "I'm sorry, AJ. I won't talk about the past."

"I want to hear it," Lisa said. She shot a look over to AJ. "I love hearing your stories about the Seafaring Girls and the lighthouse."

It surprised Kristen to hear that AJ had been talking about those things. She'd come to her Seafaring Girls meetings out of pure duty and loyalty to Kelli. At least as far as Kristen was aware.

AJ nodded, and Kristen broke off a cold end of one of her funnels. She popped it into her mouth and said, "Halloween in the eighties and early nineties was an excuse to dress rather...provocatively," she started.

Lisa snorted. "That's still true."

Kristen smiled and kept going. "AJ came to the lighthouse in the middle of the day once, straight from school."

"I'd gotten kicked out," she said. "Because I didn't meet the 'dress code.'" She put the last two words in air quotes.

"I remember that," Matt said slowly. He seemed lost inside his own head for a moment, his memories clearly blocking out the people right in front of him. "It was a milkmaid costume."

"Nothing sexy about that," AJ said with a smile.

It had been terribly sexy, but Kristen didn't argue. Everyone at the table knew she wouldn't have gotten kicked out of school for an ankle-length skirt. "Anyway, she came, and we sat down on the beach instead of up on the deck. Just the two of us."

AJ softened then. "I do remember this."

"The water looked like that." With her fork, Kristen pointed out to the waves coming ashore. They carried white tips, and they seemed to march in straight lines. They never deviated, and there was very little wind today to push them off-course. "We talked about how some things are predictable, and some things aren't. AvaJane always wanted everything to line up exactly like those waves did."

"I liked knowing the rules," she said, her eyes out on the water too. "So I could break them. So I could blow them up and try to put them back together the right way." She looked over to Kristen, her smile so kind and genuine.

"Kristen was so good to us girls, always letting us come interrupt her day, no matter what time it was."

"AJ never did like rules," Matt said.

"No." AJ laughed. "I did not. I still don't." An alarm went off, and she startled. "That's our cue to get over to the stage." She started cleaning up the plates of mostly-gone funnel cakes. "Oh, Matt-baby, he's asleep." She smoothed her son's hair off his forehead, tugged his hat lower over his face, and put the shade on the backpack in place to protect her son.

Watching her be so maternal and caring did Kristen's heart good, and as she stood, she realized Theo had cleared their trash for the both of them. He took her hand in his again, and they walked behind Matt, AJ, and Lisa as they made their way over to the mayor's stage.

It stood across the street from the beach, opposite of the Kaleidoscope Café, in the largest park in Five Island Cove. That was why the balloons launched from here, and Kristen watched as one came flying toward the earth.

"Oh, my," she said, but it landed safely, with at least a dozen people working on getting it to stop and then getting the fabric down and put away.

"They're much bigger than I imagined," Theo said.

"Welcome, ladies and gentlemen," someone said up on the stage, and Kristen's attention got diverted that way.

She easily spotted Eloise with Aaron, the two of them standing off to the right-hand side of the stage. Billie and

Grace stood with them, and both girls had grown up so much in the time Kristen had known them.

"Welcome to the Kaleidoscope of Colors Event!" The man in front of the mic was Carbon Roundy, and Kristen had known him and his family for years now. "We're pleased to have Mayor Sherman with us today, to make a special announcement."

Kristen squeezed Theo's hand as Aaron's father came forward.

"Does he do this every year?" Theo asked.

She shook her head. "Never, that I can recall."

"What's he going to say then?"

Kristen didn't know, and she tensed further as he turned and said, "I'd love for my son, the Chief of Police, Aaron, to join me. Son?"

Chapter Fifteen

Eloise coached herself over and over to keep her smile plastered to her face. She gathered the girls closer to her as their father stepped between them and headed for the podium where his dad waited for him.

Aaron looked sharper than sharp today, wearing his full police officer uniform. All the stripes. All the ribbons. Every line crisp and perfect. She loved him dearly, but she did not love this part of being his wife. Had he told her she'd have to put on a blasted skirt suit in the middle of July and stand in front of a crowd, she might have told him no when he'd asked her to marry him.

It's not the middle of July, she corrected herself. She wouldn't have told him no either. Eloise had been crushing on Aaron Sherman since she was sixteen years old, and to have her love story finally come true thirty years later had been the absolute best thing to happen to her.

It wasn't the middle of July, no. It only felt like Eloise existed one inch from the surface of the sun because of all the eyes on her. Grace cuddled into her side, and Eloise easily put her arm around the girl.

"I'm pleased to be here today," Greg said in his super-political, happy-as-a-clam voice. Eloise had talked to him when he didn't use that voice, and she much preferred it. He was so fake in front of all the cameras, the people, and the spotlight.

Aaron stood at his side, completely rigid. He'd said he wouldn't have to speak. He'd told Eloise she wouldn't have to come up to the mic at all. She was counting on him to be correct, and his father slung his arm around Aaron's shoulders.

"I'm proud to be the one to announce that the City Council of Five Island Cove, and the Police Department, run by my fine son, Aaron Sherman, will be partnering to create the Cleaner, Safer Beach Initiative. Many of you have made your voices heard, and we realize our beaches are some of the most beautiful in the world. We need to keep them clean and safe, no matter how many people come to the cove."

The crowd started to cheer, and Eloise politely brought her hands together. What she knew was that this Cleaner, Safer Beach Initiative had cost Aaron many hours of work.

He'd had to hire a dozen more officers, and there simply wasn't enough manpower to go around.

The applause died out, and Greg leaned into the mic again. "Our website is being updated as we speak, and we'll point you there—or to the FICPD—for more information." He lifted one hand into the air and waved.

Aaron did the same, and when he turned and faced Eloise, she hardly recognized him. She was used to the stern father, who doted on his daughters but also guarded and protected them fiercely. He did the same for her, and Eloise loved being within the circle of his care.

The smile melted from his face, and he rolled his eyes. Eloise grinned and grinned, because that was the man she'd fallen in love with. He practically marched back to her side, slid his hand along her waist, and pulled her close to him.

She leaned into him and put her cheek against his chest. She couldn't stand there for long, however, because the sun was directly overhead, and this stage had no tent over it. Thankfully, she'd spent an hour in the bathroom getting ready that morning, frantically texting with her evening manager, Rhonda, and griping at Grace to find her shoes so she and the girls could look pretty for five minutes.

They got herded off the stage by a few of the mayor's bodyguards, and Eloise's shoulders went down as the tension left her body.

"I have to get back to the station," Aaron said. "What are you girls going to do?"

Grace looked at Eloise, as did Billie. They both wore such hope on their faces. The problem was, they both wanted to do completely opposite things. Billie was practically an albino, and she didn't like spending all day in the sun. She wanted to make caramel popcorn, red-white-and-blue drinks, and put on their favorite movies until it was time to go to Robin's for the barbecue and fireworks.

Aaron had promised he'd be there for that, and Eloise could admit that a quiet afternoon in the air conditioning sounded amazing.

Grace wanted to go to the beach, of course. The girl was a real beach baby, and she could spend all day and all evening on the sand, building castles, running in and out of the surf, and only eating when Eloise reminded her to do so.

"Eloise," Grace whined, and Aaron looked from her to his daughter.

"Bills," he said. "You wanna come to the station with me?"

Billie certainly didn't, but she didn't deny him instantly. She too looked around the group, seemingly lost.

"We're going to go home and change," Eloise said. She took Grace's hand in hers. "We'll talk about it on the way."

Billie didn't look happy about that, but Eloise leaned in and kissed Aaron. "Robin's, seven o'clock." She met his eye, something stern in hers. "Should we wait for you at home before we go over? Or will you meet us?'

"I'll be home by four," he said.

Eloise cocked her head. She didn't believe that for a second. She wanted to, but Aaron was very busy, holiday or not. "Okay," she said anyway, and then she nodded the girls away from the stage and their dad.

"Eloise," Grace whined again.

"She's begged twice," Billie said. "I've said nothing. She shouldn't be rewarded for that."

"I'm going to text my friends," Eloise said, not addressing either girl's statement. "If I can find someone to take Grace to the beach with them, she can go." She met Grace's eyes. "Sorry, baby. I'm not up for the beach today."

Grace's face fell, and Eloise squeezed her hand. "I'll find you someone to go with, okay?"

"Jean?" Grace asked.

"Maybe." Eloise didn't know Jean's plans for the day. She might be having something at the lighthouse, as Kristen and Joel often did. She had her Seafaring Girls and her sewing students she attended to.

Jamie, who was close to Grace's age, was a bit too old for Grace to hang out with alone. She'd gotten into some issues with boys a month or so ago, and Eloise didn't need another daughter dealing with hormones and the opposite sex.

Parker was Grace's age, but he'd gone to New Jersey for the summer. The twins were too old, and Ginny had to work at the ice cream shop, Eloise knew. Alice hadn't been feeling well lately, and she'd said she was going to stay home and putz around the house until the barbecue.

There wasn't anyone else for Grace to go with, but perhaps AJ and Matt would take her if they were heading to the beach. AJ loved the sun, sand, and surf too, and she'd gladly take Grace along.

Eloise extracted her hand from the girl's and pulled her phone from her pocket. The group text string had blown up in the few minutes she'd been on stage, and she cringed at the picture of her in that horrendous navy blue suit, Billie and Grace gathered to her like she was a mother hen.

You look wonderful, dear, Kristen had sent.

Wow, go El, Robin had said. *Anyone who wants to come hang out early is welcome. I'll have drinks and appetizers before the main grill-fest at seven!*

I'll come over, Alice said. *I'm feeling a little better.*

We're going to the beach for the afternoon, AJ said. *Anyone want to join us?*

Shad and I will, Kelli said. *We'll come early too, Robin.*

The conversations moved fast in the group text, but Eloise's heart thudded and grew two sizes. "AJ and Kelli are going to the beach," she said. She looked over to Grace. "They have Asher and Lisa. Do you want to go with them?"

"Yes!" Grace leapt into the air and pumped her fist. "Yes! Can I, El? Can I go with them?"

"Let me find out which beach and when and what you need." They had to ride the ferry back to Diamond no matter what. If they had to come back here to meet up with everyone, she and Billie were looking at two hours before they'd get their quiet, air-conditioned afternoon.

Billie didn't look at her, and she grabbed onto Grace as she started to topple in her low, one-inch heels. "Calm down," she griped at her younger sister.

Eloise didn't text; she called AJ, who answered with, "You looked so proper up there, Miss Eloise." She giggled, and Eloise did smile then.

"Thank you," she said, her voice taking on a slight British accent. "Listen, Grace wants to go to the beach, but I'm wiped. Can I send her with you?"

"Of course," AJ said. "Amy's bringing her girls too."

"Oh, that's fantastic," Eloise said. Relief cascaded through her. She moved the phone away from her mouth and said, "Amy's bringing her girls, Grace."

The girl cheered again, and Eloise grinned at her. "Tell me where and when," she said. "I'll deliver her to you."

"We're going back to Diamond, right, baby?"

Eloise kept walking toward the ferry station—a whole slew of people were—while AJ tried to get the specifics from Matt. "I'll call you back," AJ said. "No one's making any decisions."

"Okay," Eloise said. "We have to go all the way home to change anyway. She's wearing a lace dress."

"Let me talk to Amy too," AJ said. "She's always telling me about this beach she knows about where not many people go."

"Let me know," Eloise said. The call ended, and she herded the girls into the ferry line. They had to wait for two before they could squeeze on, and they barely had any room to stand. She felt like she was on display, dressed as she was. Everyone else wore denim shorts and tank tops in various shades of red, white, and blue. The American flag was everywhere—but on Eloise, Grace, and Billie.

She caught several people looking at her, and she felt her political, Police-Chief's-wife smile slide onto her face. She talked to a few people, and then the ferry arrived. They'd parked in the lot that morning, so they didn't have to wait for a RideShare, and Eloise breathed easier once she didn't have so many people looking at her.

Her phone rang, and AJ's name popped up. "Hey," Eloise said after connecting the call through the stereo system.

"Diamond Island," AJ said. "Just bring her to my house. We'll go from there in an hour?"

Eloise said nothing, because AJ wasn't asking her.

"Holy cow, I want someone other than me to decide!" AJ yelled. She let out a long hiss. "An hour, El. We're leaving from my house in an hour, come hell or high water."

"Yes, ma'am," Eloise said, and she let AJ end the call. She looked at Grace in the rearview mirror. "You have to eat a real lunch when we get home."

"I will."

"You have to let me put sunscreen on before you go, and

I will text AJ to ask her to put it on you again in a little while." She held up one finger. "*No* attitude."

"No," Grace said somberly. "I won't have any attitude."

"You can eat their food," Eloise said. "But be polite about it, and remember, we're eating at Robin's tonight."

"Okay."

Eloise looked over to Billie. "What did I forget?"

"She better take her phone, and it better be charged," Billie said. "That's what Daddy always says."

"Good, yes." Eloise looked at Grace again, then focused on the road. "You'll take your phone and leave it in your bag. If I call, you answer it."

"I will," Grace promised.

Satisfied, Eloise continued through the quaint town and along the quiet streets on the east side of Diamond Island to the house she shared with Aaron and the girls. "We have to be ready to go in thirty minutes," she said.

"I'll be ready!" Grace flew from the car and toward the front door. Eloise turned off the ignition and sighed.

"Come on, El," Billie said. "I'll get out those peanut butter cookies Rhonda sent home with you last week, and I'll make the popcorn. Everything will be perfect when you get back from dropping off Grace."

She smiled, and she was so beautiful and so kind. So good. Eloise cupped her face in her hand and smiled at her. "Are you okay, Billie? It's not like you to want to stay home with an old lady like me."

Something crossed Billie's face, but she looked away. Eloise let her hand drop. "I'm fine. Just don't like the sun right now."

Eloise wanted to press the issue, but Billie got out of the car and slammed the door, the very final punctuation mark on that conversation.

"You said you wouldn't work today," Billie complained. Her blue-eyed look was enough to make Eloise's chest melt.

"I know." She still catapulted herself off the squishy couch where she and Billie had set up their camp. The popcorn had barely cooled; the movie was only ten minutes old. "Keep watching. This will be a fast call."

She swiped on the call from Julia Harper, praying with everything inside her that she hadn't just lied to Billie. The teen harrumphed, and Eloise had heard that noise before, usually when Aaron promised something he knew he couldn't keep.

"Julia," she answered pleasantly. "How are you?"

"Good." Julia sounded good; happy. "Did I catch you at a bad time?"

Eloise looked over to the TV as the volume rose...and rose...and rose. She rolled her eyes and stepped out of the living room. Billie had made her point. "Sort of," Eloise admitted.

"Are you at the inn?"

"No." Eloise scraped her bangs off her forehead, wishing she'd never cut them. "At home today. I promised the girls I'd take the day off."

"I'm sorry. I'll be fast."

Eloise pulled in a breath as she continued into the kitchen. When Julia didn't say anything, Eloise said, "Tell me you can accept the management job at the Cliffside Inn, Julia. Or are you crying because you just can't do it?"

She'd been talking to the brunette since she'd come to the cove for her best friend's wedding. Eloise experienced a twinge of guilt. She should've sent Julia to Clara. She reasoned that she had done that. She'd told her about Friendship Inn. She'd told Clara about Julia. Eloise had made sure to introduce the two of them the weekend of the wedding.

When Julia had called her a week later, Eloise had asked her multiple times if Clara had contacted her. She hadn't.

"I can take the job!" Julia squealed, and Eloise sagged against the refrigerator in relief.

She started to laugh. "You're joking."

"I'm not," Julia said with plenty of delight in her voice. "I met with my boss here on Nantucket, and she said as soon as she can find a replacement, I can leave."

Eloise knew there had to be a catch. "What if she can't find a replacement?"

"My contract is up in September," Julia said. "So at worst, I couldn't start until October first."

Eloise nodded. She was drowning right now, but she would be in October too. And November. She was missing Grace and Billie's important things, and she didn't want to keep up the lifestyle she'd been maintaining. Four or five hours of sleep. Constant texts. Even when she was off, she was working.

This phone call was only proof of that.

"I can wait until October if I have to," she said. That was three full months from now, but Eloise had been running the inn for a couple of years now. Three months was nothing in the grand scheme of things, though Eloise felt one or two breaths away from complete exhaustion.

"I'm planning to come to the cove on Monday," Julia said. "Would that work for us to go over the contract?"

"Absolutely." Eloise would hire Julia on the spot if she could leave Nantucket. "We can go to lunch or meet at the inn."

"Perfect. Thanks, El."

"You're the one doing me a favor."

"I'm excited," Julia said. "I'll see you soon."

"Yep." Eloise hung up and quickly turned back to the living room. She hustled over to the nest of pillows and blankets and gave Billie a look. "See? Fast."

Billie didn't even look at her.

"Julia is going to come work for me." Eloise picked up a handful of popcorn and put it in her mouth. "I'll be able to be home more."

"Really?" Billie lifted the remote and turned down the volume. "She is? For real?"

Eloise smiled and nodded. "As soon as she can. We'll sign paperwork on Monday."

Billie grinned widely, and it had been a while since Eloise had seen her smile like that. "I'm glad, El."

"You can come up and work on Monday too," she said. "The pool company is coming to do the pool." She threw back the popcorn, pretending not to watch Billie.

Her eyes had widened, and they sparkled in the bright light of the TV. "Yeah," she said. "Okay, fine."

Yeah, fine. Billie had a crush on the eighteen-year-old son of the owner of the pool cleaning company, and Eloise gave her a grin. Then they both focused on the movie, with their snacks, drinks, and blessed air conditioning.

Chapter Sixteen

"I knew we'd be the last to arrive." Kelli peered through her window as the RideShare driver brought the car to a stop in Robin's driveway. "This is a nice house."

Shad didn't say anything about the house. Kelli wasn't even sure why she'd mentioned it. Her stomach ached, and she wasn't sure why. She hadn't eaten much that day, and she hated doing all of the summer fun things that families did without her son.

"Come on, honey," Shad said. "Are we going in?" He poked his head back into the car, and she realized he'd already paid and gotten out.

"Sorry." She got out too, and he met her and took her hand in his.

"You okay?" He looked at her with compassion and concern.

"Yes." She gave him a smile. "I just miss Parker."

"I know."

They walked up the sidewalk and right into the house. Kelli wouldn't have knocked anyway, but the door had been left ajar. Laughter filled the air, and it started to infuse into her soul too. Of course she wanted to be here. Everyone she loved was here.

Maybe not her sisters, or her mother, but everyone else Kelli had surrounded herself with lately.

"Kelli and Shad are here!" Robin yelled, and if it had been Alice or AJ, Kelli would've suspected them of having too much to drink already. But Robin? She didn't normally drink, and the party wasn't even supposed to start for another hour. Kelli and Shad had come "early" to help and hang out.

Alice and the twins stood in the kitchen, cutting up watermelon. Charlie looked like he might use the knife on his twin, and Mandie snatched it away from him. "Enough. You two are officially separated for the rest of the night."

"Hey," he said.

"I'm not going to listen to you snipe at each other anymore." Mandie looked like she meant business, and she pointed with the tip of the knife for Charlie to leave the kitchen. He glared at her and then gave Ginny a terribly loud death look before he stomped out of the kitchen.

"You go, girl." Alice grinned at Mandie. "I've been trying to get them to get along all summer."

"Sorry, Mandie," Ginny said.

"It's fine." Mandie sliced through a chunk of watermelon like it was anything but fine. "I'm just sick of it."

"Kelli," Kristen said. "Shad. Did you guys go to Bell Island today?" She stepped into Kelli and gave her a quick hug.

"No," Kelli said. She exchanged a quick glance with Shad and slipped her arm through his. "Shad ran the half-marathon on Diamond, and we stayed there for breakfast." They'd then gone to Rocky Ridge and spent a few hours with one of his co-workers. They had a huge house overlooking the black-sand beach, and Kelli told herself the extra exposure to the sun had definitely drained her.

She gave Kristen a smile and moved to say hello to Alice and then Jean and Clara. She stood next to Jean and nudged her. "Do you have time for lunch this week?" She smiled at her. "Or next week. We can ask AJ too. I know she's doing more freelance stuff now."

"Yeah, sure," Jean said. "My sewing lessons aren't going this summer, but the Seafaring Girls are starting up again."

Kelli nodded and said, "I'll talk to AJ." She looked past Jean to Clara. 'How's the inn coming, Clara?"

The woman quickly swallowed her mouthful of soda and nodded. "Good," she said with a smile. "Will Bridge finally agreed to build up the dock again and add a ferry that will go back and forth."

"He did?" Kristen asked. "When did he do that?"

"Today." Clara started to laugh, and Kelli could feel her joy as it filled the room. It was nice to see and hear, because Clara had seemed so miserable since she'd moved to the cove over a month ago.

Her husband stood over by the sliding glass door that led outside with Arthur, and he'd always been personable and warm. Duke was in Alaska, and perhaps that was why Robin was being so loud tonight. She hated her husband being gone, and maybe the holiday had triggered an extra dose of missing him.

Clara continued to detail how with the ferry services restored, she'd be able to get restaurants to come to the inn. She'd be able to hire people and they'd be able to get to work. She laughed and kept popping chunks of pineapple into her mouth as she talked.

Kelli liked being involved in her happiness, and she certainly didn't have anything to add to the conversation. She noted that Eloise and her family hadn't arrived yet, nor had Laurel and Paul or AJ and her people.

"Knock, knock," someone called, and Kelli turned as Tessa Simmons and her boyfriend came into the house. Kelli smiled at her and moved to embrace her. "Hey." Tessa smiled as they separated. "Shad, how are you?"

"Good, good." He hugged her too, and they both faced her boyfriend.

Tessa jumped to attention. "Guys, this is Abraham

Sanders. Abe, these are some of my new friends here on the island. Kelli and Shad Webb."

"Great to meet you," he said, and he had a quick smile and bushy eyebrows that reminded Kelli of her grandfather. He put off a good air, and she shook his hand and welcomed him.

"I mean, it's not my house." She smiled over to Robin. "It's Robin's. She loves throwing a good party."

"Who wants a red, white, and blue drink?" she called in that moment. A swell of voices filled the air, and Robin grinned around at everyone. "Girls, let's get them made."

She really was on something tonight, but Kelli had never known her to be anything but responsible. She joined Robin and her girls at the island in the kitchen and watched as they poured a cranberry-watermelon drink into the bottom of a glass filled halfway with ice.

"Then," Robin said. "You pour in a little bit of heavy cream. Just a little. Right down the side." She demonstrated it, and the white liquid sat on top of the red.

She put down the carton of cream. "Then, Sprite." Mandie handed the can to her, the top already popped open, and Robin poured it in. "And Gatorade Zero." Her younger daughter, Jamie handed her that bottle, and Robin topped off the cup with the blue liquid.

It really did stay separated, and for some reason, the red, white, and blue drink made Kelli grin and grin.

"Non-alcoholic," Robin called. "Everyone can have one."

Kelli joined the fray of people making the drinks, and she took one to Shad and then Tessa and Abe before she made one for herself and joined them in the quieter corner of the living room. Charlie slouched on the couch nearby, his attention on his phone even after Alice brought him a festive Fourth of July drink.

Kelli cheered when Eloise, Aaron, Billie and Grace arrived, and she couldn't help noticing the glow that accompanied Laurel when she arrived with Paul. The house seemed to swell with friendship and love, and Kelli was so glad to be part of it.

She sipped the last of her drink and looked around the room. Robin laughed too loud—that meant something was up. Something she was trying to cover up.

Alice seemed more subdued, and that was usually never good either. The year she'd gone through her divorce, she'd wasted away, physically and emotionally. She was so much better with Arthur, and he never got too far from her. He leaned down and spoke quietly to her a couple of times, and Kelli wondered what that was about.

AJ and Matt arrived after Scott, Aaron, and Mandie had gone into the backyard to start grilling hamburgers and hot dogs, and they didn't have Asher with them. She raised her eyebrows and moved toward AJ. "Where's your boy?"

"He was exhausted after the beach," she said. "Lisa said she'd stay home with him."

Matt took AJ into his arms, and she giggled and looked back at him. "He was asleep before we left." Matt grinned at Kelli, and she smiled back. He'd always been good to AJ, and they sure did love one another.

"Oh, there's drinks," AJ said, and off they went in search of food and drink before the main dish.

Kelli returned to Shad's side, a throbbing in her temples she didn't understand. Kristen and Theo sat at the dining room table with Lena, Jean, and Clara, chatting about something.

Charlie perked up when Mandie came back into the house and sat beside him on the couch. Shad and Abe were talking about something, and Kelli eavesdropped on the teenagers.

"Sorry I yelled at you," Mandie said.

"It's fine," Charlie said. Kelli finished her drink as she watched them but pretended not to. Charlie took Mandie's hand in his. "It was kind of hot."

Mandie smiled, her head dropping as she did. "Stop it."

"Why won't you go out with me?"

"Because." She didn't say more, and Kelli couldn't keep staring at them. She looked away right as Charlie looked up at her, and praise the heavens, AJ waved to her. Kelli went that way, glad she could escape having to explain to the teenagers why she was so interested in their lives.

She wasn't, not really. At the same time, she was, because they'd dated before. She knew Robin and Alice had concerns about the relationship, but in her eyes, it sure seemed like Charlie and Mandie liked each other and would be good for each other.

"What's up?" she asked as she arrived at the counter where AJ stood.

She glanced around like they were about to do a covert mission together. Kelli's stomach swooped and tightened. "I don't like that look, AJ."

AJ grinned at her. "We don't have our baby tonight," she said. "Do you think Robin would be upset if we left?"

"Left?" Kelli didn't compute. "Why would you leave?" AJ and Matt went out all the time. Kelli knew, because she babysat for them sometimes. Jean did. Matt's mother did.

"There's a dance at the park." AJ's eyes held wonder, like she was sixteen again with her first boyfriend.

Kelli said, "You do what you want, AJ." She always had. Her attention got diverted when Arthur opened the back door and yelled, "The Chief says we're ready to eat!"

People moved then, and Robin started giving directions for where to sit, where to find plates, and where to get condiments. Kelli got joined by Shad, and she picked up a paper plate. She wanted to be here, and she went through the line, loading her plate with baked beans, macaroni salad, and watermelon. Outside, she told Aaron, who manned the grill, that she wanted a hot dog, and he gave her one right inside her bun.

She said, “It’s good to see you, Aaron,” and he looked at her. Really looked.

“You too, Kelli.” He relaxed, and Kelli wondered if he ever just got to be himself. She sometimes felt like she couldn’t just be, and all she did was run a yoga studio. Aaron had to be tired a lot of the time, and she noticed how sweet El was with the girls. She saved Aaron a place, and he joined them at the big picnic table in the backyard.

Kelli wasn’t surprised to see that AJ and Matt didn’t come outside. They really had left. She shook her head mentally, and then told herself to be present. She chatted with Eloise and the girls, then Kristen and Lena, who’d sat across from her and Shad.

Shad worked in politics, so he could talk to anyone. He did too, and she thought he got along really well with everyone there.

“I have an announcement,” Eloise said once the eating had started to wind down. It wouldn’t be dark for hours yet, but knowing Robin, she’d planned some sort of game, movie, or activity. Probably all three.

She looked to Aaron, who seemed just as surprised as everyone else. Eloise waited for all the chatter to stop, and then she beamed out a brilliant smile at everyone. “Julia Harper agreed to come work for the Cliffside Inn as our day manager. She's coming on Monday to sign the contract, and she'll be here no later than October first."

"Oh, that's wonderful," Kristen said, her voice only the first of many which started congratulating Eloise.

Kelli got up and hugged her, then said to the girls, "That'll be good, right? To have your mom home more?"

"Definitely," Billie said with a smile.

Grace bounced in her seat in excitement, and Aaron put his arm around Eloise and touched his mouth to her cheek. Kelli loved watching them, and she'd be lying if she said she didn't feel a touch of jealousy.

She had a good life too, and she loved her husband. She'd always wanted a little girl, but getting pregnant had been terribly difficult for her.

Jean raised her hand and actually got up on her chair as she said, "We have an announcement too." She looked at Reuben, who stayed seated and smiled up at her. Her eyes filled with tears, and she looked at Kristen for a long moment. Then Robin, Alice, Laurel, and finally Kelli.

"A birth mother has chosen us to be the parents of her baby girl."

A hush settled over the backyard, and then it was like a cheering bomb had been launched and exploded. Kelli cried out and jumped to her feet again. She clapped her hands, because she knew how very much Jean wanted to be a mother.

"A girl," she said to Eloise, who'd also gotten to her feet.

Kelli grabbed her in a hug, and they bounced up and down together. "She's always wanted a girl."

They went to hug and congratulate Jean and Reuben, and Kelli really wished AJ had stayed. She'd be mad she'd missed these announcements, but Kelli had never been able to sway AJ, despite what the other woman said.

She loved her endlessly, but she didn't understand why she wouldn't want to be here. Kelli did, and she was supremely happy that she'd returned to the cove, taken control of her life, and started down a new path toward happily-ever-after.

A couple of weeks later, Kelli closed the door to her office at Whole Soul. Something wasn't right, and she needed to figure out what it was. She hadn't felt well —entirely well—in at least a month. She'd just finished a yoga class she'd taught at least a hundred times before, and she was sweating profusely.

The yoga had been hard. She currently felt very close to passing out. She stumbled to her desk and collapsed into the chair. She sucked air in through her nose and carefully pushed it out of her mouth. With her head down on her desk, eyes closed, the world stopped spinning.

Her stomach ached, and her back spasmed from the workout she'd done so many times it shouldn't have fazed her. Today, it had. She didn't have a doctor here in the cove yet. Parker had a pediatrician, but Kelli rarely got sick.

When she felt like she could lift her head, she did. She picked up her phone and called her husband. "Hey, hon," he said, his voice upbeat and bright. "What's up? Finished for today?"

Normally, she would be. Today, she wasn't sure she could get home by herself. "I don't feel well," she told him. This wasn't the first time. "Something's wrong. I almost passed out during class."

"That's not good." Gone was the upbeat nature of his voice. "I'll come get you, and we'll go see Doctor Dave."

"Doctor Dave?"

"He's an old friend," Shad said. "I'll call him right now."

"Is he an actual doctor?" Kelli asked.

Shad laughed. "Yes, Kel. He works at the hospital here in the cove. I always call him when I need something."

"All right. I'm in my office." She stayed there until her husband came, at which point, a sense of silliness had crept into her. "I'm fine." She got to her feet as he entered. "I'm sorry. I shouldn't have called. I feel fine now."

"You're not fine." He ran his hands up her arms. "This has been going on for weeks. Come on." He lovingly put his arm around her and led her outside to the waiting Ride-Share. It was a quick jaunt to the ferry, and Kelli did need to sit once she got on the boat.

She didn't normally get seasick, but today, she felt like she might hurl with all the undulating, moving water. Thankfully, she didn't, and by the time they'd arrived at the hospital, checked in to see Dr. Dave, waited, and then been brought back to the small exam room, Kelli was ready for a nap.

Definitely something wrong.

A tall, dark-haired man came into the room laughing. He grabbed onto Shad with a, "Hey, brother," and a healthy back slap. "What are you doin' here?" He spoke like a Westerner, and his huge personality filled the room.

"My wife doesn't feel well." Shad grinned about it like this was great news.

Dr. Dave looked at her, his smile staying in place though the energy surrounding him started to dim. "Hey, Kelli. I don't think we've met."

"No." She extended her hand for him to shake.

"It's great to meet you finally. Shad likes to hide his greatest treasures away from the rest of us." He grinned at her, and Kelli listened to her husband chuckle.

Dr. Dave leaned against the countertop in the room, which ran down a few feet to a sink. He didn't hold a clipboard or a chart at all, and two other men had accompanied him into the room. "I'm being shadowed today by Dr. Diesel and Dr. Allen. Are they okay to stay?"

Kelli couldn't see why not. "Okay," she said.

"Tell me what's goin' on."

She swallowed. “I haven’t felt well for a few weeks. I’m tired. Way more tired than normal. My stomach hurts sometimes. I have headaches.” Her mouth turned dry, because she didn’t want to sit here and list these symptoms. It sounded like she needed some ibuprofen and a nap.

Foolishness filled her again, and she took a deep breath.

“How old are you, Kelli?” he asked. He accepted the chart from one of the other doctors and flipped it open.

“Forty-six,” Kelli said at the same time he did.

Dr. Dave peered over the top of the chart. “How long since your last menstrual cycle?”

Shock filled her from front to back, top to bottom. She opened her mouth to respond, but laughter came out. “I’m not pregnant.”

“You’re not too old,” Dr. Dave said. “It’s been known to happen. Successful pregnancies too.”

She shook her head. “No. After I had my son, my doctor in New Jersey said I’d never get another baby.” She looked over to Shad, her throat raw from that single sentence.

He took her hand and squeezed. Turning to Dr. Dave, he said, “What else could it be?”

“I’m not sure,” he said with a long exhale. “Let’s get some blood and run some tests.” He scribbled something on the chart, and the next thing Kelli knew, two nurses had entered the room and were taking two thick vials of blood.

Dr. Dave came back in after several more minutes, and

he smiled at Kelli and then Shad. "Blood work's off. We'll be able to see the enzymes and readings in a couple of days."

Kelli nodded, wondering if there was anything she could take over the counter to feel better, sleep better. She started to ask when Dr. Dave added, "We ran a pregnancy test, just in case. And Kelli and Shad..." He looked between the two of them, his face practically glowing. "Congrats, guys. You're gonna be parents."

Shad made a strangled noise, which was nothing compared to the complete and utter surprise moving through Kelli. She couldn't vocalize at all.

"Are you sure?" Shad asked.

"Quite sure," Dr. Dave said. "Your hormones are off the charts, Kelli."

"I'm not sick in the morning," she said. "It's more like lunchtime."

"Everyone's different." He wrote something else on a pad. "Prenatal vitamins. Do you have an OBGYN?"

Did she have an OBGYN? Why in the world would Kelli have an OBGYN?

She couldn't even shake her head no. Shad said it for her, and Dr. Dave said he could recommend someone. Kelli stopped listening at that point. Rather, her ears stopped taking in information. She'd absorbed too much for the day as it was.

The next thing she knew, Shad was opening the car door for her. They got in the RideShare, both of them silent.

Neither of them spoke a word all the way back to their townhouse on Pearl Island.

Shad led her inside and closed the door behind her. He faced her, his smile growing now. “Kelli,” he whispered. She melted into his embrace, her tears flowing hot and fast now.

“I can’t believe it,” she wept. “I don’t—I can’t—” She couldn’t make full sentences, and Shad simply held her. After a few seconds, he pulled away and wiped her tears.

“Are you happy?” he asked.

She nodded, because how could she not be? Worry ate at her. “Are you?” She’d told him she couldn’t have kids. Her age had been a factor, and she and Julian had tried for *so* long before they’d gotten Parker. She’d honestly believed she couldn’t get pregnant.

“Yes,” he whispered. “This is a miracle, honey.” He kissed her, the lightest touch of his lips against hers. “Of course I’m happy.” He kissed her again, this stroke becoming deeper and more meaningful.

He pulled away, his smile quickly adorning his face. “Are you going to stand on a chair at a party and tell everyone?”

She half-laughed and half-cried. “No,” she whispered. She leaned her forehead against his. “I love you, Shad.”

“I love you, too, Kel.” He moved into the kitchen. “I’ll make tea and tell you everything you zoned out on.”

She followed him. “Like what?”

“Doctor Dave said if you’ve been feeling this way for over a month, you’re probably already ten or eleven weeks along," he said. He filled the kettle with water and set it on the electric element. "So that means you're due in March."

"March," she repeated.

"He's estimating. We'll go see Doctor Willis, and then we'll know more." He got out a couple of cups and draped teabags in them. "I got a prescription for prenatal vitamins and some anti-nausea pills. I can pick them up during my lunch tomorrow."

Kelli's mind began to wander again. "What about Whole Soul?" she asked.

"What about it?" The electric kettle boiled quickly, and he lifted the already-bubbling water in the teapot from the element.

"I won't be able to do my yoga classes as I get bigger."

"Then you'll develop a yoga class for expecting moms," he said. "It'll be a hit." He smiled at her after he poured the water over the teabags. He put down the kettle and came toward her. "Don't worry, hon. We have lots of time to work it all out."

He put both hands on her shoulders. "Okay? I can see you disappearing again."

"I'm trying not to."

"Stay here with me," he whispered. "You're tired. Let's go lie down. I'll lay by you until you fall asleep."

She nodded, and they left the tea behind in favor of climbing the steps to the master bedroom. Kelli let him take off her shoes, and she stepped out of her yoga clothes while he turned down the bed.

They did lay down together, and Kelli sighed as her eyes drifted closed. Shad kept her close to his heartbeat, and Kelli couldn't believe everything she'd been told that day.

It hit her all at once, and she pushed herself up onto her elbows, pure adrenaline coursing through her veins. "Am I really pregnant?"

Shad laughed and nodded. "Yes, Kel. You really are."

She leaned down and kissed him then, the urgency in the action more than she'd anticipated. "Make love to me," she whispered against his lips, and Shad had never denied her when she'd wanted him to be intimate with her.

He didn't this time either.

Chapter Seventeen

Clara emerged from the bedroom and went down the hall to the kitchen. Lena sat on the couch, one of her favorite television shows playing at a low volume. She didn't look over to Clara, who went over to her husband.

Scott sat at the bar, the way he usually did in the morning. He'd brewed coffee and scrambled eggs while Clara had been in the shower and getting ready. "Morning, hon." Scott barely glanced at her, then did a double-take. "Whoa. What are you all dressed up for?"

His eyes slid down to her shiny black pumps and back to her eyes. Clara wore a deep, dark pencil skirt with a black and white checkered blouse tucked into it. She wasn't exactly thin, but she'd accepted her body a long time ago, and she had lost some weight in recent months.

"I have a meeting today," she said. She swallowed and licked her lips. She currently wore far too much makeup, and a measure of ridiculousness moved through her. She'd met Jennifer before, probably looking nearly homeless—because at the time, she had been. "With Jennifer Golden."

"Our landlord?"

Clara twisted her hands together, then realized she was doing it and pulled them apart. She wiped her palms down the front of her skirt. "She called a month or so ago. She said she wanted to meet with me about possibly coming on as an investor."

Scott's wide eyes got wider, though he frowned. "When?"

"I don't know," she said. "End of June. I've been putting her off, because there's something...strange about it." She went into the kitchen and got down a coffee mug. "She said I couldn't tell anyone. Like, not even you." She poured herself a cup of coffee and faced him again.

"I finally got her to let me bring Tessa, because I need someone else there."

"I'd have gone," Scott said. "I thought your mother was funding a lot of the renovation."

"No," Clara said. They'd talked about this so many times, and a sense of exhaustion pressed behind her perfectly lined eyes. "She helped us buy the inn in the first place. The renovation funds have been coming from the grants I've been getting. And the construction loan." She reached for the sugar spoon with a shaking hand. "And it's not enough, Scott," she added quietly.

He stood, his barstool scraping along the linoleum flooring. "I know the demolition has been taking forever. That's a lot of labor."

Clara nodded, but it was more than that. "And the commercial appliances. And the new staircase—thank goodness that's finally done, though." She'd paid the bill, seen the dangerously low amount in the loan, and called Jennifer to set up the meeting for today. "We need more money to keep things going. A lot more. She said she'd like to meet with me, see the business plans, and she'd see if she'd like to invest."

Scott joined her in the kitchen. "You're telling me." He lifted his eyebrows in a silent question mark.

"I figured she can't tell me to keep a secret from my husband." Clara scooped sugar into her coffee and looked up to her husband. "I figured it would be okay if Tessa came."

"I want to come," Scott said. A hint of impatience and frustration entered his eyes. "I'll go get changed. Looks like we're dressing for a fancy party." Without waiting for her to respond, he turned and walked out of the kitchen.

Clara looked over to Lena, a buzzing firestorm in her chest. She should've told Scott sooner; Clara knew that.

Sometimes doing things with him was harder than doing them alone, as they'd never worked together before. She felt like she had to explain things over and over to him, because she handled the finances and made most of the decisions, and not just surrounding Friendship Inn. But in all aspects of their lives.

"Lena," she said, making her voice bright. "Are you ready to go to Jean's? She's taking you out on the boat today." Her daughter had a beach bag that was always filled with what she needed to spend the day on the sand. "I'll get you a water bottle."

"Dad made lunch," she said.

"Good." Clara opened the fridge and pulled out a couple of cold bottles of water. She tucked them into Lena's blue-and-white striped bag and straightened. "We have to leave in a few minutes. Get your shoes on, okay?"

"Okay." Lena scooted to the edge of the couch and pushed herself to standing. She went around the corner and down the hall to her bedroom, and Clara ran her hands through her hair.

"Scott," she called. "We have to go."

"Two minutes," he yelled back, and it sounded like he had a toothbrush in his mouth.

Clara texted Jean that they were leaving, and then she texted Tessa the same thing. *I'm already on Diamond*, Tessa said. *Just walking the shops until it's time to go over to the restaurant.*

Clara smiled, her fondness for Tessa deepening. *Thank you*, she sent to her. *Scott is coming.*

So you decided to tell him.

Yes, Clara said. *It didn't feel right to not tell him, and I couldn't lie once he saw what I'm wearing.* Worry ate through her, but Clara didn't know what to do about it. Taking money from a private donor wasn't a crime. People invested in businesses each and every day. If Jennifer Golden had the money she wanted to risk, that was up to her. Wasn't it?

What Clara didn't understand was why she couldn't tell Robin about it. Or anyone. Scott, even.

His footsteps came down the hall, and he paused and said, "Come on, Lena-Lou. Time to go."

They both walked back into the main area of the house, and now Scott wore black slacks, a white, long-sleeved shirt, and a crisp blue tie with a paisley pattern on it. He used to wear professional office attire five days a week for work, and sometimes on Sunday when they opted to go to church.

"You look great," Clara said, and she meant it. She stepped over to him and spread her palms over the corners of his collar. She'd done this every morning for many years. He put his hands on her waist and drew her closer to him. Clara went gladly, surprised at how good it felt to be in his arms again.

It had been a long time.

Her heart softened, and she tilted her head back to indicate she wanted him to kiss her. A hint of surprise entered his eyes for only a moment, and then he leaned down and touched his mouth to hers. He'd kissed her quickly sometimes when he was running late for work. Sometimes it was filled with passion, an indicator of what he wanted to do later, when the job wasn't waiting for him. Sometimes it was just a kiss, a "I'm off to work, love you, hon," type of thing.

This kiss was like kissing him for the first time all over again. Joy dove through her, as did a fair amount of heat. He tightened his grip on her body, a growl starting somewhere below his throat. "You don't have to do everything alone," he whispered, barely breaking the kiss to say the words. He matched his mouth to hers again, and Clara matched him stroke for stroke, hoping all of her flaws could simply be kissed away.

She knew they couldn't. She kept things too close to herself sometimes. She didn't tell him everything. It wasn't that she liked suffering alone; it was that she simply didn't know how to communicate very well.

He finally broke the kiss when her phone rang, and Clara turned her head to fix her lipstick while Scott cleared his throat. They'd been sleeping in the same bed since they'd moved into this house, but that was all that had been done —sleeping.

She came to bed after him, usually, and he was either asleep or watching TV with his headphones in. Clara looked at her phone and saw Tessa's name there. With an inferno still raging in her veins, she swiped on the call. "Hey, Tess."

"You're probably in the car," she said. "But we just got the email from Vanity Fabrics. They're going to donate everything for the bedrooms!" She started to laugh, but Clara could only stand there in her rented living room and stare.

"They are?" she asked, the whisper falling from her mouth.

"Yes!" Tessa giggled again. "I told you we should be asking for donations for everything. There are companies who do charitable things as tax write-offs. It's advertising for them, besides. I'm going to make a list of other places we can ask. Maybe we can get this inn open after all."

Clara didn't like those last two words, but she could at least acknowledge them now. Everyone around her had been watching her efforts with the inn with some level of wariness, including herself. Scott too. It had been him who'd finally told her that they might not be able to finish the project and get it open.

She'd been angry. Anything Clara didn't like, she got angry about. In the end, she almost always came around to the truth, though. This was just one more instance of it.

"Thank you, Tessa," she said. "This is incredible." She turned to face Scott, who cocked his brows again. "We just got all of the linens donated from Vanity Fabrics."

He simply blinked at her, and Clara laughed this time. Giddiness pranced through her, and she said, "We're on the way. We might be a minute or two late. Wait for us, okay?"

"I will," Tessa promised, and Clara ended the call.

"Come on," she said. "We're a tiny bit late, so we need to hustle." She did just that, curbing her impatience at the extra seconds it took Lena to get in the back seat. Scott ran her into the lighthouse, and he jogged back to the car.

"Ready?" he asked. He started driving before he buckled his seatbelt, and Clara reached over and took his hand in hers.

"Ready." She squeezed his hand. They'd once embarked on a terrifying journey together called life. Finishing college. Marriage. Moving from New York to Vermont, then to Five Island Cove. "We've been through a lot together," she said quietly.

"That we have." He kept a firm hold on her hand all the way from the east side of the island where the lighthouse was to the west side, where the newer, nicer restaurants were. Clara said nothing, because when she got nervous, she clammed up.

Scott parked and looked at her. "I love you, Clara. I know who you are, and I get why you didn't tell me."

She nodded. "I'm trying, but I've reverted a little bit."

"I know you have." He stretched over and kissed her, and it was just as explosive as earlier. "Are we not going to the island today?"

"Depends," she murmured. "On how well this meeting goes."

"Because if not, I'd love to take you home and kiss you

some more." Desire rode in his dark eyes, and it strung through Clara too.

"If not after lunch, then tonight," she promised, and they got out of the car together. They joined hands again, and Tessa met them on the sidewalk.

"Not too late," she said. "I haven't seen her either."

Clara nodded, took a deep breath, and made for the entrance to The Glass Dolphin. She hadn't eaten here yet, though Kelli and Alice had both testified that the food was great. One of Tessa's good friends, Maddy, worked as the manager here, and in fact, it was the blonde woman who looked over to them as they entered.

"Tessa," she said pleasantly. She abandoned whatever task she was currently doing and came over to them. "Clara, Scott. It's great to see you." She wore a skirt and blouse too, everything about her professional and neat. "Just the three of you?"

"We're meeting a fourth," Clara said. "I don't think she's here." The Glass Dolphin was airy and bright, and she could see many of the tables. Not all of them, as a gigantic fish tank did obscure part of the space. "Jennifer Golden?"

"Oh, she's here." Maddy smiled and picked up three menus. "Come with me." She exchanged a glance with Tessa that Clara couldn't decipher. Then, she didn't have time. She minced her way over the smooth tiles in the restaurant, praying with everything she had that she wouldn't fall.

Maddy led them past all the tables, full or empty, and opened a door on the far left wall. "Here you go."

Clara entered first. The room wasn't as bright as the one they entered from, as curtains had been drawn over the windows. Only a few tables stood in this room, and they'd each hold at least twenty people.

She edged into the room to leave space for Scott and Tessa, but she didn't see Jennifer. Perhaps there was another secret room off of this one.

"There you are," someone said, and that was when Clara saw Jennifer. The woman rose from the far end of the furthest table, the one furthest from the windows.

"Oh, I didn't see you." Clara gripped her folder tighter as she nearly ran to Jennifer. Her heartbeat sprinted beneath her ribcage, and she told herself to calm down. Her adrenaline had already spiked, but she did slow her step and hitch a smile to her face. "Sorry we're a tiny bit late."

"Not at all." Jennifer shook her hand and indicated the table, which had been set for three.

"My husband is joining us," she said. "Scott, you know Jennifer. And have you met Tessa?" She indicated the other woman.

Surprise colored Jennifer's face, but she gracefully shook Scott's hand and then Tessa's. "Lovely to meet you all." She glanced over to Maddy, who'd already started setting a fourth setting. "Thank you, Madeline."

"No problem." Maddy worked quickly, gave Tessa and

Clara another glance, and left the room. As Scott pulled out Clara's chair for her, she recognized the look on Maddy's face. She met Tessa's eye, and the same wariness sat there.

Maddy had been warning them of something. Tessa looked terrified. Clara's pulse kicked up a notch. What had she gotten herself into?

And how did she get herself out?

Chapter Eighteen

Alice put her hand over her coffee cup as the waitress approached. She gave the woman a smile, and they exchanged an understanding. She leaned into the table, where she sat with Laurel. "It's all beautiful, Laurel. Your mother is doing all of that?"

She nodded and put one hand on her belly. "She's friends with the owner of The Holiday House, and I guess the furniture is all seconds. I don't care. I think it looks great." She picked up her phone, where she'd shown Alice all of the nursery furniture.

"It does," Alice said. "I remember setting up a nursery for the twins." She sighed as she leaned back into the booth. "It was so much fun. We didn't know if we'd have boys or girls, and I think you know me well enough by now to know what that meant."

Laurel grinned at her. "You overbought." She held up one hand as Alice laughed. "Wait. No. Everything you bought was white."

Alice pealed out a long string of laughter, because Laurel had hit the nail on the head. "White," she said, still laughing. "Guess how long that lasted?"

"Five seconds." Laurel laughed with her, and Alice sure did love her. They'd been through a lot in the past couple of years, and Alice had never been so close with another woman outside of the Seafaring Girls. In her previous life in the Hamptons, she didn't have real friendships. She had competition-ships. It was always if she was doing better than them, or they than her. Not here, and Alice loved her life in the cove now.

"All right," she said. "So Robin and I will do a shower just after Labor Day, because you'll know by then what you need and what you don't."

"That would be great," Laurel said. She gathered her hip pouch, as she didn't carry a purse, not even on her day off. "Thank you, Alice. Really." She paused and met Alice's eye. "My mom will do a shower in Nantucket too. I'll have everything I need."

"I'm sure you will." Alice took the last swig of her coffee and picked up her own purse. "Thanks for coming to lunch with me on your day off."

"Too bad AJ couldn't make it."

"Yeah." Alice slid out and got to her feet. "She was going

out to Bell to see her sister and dad. I guess it's some sort of anniversary for them." She wasn't entirely sure, as AJ had been vague on the details. Alice felt torn when it came to AJ right now, which was why she'd invited her in the first place.

She and Matt had snuck out of Robin's picnic and fireworks show on the Fourth, and Robin hadn't been terribly happy about it. She'd complained to Alice a little bit, and Alice could see her point. At the same time, Alice considered AJ a capable adult, and if she wanted to go out with her husband alone, she should and could. She didn't have to check with Robin first.

She tried to be neutral when it came to silly things like this, and she hadn't said anything to AJ about it. She figured she could at least see her again and get a feel for how AJ was doing, but it hadn't worked out.

As Laurel struggled to get out of the booth, Alice looked past all the tables to a couple of people walking toward them. Four people. She knew them all.

She sucked in a breath at the sight of Clara and Scott Turner, Tessa Simmons, and Robin's mother, Jennifer. She put one hand on Laurel's forearm as the woman stood. "What is going on there?"

Laurel turned to see what Alice was talking about. She shook her head, her long hair—which she usually kept up in a ponytail, bun, or braid—swinging. "I don't know. Is that Robin's mother?"

"With everyone involved at Friendship Inn," Alice

murmured. In the next moment, Jennifer's eyes met hers, and Alice put a bright smile on her face. Probably the brightest one she'd ever given someone. "Jennifer." She swept toward her. "How are you?"

"Good." Jennifer received her into a hug and gripped her tight. "How are you, Alice?"

"Great." Alice stepped back and looked over to Clara and Scott. They both wore a look of mild horror, though they'd been smiling a moment ago. Tessa stood behind them, clearly out of the way, hoping she'd be out of Alice's mind.

She was not.

Something was afoot here.

"Did you enjoy lunch?" Jennifer asked easily, not bothered by anything. She kept walking, and Alice fell into step beside her as they headed for the exit.

"Yes," Alice said diplomatically. She knew so many stories about this woman, all of them through the Robin-lens, but still. "The roasted beet salad is *so* good. Have you had it?"

"I did today," she said. "The candied walnuts are my favorite."

"I liked those too." Alice pushed open the door, because Jennifer wasn't going to do it. She did exit first, and Alice wasn't sure what planet she'd stepped out onto. She followed Jennifer and said, "Well, it was good to see you. Robin says you're going on another cruise this Christmas?"

"Yes," Jennifer said. "I love them, and the holidays are the perfect time to travel." She smiled at Alice and waved. "Good to see you, Alice." She said nothing to Clara, Scott, or Tessa as she walked away. After a couple of steps, she turned back. "Oh, and good to run into you, Clara." She actually came back up onto the sidewalk and looked blankly at Scott.

"Sorry," she said. "I don't remember your name."

"Scott," Scott said. He shook Jennifer's hand as if they'd just met, but a strange vibe in the air told Alice they had not. Not only that, but Scott and Clara rented their house from Jennifer. Surely she knew them.

Maybe she's only dealt with Clara, Alice thought.

She hadn't seen them eating together in the restaurant —any of them—so it *was* possible they were just walking out at the same time and had started talking.

"Yes," Jennifer said smoothly. Her eyes crinkled as she smiled, and Alice had a brief memory of her own mother's eyes doing that. "Lovely to see you." She did walk away then, and Alice watched her go until she settled into her SUV.

"How do you know Robin's mom?" Laurel asked casually. She shaded her eyes with one hand, looking in the direction Jennifer had gone.

"We rent the house from her," Clara said, her voice even and far too cool. "I'm surprised she didn't remember Scott."

She cast a worried look to her husband that Alice couldn't decipher.

She watched Clara, but the other woman wouldn't meet her eye. For Clara, that wasn't that abnormal. When she was excited about something, she could talk and talk. But initiating a conversation wasn't her strong suit. Participating in one that bored her wasn't either.

They left, and Alice noted how nicely they were dressed. She chin-nodded to them and said to Laurel, "Why are they all dressed up?"

"Maybe it was their anniversary too?" Laurel guessed. "I thought they worked out on Friendship Island every single day."

"The usually do," Tessa said, and Alice looked over to her. She smiled, said, "It's fun that you two get to go to lunch together sometimes," and then she departed too. She too wore a black skirt with a flowery top, and Alice definitely suspected they'd just had a business lunch.

Whether that was with Jennifer or not, she didn't know.

Alice wasn't sure if she really meant that or if she'd somehow jabbed at Laurel and Alice about going to lunch together.

They were allowed to be friends outside the main group. Alice went to lunch with a variety of people, especially when Arthur worked at the school. Counselors had gone back already, as one of their busiest times at the high school was the few weeks leading up to the first day of school.

"I go out to lunch with Kristen sometimes," Alice said, her chest stinging. "And Jean and AJ and Kelli. Everyone."

"I don't feel left out," Laurel said. Their eyes met, and Laurel's filled with worry. "Do you think others feel left out?"

Alice had no idea, and she'd never thought of it. "Kelli's at work today. I invited AJ, but she was busy. Jean's doing her Seafaring Girls day camp." She started holding up a finger for each person. "Robin and Mandie are doing that consultation. Eloise is recording videos for Julia. Kristen said she was too tired."

She looked down the sidewalk where Clara and Scott had gone. "The only person I didn't think to invite was Clara, and I figured she'd be out on Friendship...with Tessa."

Tessa wasn't truly in the core group anyway. She'd come to the Fourth picnic, but she hadn't been added to the group text.

"I should've invited Clara," Alice said. A twinge of guilt cut through her. "I will next time, now that I know she's not out on Friendship all the time." Clara could've told everyone that, but she hadn't. She'd opened up a little bit, but not much, and Alice couldn't force friendship on someone.

"Don't feel bad." Laurel linked her arm through Alice's. "They obviously wouldn't have been able to come anyway." They went toward Laurel's car, as she'd picked up Alice that morning for shopping and lunch. "It's dangerously close to my nap time, so we have to get going."

"Plus, it's too hot to stand out in the heat and second-guess ourselves." She smiled at Laurel, who nodded emphatically. Alice really tried hard not to do that. She'd spent so much of her life on second and third guesses, and she didn't want to do that anymore.

"I can't believe the twins are leaving in less than a month." She sighed. "Tell me the truth: Am I handling it better than Robin?"

Laurel shrugged one shoulder and released Alice's arm. "I'm not going to answer that. I have no idea how to rate how you're handling anything. You're different people."

That was a perfect answer, and it reminded Alice that she didn't need to handle her twins leaving home and going to college like someone else. She only had to do it her way.

At home, she found Charlie sitting at the counter, an empty bowl in front of him. It had obviously contained cereal at some point, and she picked it up. "Done with this?"

"Yeah, thanks, Mom." He didn't look away from his phone until the bowl clanged in the stainless steel sink as she set it down. "Hey, I wanted to ask you something."

She turned toward him, a zip of adrenaline pulling through her. "Yeah?"

"I've been talking to my roommate at NYU, and he said we can upgrade our Internet for only ten bucks a month."

"Okay," she said.

"I was wondering if you'd be willing to sponsor that for us." He put a big, goofy, Charlie-grin on his face.

Alice did not return it. She put one hand on her hip instead. "Depends."

His smile slipped, as he'd clearly been expecting her to say yes. Even if she hadn't up-front, Alice didn't normally strike deals with her kids. "On what?"

"On what you say next." She prowled over to the counter top, and with only four feet separating them, she looked her son right in the eyes. "Who did you go out with on Friday night?"

He hadn't told her. She hadn't even known it was a date until he'd gotten home—at one o'clock in the morning—and he'd let the word slip.

He blinked and swallowed. "This isn't a big deal," he said.

"The fact that you have to preface her name with that means it's a big deal." Alice folded her arms. "I just want to know if it was Mandie or Sariah." That wasn't entirely true. She wanted to know that, and then she wanted to know why he thought starting up a relationship with either one of them again was a good idea.

He was leaving in three weeks.

So is Mandie, she thought, the words a whisper. They were going to the same school, living in the same city. It would be easy for him to continue a relationship with

Mandie. Alice didn't entirely hate the idea, but she wanted to understand where her son's mind was.

He swallowed again. "Mandie."

"Did you kiss her?"

"You said you just wanted to know if it was her or Sariah."

"Now I want to know more."

He glared at her. "I don't have to tell you everything." He collected his phone and got to his feet. "I have to get to work." He left the kitchen, and Alice let him go without calling anything after him.

"He definitely kissed her," she said to herself. Now she had two things she didn't want to tell Robin, and she sighed as she followed her son. She bypassed the steps he'd gone up and went into her front office. She sat at her desk and looked at the case she needed to finish that afternoon.

She tried, but her mind kept wandering. She kept seeing Clara, Scott, and Tessa with Jennifer. She kept imagining what the future would be like if Charlie and Mandie got married.

At least she'd already know the bride's parents, and that thought alone got her through the dull documents and hours until Arthur got home.

She got up to meet him in the kitchen, and he took her into a smiling hug and said, "Hey, how was your day?" just before he kissed her.

Alice didn't want to tell him about any of the confusing things, so she just kissed him back. "Good," she said. "You?"

"Good enough." He stepped away from her. "The twins are both working tonight?"

"Yep."

"Let's go get tacos and sit on the beach." He grinned at her. "You want to?"

"Absolutely, I do."

He unknotted his tie and said, "I'll go change," and a moment later, Alice's phone rang.

Robin.

Her gut clenched, and her heart sank all the way to her heels. Then she swiped the call to voicemail. She didn't have to answer every time her best friend called. Nerves and guilt combined inside her, and Alice paced the kitchen for a few seconds.

"If she calls back, then you'll answer," she told herself. "She could be calling about anything." She looked at her phone, and it didn't ring again. She also didn't get a voicemail notification, which meant Robin hadn't left a message. Couldn't be that serious. Before, when she'd been concerned about Mandie and Charlie's relationship, she'd left messages in her Very Stern Voice for Alice to call her back.

Right when Arthur came out of the bedroom and said, "Ready," Alice's phone rang again.

Robin.

Chapter Nineteen

Robin frowned at her phone as her call to Alice went to voicemail for the second time. With Mandie off shopping for pastries for a wedding that would happen after she left for college, and Jamie down the street babysitting, Robin was home alone.

She hated being alone. Duke was three hours behind her, and he'd be out on the boat at this time of day.

"Arthur just got home, I bet," Robin said. She shoved her silent phone in her back pocket, but something seethed inside her. She'd seen her friends a lot this summer, but they didn't feel as connected.

Kristen was dating someone new, and her daughter had returned to the cove. Robin opened her freezer and pulled out a bag of chocolate chip cookies. She could run these over to Kristen and see how she was doing. Maybe then Robin wouldn't feel so disconnected from everyone.

Eloise had texted that morning to say the same thing Robin felt. Once she had Julia here and working full-time, she wouldn't be so consumed by the Cliffside Inn, but until then, El had said, *I feel so out of the loop. What's everyone up to?*

Robin hadn't truly known. Life was life, and it felt like they did talk, but that there were definite secrets between all of them too.

She pulled her phone from her pocket. *Beach weekend*, she typed out. *Everyone needs to come. I feel like we haven't really hung out together this summer. Bring the kids, bring your coolers, and let's chat and relax together on Sunday afternoon.*

She took off the last period and made it an exclamation point. That felt more exciting, and more like she wasn't calling them out for living their own lives. She'd known things would change a little bit when there were four weddings last summer. That was inevitable.

"It's something else," she mused, and she quickly tapped to send the message to the group before she could change her mind, worry about what people might think of her, and erase the text.

I'm in, Eloise said. *I'm texting Aaron right now.*

Matt will be off-island, AJ said. *But Lisa and Asher and I will be there. Great idea, Robin!*

Robin loved being praised for her ideas. Just once, however, she'd like someone else to plan the beach weekend. She set the cookies on the counter and pulled over a notebook. If they were going to the beach in only a few days, Robin needed to start prepping food, supplies, and drinks.

By the time she made it back to her phone to text Mandie and Jamie about their beach afternoon, the group text had blown up. She read through the messages quickly and answered Kristen's question with, *Of course you can bring Theo. Everyone is invited.*

Her pulse skipped and flipped in her chest, but her thumbs flew across the screen. *I'm calling a Tell-All. I feel disconnected from everyone, and I want to know what's going on in everyone's lives.*

The Tell-All meant everyone would have to share something, and usually something big. Something secret. Something they were afraid of or worried about. Something they maybe hadn't revealed yet.

Robin read over the text and decided if she couldn't tell her best friends that she felt disconnected from them, there was a problem. She sent the message as she drew in a breath and held it.

Seconded, Alice said almost the moment Robin's text showed as going through.

Traditionally, with the five of them, they needed three people to agree to the Tell-All or it didn't happen. With as many as they had now—nine or ten people, they really should have five or six people agree to achieve the majority.

Third, Laurel said, and Robin smiled fondly at her phone. She wasn't the only one feeling like she hadn't spoken to everyone, and right on top of Laurel's message came El's. She wanted the Tell-All too, and satisfied, Robin picked up the cookies and headed over to Kristen's condo.

Once she arrived, she drank in the silence of the senior community. If she listened hard enough, she could hear the waves coming ashore from the ocean just beyond the last building, where Kristen lived.

She knocked on the door and stepped back. She couldn't tell if Kristen was home or not, though she'd spied her minivan in the parking lot. But she could be anywhere here at her condo, as they had activities and beachfront access. She couldn't hear anything from inside the condo. She could potentially leave the cookies, but they'd be melted if Kristen was gone for any length of time.

"Meow."

Robin looked over to find a gray and white cat peeking around the corner of the building. It didn't look exactly tame, and Robin clutched her cookies a little tighter. Then she told herself not to be ridiculous. The animal was a cat, not a chocolate-chip-cookie-eating lion.

She looked back at Kristen's door and pushed the door-bell. It clanged inside, and a moment later, Kristen said, "Coming!"

Relief punched through Robin for some reason, and she waited a few moments until Kristen opened the door. She ran her hands through her hair, and she looked a bit... disheveled. "Robin, hello."

She held up the bag of cookies. "I brought you a treat."

Kristen's face brightened, but she glanced over her shoulder. "Thank you. Come in." She backed up, and Robin crossed the threshold of the condo. To her left, she found Theo sitting on Kristen's couch. The TV wasn't on. No radio. He was just sitting there.

All at once, Robin knew she'd just interrupted them doing...something. Embarrassment filled her too, and she bustled into the kitchen. "Hello, Theo."

"Robin," he said. He groaned as he got to his feet.

Robin threw the cookies on the counter. "I won't stay. I was just dropping by." She couldn't even look at Kristen for some reason.

"I have to get to the office," Theo said. "So don't rush off on my account." He moved over to Kristen and took her into his arms. Robin didn't mean to, but she couldn't stop staring at them. "See you later, Kristen?"

"Mm, yes," she said.

Theo leaned down and kissed her, right in front of Robin, and then he turned and left the condo through the still-open door. Kristen moved to close it, and she pressed her back into it as she faced Robin.

She had no idea what to say. Only a few feet separated

them, but the silence was as thick as rubber. "I..." she started. "I didn't mean to interrupt."

Kristen's face formed into a smile, and Robin felt hers doing the same thing. "So we're kissing Theo now."

Kristen nodded but still said nothing.

"How long has this been going on?"

"A little bit," Kristen said as she finally pushed away from the door. "He's coming to beach day."

"That's fine," Robin said. "Great." She watched as Kristen opened the bag and took out a cookie. "Are you going to tell everyone at the Tell-All?"

"I suppose I'll have to," Kristen said. She took a bite and her eyes rolled back in her head. "Robin, you're a blessing."

Robin giggled and said, "Even if I did interrupt you kissing your boyfriend."

"Oh, hush." Kristen swatted at her, but her eyes held such life. Life like Robin hadn't seen in her Seafaring Girls leader in a long time. She finished her cookie and asked, "Should I bring my potato salad to the beach on Sunday?"

"Is that even a real question?" Robin grinned at her, hugged her, and added, "I just miss everyone." She didn't walk with Kristen, Lisa, and AJ in the morning. She worked a lot in the summer, and she was glad she'd had the time with Mandie this year, but that didn't erase that she wanted to connect with her friends.

"Beach day will be great," Kristen said, and Robin could only hope she was right.

SUNDAY AFTERNOON CAME, AND ROBIN LOADED the cooler into the back of her van. "Jamie, get the peanut butter bars, okay?" They needed to go on top, and Robin had forgotten to grab them.

AJ had texted the location of the super-secret beach that her sister loved, and Robin had burst her bubble and said they'd been going there for years. AJ had never responded, and Robin only slightly regretted sending the text. She felt very removed from AJ and what was happening in her life, and some of that came from AJ herself. Some of it happened because Robin couldn't just let things be.

Mandie brought out the towels, her beach bag, and all the sun hats. They got put in the van, along with the food, the umbrella, and the chairs Robin had packed that morning. Jamie finally came skipping down the steps with the peanut butter bars, and as she handed them to Robin, she asked, "Can I invite Damien to the beach?" She reached up and twirled one lock of hair around her fingers.

Robin's first instinct was to say no. "The boy you kissed in the grocery store?"

Jamie didn't answer, other than to lower her hand and narrow her eyes. Robin hadn't caught them; Duke had, and that had been worse, she knew. She hadn't spoken to Jamie much about him, other than to check her phone and keep up with where she went and who she went out with.

"Yes," Mandie finally said. "The boy she kissed in the grocery store. She kisses him every time they're together."

"Hey," Jamie protested. "I didn't blab about your kissing."

Robin's gaze flew to Mandie. "Who are you kissing?"

"Charlie," she and Jamie said together.

Robin backed up a step. "What? When did this happen?"

"I went out with him last week," Mandie said. She wasn't embarrassed or anything. She looked at Jamie. "It's always easier if you just tell Mom what's going on."

"You didn't tell me you went out with him." Robin planted her hands on her hips.

"You had a training session," Mandie said. "And I'm an adult." She turned and walked to the front of the van, opened the passenger door, and got in. "We'll be late," she called.

Robin looked at Jamie, who blinked back at her. She had no idea how to fight the tide of boys in her daughter's lives. She probably didn't need to. Someone should tell mothers they only got fourteen years to raise their daughters, though, not eighteen.

"Okay," she said. "On one condition," she clarified as Jamie squealed. She quieted and nodded. "You two will stay within my sight at all times. You will introduce me to him as your mother, using my name and his. You will not ignore the other people there because of him."

"Okay," Jamie said.

Robin studied her for a moment. "Okay."

Her daughter squealed again and went to get in the van too. Robin reached to close the back hatch, and she looked up to the ceiling in the garage. "Duke, I wish you were here to help with this."

But he wasn't, and Robin could've wasted her whole life on wishes. Instead, she drove them to the "super secret" beach and started trekking across the sand to get everything set up. To her great surprise, Alice, Arthur, and the twins were already there. They'd already staked out a large portion of sand and set up two shades for people to sit under.

Mandie didn't run to Charlie, but they definitely greeted one another in an intimate, flirtatious way. She smiled at him and let him sweep his lips across her cheek as she said, "Hey, Charles."

"My Mandie," he said, and they laughed. They both worked to set up chairs and move coolers while Robin met Alice's eye.

"I've only know for a few days," Alice said by way of hello. "He's an adult. She's an adult. I didn't know what to do." She looked nervous, and Robin didn't want that. She waved away Alice's concern.

"It's fine," she said. "You're right. They can do what they want." She watched them for another moment, and then Kelli called for help. Robin turned to go grab the bag of food swinging precariously from her arm, and from then on, a steady stream of people Robin loved showed up one after the other.

With all the shades, they'd essentially made a place where they could sit in a circle instead of a long line or two rows, and Robin took her seat and opened the cooler while plenty of people still worked on finding their place.

Eloise sprayed her girls with sunscreen, sent them off to the water, and collapsed into a chair beside Robin. She sighed and then smiled. "This was such a good idea."

Robin gave her a smile in return. "Yeah, I hope so."

El met her eye. 'Why wouldn't it be?"

"It's a Tell-All," Robin said, a new kind of excitement generating in her stomach. "You never know what someone is going to say."

"True." Eloise looked around at the group. AJ had settled across her and El, with Kelli right beside her. Her step-daughter held Asher on her lap as she rubbed creamy, white sunscreen into his white-white baby skin.

Laurel sat under an extra umbrella, and Paul wafted air toward her with an oversized fan. Robin smiled at them, but Laurel wasn't looking at her. Rather, Alice had sat beside her, and the two of them were already engaged in a conversation. Jean and Reuben took up spots next to Alice, and then Theo and Kristen, who'd taken the place next to Robin.

"Are these open?" Clara asked of the seats on the other side of El, and she nodded.

"Yep." She got up to help Clara and Lena, as Scott hadn't come due to a migraine.

Once all the kids had gone off to the surf, Robin felt the weight of every eye on her. She supposed she had called the Tell-All, and she looked over to where El held hands with Aaron. El nodded at her, and Robin drew in a deep breath.

"All right," she said. "Let the Tell-All begin."

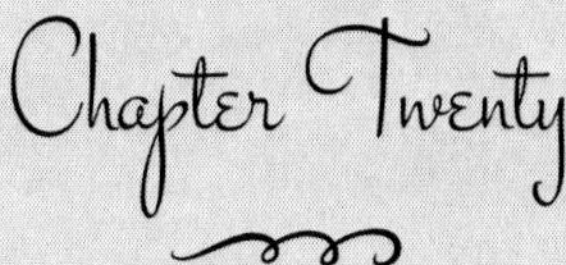

Chapter Twenty

Eloise could only grin. No one said anything. The breeze and the distant call of kids in the ocean was the only thing she could hear, and she shook her head. Leave it to Robin to call the Tell-All and then say nothing.

"Why don't you go first?" she prompted.

Robin looked at her with wide, blue eyes. "I have to go first?"

"You called it," Alice said.

Eloise didn't need to point out that she and Alice had seconded the Tell-All. Everyone knew, no matter how many messages had flown back and forth since then.

"I'll go first," Kristen said. She cleared her throat as all eyes moved to her. "I kissed Theo on the Fourth of July." She nodded like that was that. Theo grinned at her and then around at everyone else. He deliberately lifted her hand to his lips and kissed it too.

Eloise found him charming and perfect for Kristen, and she turned in surprise as Aaron started clapping. "Good job, Kristen," he said.

Eloise tried to grab his hand and stop him from clapping again. "What? This isn't what you do at a Tell-All?"

"No," she hissed at him. "Stop it."

He grinned at her, but thankfully, he did stop. He was relaxed, casual, and oh-so-sexy. Eloise didn't think he fit with all the tension radiating under the tents.

"I have something," Laurel said. "I've only told Alice, but Paul and I are having a boy."

"I knew that," AJ said, frowning. "You told us on the group text."

"Let her finish," Alice said.

Laurel smiled at AJ, and Eloise was glad at least one of them didn't get offended at the slightest things. "We've had a hard time coming up with a name," Laurel continued. "But we think we've finally landed on one."

She looked at Paul, but he zipped his lips. Laurel laughed lightly and said, "Fine, I'll tell it."

"It's your Tell-All," Paul said.

"We're going to name him Jamison," she said. "Probably call him James."

"Oh, that's perfect," Eloise said. "James Lehye." She tried out the name in her mouth, and it fit nicely.

"And I'm probably going to quit the police force when he comes." Laurel sat back, the waves of stunned silence now rolling through the gathered crowd.

Eloise jerked her attention to her husband. "What?" she asked at the same time he sat forward.

"You're quitting?" he asked.

"Surprise," Laurel said, her eyes glued to Aaron's. "I was going to tell you. I just hadn't figured out how."

Aaron sure did seem stunned, and Eloise knew he didn't like surprises. She started to clap, and that drew him out of his dumbfounded state. "That's great, Laurel," she said. "I'm happy for you."

No one else started clapping, and Eloise quickly stopped. "So mine is pretty well-known. I'm stressed with the inn and everything it requires. But I haven't told anyone —except for Aaron—that Julia Harper is starting earlier than I anticipated." She beamed around at everyone. "She'll be full-time on August thirtieth. Less than a month."

Congratulations lifted into the air, and Alice, AJ, and Kelli all applauded this time. Eloise grinned around the smashed circle, which was really an oval, and waited for someone else to go.

Shad elbowed Kelli, but she shook her head. He leaned toward her and whispered something, and Eloise wasn't sure what she was waiting for. A Tell-All was a Tell-All, and all told. Not a Tell-Some, or only required some to tell.

"I thought my appendix had burst," Alice said. "Back

when everyone moved. When Jean hit me with that box—" She glanced over to the other woman. "It was fine, honestly. But I had all this pain for a while. So Arthur finally took me in, and it wasn't my appendix."

"What was it?" Robin asked. Eloise knew she hated being left out of the loop, and Eloise didn't blame her. For Robin, she shared everything. She shared so much, no one ever needed to call a Tell-All for her. She didn't understand people who didn't share the way she did, and sometimes she felt betrayed that they didn't.

Eloise reached over and took her hand in hers. "It's okay," she said. She wanted to add that Alice hadn't "betrayed" them by not sharing her medical news. Everyone dealt with things in different ways, and Robin had gotten better at accepting what people told her, when they felt like they could.

"I need to have a hysterectomy," Alice said. "Things aren't going well up there." She smiled. "I have another appointment once the twins leave for college, and then we'll probably schedule it."

No one clapped this time, and by the look on Laurel's face, not even she knew this.

"I can't believe Laurel is quitting," Aaron said right out loud, and Eloise shook her head.

"You're a few behind, baby," she said to him.

"Speaking of babies." Kelli cleared her throat. "Shad and I found out that I'm..." Tears fell down her face, and by the time she spoke the last word— "...pregnant," her voice had become a whisper.

"No," Robin said. She then launched herself out of her chair and across the oval to Kelli. "Kel, this is so great." She hugged her tightly, and all the other women lined up to do the same. Even AJ looked like she'd been hit with a brick, and Eloise felt that way down in her soul.

She looked over to Aaron. "Did you hear that?"

He wore an odd look. "Yes," he said.

"Maybe I could get pregnant," Eloise said. She'd honestly never thought of it. She'd considered herself too old. But AJ had had a baby last year, and now Kelli... Eloise got up and padded through the sand to Kelli. She held her tightly and said, "Congratulations. I'm so, so happy for you."

Jean was crying too, Eloise noticed, and she gave her a squeeze too. "I'll go next," she said before Eloise had regained her seat. "Reuben and I have a lunch to meet our birth mother." She swiped at her eyes and shook her head. "I practiced at home and everything, but I just can't say it without crying."

"You should cry," Clara said. "This is so amazing, Jean."

Eloise suddenly saw the woman in a new light. She'd always been a touch stand-offish. She didn't participate much in the conversations unless someone asked her a direct question or it was something she was sharing about the inn. But she and Jean were clearly close, and Clara hugged her tightly, and when she stepped back, both Jean and Clara were weeping.

Eloise couldn't stand the sight of that, and she brushed quickly at her own eyes. She couldn't wait to meet the new babies that would come to their group in the next several months, and her own desire to have a child reared its head.

She'd done such a good job of burying it all these years. She loved Billie and Grace with her whole heart. She had Aaron, and she truly hadn't needed a baby of her own. With her current lifestyle, a baby would undo her completely.

Aaron held her hand and said nothing. Robin checked over her shoulder for her kids, and Lisa came back to the tent to get an applesauce pouch for Asher.

"All right," Robin said. "Who hasn't gone?"

"You haven't," Alice said.

"I'm an open book," Robin said. "I'm missing Duke all the time. I'm falling apart because Mandie is moving out. Jamie brought her freaking boyfriend to beach day. What else is new?" She rolled her eyes as several people laughed.

Eloise did not. She knew all of those things *were* terribly hard for Robin. So what if they were first-world problems? They were still *her* problems.

AJ raised her hand. "I'm like Robin. Life is pretty even for me right now. I don't have much to tell." She shrugged, and Eloise could appreciate that. It was probably nice for AJ not to have much going on in her life right now, besides the good things. Her life certainly hadn't been like that very often.

"Oh, but Asher's first birthday party is in about ten days." She beamed out at everyone. "You're all invited, and I've been practicing my baking skills. That's about all that's new with me."

She gave the date and time, and everyone put the party in their calendars. Eloise would try to make it, but if she couldn't, she'd send the girls with a gift. Both Billie and Grace loved Asher, and Billie had offered to babysit for AJ whenever she needed it.

"I'm afraid of living at Friendship Inn," Lena blurted out.

Eloise swung her attention to the young woman seated beside her mother—who also hadn't said anything.

"Lena," Clara said, her voice almost a chastisement. "You'll be fine there."

"It's dark," Lena said.

"It's dark in the lighthouse too," Jean said. "Remember how dark it gets underground, Lena?" She locked eyes with her niece. "And you do okay there."

"Yeah," Lena said. "I do okay there."

Silence settled in the shade again, and Eloise found herself looking at Clara. Everyone was, and finally, Kristen said, "It's your turn, dear."

Clara shook her head. "No, I don't have anything."

"At least update us on the inn," Robin said.

A wild look entered Clara's eyes, and she surveyed the group. "I..." she started, but it was like she couldn't get her voice to work. Her throat worked; her mouth opened and then closed again.

Eloise felt sorry for her, and she wanted to get up and say it was all okay. She didn't have to say anything at all.

"I honestly don't know if the inn will ever open," Clara finally managed to push out of her throat. "It's so hard to say that, but there it is."

"I thought it was going okay," Jean said. "You got all the linens donated."

Clara had put that on the group text, and Eloise nodded with several others.

"There's just so much," Clara said. "Scott's started to look for other jobs. We need a way to pay our bills." She looked down helplessly at her hands. "So I don't know. I really don't."

"You still go out there every day, don't you?" Robin asked.

Clara nodded, but when she looked up, only misery sat in her eyes. "Yes, because what else do I have to do?" She sounded absolutely pathetic, and Eloise got up and went to hug her. No one should have to feel so alone and so helpless, and Eloise couldn't stand the thought of Clara shouldering all of this by herself.

If she could carry some of it, she would.

"Thank you, Eloise," Clara whispered.

"I should've hired you to be my daytime manager," Eloise whispered back. Regret lanced through her. "I didn't know you needed a job." She pulled away and looked into Clara's watery eyes. "I swear, I didn't. I thought it was going well."

Clara shook her head. "Not your fault. We'll find something."

Kristen came over, then Alice, and Robin, and Laurel, and before Eloise knew it, she found herself pressed into the middle of a big group hug. Plenty of people sniffled, Eloise included, and she realized just how included she was.

She belonged with these women, and they belonged with her. Not just with her, but *to* her. Because she felt it so strongly, she said, "You guys belong to me, and I'm so glad."

"Me too," Robin murmured.

"And me," Alice said.

"I feel the same," Laurel said. "I'm going to need so much help once the baby comes." She wiped her face and took a big breath. "Promise me I won't have to do this myself."

"You won't," Kelli said.

"Not for a second," Jean added.

"I'll help you, Laurel," AJ said.

Clara said nothing, but she didn't need to. Kristen smiled at everyone and said, "I love you, all my girls."

"Mom," Mandie said, breaking the moment. Robin turned toward her. "Jamie and Damien just left."

"What?" Robin charged out of the circle like a rhinoceros on a rampage, and Alice rolled her eyes.

"Here we go," she said dryly. "Now that the Tell-All is over, can we break out the mocktails? I was promised mocktails."

"As was I," Laurel said.

"Comin' up," Arthur announced, and Eloise returned to her husband. Instead of sitting in her own chair, she sat in his lap.

"Are you going to die without Laurel?"

"Yes," he said simply. "She's a good cop. She can't be replaced."

Eloise watched as everyone livened up. Snacks and drinks and food got taken out and passed around. She loved beach day so very much.

"Do you want a baby, El?" Aaron asked, his mouth very close to her ear. "If you want a baby, I'll do what I can to help you get one."

"I don't know," she murmured, which was the truth.

"We can work on it tonight if you want."

She smiled and turned to face him. "I think that's what *you* want."

"I can't help it if my wife is the sexiest woman alive," he murmured just before kissing her. Eloise loved how he treasured her, and she kissed him back briefly. No need for a show on the beach. She sighed as she settled her head against his shoulder and thought about what a baby with half of her genes and half of his would look like.

Not like Billie and Grace, she knew that. She also didn't want those girls to think they weren't enough for her. But a baby of her own... Eloise would definitely have to think about it.

Chapter Twenty-One

Jean pushed through the door at the top of the lighthouse, where Reuben worked. She hadn't even tried to understand the monitors, screens, and controls he operated, but she smiled at him as he twisted in his chair to see who'd come to join him.

Spoiler alert—it was always her. He locked the door to the top of the lighthouse at the base of the stairs right past the entrance to their living quarters, and only Jean had the key.

"Hey." He got to his feet and came toward her. In three steps, he arrived and kissed her quickly. "What are you doing up here?"

"I just checked in for our flight," she said. "And we need to send our top choice name to Becky."

His eyebrows went up, and nerves raced through Jean. "I just got an email from her," she explained. The young woman was nineteen years old, pregnant for the first time, and currently lived in Boston. She'd just finished her first year of college, and she had big plans and dreams for her future. She didn't want a baby right now, and when her boyfriend had bailed, Becky had started looking at adoption options.

She'd tried to get Reuben and Jean to text with her off the Chosen Family website, which she wasn't supposed to do. Jean hadn't been comfortable with it, and Miranda had told her not to participate until the adoption was all the way complete. Finalized, and there was no way Becky could somehow take them to court and remove the placement.

She simply messaged through the agency, and Jean checked several times each day, as Becky seemed to have a lot of questions. "What if we tell her a name she hates?"

Reuben didn't laugh, because he'd known Jean long enough to know he shouldn't. "Honey, she's not going to choose someone else because she doesn't like our top name. It's our baby."

"But it's not really," Jean fretted. "What should I tell her?"

"I thought we'd decided on Heidi," Reuben said. He twisted and picked up his can of soda pop. "Right?"

"I do love Heidi," she murmured. But would Becky?

She had the email open—she'd come up specifically to talk to Reuben about this—and she quickly tapped in the letters of Heidi's name and sent the message.

Her anxiety didn't lessen with the task done. "I'm going to go finish up that jumpsuit for her. Then, I'll get everything packed." They were leaving in the morning, and Jean didn't think she'd be able to sleep tonight at all.

"Leave me something to do, sweetheart," he said. "Okay? You don't have to do everything."

Jean nodded and said, "Okay," and left him in the uppermost part of the lighthouse, windows for three-hundred and sixty degrees. As such, the room could get unbearably hot if they lost power for any amount of time at all.

Jean hunched over her sewing machine until the jumpsuit for Becky was complete. She ironed it. She packed her clothes, some snacks, her electronics, and any toiletries she wouldn't need in the morning. She only got out a bag for Reuben, leaving him his own packing to do.

She texted with her mother to make sure she knew their flight numbers and that they'd be in Long Island in three days. Becky wasn't due for another two months, and that put her due date dangerously close to Laurel's.

Three weeks ago, Jean hadn't had anything for a baby, but since she and Reuben had gotten the news that Becky had selected their profile, she'd been making blankets, bibs, and burp cloths. She'd sewn onesies in various shades of pink, purple, and white, and she'd stitched on rattles, ladybugs, and baby mammals.

Once she returned from the mainland, Jean had plans to start on an army of dresses and leggings, as she could whip out a set of those in a morning or an afternoon, even with her lessons and her Seafaring Girls.

She wouldn't be able to do nearly as much once they brought their baby home, and on her way past her sewing studio, Jean paused and looked inside. The room would hold a crib and a rocking chair and not much else, and all of her sewing supplies would have to be moved up a level.

Tears came to her eyes, because she would move heaven and earth to have a baby and be a mother, and she pressed one hand over her heart and whispered, "Please let this work out."

She'd been on the floor in the bathroom, sobbing and heartbroken before. She couldn't go through that again, and with any luck and a lot of miracles, she wouldn't have to.

Today was not a good day to be idle, so she cleaned up the kitchen and started on lunch. Reuben came downstairs every day, and Jean couldn't wait to watch his face light up at the sight of their daughter.

She fed him honey chipotle fried chicken tacos, and he went back upstairs. Parker was still off-island, and AJ hadn't asked Jean to babysit in a while. She'd been calling Jamie instead, and Jean couldn't say she was upset about it. She missed talking to AJ and cuddling with Asher, but she had plenty of projects around the lighthouse to keep her busy.

To stay busy, she went outside and worked on the flowerbeds and rose bushes that encircled the wide base of the lighthouse. Sweat beaded and ran down her face, but Jean didn't mind the heat and humidity.

Before she knew it, her girls came, and Jean had to run inside to get their treats for that day. "Wait here," she told them, and she darted downstairs to get the grapefruit pistachio cheesecakes she'd made before Reuben had even gone upstairs that morning.

She'd stacked them on a tray and stowed them in the fridge, so they were easy to grab and go. Outside again, she grinned at the girls. "I want you to taste them without knowing what it is." The cheesecakes definitely had a slight pinkish-orange hue, but Jean wasn't sure she'd know what it was just by looking if she didn't already know.

"That's my dad's favorite nut," Cheryl said. "It's pistachio."

"I love those too," Bri said, her eyes never leaving the tray. "We each get one, Miss Jean?"

"Yes, you do." She held the tray as steady as she could as the girls each took a little jar and a spoon to go with it. "We're going down to Sea Lion Beach today," she added. "After we snack and chat."

Once everyone had a cheesecake, Jean still had one on the tray. She looked around and started reciting names. She'd combined her three groups into two for the summer, as a few girls had dropped out, and she didn't want to do lessons on the weekend in the busy summer months.

"Where's Tara?" she asked. Neither the girl nor her mother had texted Jean to say she wouldn't be there that day. Jean looked across the parking lot, but all she found were bikes and scooters the girls had ridden to get to the lighthouse.

"Haven't seen her," Karly said.

"I think she went to her dad's," Halle said.

"No." Jean shook her head. "That was last week." She watched the rise in the road, expecting to see Tara come pedaling up. She didn't, and Jean bent to set the tray on the ground. "I'm going to call her mother."

She did just that, pacing away from the girls as they chatted about beaches, boys, and how utterly beautiful their latest celebrity crushes were.

"Jean," Mrs. Tailor said. "How are you?"

Worry needled Jean. "I'm great, Mrs. Tailor. Have you sent Tara? She hasn't arrived."

"She hasn't?"

Jean shook her head, remembered she was on the phone and said, "No, she's not here."

"I'll see where she is and call you back." She hung up,

and Jean hoped she hadn't caused a big problem. At the same time, if her fifteen-year-old daughter hadn't shown up where she was expected to be, Jean would want to know.

Tara never did come to Seafaring Girls, and Jean took the girls to the beach. She ate dinner with Reuben. She lay in bed and tried to fall asleep. She eventually did, as she woke to an alarm.

She and Reuben made it through security at the airport, and they flew to Boston. Jean felt like she was robotic, her lungs only breathing because that's what lungs did. She didn't remember or recognize any of the breaths. She had no memory of what she'd done on the plane or what she'd been thinking about two seconds ago.

Before she knew it, she and Reuben entered an unremarkable building made of dark brown stone. A small sign proclaiming that they'd arrived at Chosen Family greeted them, and Jean ran her finger across the top of the sign.

Reuben kept his hand tightly in hers, and Jean saw the stress in his jaw. He was as nervous as she was. Then, a familiar face smiled at them, and Jean felt like the block of ice her chest had been encased in had finally broken.

"Jean," Miranda Heller said. "Reuben. Right on time." She rose from her chair, and she was much taller than Jean had imagined she'd be. They'd never met in person, and Jean couldn't help the rush of emotion that flowed forward at the sight of this angel who'd helped them find a baby.

"Miranda," she said as she ran the last few steps to the woman and wrapped her in a tight hug. She wanted to say thank you, but she couldn't get her voice to work. When she thought she wouldn't fall apart, she stepped back.

Reuben tucked her against his side, so she didn't have to be strong, and he shook Miranda's hand in a much more professional way. Jean wiped her eyes, determined not to blubber through the whole meeting.

"Come on." Miranda wore a bright smile on her round face and in her electric blue eyes. "She's waiting for you over here in greeting room two."

"She's here?" Jean's gaze flew to the doors lining the wall opposite of the desks.

"She sure is." Miranda led the way, her long legs eating up twice the distance that Jean's short ones did. "We always bring our moms in before the couple. Most of them like to see you before you see them, and all of our greeting rooms have one-way glass. You can see out; we can't see in."

She spoke over her shoulder, her long blonde hair reminding Jean of AJ's. Miranda had to be in her late thirties or so, and Jean noticed she didn't wear a wedding band. She had no idea what kind of internal fortitude it would take to do Miranda's job. When she'd had to call Jean last year...

She took a deep breath as Miranda paused outside a room with a clearly marked two on it. She told herself she was meant to be this baby's mother, no matter what she encountered on the other side of the door.

Her mother had told her she could do hard things, and Jean thought this might be the hardest thing of all for her. Meeting new people for an introvert could almost be considered a form of torture, and yet, here Jean stood.

Kristen had told her she'd be the best mother in the world, and Jean had believed her. She clung to that right now, as the door swung open to reveal a young woman a few inches taller than Jean.

Her belly stuck straight out from her likely-normally thin frame, and she rested one hand on it while she smiled at Jean and Reuben. Other than the height and the obvious pregnancy, Jean could've been looking in a mirror. Becky was obviously younger. She'd braided her hair into two French braids that went down the back of her head, the ends of them falling over her shoulders.

She wore a flowing maxi dress in black, and Jean couldn't see her feet to know what shoes she'd put on that morning. She didn't have much makeup on, and she was a classically beautiful young woman.

"Hello, Becky," she said, and she appreciated how Miranda melted out of the way. Jean went by her and into the greeting room, which had been wallpapered in fun, bright colors. She hadn't been expecting that, and she took a quick sweep of the room before she reached Becky. "Do you hug strangers?"

"I do," Becky said with a smile. She opened her arms, and Jean stepped right into them. Tears burned behind her eyes, but she didn't let them out. She didn't shake. She simply held the young woman who had made all of her dreams come true.

Thankful she'd been able to maintain control of her emotions, she stepped back and said, "This is Reuben, my husband."

"Hello." Becky lifted one hand in a wave, and Reuben swooped in and hugged her too. The tension broke as they both laughed, and then both Jean and Reuben looked at Becky's belly.

"I'm not as uncomfortable as I look," she assured them as she moved over to the couch in the room. A table had been pushed in front of the one-way glass, and a wingback chair stood next to it. Reuben took that, leaving Jean to perch on the edge of the couch opposite from Becky.

She handed her the wrapped jumpsuit. "I made you this," she said. "For after the baby is born."

Becky took it, her eyes wide. "Thank you." She started to unwrap it, but Jean shook her head.

"You don't have to open it now. It won't fit or anything, but Miranda said you liked fashion, and I can't imagine it'll shift that much in the next couple of months." She shot Reuben a nervous look, her mouth suddenly so dry.

"Tell us what you're studying at BU," Reuben said, his smile warm and personable.

"Biology," Becky said as she set the gift aside. "I want to be a doctor." She smiled, and Jean returned it. "I took some concurrent enrollment courses during high school, and I did a summer camp at BU a few years ago."

"Wow," Jean said. "You must really love it."

"I loved my professor at BU," Becky said. "You might know her. She's from Five Island Cove, and she used to tell us stories of the islands and growing up there."

Jean's mouth dropped open. "You're kidding."

Becky shook her head and looked down at her hands, which she'd folded neatly in her lap. "To be honest, I chose you because I've always wanted to go to the cove. I loved her stories. It sounded so...perfect." She looked up. "It was Doctor Hall. Do you know her?"

Jean swallowed, but the lump in her throat would not go very far. "Eloise is one of my very best friends," she said. "She's back in the cove. She owns and operates the Cliffside Inn."

Becky nodded. "I know. I keep in touch with her every now and then."

Jean nodded to her belly. "Since this?"

Becky shook her head. "No, ma'am. I haven't told her about this."

Reuben cleared his throat, and Jean looked at him. They'd talked about topics they could each bring up, but Becky had thrown a wrench right at Jean's head. She looked back to Becky and reached over to take one of her hands.

"You'll have to come to the cove all the time," Jean said, her eyes filling with tears again. "To see it and experience it… and to see Heidi."

A tear slipped down Becky's face too. She swiped at it with her free hand and said, "I'd like that."

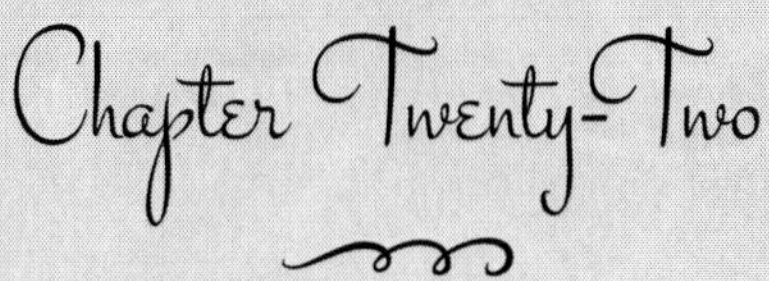

Chapter Twenty-Two

Clara rolled over as her alarm went off. The weight of the day already pressed on her chest, and she couldn't get a proper breath.

Jennifer wanted an answer on her offer to invest in Friendship Inn.

Clara needed to get out to the island and go through the expenses before she could say yes. Jennifer wanted all the bills that were accumulating, and Clara left everything at work so she didn't have to deal with it at home.

Heaven knew she had enough going on here to fill the hours. Lena had decided she didn't like riding two ferries to get to the inn, and she'd refused to go every day this week. That complicated things, because while she could live alone, Clara and Scott had never left her for longer than a few hours at a time. Certainly not all day long.

She could cook a few things—scrambled eggs and toast. She loved the toaster waffles with a lot of butter and syrup, and she could pour herself a bowl of cereal. Hot dogs, sandwiches, Lena could do all of that.

She and Scott had been going in shifts, with Clara getting on the first ferry off Diamond Island and working until early afternoon. Scott would show up about eleven, and that left Lena at home for almost four hours by the time Clara returned.

When she did, it wasn't nap time. It was clean up time, and emotional management time, and lecture time, and frankly, she was exhausted.

She kept her eyes closed, because not only did the biggest decision of her life need to be made today, but it was Asher's birthday party that afternoon. Clara hadn't RSVP'ed though AJ had texted her privately to ask if she'd be there.

She'd managed to buy a gift through the miracle of online shopping, and she'd been up late last night pacing the kitchen when she remembered she hadn't wrapped it yet. She'd done that, and she was all set to go to the party.

She didn't want to go, though. She reasoned that she'd only met AJ a few months ago, and surely the woman wouldn't care if Clara was at her one-year-old's birthday party. He'd get the gift either way.

Scenes from beach day last weekend filtered through her head, and Clara could admit she'd enjoyed herself. She loved how accepting everyone had been of her and her family, but she didn't feel truly close to anyone in the group outside of her mother and Jean.

Maybe Eloise, she thought, as she'd asked her questions all summer that Eloise had readily answered. Or Kelli. She'd always stood or sat by Clara at parties, always said hello to her early on, and generally seemed to want to get to know Clara.

It was Clara who didn't like people much. She knew it. She knew it took her an extraordinarily long time to make friends and learn to trust people. She'd always labeled herself an independent person, and that was definitely part of it. But also, she'd grown up six years younger than Reuben, and that was enough distance to put them in two different generations.

She'd dealt with her father alone as a teenager, her mother too passive to do much to curb their shouting matches. She'd dealt with her assignments and grades alone, the perfectionist in her not allowing anything but absolute perfection.

She wanted the same for the inn, and deep down, she knew she'd never achieve it.

A sigh slipped from her mouth, and she forced herself to sit on the edge of the bed. "You're going today?" Scott asked, his voice deep and husky from sleep.

"Yeah," she said. "What else do I have to do?"

"Relax," he said. "Take Lena shopping. Go to the birthday party."

She stood and gave him a dirty look. "Shopping?" *With what?* she wanted to ask him. Three of their credit cards were maxed out, and Clara couldn't really justify putting ice cream and shorts they didn't need on another Visa.

Scott didn't respond, and Clara stepped into the shower. She stared as the water went down the drain, wishing all of her problems could just as easily disappear. Go down a pipe to who-knows-where, where they were out of sight, out of mind.

She had no idea if the pipe taking the water from her shower was strong and secure, or if it was two showers away from leaking into the foundation of the house. It could go either way, because she couldn't see it. Didn't have to deal with it until it burst.

Clara was the one about to burst, and she knew it. She could feel the emotion simmering in the bottom of her stomach. It might be Lena whining about something that set her off, or it might be something even simpler, like the ferry being late or full.

Her frustration built and built inside her, until she blew, and she didn't know how to stop being like that. "Therapy," she said to the water going down the drain. She'd seen a therapist for many years in Montgomery, and she'd really enjoyed working on herself. She'd definitely slipped since everything with Scott had exploded her nice, quiet, normal life in suburbia.

She went through the motions of the morning—brushing her teeth, brewing coffee, brushing Lena's bangs out of her hair and saying she'd be home later—and before she knew it, she'd stepped onto Friendship Island.

The construction crew wasn't there that day, and Clara simply stood still and breathed in the stillness of this place. It was quiet and serene, and she owned almost the entire land mass she stood on.

She could sell it too, and then maybe she and Scott would be able to take Lena to get an ice cream cone without a terrible pinch beneath her ribs. She couldn't describe the feeling of worry that surrounded her all the time. Always about money. What excuse would she use when the next card filled up? Which one would she pay this month with another one, just to buy herself thirty more days?

Pure desperation filled her, and Clara stood on the rebuilt dock and sobbed into the silence. She cried and cried, her chest aching and her throat sending dry, stabbing pains through her head and down into her shoulders.

She looked around for help, and there was none. No one.

Clara was absolutely alone in this venture, on this island, and she could turn in a full circle and only see sky and ocean. She felt terribly insignificant in that moment, and she didn't want this island to be her life.

She seized onto that thought and used it to propel herself toward the inn. She and Scott had been working tirelessly on it for almost three full months. They'd put every dime of the construction loan into it or into paying the bare minimum of their bills, and Clara could see the improvements.

The rickety half of the inn was gone now. Most of the debris had been removed too. No foul smells came from the interior of the inn, and when she went inside, the grand staircase at the back of the lobby stole her breath.

It had been solidified and fortified, and the rest of the lobby welcomed her in a similar way. The administration part of the inn was ready, with a check-in counter and offices down the hall behind the chest-high counter.

All of the rooms on the first and second floor had been stripped and cleaned. The restaurant spaces had likewise been scrubbed and sanitized, but Clara could not afford appliances. She'd gotten linens donated, but no one had come through with furniture yet. She couldn't even afford to buy herself a new couch; there was no way she could furnish the thirty-one rooms that stood waiting for beds, dressers, couches, chairs, miniature refrigerators, and more.

So much more, Clara didn't even know what the "more" was.

"Irons," she said to herself as she walked over to the check-in counter. "Hangers. Safes." *Oh, my.*

She didn't know what sixty irons cost, but she knew it

was more than she had. Unless she took Jennifer's offer, Clara couldn't move forward on Friendship Inn.

She went past the counter and through the door. Her office sat at the end of the hall, and the open doorway beckoned to her. She imagined herself this magnificent CEO of a huge company, managing dozens of people and hundreds of moving parts. If she could get Friendship Inn off the ground, that would be who she was.

As she entered her office, her head held high even as the tears on her cheeks cracked, Clara wasn't sure she was that woman. She paused just inside the office and looked around.

It was nothing special, because Clara couldn't afford special. She'd used to spend her days picking out curtains and wishing she could replace her perfectly good countertops with something better. Quartz or granite or even bamboo.

Now, she was just so grateful she had a house to live in.

Moving quickly, she strode to the old desk she'd cleaned and repaired herself so she could use it. Her mind shouted thoughts at her, and she pulled open the drawer. It squealed, as usual, but Clara barely heard it.

She yanked out a notebook and picked up a pen.

What's most important? she scrawled across the top of a clean page.

Her fingers kept moving as her thoughts swirled.

Scott

Lena

Mom

Reuben

Jean

Their new baby

Theo

Eloise

Robin

She paused there, her fingers aching from how hard she'd been holding the pen. She re-read what she'd written, sure that wasn't her handwriting. It was far too rushed and way too messy.

But it was hers. Her brain vomit. What was most important to her.

Friendship Inn wasn't on it. The inn wasn't even in the top ten, because if she'd continued, she'd have written down the names of each woman she'd met and spent time with here in Five Island Cove.

Tessa

Alice

Kelli

AJ

Laurel

In fact, everything on the list was actually an every*one*. People.

"Maybe I do like people," Clara whispered. At the very least, she didn't want to have to do everything herself anymore.

She switched out the notebook for her ledger. She knew these numbers by heart, though she certainly wasn't a math major. She needed thousands just to finish what she'd started, and that didn't include anything new, like commercial appliances, landscaping, the parking lot, or staff.

Clara actually felt like throwing up at trying to hire and pay the staff necessary to run this place.

Her throat narrowed, and she was sure any sane person would've called Jennifer Golden weeks ago and said they'd sign anything she wanted in exchange for the money.

She stared at the ledger, leafing through the pages where she'd left herself notes. She didn't read them; the blue ink lines blurred as her mind wandered.

With a snap, she shut the book and got to her feet. "I'm not taking the investor." Her voice echoed in the nearly empty room—it wasn't at all the post CEO's office she imagined for the woman who ran Friendship Inn.

No, she'd have curtains on the windows. Clara didn't.

She'd have a deep, dark brown leather couch in the corner, with a wet bar directly beside it. Clara looked to the corner where she'd envisioned the couch, and all she saw was dirty sheetrock she'd had to pull apart to fix a leaking pipe. She hadn't fixed it yet, because honestly, a four-foot section in this back room that no one would see wasn't at the top of her list. It never would be if she continued here.

"I don't want to continue here."

She sat back down and opened her laptop. Instead of

going into her monster-long to-do list for the day, she clicked open an Internet browser, and she searched for real estate agents in her area.

She scribbled down a few names, closed the computer, and picked up her phone. A moment of hesitation had her almost giddy with excitement. With just a couple of calls, she could be free of everything.

Her finger hovered above the screen, and then she dialed.

CLARA LOOKED UP AS FOOTSTEPS CAME DOWN THE hall. She knew her husband's gait, and she got up to meet him when he came inside. He lifted a brown paper sack and said, "Ryan's waiting."

She rounded the desk and took the bag from him. After stretching up to kiss him, she asked, "Do you think he'll wait while we do a few things?"

"What things?" He held her onto her hips, and Clara wanted to smile at him. She couldn't; not yet.

"I've been researching real estate agents," she said. "But I think we should call my mom and talk to her. She'll know the best in the cove for this anyway, and I don't know... I want to talk to her about it."

"I think he'll wait for us to make a phone call."

Clara did smile then, and Scott added, "I'll text him,"

while she turned to go back to her desk. She sat down and pulled out the salad her husband had brought for her. It wasn't exactly breakfast food, but it was about mid-morning, and she'd only had coffee before leaving the house.

She tapped to call her mother, then opened the salad while the line rang.

"Good morning, dear," her mother said, her voice so calm and so soothing.

"Mom," Clara said. She snapped off the top of the ranch dressing and poured it over her salad. "Listen..." She suddenly didn't have the words. Growing up, her father had drilled into her and Reuben to *never, ever quit. Always go down with a fight.*

In the end, he'd gone down. Everyone died. Everyone would go down, no matter how hard they fought.

The enormity of Clara's situation rolled over her again, and she tried to breathe, but couldn't.

"Kristen," Scott said, and Clara looked at him. He gave her an encouraging smile. "The inn is too much for us. We'd like to list it for sale, and you know all the best real estate agents in the cove."

"We'll pay you back," Clara blurted out. "All of it, Mom. We've made so much progress here. Someone else is going to buy it and fix it up the way it needs to be."

Her mother said nothing, and Clara couldn't even stir her dressing into her salad. She opened her mouth to say something more, but Scott shook his head. She appreciated his gentle guidance, and she snapped her lips closed again.

Her default was to explain more, and she'd been working with Scott to curb that instinct since the day Lena was born. She didn't need to hear anything twice. She simply needed more time to process.

"Well," Mom said. "I think...I think that's probably the best thing to do."

Clara's shoulders slumped as relief filled her. "Really?"

"Yes, Clara," Mom said. "You don't have to prove anything to anyone."

"We'll pay you back." The last word caught in her throat, but Clara would pay her mother back every dime if it was the last thing she did.

"I'm sure you will," Mom said. "Let me see who would be best for this type of sale."

Clara smiled at her husband and started to stir her dressing into her salad. When she'd called him and told him all of her thoughts, he'd questioned her. Asked things more than once just to be sure.

Clara was sure.

She didn't want to do this anymore. She felt like she'd put in a decent effort, but the enormity of it was too much for her. Too much for her and Scott combined. Friendship Inn needed a big company, one that knew how to restore old buildings and run hotels, with someone at the helm of it who had far more experience than they did.

"Sampson Winslow," Mom said. "He's the best in the cove."

"Thanks, Mom," Clara said, and her voice came out quiet and reverent.

"Of course, dear," Mom said, and Clara appreciated how even she always was. She'd been like that growing up too, and she'd been the peacemaker in their home between Clara and her father. She'd evened out both of them, sanded away at their rougher edges until they'd become more refined and less reactionary.

"Will you be at Asher's party?" Mom asked.

"Yes," Clara said with a strong, sure voice. "I'll see you there."

"I love you, dear."

Clara's throat closed again, for she knew how unloveable she was sometimes. "I love you too, Mom." The call ended, and the lump of emotion remained in her throat for a few moments while the screen stayed lit.

Then she took her first bite of salad as Scott said, "I've got Sam's number right here." He met her gaze. "Should we call him right now?"

"Yes," Clara said. "Then, when I'm finished eating, we'll head back to Diamond Island. I need to run home and get baby Asher's gift before the party."

Chapter Twenty-Three

AJ couldn't stop snapping pictures of her son. He was simply the cutest one-year-old who'd ever lived, and she wouldn't believe otherwise. Jean had made him the cutest little sailor outfit for today, and as he gave her another two-toothed grin, AJ took yet another picture.

She heard the rumbling of the garage door, and she brightened. "Oh, guess who that is?" She scooped Asher off the floor and into her arms, which caused her to groan. He was a year old now, and at least twenty pounds. "Daddy's home!"

Matt walked into the house about a minute later, and he carried the biggest box AJ had ever seen. It was wrapped in white paper with tons of blue umbrellas on it, and AJ grinned at him as he put it on their dining room table.

"Look-it who it is," she said to Asher. "Wave hello to Daddy."

Asher kicked his feet and babbled in his baby-tongue. Matt chuckled and came toward them. AJ passed their son to him, and Matt leaned down to kiss her. "Smells good in here, sweetheart."

"Thanks," she said. She'd spent the morning cleaning while Lisa had run to the grocery store. Then, they'd put the beef roast in the slow cooker, and AJ had made a cold corn salad, corn muffins, and corn salsa.

It was never too early to celebrate her son's favorite foods, and right now, that was corn.

"How's the course?" she asked. The moment she did, she hated the question. It felt so...rote. She asked Matt every day when he walked in how the golf course was.

He said the same thing every day too. "Good enough," he said, mimicking the words she heard in her head.

She looked over to him. "Sorry."

"It's habit." He gave her a smile. They'd snuck away from Robin's picnic on the Fourth of July, and AJ knew Robin wasn't very happy with her because of that. AJ had shouldered a lot of displeasure over the years, and her therapist told her that sometimes she had to take care of herself first.

That was what she and Matt had been doing that night. They'd been taking care of their marriage. They'd gone to Mort's and gotten lobster rolls to go. They'd found a patch of beach and watched the sun go down while they ate them. They'd talked a lot. About their relationship. About what they wanted from the other. About how they could keep working on building something they both wanted.

Then, since Lisa was watching Asher, and the boy was already asleep, Matt had called around until he'd found a hotel that had an available room, and they'd stayed a single night away from their son.

By the time Asher woke in the morning, AJ was there, as if she and Matt had come home when they hadn't. She'd told him she didn't need a whole lot more than that, but that she hated asking him about his day. She wanted more than that. She wanted real connections, with real conversations. She wanted a staycation with her amazing husband too, and she wanted him to make love to her the way he did when his daughter wasn't in the next room over, and she wanted the two of them to continue to be "the two of them."

"What's going on with the turf install?" she asked, the question she should've asked the first time.

"It's slow," Matt said. He grinned at Asher and bounced the boy on his hip. "You're slobbering, buddy. Did you tell Mama you're getting another tooth?"

"Ice cream," Lisa called, and AJ's attention divided between checking out her son's new tooth and helping her step-daughter bring in the melting frozen foods. She took

Asher from Matt, who went to help his daughter, and the alone-time she had with Matt disintegrated.

Lisa was only the first of many people who started arriving, and after another half-hour, AJ stood in her kitchen with all of the assembled guests.

Robin, Mandie, and Jamie had come, of course. Jamie had been babysitting Asher more and more while AJ wrote her freelance articles. Alice had come alone, twin-less and Arthur-less. Eloise had brought the girls, and Amy had brought hers too.

Kristen had come with Theo, and he currently tried to sneak a sugar cookie that Jean swatted his hand away from. He chuckled, but Jean gave him a stern look. Reuben had come too, a rare afternoon away from the lighthouse—for Asher.

AJ's heart filled with love.

Her father stood with Asher in his arms, and AJ said, "Dad, put him in his chair, okay?"

The doorbell rang, and Laurel entered a moment later, panic on her face. "I'm not too late, am I?" She saw them all assembled in the kitchen, and her fair face flushed. "Sorry. I couldn't get back from Sanctuary. You would not believe how many people are trying to come to Diamond Island."

"Aaron said he might close it," Eloise said.

"Close the island?" Alice asked. "Can he do that?"

"He can if people are here without anywhere to stay,"

Eloise said. "So if they have a room at Cliffside, they have to stay on Sanctuary."

"Wow," Robin said. "It's that bad?"

"He can't keep up with the needs," Eloise said. "Manpower for safety, but also clean-up. Everyone here on Diamond makes a huge mess for the Parks Bureau."

"Shad's been talking about that too," Kelli said, and she stood right next to AJ. She always had, and AJ reached over and took her hand. Shad hadn't come, because he hadn't been feeling well, and Kelli herself looked a little worn out.

AJ had been when she'd been in her first trimester, so she understood. She drew in a breath as her father snapped the last strap around Asher. "All right," she said. "I think we're ready to sing."

She nodded to Matt, who lifted the single-layer chocolate cake she'd made for Asher. Kristen had baked a much bigger one for everyone else, but AJ wanted all the first-year pictures. Asher with cake all over his face. Asher going in with both fists. The pure joy of getting a whole cake to himself.

She looked around one more time, overcome with emotion, and realized that Clara wasn't there. She hadn't gotten terribly close to Clara over the past three months since she'd been living in the cove, but even Robin hadn't become buddy-buddy with Clara.

Jean was the closest with her, as she'd known her for

years and years now, and even then, Clara sometimes would barely say anything to Jean.

"Do you want to lead it, hon?" Matt asked. "Or do I just give him this and we go for it?"

AJ blinked and looked at her husband. "You have to light the candle. Then we'll sing."

He did that, and AJ started them out with, "Happy Birthday to you," in a loud voice. She then let hers fall silent as everyone else picked up the song. Tears filled her eyes at all the voices, all the shining eyes looking at Asher, all the love she felt here in the house.

Her house.

Her house, with her husband and son.

AJ had gotten everything she wanted, and it hadn't come easy. None of it would continue to be all that easy, as evidenced by her rote question from earlier. She wanted to keep working at her relationships, on herself, and at being a good wife and mother.

The song ended, and Matt set the cake in front of Asher and crouched in front of him. "Happy birthday, bud," he said.

The boy looked at his daddy, confusion in his face. He reached for the candle, and Matt laughed as he brushed his hand away. "You have to blow it out. Watch." Matt huffed on the candle and the flame flickered. He blew harder, and it went out.

He plucked the candle from the cake so it wouldn't

burn their baby, and AJ said, "Go on, Ash. It's cake, and it's yours." She held her phone up, ready to take a whole series of pictures. Then a video.

"I'm so sorry we're late," Clara said, and AJ looked away from her phone and her baby.

Clara, Scott, and Lena bustled into the house, and Lena went right over to Asher. "Did he blow out the candle by himself?"

AJ smiled, because no, a one-year-old didn't blow out their own candle. Lena looked around at everyone. "Did you sing?"

AJ didn't want her to be upset, and Clara tried to get Lena to come stand out of the way.

"Nope," Matt said. He flicked on the lighter again, and AJ watched as he re-lit the candle he'd stuck back in the cake. "You're just in time."

He beamed at Lena, who lit up as brightly as the sun. She sang loudly, and AJ couldn't stop the smile on her face, nor the happiness filling her over and over again.

Matt put the cake on the tray again, and Asher looked at it again.

"You blow on it," Lena said.

"Show him," Matt said, and AJ actually watched Clara as Lena bent down and snuffed out the candle with her breath.

She stood in Scott's arms—that was new—no tension in her shoulders or face. She smiled at Lena when AJ had really only ever seen her try to sweep the young woman to the back of the crowd, out of the way.

"He's eating it, babe," Matt said. "Are you filming this?"

AJ jolted again, lifted her phone, and started recording as Asher finally figured out what the dark brown thing in front of him was. "Cake," she said as his eyes filled with delight and he went back for another, bigger fistful.

Chatter broke out then, and Kelli started serving the cake for the adults.

"There's shredded beef sandwiches," Kristen called. "Corn dip and corn muffins. What else?"

AJ let Robin take over the food part of the party, because she just wanted to enjoy herself. They'd all brought gifts in blue bags and boxes, but that wasn't the special part of today.

The food was good, but again, not the most important thing.

No, the most important thing about today wasn't a thing at all. It was the people who'd taken the time out of their lives to be in her house, with her, celebrating her son.

She took a few more pictures and moved over to where Clara stood with Eloise. "...just loves birthday parties," Clara said. She glanced over to AJ and backed up to make room for her. "Hey, AJ. Sorry we were late. The ferry coming from Sanctuary was a nightmare."

"Laurel said that," AJ said. "I'm surprised you came. You didn't need to."

Clara blinked at her, a bit of surprise riding in her eyes. "Would you say that to Kelli?"

AJ felt like she'd been punched in the lungs. "Uh..." She looked over to Eloise.

Clara sighed and fell back another step. "I'm sorry. That was so blunt." She put a smile on her face. "I came, because I do want to be here. I want to be part of this." She gestured her hand around the house, and AJ totally understood what she meant. "I belong here."

She exchanged a look with Eloise. "I was just telling Eloise that I've been shifting around some of my priorities."

"I told her to just start responding to the texts, and she wouldn't be able to get rid of us." Eloise grinned and turned slightly toward Billie as the teenager handed her a plate. "Thanks, baby. Did you get some?"

"I'm getting it now," Billie said. "Clara? You want something?"

"Scott is getting it." Clara wore a completely new suit, from head to toe, and AJ barely recognized her. Perhaps something amazing had happened at Friendship Inn this morning.

"Aaron just closed the island," Eloise said, holding up her phone. "You have to show proof of where you're staying or your address to get on the island."

"What about getting off?" someone asked, and AJ turned at the new voice.

Tessa stood there with her boyfriend, Abe, and Maddy

Lancaster. She stood with a drop-dead gorgeous man that AJ had seen before. Maybe at the wedding? Her memory fuzzed, because she wasn't as young as she once was, and she'd only met Maddy's boyfriend once.

"We're a little late," Tessa said. "You should *see* the ferry station."

Eloise moved over to Tessa and hugged her. "You can get off the island, no problem," she said. "It's only for people coming onto Diamond. The other islands aren't an issue."

"Oh, they're an issue," Laurel said almost under her breath. She looked at AJ, and AJ went over to her.

"How are you feeling?"

"Good," Laurel said. Her hand went to her belly. "Tired. There's not enough cops on Sanctuary either. That's all I'm saying."

AJ put her hand on Laurel's belly too and smiled. "I'm sure there aren't." She looked up. "Won't be your problem soon enough, right?"

Jean joined them, as did Kelli, and AJ loved how the women who'd be moms again soon had banded together, almost like having a child close to the same age was an unspoken bond that formed between women.

"Something's going on with Clara," Kelli said.

AJ turned and looked at her. She laughed with Alice and Robin, and that definitely was unusual.

"Maybe she's just coming out of her shell," Laurel said. "Trust me when I say this group is hard to break into."

"We are?" Kelli asked.

"There's just a lot of you," Laurel said. "Us. There's a lot of us."

AJ couldn't disagree with that, and with Maddy and Tessa, and their significant others, the group simply kept growing. She grinned into the vibrancy of the energy in her house and fed off of it.

"If she is opening up," Jean said, still watching Clara. She now ate cake and talked with Tessa and Maddy. "We'll find out soon enough what's going on."

Chapter Twenty-Four

Robin led the way, the suitcase she towed behind her bumping along with her. Mandie struggled under the weight of her duffle bag, but Robin had told her it would be hard to carry it. Her daughter was headstrong and responsible, and she had a lot of lessons to learn her way.

Carrying a bag through a very busy airport in New York City when she could've packed a rolling suitcase instead apparently counted as one such lesson.

"Mom," Mandie said. "We lost Alice and the twins."

Robin slowed down and turned back to Mandie. "They were with us."

"It's not a race." Mandie gave her a look that Robin didn't appreciate, but the truth was, Robin did want this to be over as quickly as possible. The day had just begun, and they had a long way to go before the three teenaged adults she, Duke, and Alice had traveled the twelve miles from Five Island Cove to New York City with would be settled and in their new homes.

Twelve miles, Robin thought. On land, that was nothing. A drive she could probably do in fifteen or twenty minutes, through a school zone.

But across the ocean? It felt *so* far to Robin, and she had to take a deep breath every time she thought about it.

Duke stopped next to her and looked behind them too. "There they are." He pointed to the left. "Looks like Charlie found something to fix his backpack."

"He just needs to buy a new one," Mandie said, a touch of irritation in her voice. "He has this weird thing about using that one."

"Why?" Robin asked. She liked tradition and superstition as much as the next person, but even she could see Charlie needed a new backpack.

Mandie sighed as Alice and the twins came toward them again. "He says he's had it since sixth grade, and it's a relic now."

"I don't think a backpack counts," Duke said with a chuckle.

"Apparently it does." Robin gave Alice, Ginny, and Charlie a tight smile. "We have to get to the RideShare pickup."

"It's not called RideShare here," Mandie said. As if Robin didn't know.

She gave her daughter a look, turned, and kept walking. Duke matched her pace this time, and Robin did slow down a little. She didn't want this day to be a bad memory for Mandie—or anyone else—and she managed to rid herself of the frustration before they got their bags. She and Duke would only be staying in the city for a single night, so they'd brought backpacks. They each towed a suitcase after they'd stopped at baggage claim, and all the contents of those bags would stay with Mandie in her new dorm.

The city had stores too, and Robin swallowed back another round of nerves. She let Duke lead them to the ground transportation pick-up, the noise of so many people assaulting her on all sides. Mandie glowed as she looked at everything around her, and she turned to Robin with stars in her eyes.

"I love the city, Mom."

Robin gave her a smile. "I know you do." And she did. She could only hope and pray she wouldn't lose her daughter to the allure of a big city. Even if Mandie moved here permanently, Robin held hope that she'd come visit the cove far more often than her friends had once they'd left.

"All of this?" the driver asked, his eyes drinking in the six of them. And the seven suitcases. "You need two cars." He reached for Mandie's first bag.

"This is an extra-large," Duke said. "It says we'll fit."

"You have seven suitcases, man," he said.

"I'll hold one," Ginny said.

Robin said nothing, and she herded the girls into the van. If they all got in, maybe it would be okay. It did take some rearranging and some stacking, but all the people and all the bags got loaded.

They had three stops to make, and Robin wouldn't want to be in Alice's position. Her kids had secured housing in two different buildings, and she'd asked Duke to go with Charlie initially. Just to see how things would go. Just so she knew he wouldn't be trying to find his dorm by himself.

They were the first stop, and thankfully, they'd planned for that, and no one had to get out and get back in. His bags had been put on top, and Duke lifted his hand in a wave as the van door slid closed.

He seemed so relaxed and calm about the whole thing, and Robin did like having him as an anchor and an example to look to. Not only that, but he was home for the season, and Robin couldn't wait for their lives to settle down too. Once Mandie was all moved out and school had started, she'd feel better.

She and Mandie got out at the next stop, and she looked back at Alice. "We'll be in touch."

Alice gave her a smile that looked like a façade. Robin saw right through it, because she'd been putting on the same brave front for a week now. Heck, all summer. "I'll text you," Alice said, and Robin nodded.

She pushed the button to close the van door, and then took the suitcase she'd been towing since they'd deplaned.

"All right." She gave Mandie a bright smile. "Let's go find your dorm."

All three of them had traditional halls, meaning there would be no kitchen. They'd have to share shower and bathroom facilities with others on the floor, as well as a communal kitchen. Mandie had said she couldn't wait to try all the food in New York City, and Robin hadn't had the heart to tell her how much that would cost.

Her daughter had been working for years, and she had some money saved. Her rent was paid for the year, and her scholarship covered her tuition—at least for this first semester. If she kept her grades up, she'd be fine.

Robin's chest vibrated in a strange way, but they went in Brittany Hall, where plenty of activity was happening. A woman approached them, her smile made of sunshine. "Good afternoon," she said. "It's moving day. What's your name?" She barely looked at Robin, and Mandie gave her name.

"You're on the sixth floor," the woman chirped. "We've got Alex who can take you up." A young woman probably only a couple of years older than Mandie approached, and she smiled with beautiful white teeth against her dark skin.

"Six-seventeen," the woman said, and Alex nodded.

"Come with me," she said. She started toward an elevator bank in the back. "Do you know your roommate?"

"No," Mandie said. "Sort of?" She glanced over to

Robin. "I got her email a few weeks ago, and we've talked a little bit. Her name is Jessa."

"Okay," Alex said, then she launched into the history of the dorms and apartments for NYU students. Robin actually liked it, but she could tell Mandie was zoning out.

"Do you know anyone at NYU?" Alex asked.

"Yes," Mandie said. "My boyfriend is in Goddard Hall, and my best friend is in Third North. They're twins."

"Oh, perfect," Alex said. "Third North is nice. I lived there my first year." She smiled and then gestured to a door. "Your roommate isn't here yet, so go on in and pick a bed. Get unpacked." She tapped her shirt right above her heart. "Look for any of us with the purple shirts if you need something. We'll help."

"Okay," Mandie said.

"Kitchen and dining area down the hall," Alex said, nodding the way they hadn't been yet. "Bathrooms on both ends of the hall too."

Mandie nodded, and Alex handed her a keycard. They hadn't stayed in many hotels, but it reminded Robin of that. Mandie held it to the lock mechanism. It clicked, and she pushed the door open.

Robin expected to find a cramped room with two twin beds, two desks, two chairs, and two closets. That was exactly what she saw, and she wasn't surprised at all that Mandie entered the room and started soaking everything in.

A window took up the wall between the two beds, and

four shelves have been affixed to the wall parallel to the beds. Another acted as a headboard above the bed.

She looked to the right side, and Robin would be surprised if she chose that. It was closer to the door, and Mandie never liked being the closest to the entrance of a bedroom.

She looked left, and Robin wondered what she was trying to figure out. "This side." She turned to the right and finally dropped her duffel bag on the bed. She groaned loudly as Robin tugged in the suitcase and closed the door.

"Why this side?" she asked.

"It has a bigger closet." Mandie smiled at her, unzipped the duffle, and added, "All right. Here's my sheets. Let's get this room set up."

ALICE MARVELED AT HOW EFFICIENT GINNY WAS. In no time at all, her bed had been made up, her clothes unpacked, and her suitcases stowed under her bed. She'd never had a lot of posters or knick-knacks in her room, and she stood at the end of the bed looking at the mostly bare walls.

She had brought a picture frame that held three pictures —one of her, Charlie, and Alice. One of her and Ray, her boyfriend who'd moved to Maryland to attend college, and one of her and Charlie.

Her backpack sat in her desk chair. She'd put her retro alarm clock and a neat row of her favorite paperback books on the desk too.

"I need a plant," she said, turning to Alice. "And I could put a bean bag here." Ginny loved bean bags, and Alice gave her a nod.

"All right," she said. "We have to go to the store no matter what. We'll see what they have." Her stomach churned, and not only because she'd had to pick which twin to go with. Her ex-husband lived in the city, but he'd bailed on helping the twins move in. Alice couldn't help thinking that he'd somehow poison the twins now that they were so much closer to him. Alice had asked Duke to go with Charlie so they could get everything moved in quicker.

"Your room is definitely the nicest," Alice said. She held out her phone to show her the pictures Duke had just sent. "That's your brother's room."

"It's so dark," Ginny said, peering at the photo on Alice's screen.

"His window isn't very big," Alice said. "And he's right next to another building."

Ginny looked up, concern in her eyes. "I feel bad."

"Why? You don't need to feel bad. Charlie changed his mind a bunch of times. He's lucky he got on-campus housing at all." She pocketed her phone. "If you're ready, though, we can head over there. I'll text Robin."

She'd sent pictures of Mandie's room too, and it was

fairly nice. The kitchen facility looked good too, and Alice did hold out hope that Ginny would maybe do a little cooking. *At least in the microwave*, she thought.

They turned to leave just as the door opened. A blonde woman stood there, and she said, "Oh, hello," in a falsely bright voice. "She's already here," she yelled over her shoulder. When she faced Alice and Ginny again, she painted over the obvious disgust in her tone with that fake smile. "You must be Ginny."

"Yes," Ginny said. "You're...Constance's mother?"

"Step-mom," another voice said, and Alice looked to the younger woman behind the blonde. She was about as opposite of a blonde-haired, blue-eyed person as someone could get, and Alice couldn't help smiling at the dryness in her voice.

"I got it, Linda," she said to the woman. "You can go."

Linda opened her mouth, then closed it again. "I'll go check on Reginald."

"You do that," Constance said.

Linda left, and Alice wanted to as well. Constance wore a pair of black jeans with so many holes and rips in them, Alice wondered how she could get her toes and leg through without ripping something wide open.

She wasn't overly tall or short, nor necessarily thin or not thin. She did have a larger-than-average chest, which she'd stuffed into a black tank top. Her dark hair fell over her shoulders, and she wore steel-toed boots with the jeans, no makeup, and bright pink nail polish. That last one really threw Alice, and she wished she had half the tact Arthur did for dealing with teenagers.

Ginny squealed and took the three steps to Constance. They hugged, both of them laughing, and then Ginny faced Alice. "Mom, this is Constance." She smiled at her and then Alice. "My mom, Alice."

"It's lovely to meet you," Alice said.

Ginny and Constance giggled again, which Alice so didn't appreciate. She gave Ginny a look she ignored, and she supposed she should be happy her daughter had a roommate she got along with.

"Mom, can she come with us?"

Alice hadn't been expecting that. "Oh, uh, don't you need to move in, Constance?"

"No," she said. "My step-mom will do it. Well." She rolled her eyes. "She hired someone to do it."

Alice's eyebrows went up. "She hired someone to come move you into your dorm?"

"Mom," Ginny said, and Alice switched her gaze to her.

"What?"

"Can we go? Charlie has to be done by now." She opened the door again and stepped out into the hall, Constance right behind her.

"Okay," Alice muttered. "I guess she's coming with us." She wasn't very happy about that, but she had another child to attend to, and then she'd have to deal with a meal in the city, and then Robin and Duke at the hotel they'd booked.

Her day was far from over, and it didn't really matter if Constance came with them or not. She and Ginny chattered the whole way over to Charlie's building, and she texted him that they'd arrived.

He and Duke came down to get them, and then they rode the slowest elevator Alice had ever stepped foot in to the seventeenth floor. Charlie's room was all made up too, and his roommate sat at his desk, headphones on while he played a game on the Internet. Alice was happy to see her sponsorship for the higher-speed service was already getting good use.

"It looks good." She grinned at Charlie. "Got your own trashcan. That's important." She ran her fingers along the shirts he'd hung up. "Clothes put away."

Her son grinned back at her, and feeling his energy, all of her doubts about him moving out and going to college evaporated. Sure, he might fail. He might hate it here. He might break-up with Mandie and be miserable.

But...he might not. He might thrive on his own. He might love the vibe of the city and learning what he wanted to learn. He might fall madly in love with Mandie, or meet someone else. The possibilities for both of her children were endless, and Alice could feel how exciting that was for them.

"Where are you from, Constance?" he asked, drawing

Alice's attention away from the way he'd stacked his school supplies haphazardly on his desk.

"The Hamptons," she said, and Alice's blood turned to ice. She met Charlie's eye.

"Oh." He swallowed. "We're from Five Island Cove." He indicated himself and Ginny, and she nodded. Alice wanted to hug them both right there on the spot, but she didn't want to be the embarrassing mom.

Thankfully, Robin texted in that moment, saying they were done too. "All right," she said. "Let's go get something to eat."

The kids exited the room as Alice responded to Robin, and she looked up at Duke, who stood out in the hall. "Thank you, Duke."

"Of course," he said. "Happy to do it."

"Did you see Mandie's room?"

"From about thirteen different angles," he said, smiling.

Alice grinned too. "I'll bet."

"My wife is a unique individual," he said.

"And we love her for it," Alice said.

HOURS LATER, AFTER DINNER, AFTER DROPPING each person off at the building, and after she, Robin, and Duke had checked into their hotel, Alice lay in bed, utterly spent. She'd told Arthur about the whole day, from the flight to the "death van ride" to the roommates to everything.

A knock sounded on her door, and she knew that would be Robin. She got up to answer it, and sure enough, her best friend stood in the hallway holding a bottle of wine and two glasses.

"Are you trying to romance me?" Alice joked.

Robin grinned and simply went past her and into the room. Once the door had closed, she said, "We've earned this."

"Yes, we have," Alice said, following her to the small table-for-two in front of the window.

Robin popped and poured, and she handed Alice a glass of red wine. "I think I handled it decently well too."

"I think you did." Alice smiled at her and waited for her to finish pouring her own glass. They lifted their goblets into the air, clinked them, and then sipped simultaneously.

Alice sighed as warmth moved through her. "My house is going to be so quiet."

"Did Em get moved in okay?"

Alice nodded. "She texted Ginny a bunch of pictures. They're going to breakfast in the morning with their roommates." She was relieved Emily had been able to get out of her house, and that her mother had been the one to bring her to the city. She hadn't been able to do much about the situation at home, and her mother had allowed her to stay at Alice's over the summer.

Robin sipped her wine and said nothing, and Alice's mind wandered. All she could see was Clara and Scott talking to Jennifer Golden, and she glanced over to her best friend.

"Have you heard anything about the inn?" she asked.

Robin met her eye. "The inn? Friendship Inn?"

Alice nodded and hid behind her wine glass.

Robin shook her head. "Clara's really chatty on the text now, but she hasn't mentioned the inn."

Alice swallowed and committed to getting this secret off her conscience. "I have to tell you something."

Robin looked over to her, her eyes halfway closed. She was probably so tired. Alice knew she was, and she didn't feel things as deeply or as personally as Robin. "What is it?" she asked.

"I don't know if it's anything," Alice said. "But I saw Clara and Scott and Tessa with your mother at The Glass Dolphin a few weeks ago."

Robin's eyes rounded. "What do you mean?"

"I mean, I saw them leaving the restaurant together." Alice set down her wine glass. "It was really weird, because your mom acted like she barely knew them, but it's plain that she does."

Robin's face screwed up as she frowned. "She rents her house to them."

Alice nodded and gazed into the distance. "Why would she pretend not to know them then?"

Robin's frown deepened. "I don't know."

Alice didn't know either, and she didn't know what else to say.

"I'll ask her," Robin said. She sighed, then threw back the last of her wine. She met Alice's eyes, pure energy in hers. "Thank you for letting us tag along with you today. I think it made it much easier for me to leave her in that dorm, knowing you were doing it times two." She smiled at Alice, who returned it.

"I think I tagged along with you," she said.

Robin shook her head. "Either way." She got up and hugged Alice, then took the wine and her empty glass with her as she left. Alice finished her wine alone, hoping she'd done the right thing by telling Robin about her mother.

Chapter Twenty-Five

Robin pulled up to her mother's house, her heartbeat already pounding out of control. It had been for a week, and Robin couldn't keep living with the palpitations.

She'd mentioned her conversation with Alice to no one, not even Duke. Alice hadn't brought it up again, which made her a very good friend.

Robin looked up to the front door, but she couldn't see it from her position in the driveway. It sat past the garage, which protruded out from the front of the house, and around the corner.

Everything about her mother's house was flawless. She made sure of that with her love of gardening, as well as quick and consistent repairs to anything that would bring stain or spot to her reputation or image.

"How you've managed to live in the cove all this time is

a mystery," Robin muttered to herself. Out of her siblings, Robin was definitely not the most accomplished.

She finally gathered the courage to get out of the minivan and head up to the door. She knocked and then opened the door.

"Mom?" she called. "It's just me."

Just me.

Robin felt so insignificant with those words. The idea that her mother had...Robin didn't know what. But she knew that her mother had more than a landlord/tenant relationship with Clara and Scott Tanner.

She trusted Alice explicitly, and Alice was an excellent judge of character. She saw details others missed, and Robin just needed to ask a few questions.

"Robin," her mother said as she came out of the kitchen at the back of the house. She carried a dishtowel and wiped her hands with it. "What are you doing here?"

Robin tried to smile, but the gesture felt shaky on her lips. "Uh, just came to see how your garden was doing."

In September, her mother started to harvest cucumbers, lettuce, and green beans. She'd been eating peas all summer, and her peaches should be ready soon too.

Her mother's face lit up, and Robin wasn't sure if she was being genuine or not. She couldn't really sit around and garden all day long, could she?

She works at Dr. Benson's office, she told herself. *Part time.*

Robin's father had passed away fifteen years ago, and her mother hadn't remarried. She'd dated a little bit a year or so ago, but when that relationship hadn't worked out, she hadn't gotten another boyfriend.

She'd been working at the dentist's office for years as well, starting after her husband's death, but she'd never wanted for much.

Robin's dad had been a surgeon at the hospital here in the cove, and Robin hadn't known they had money growing up, but her mother had started demonstrating as much after Dad's death.

Her mother wore her scrubs already, and Robin was actually glad. This conversation wouldn't be able to go on and on if Mom had to get to work.

"What's up?" her mom asked as she turned. She hung the towel on the handle of the oven door and faced Robin again.

She wore a placid expression, and Robin couldn't believe that she would do anything to upset Robin.

Of course, she'd done plenty of things that had hurt Robin over the years. Either intentional or not, Robin wasn't sure. She'd like to think her mother wouldn't deliberately cause her pain or grief, but she had demonstrated some selfish behavior in the past.

"I have to leave for work in a few minutes," her mother said. "I can't sit and chat this morning." She gave Robin a smile as she said it, but her meaning was clear.

Get to the point.

Robin took a deep breath. "Mom, are you doing something with the Tanners?"

Her mother blinked. "Doing something?" Her voice was somewhat even, pitching up the way anyone would when they asked a question. "They rent my house from me."

"Alice said she saw you with them at The Glass Dolphin." Robin pressed her hands together and inhaled. "I mean something more than them renting the house."

She'd made Duke and Robin pay rent for years too, and Robin hadn't minded. She didn't want her mother to be able to hold anything too heavy over her head.

"I'm sure Alice was wrong," her mother said coolly.

Robin knew in that moment that she wasn't. "Mom, tell me the truth."

"I am."

"I know you're not." Robin folded her arms. "What's going on?"

"Nothing."

"Mom." Robin practically barked the word.

"Robin, I don't owe you any explanations." She pulled her scrub shirt down and gave Robin a fierce look. "I'm late for work, and I don't have anything to tell you about the Tanners."

She picked up her purse, shouldered it, and started for her

garage exit. A sense of helplessness filled Robin, but she should've known better than to talk to her mother. She could be particularly stubborn, and Robin watched her open the door.

"Why can't you tell me?" Robin asked.

"I don't tell you anything about my finances," her mom said.

"Your finances?" Her mind raced. She knew precious little about her mother's finances, that was true. Why would she be doing anything...*financial* with the Tanners?

"Robin."

"Just tell me," Robin said. "Clara is my friend. She hangs out with me and all of my friends. If there's something going on, I deserve to know about it."

"Deserve?"

"Yes," Robin said. She lifted her chin and took a step toward her mom. "It won't take you long to tell me."

Her mom turned back to her. "I'm not going to explain anything when there's nothing to explain."

Robin searched her mom's face. She wasn't going to give in on this. "I'll ask Clara," she said. She started down the hall toward the front door. She'd have to pull out of the driveway in order for her mom to get out anyway.

"Robin," her mom called after her.

"It's fine, Mom. I get you don't want me to know anything about your life. You've entrusted everything to Stuart instead of me, though I've lived here my whole life and could be more in-the-know." She turned back to her, even took a couple of steps that way.

"I could've handled your affairs. We could've had a closer relationship. You chose everyone and everything over me, and Stuart doesn't even care about what you're doing here. There's a reason he never comes to visit."

"Stop it," her mom said.

Robin felt wild and out of control. "Even my daughters don't like being around you. They know how fake you are. Even they see right through you." She yanked open the front door and started outside.

"I offered to invest in the inn," her mom blurted out.

"Great," Robin said over her shoulder. Her ears were working, but they didn't make connections with her brain. She stomped toward her car, and it wasn't until she was several blocks away from her mother's that she realized what she'd said.

"She offered to invest in Friendship Inn?" Robin knew her mother had money, but she didn't know she had that much. The inn needed hundreds of thousands of dollars to get it to the point of opening, and Robin had thought Clara and Scott had a construction loan.

She'd have to look through hundreds of texts, and back months, to find the message where Kristen had said that. Her memory tickled, and she definitely remembered seeing Kristen's message about the inn and the construction loan.

Otherwise, the Tanners had no way to pay their bills.

She thought of Clara's news that she'd gotten some companies to donate goods. In essence, they'd sponsor the inn, and Robin had thought the renovation was going well.

"Doesn't mean they don't need money," she said.

She hadn't been paying attention to where she was driving, and she realized as she went up a rise that the lighthouse pierced the sky on her right.

She'd driven to the lighthouse. The one place she'd always felt safe and cared for. Most of that had come from Kristen, but she wasn't here anymore.

Robin pulled into the parking lot anyway, and all of the spots sat open and available. She went to the far end of the lot and parked. Out the windshield, she could see the ocean beyond the bluff.

It went on and on, and Robin tried to find a solution to the unrest in her soul.

Regret lanced through her. She should've known better than to go to her mother to get answers. She should've started with Clara.

For some reason, she expected her mother to lie to her, and she didn't want to put Clara on the spot. She'd just barely started to warm to the group in the last month or so, and Robin wanted her to continue to find her place with them here in the cove.

Her phone buzzed, and Robin didn't dare look at it. It would probably be her mom, demanding an apology. She never offered one first, and Robin had stopped hoping for that a long time ago.

She wasn't sure how long she sat in her car, but she caught movement in her rearview mirror and saw Jean crossing the sidewalk and coming toward her.

Emotion surged up her throat, and Robin wanted to disappear. She wasn't sure why. Jean was the nicest person on the island, and she wouldn't judge Robin.

She got out of the car and tucked her hands in her pockets. "Hey," she said.

"I thought it was you, but you didn't answer when I texted."

"I was just thinking." Robin faced the water again. "I used to come here to do that, and I just...showed up here."

Jean came to her side, and they stood there, the two of them. Silent.

"I don't get along with my mother," Robin said, her voice almost a whisper. "She's...I don't know what. I need to talk to Clara, but I don't want to."

"Clara?" Jean asked.

"My mother said she offered to invest in Friendship Inn," Robin said. A storm started in her soul. "I don't know why it bothers me, other than she's never offered to invest in me. When a tsunami hit the island, we got a loan to replace Duke's boat. If she had money to give to Clara, why couldn't she offer it to us?"

She wept, and she hated the heat in her eyes. The weakness in her heart. She'd thought she'd worked through these feelings already.

Apparently not.

"And why Clara? How could Clara take her money and not say anything to me? To the rest of us?"

Jean said nothing. She put her arm around Robin and let her lean into her, which Robin did.

After a minute or two, she said, "Kristen invited me to lunch at her condo today. Let's go."

Robin sniffled and shook her head. "No, I'm not going to encroach on that. I'm okay." She tried to step away from Jean, but the other woman held her.

"She won't mind," Jean said, her dark eyes burning. "Maybe she'll have some answers for you."

Robin searched Jean's face. "What do you mean?"

"Clara's her daughter," Jean said simply. "Maybe she can help you know how to talk to Clara."

"I don't want to push Clara away," Robin said. "She's just started to participate."

"Clara's her own person," Jean said. "She gets to make her own decisions."

Robin wasn't sure why this stung so badly. All she knew was that it did.

Maybe she should go talk to Kristen. Perhaps she could learn more about Clara, get more information about the investment, and find some peace.

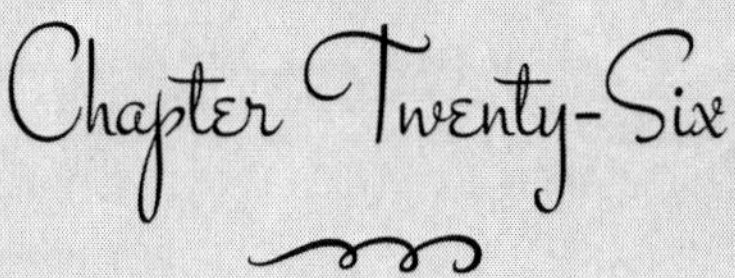

Chapter Twenty-Six

Kristen had just set down a bowl of Caesar salad when the doorbell rang. "It's open," she called.

"Mom," Lena said.

"I bet it's Aunt Jean," Kristen said to her granddaughter.

Sure enough, Jean came through the door, her slight frame doing nothing to hide the woman behind her. "And Robin."

Kristen smiled and went to say hello to both of them. "Robin," she said.

"I hope it's okay I came," she said. "I was..."

"She was at the lighthouse when I was leaving," Jean said. She stepped into Kristen and hugged her. She didn't say more, but Kristen heard some unspoken words.

"The lighthouse?" She raised her eyebrows at Robin.

"I just ended up there," Robin said. "I don't know why."

Kristen knew why, but she didn't say so. "Come in. I'll grab another plate."

"I don't want to crash your lunch."

"Nonsense." Kristen would welcome Robin into her home at any time. "Clara is out at the Cliffside Inn right now, so I thought a nice lunch was in order."

"Clara's at Cliffside?" Robin asked, her voice sharp.

Kristen glanced over to Jean. "Yes."

"Why?"

"Come sit down, Lena," Jean said. She led the girl over to the table. "Did you help Grandma with lunch?"

"I made the pasta salad," Lena said.

Kristen couldn't escape Robin's glare, and her eyes returned to her. "Come sit, dear. Let's at least get something to eat before you start telling me what's wrong."

Thankfully, Robin held her tongue until they all sat at the table. Kristen took a hot ham-and-cheese sandwich and passed the platter to Lena. She planned to take the leftovers to AJ and Matt, so she'd made extra. Having Robin here wasn't an issue at all.

"How is Mandie doing in the city?" she asked, spooning pasta salad onto her plate.

"Good," Robin said. "She survived the first week, and she said she likes her psychology class." She flashed a tight smile, and Kristen thought it would take a lot more than food and a listening ear to get Robin to relax.

Jean chatted about her new Seafaring Girls, saying, "Billie is seriously the cutest one. She doesn't say much, but she's clearly a leader."

Kristen nodded and smiled, glad Jean had something to give her purpose and enjoyment. "What are you going to do when the baby comes?"

"Oh." Jean reached for a napkin and wiped her face quickly. "I didn't tell you. The city got me an assistant, so I can have some time off with the baby."

Kristen looked over to Jean. "Oh? That's great. Who is it?"

Jean grinned and looked over to Lena. "Well, I got two of them, actually. They both already have part-time jobs in the morning, so they have some free time in the afternoons."

Kristen thought she was being a bit vague, and instead of asking again, she waited for Jean to spill her secrets. She looked over to Robin, but she didn't even seem to know another conversation had started at the table.

"Did you tell her?" Jean asked Lena.

The girl shook her head.

Jean grinned at her with clear pride in her eyes. "Good girl, Lena." She looked over to Kristen. "It's Lena and then Tessa."

Kristen had just taken a bite of her sandwich, and she

very nearly choked on it. "Lena?" she said around the hot bread, ham, and melty cheese.

Lena giggled with Jean, and Kristen was so, so grateful the girl had her for an aunt. "I kept a secret, Grandma."

"I'll say," Kristen said.

"Good for you, Lena," Robin said, and Kristen glanced over to her too. "That's great. What are you doing in the morning?"

"I'm back at the grocery store," she said.

"Not the one in Vermont," Kristen clarified.

"It's just a couple of blocks from my house," Lena said. "I ride my bike after Mom goes on the ferry."

Robin nodded, and Kristen swallowed her food and reached for her glass of water. "Start at the beginning, Robin."

Tears filled her eyes. Actually tears, and Kristen knew how much it took to make the woman cry. So much, Kristen had wondered at times if she didn't bottle everything too tightly.

"My mother," she said. "I think she offered to invest in Friendship Inn."

This was news to Kristen, and her eyes widened. She tried to recover quickly, but Robin was an observant woman. "Clara has..." She looked over to Jean, who also wore wide eyes on her face.

"She quit Friendship Inn," Jean blurted out. "She and Scott are going to sell it."

Robin swung her attention to Jean in an instant. "What?"

"She didn't give me all the details," Jean said. "But that's why she's at Cliffside today. She's taken a job there, with Eloise, Julie, and Rhonda."

"Eloise has needed the help for a while," Kristen added quietly. She'd once had two more managers, but they'd both quit at the beginning of the summer, so Kristen was glad El had found the help she needed.

She didn't want to discount Robin's turmoil, because she knew the relationship between her and her mother had been strained for four decades.

"So she didn't take the offer," Robin said. She had eaten very little, though her plate held plenty of food.

"I don't know what the offer was," Kristen said. "Or if there was one. If there was, I don't think Clara took it."

"She never told you about it?" Robin zeroed in on Kristen, who shook her head, and then Jean, who did likewise.

Robin visibly relaxed, and she poked her fork into a bowtie and lifted it to her lips. "Alice said she saw them at The Glass Dolphin, that my mother pretended not to know Clara and Scott."

Kristen reached across the space between them and covered Robin's hand. "This bothers you, because you don't like things to be unjust."

Robin shook her head, her tears shining in her eyes again.

"And you wish your mother would invest in you."

Robin let a single tear slip down her face, and she quickly wiped it away. "I'm fine."

Which meant she wasn't.

"Of course you are," Jean said. "But it's okay to want your mother to confide in you."

"Or give you a rent break when you need it," Kristen said.

"Or loan us the money for Duke's boat," Robin said. "I just..." Her shoulders slumped. "You don't think Clara took it?"

"If she did, it wouldn't make sense," Kristen said. "She's really not going to continue with the inn."

"When did she tell you that?" Robin asked.

Kristen's memory wasn't as good as it once had been. Then it fired, and she said, "The same day as Asher's birthday party."

"That was almost a month ago," Robin said. She looked between Jean and Kristen. "Why hasn't she told any of us?"

Kristen didn't have an answer for that. She knew her daughter well enough, and opening up for her might actually cause her to break out in hives.

"She's...working on that," Jean said.

"You two knew." Robin wasn't asking.

"I only found out because she asked me to help with Lena in the mornings," Jean said.

"I stay with Aunt Jean in the mornings," Lena said.

Kristen smiled and pulled her hand back. "That's right, dear. You get to go help Aunt Jean with breakfast in the mornings." She threw a smile in Robin's direction too. The woman had calmed, and she took a bite of her sandwich now.

Things weren't all the way fixed, or even close to right, but she wasn't wound all the way to one hundred anymore, and Kristen hoped this wasn't the calm before the storm.

A COUPLE OF EVENINGS LATER, SHE SMILED OVER to Theo as he laced his fingers between hers. "What are you smiling about?" she asked.

"I have a surprise for you," he said. He'd come to pick her up at her condo, saying he wanted to take her to dinner. She was extraordinarily bad at cooking for one, and she'd never say no to someone who wanted to take her to dinner.

Deep down, she knew it was more than that. She wouldn't just go out with any man. She sure did like Theo, and as their relationship had started into its fourth month, Kristen had started thinking about the end game of it.

What was she going to do? Date him until one of them passed away? Could she get married again? Was he thinking along those same lines?

She hadn't asked him any of those questions, and he hadn't brought them up either. They walked together almost every morning, and he held her hand as they traversed the sand. He took her to breakfast, lunch, or dinner, and she sure enjoyed kissing him goodnight or goodbye for the day.

It was nice to have someone to talk to who was relatively drama-free, as her lunch with Robin, Jean, and Lena had been filled with tension. Since then, she'd heard nothing from Robin—or Clara. Or anyone.

School had started again. Routines had settled over Five Island Cove. New classes, new teachers, new patterns of behavior. The beaches still filled in the afternoons, but only with locals. The construction on new buildings and restaurants continued, but Kristen and Theo didn't have to fight the crowds to try them.

"I thought we were going to dinner," she said.

"We are." He threw her a playful look. "After the surprise." He took her down the sidewalks in their fifty-five-plus community, clearing leading her toward his place.

She didn't ask him any more questions, and he opened his condo door without a key. Kristen heard the mewing immediately, and her gaze flew to him. "Theo," she said, really drawing out his name with plenty of warning. "What's going on?"

"My friend's daughter's cat had kittens." He left the front door open and moved over to a cardboard box that rested next to the dining room table.

He lifted a pure gray kitten, save for a white patch in a

triangular patch between its eyes, from the box. He smiled at it and stroked it with two fingers. "Isn't she so cute?"

She so was. "You're going to raise a kitten?"

"No." He grinned at her. "I got her for you."

Kristen's eyes rounded. "You got her for me?"

"Michelle is willing to raise it and keep it until she's a little older," Theo said. "Then you can have her."

Kristen moved over to him and took the adorable kitten from him. She snuggled right into her chest, and Kristen ducked her head and smiled at the feline. "Oh, I love her."

"So do you want her?" Theo asked.

Kristen looked up, her eyes looking deeply into Theo's. He wore happiness and hope there, and Kristen felt herself doing something she thought would not happen for her again—she was falling for him. Falling in love.

"Yes," she whispered. "Thank you so much." She cradled the kitten close and tipped her head back so she could kiss Theo. He lowered his head and met her mouth.

The kiss was sweet and tender, yet said so much. Passion infused the action too, and Kristen only pulled away because her kitten mewled at her to do so.

"Sorry, baby," she said to the kitten. She put her back into the box, which had a small blanket and a couple of plastic rings. The kitten cried again, but without her in her arms, Kristen could kiss Theo properly.

So she did.

Chapter Twenty-Seven

"Parker," Kelli called up the stairs. "Come on. Your father's on the computer." She turned away from the view looking up to the landing and went back into the kitchen.

Julian waited on the screen, looking down at his phone. Parker's footsteps landed overhead, and Kelli's stomach twisted and flipped.

Her son had flown home alone a couple of weeks ago, and Kelli had cried and cried when he'd been escorted past security to her and Shad. Some of that came from her increased hormones due to her pregnancy, and some of it came from the sheer love she had for her son.

"Come on." She waved him forward as he finally came into the kitchen.

"I'm coming," Parker said, his voice halfway tainted

with teenage attitude. She threw him a sharp look, and he deflated as he slid onto the barstool beside her.

The past couple of weeks hadn't been easy in her house, as Parker had moved into junior high, and his summer in New Jersey had only seemed to fuel his attitude.

Kelli had had to remind him who she was, and that as his mother, *she* was in charge around their house. He would show her respect, and if he couldn't, there would be consequences.

She'd grounded him for the first time in his life, and it had been torture for her too, to not be able to take Parker to Jean's for a welcome-home lunch the woman had planned specifically for him.

She'd done it a few days later, and Kelli had threatened Parker to within inches of his life that he better not treat Jean with a single ounce of attitude, or Kelli would *never* take him to the lighthouse again.

Jean had reported that he'd been great, and Kelli hadn't questioned her or Parker further.

"Dad," Parker said, and Kelli looked at the screen too. Julian lifted his head and smiled at his son.

"Heya, buddy. How's school?"

"Boring," Parker said. He threw a look to Kelli. "But I like my percussion class."

"That's great." Julian looked at Kelli, and the weight of this video call settled on her.

She'd called it, and the words she needed to say suddenly fled her mind.

"What's up, Kel?" Julian asked.

She looked over to Parker, and then back to Julian. "I have something to tell you both," she said. "I'd have done it when Parker got home, but you didn't come with him."

Julian's gaze hardened, and Kelli didn't mean to criticize him. She looked down at her hands.

"I'm pregnant," she said. "Shad and I are going to have a baby in the middle of March." She wasn't sure why she wanted to tell them together. She didn't have to tell Julian at all.

"That's great, Kelli," Julian said.

She lifted her eyes to meet his through the video chat. Her eyebrows went up as she tried to truly judge his reaction. They had worked so hard to get Parker, and it had been the trial of her life—at the time. His too, she'd thought.

"Thank you," she said. She looked over to Parker. "So you'll be a big brother." She smiled and tousled his hair.

He let her, which reminded her that Parker was still her little boy. He didn't seem excited or upset, and Kelli wasn't sure if she liked his lack of a reaction.

"Are you okay?" she asked.

His brow furrowed then. "Yeah," he said. "Why wouldn't I be?"

"I don't know," she said. "You're going to be a lot older than your brother or sister."

"Yeah," he said. Then he brightened. "Can I help you and Shad pick out the name?"

Kelli hadn't been expecting that question at all, and she blinked as Julian chuckled from Jersey. "I—maybe," she said.

Kelli didn't know what else to say. Neither Julian nor Parker found it all that significant that she was pregnant, and to Kelli, it was literally the second biggest miracle of her life. Parker being the first.

"Okay," she said, not sure why her chest stung. This was her ex. She didn't need his approval or congratulations.

"Thanks for jumping on Julian."

"Can I talk to Dad for a few minutes?" Parker asked.

Kelli looked at her son and saw him growing up right before her eyes. It was like a slow-motion movie, and she saw the first twelve years of his life in only a few seconds.

She reached over and pushed his hair to the side. "Yeah, sure," she said fondly. "You look so old, buddy." She gave him a smile, which he returned.

She slid from the barstool and left her son to chat with her ex-husband. Gladness spread through her that they had a relationship. She wanted that for them, and she was also glad Parker had Shad here full-time to help her parent him properly. He also had the influence of Jean and Reuben, whom he loved. And Kristen. Robin, Alice, Eloise, AJ,

Laurel, Kelli's mother, and even Clara would take Parker anytime Kelli needed them to. She had friends at Whole Soul who would as well.

It truly did take a lot of people to raise a child, and Kelli's chest constricted as she thought about all the supportive people she had in her life. She wasn't alone, and she never wanted to feel like she was again.

She went past the steps and out the front door to the garden patio that sat in front of the twinhome where she and Shad lived with Parker.

Shad sat at the metal table, the shade from the umbrella keeping him safe from the sun and cool at the same time. He looked up as she closed the door behind her. "Hey." He got to his feet. "How did it go?"

Kelli nodded. "Good enough."

"Why do you look like you're going to cry then?" He wore compassion and concern in his face and he took her into his arms.

Kelli clung to him, her solid place when things got really shaky, and closed her eyes. "They didn't seem to care."

Shad didn't say anything, probably because he didn't know what to say. Kelli didn't blame him. She had no idea why she'd expected them to be flabbergasted by her pregnancy news.

She stepped back and studied the patio pavers at her feet. "I don't know why, but I wanted them to be, I don't know, wowed or something." She shook her head. "It's silly."

"*I'm* wowed," Shad said. He bent down and ducked his head, then lifted hers until she looked into his eyes. "This is the most amazing, most life-changing, most wow-ful thing that's ever happened to me." He grinned at her. "Okay? This—between me and you—we're the only ones who have to be wowed."

Kelli fell in love with him all over again with those words. She nodded, the pinch leaving her chest. "You're right." She touched her mouth to his. "Thank you."

Shad led her to the table. "Besides, your mom is almost here, and she'll be thrilled, I'm sure."

Kelli picked up her ice water and took a sip. The cold liquid carved a path through her, and she'd barely set her glass down when a car pulled to the curb. Her mother got out of the backseat, her sights already set up the steps.

Kelli lifted her hand in a wave, and Shad got up to go greet her. "Paula," he said, laughing as he went down the steps. He hugged her, took the food she'd brought in two white paper bags, and brought her up to the table, where Kelli also stood to hug her mom.

"Where's Parker?" her mom asked, looking toward the door.

"He's talking to Julian," Kelli said. "He'll be out in a few minutes." She looked at Shad, who started unpacking the food.

"Cobb salad," he said, sliding that in front of Kelli. "Mac and cheese." He put that in front of the last seat at the table, where Parker would sit.

Once he'd passed out all the food, Kelli removed the plastic top on her salad and lifted the small cup of dressing. "Mom," she said. "Shad and I have some news."

She looked over to her mother, filled with love for her too. Her life hadn't been easy, and Kelli had just started rediscovering how amazing her mother was. How much she'd protected her from in the past. How selfless and how sacrificing she'd been.

Her mother looked over to Shad, who wore a smile with the wattage of the sun.

"We're going to have a baby," Kelli said.

Her mother's eyes widened, and a shaking hand shot to her mouth. "You're kidding."

Kelli shook her head. "Not kidding. We're due in March."

Her mother wasn't one for shrieking, but she made a squealing sound now and lurched out of her seat again. Kelli caught sight of her tears as she hugged her one more time. "Oh, how exciting," she said. "What a huge blessing for you both." She pulled away, her joy emanating from her in three-hundred-sixty degrees. "I'm so very excited for you."

She sat down and looked over to Shad. Kelli did too, and

he was just pulling his hand away from his eyes. "Are you excited to be a father?" her mom asked.

"More than I can say," he said, and Kelli didn't need Parker or Julian to be happy or excited for her. She knew they were; of course they were.

Shad and her mother were—and Kelli already loved the life growing inside her to bits and pieces—and they'd provided the reactions she wanted. Over and over, Shad did, and Kelli was so glad she'd moved in next door to him and then taken a chance when she'd been scared to do so.

Chapter Twenty-Eight

Laurel stepped into Aaron's office, Paul right behind her. He carried the last box of her things, and Laurel wasn't sure how to even speak.

Aaron Sherman, tough, tall, Chief-of-Police whom Laurel had once found so attractive looked up, then stood. "You're all set?" He didn't smile, and Laurel didn't either.

He was married to one of her best friends, and they saw each other socially and casually.

She nodded. Aaron noticed her silence, or maybe the way her chin trembled, and he came around his desk and drew her into a strong hug. "Hey," he said, his voice not nearly as gruff as it usually was inside this office. "You can come back any time you want, Laurel. Okay?"

She nodded as she gripped his shoulders. She had no idea she'd react this way. She wanted to quit her job so she could be a full-time mom. Her baby was due tomorrow, and Laurel had no idea if the boy would come in the next twenty-four hours. She had some unpacking to do from the baby shower her mother had thrown for her in Nantucket, and she got started on that.

Her parents had then come to the cove to be here when the baby was born. Kristen had filled her fridge and freezer with food, and Jean had carefully and lovingly placed at least a dozen outfits in the top drawers of the dresser Paul had finished putting together last weekend.

Robin and Alice had hung the drapes in the nursery, then set up the rocking chair and changing table. Kelli had commissioned art from a co-worker at her yoga studio who painted on the side, and she'd filled one wall of the nursery with baby animals curling themselves around the letters in Jamison's name.

AJ had prepared a "first week of motherhood" kit for Laurel, claiming no one could really predict what those first several days would be like, but that she had a few things that could maybe make Laurel's life easier once she brought her baby home.

Aaron had given Paul the next two weeks off, barring any emergencies that might come to the cove, and both Laurel and Paul had been praying there wouldn't be any.

Eloise, Julia, Maddy, and Tessa had given her a coupon book for free baby-holding, even in the middle of the night, and Eloise had cried honest-to-goodness tears when she'd given her the booklet and said, "I would literally sell my soul to sit and hold your baby. Please, please call me when you need a nap." She'd pulled away and said, "Or I'll just come over in the afternoon and take him and force you to lie down."

Laurel had only been able to nod then too. Two or three years ago, she couldn't even imagine the life she had now. The friends who'd come into her life. The care for her—for her—they exhibited. She couldn't fathom it, and her relationship with Paul was the same.

"Any time," he said. "Just bring the baby in to show us." He gave her a warm smile and looked past her to Paul. He stepped that way, and Laurel ducked her head and wiped her tears. She was looking forward to not having so many raging hormones in her body. Then maybe she wouldn't tear up at the mere thought of everything, from leaving her job, to her friends, to Paul stopping to buy her a cheeseburger on the way home from work.

They left, got the cheeseburgers, and headed home. Laurel thought she might feel different, but she wasn't sure how she should feel.

"Well," she said to Paul. He looked up from his French fries. "I'm unemployed now."

He gave her a smile and covered her hand. "Hon, you're going to be so busy. Being a mom is a full-time job."

She nodded, and she let Paul take care of her that night. The baby wasn't born overnight, nor did he come the next day. She and Paul finally stopped sitting around the house, waiting for her to go into labor, and decided to go to dinner.

Laurel felt absolutely huge as she pulled a shapeless dress over her head. The only things she could wear were big rectangles of fabric, and she hated how it bumped slightly over her breasts, and then swelled to epic proportions over her belly.

"I hate leaving the house," she said to Paul as he came out of the closet, a fresh polo covering his torso now. "Everyone is going to ask when I'm due or make some comment about how uncomfortable I look."

He smiled at her and said, "I can run in somewhere and we'll take it to the beach."

Hoped filled Laurel's heart. "Would you?"

"I've already got the chairs in the back of the car." He pulled her close to his side, and she looked at the two of them in the mirror as he planted a kiss against her temple.

His impish grin appeared and he whispered, "My word, Laurel, you look *so* uncomfortable. When are you due again?"

He shoved him away from her as he laughed, and he barely moved. He came right back to her side, his happiness contagious.

"I love you," he said next, and Laurel couldn't stop herself from smiling at that. She'd never tire of him saying it, of feeling it move through her, of letting their love dictate her life.

The moment paused, and then life rushed on. Paul stepped away from her, and Laurel reached for his hand at the same time he extended his toward her. They left the house together, and in the car, Laurel buckled her seatbelt around her baby for hopefully the last time.

Paul closed her door, and she put both hands on her enormous belly. "You have to come soon," she said to the baby. "Today would be ideal. Tonight. Heck, right now."

The baby squirmed inside her, and she smiled as she looked over to Paul. "I told him he has to come, and he's kicking me."

He chuckled, and Laurel kept her hands on her belly as the baby caused a band of tension to form across the top of it.

Paul drove them toward Mort's, and Laurel shifted as the tightness in her body flowed down over her belly. It rippled almost, and since she'd never been in labor before, she had no idea if this was a normal part of it or not.

In talking to Robin, AJ, Kelli, and Alice, she'd learned quickly that there was no "normal." There was her water breaking, and then she'd know she was in labor for sure and she should get to the hospital. Otherwise, labor pains could start in her back like Alice's had, or be sharp sensations through her midsection like Robin's. AJ's water had broken without any labor pains at all, and Kelli said she'd been in labor for four days before she thought it was bad enough to go to the hospital. Even then, her delivery with Parker had taken twenty hours.

She groaned as the discomfort continued, and Paul looked over to her. "Laurel?"

"It's just tight," she said.

He said nothing to question her further, and he pulled up to Mort's. "Crab cake sandwich?"

She gave him a smile. "Yes, please. Extra tartar sauce and ketchup." She liked to mix them together to make a sauce for the sandwich, and she dipped her fries in it too.

"You got it, my wife." Paul got out of the car, left it running so Laurel would be comfortable, and headed inside. Now that the busy tourist season was over, they'd have no problem getting dinner and finding a spot on the beach.

Laurel leaned her head back and closed her eyes. Her mind automatically started reviewing what she needed to do tomorrow, and then she remembered she didn't have a job.

Relief and a sense of peace moved through her, and the barest of smiles touched her lips. In that moment, her belly tightened again, this time much faster. Painfully fast.

She gasped, her eyes flying open. She gripped her belly now, both hands pressing into the firmness of her body. Pressure built between her legs, and Laurel couldn't stay in the car.

She unbuckled her belt and opened the door, and in the few seconds it took her to do that, the pain and pressure had increased so much, tears came into her eyes.

She gripped the sides of the car and boosted herself to a standing position. The pressure lessened, thankfully, and Laurel breathed out.

Then wetness ran down her legs. She looked down, surprised, but her belly hid her legs and feet, and had for weeks. She wore a dress, so she couldn't see if it was wet.

"You're wet," she told herself. Pressure built again, and Laurel gripped the top of the door now. She turned toward the fish shop, but Paul had gone inside.

A car pulled up, and Laurel took a step toward it. White, sharp, instant pain slid down her right hip, causing her to cry out.

She froze, her body's way of telling her not to move again. If she just stood still, everything would be fine.

You're having a baby, she thought. *You're not fine! Get Paul!*

A man got out of his car, and Laurel yelped, "Hey," at him.

He looked toward her, his step pausing. She had no idea what she looked like, but the wariness slid from his face in the next moment. "Ma'am?"

"My husband is in Mort's," Laurel said, speaking rather quickly as she wasn't sure what would happen next. "His name is Paul. Will you tell him my water broke and we need to go?"

He looked to Mort's and back to her. "Paul. Got it." He took off for Mort's, and Laurel appreciated the urgency. She had the thought that she should sit back down, get buckled, and be ready for when Paul came out, but she couldn't make herself do it.

Her legs ached now, and a general sense of exhaustion overcame her. Her mind fuzzed as her head swam, and she held tightly to the door so she wouldn't fall.

"Laurel." Paul rushed toward her. "Get back in the car, babe."

"It hurts," she said, looking to him for relief. He'd always taken all of her pain and held it for her until it was fixed and gone.

He grabbed onto her arms. "Hon, you have to get in the car so we can go." He wore urgency in those beautiful eyes, and Laurel tried to think through the haze still enveloping her.

Pain tore through her abdomen, and her face crumbled. She started to cry, once again hating that weakness. This pain. That she couldn't unfreeze her muscles.

Paul got very close to her and said, "Baby, I need you to get in the car right now," in his don't-mess-with-me-I'm-a-cop voice. He sometimes talked to her like this while they made love, and she adored the fantasy he created in their bedroom.

Out here, her body apparently listened the same way it did in the bedroom. She sank into her chair, and Paul helped her get her legs in. "Buckle up," he barked at her, and then he ran around the car.

By the time he got in, Laurel had regained her senses. "Sorry," she said. "There was so much pressure that I had to get up."

"You zoned out," he said.

"I was in quite a bit of pain," she said. "It's subsided now."

"Your water broke?" He backed out fast, and Laurel reached to hang onto the handle on the roof.

"Yes," she said, feeling the warm wetness again.

He drove quickly, the tension in the car more than Laurel liked. But she was having a baby, and she didn't want to get to the hospital any later than necessary either.

Paul grinned at her and reached over to rest his hand on her belly. "Your son listened to you, hon. He's coming."

Laurel had a brief moment to return his smile, then another blinding wave of pain burned a path through her. So hot and so quick, Laurel cried out and closed her eyes almost like she could avoid the pain if she couldn't see.

When she woke up, all she could hear was Paul's voice. "Come on, Laurel," he said. Not the tough cop who wanted her to wait, and not the sexy, sultry voice of the man who wanted to take her to dinner. This tone only carried panic, and Laurel didn't like it. Paul didn't panic. Paul approached everything with an even demeanor. He only let stress get to him later, at home, when the situation was over and the doors closed.

She groaned again, her throat beyond dry.

"There you go," he coached, plenty of anxiety still in his voice. "Wake up, Laurel. Open your eyes and look at me. We're almost there."

She felt like she'd been dropped onto hard pavement. Every muscle in her body was on high alert, tight and tense. As discomfort moved through her core, she remembered what was going on.

Her eyes opened, and the world stayed blurry for a moment. Paul continued to encourage her, telling her every turn he was making.

"We're here. I'm getting out. Stay right there."

Laurel couldn't move anyway, so obeying Paul was easy. He didn't come right around the car, though. Laurel wasn't sure where he'd gone, and she tried lifting her hand to open the door.

She didn't have the strength. It felt like she'd been asleep for a very long time, but she couldn't have been. The trip from Mort's to the hospital wouldn't take more than ten or fifteen minutes, depending on the traffic.

"She's out again," Paul said. "Laurel."

"We'll get her out, Mister Leyhe," a woman said. "Back up."

"She said her water broke."

"You said that."

Laurel could hear them, and she wanted to tell Paul she was okay. She couldn't see him, however, and she honestly wasn't sure if she was okay. Why couldn't she see?

Firm hands gripped her, and she got lifted from the soft seat where she sat.

"No," Paul said. "Look at all that blood. Is that normal?" No one answered him, and a couple of voices started talking over one another.

"Laurel," he said. "I'm right here." His fingers slipped between hers, and she wanted him to know she heard him. That she was right there too, and he needed to hold on so she didn't drift away.

She squeezed as hard as she dared, and Paul said, "You're okay, my love. Okay? We'll get the baby out, and you'll be okay."

Chapter Twenty-Nine

Clara held Lena's hand as they entered the hospital. Her daughter carried a bright blue plush elephant, and Clara would honestly be surprised if the girl gave it up for the baby.

Lena had several plushies she loved dearly, and at least three of them were elephants. She loved the trunked animals so much, and Clara hadn't been surprised when she'd selected it for Laurel's baby.

Jamison had been born two days ago now, and Laurel was finally feeling well enough to have visitors.

She'd had a blood transfusion after she'd lost too much when her water had broken and she'd started bleeding at the same time. She'd had a tiny tear in her uterine wall, and through a miracle and the grace of God, her little boy had been delivered via Caesarian section only forty-five minutes later.

She'd been out for all of it, and her doctors had been monitoring her closely since. She'd made quite a good recovery overnight, and the texts Clara had gotten that morning had brought her great relief.

She was sure she'd be the last one to arrive at the hospital to visit, which was fine as Laurel could only have two visitors at a time and she'd have to go in with Lena.

Robin, Alice, and Eloise had taken shifts here at the hospital since the moment Paul had called Aaron to tell him about Laurel. He'd told Eloise, and someone had been here since.

Clara rode the elevator up to the maternity ward, only mildly surprised to find everyone there. Mom and Jean turned toward her with smiles. Lena held up the elephant, and Jean grinned at her.

AJ sat on a loveseat with Kelli, and Robin and Alice stood behind the pair of chairs where Eloise sat. They all looked at her, and Clara told herself not to be self-conscious. These women were her friends, and they wanted her here.

"There you are," her mother said.

"I didn't know you'd all be here." Clara looked around at everyone, noticing something tight on Robin's face. She wasn't sure why, but Robin's expression changed a moment later.

"We were leaving," Jean said. "Right when Kelli and AJ got here, and we've just been visiting." She now held the elephant, and Clara marveled at how much Lena had grown and changed since she'd come to the cove.

Jean took her to work every morning now, and she'd not reported a single melt-down from Lena. She helped Jean with breakfast, mostly because Jean got out recipes from her mother and grandmother and taught Lena how to make them. She let her put together doughs and batters on her own, and she didn't get upset if things didn't go right. She just got out a gallon of milk and a box of cereal on days when the waffles had a couple of tablespoons of salt in them instead of sugar.

Clara had felt bad about her impatience to allow Lena to cook at home, but Jean had reminded her that Lena simply needed different experiences with different people. It wasn't a commentary on Clara at all.

She'd enjoyed her mornings—early as they were—at the Cliffside Inn, and her gratitude for Eloise only grew with each passing day.

Right now, she smiled at the dark-haired woman as she rose from the chair. "She'll be thrilled to see you and Lena," Eloise said. She gave Clara a quick hug and stepped back. "Her parents are back there with Paul right now. The doctor was supposed to come in and give them an update, and then Paul said he'd come tell us."

Clara nodded and said, "It's okay if we can't go see her. Lena wanted to bring her something for the baby is all."

"You have to see the baby," Alice said. "He's the cutest little thing in the whole world."

"He's got Laurel's cute face," Mom said. "With Paul's darker hair."

Clara had seen pictures of him, but she could admit there wasn't anything as special as a holding a newborn baby. Her heartstrings hummed, and she smiled around at everyone. "I'd love to see him." She met Robin's eye, and once again the woman wasn't smiling.

Clara hadn't seen her in person for a few weeks, as making yet another crazy ninety-degree turn had been happening in her, Scott's, and Lena's life.

She now got up at three o'clock in the morning and got on the first ferry—at five a.m.—to go to Sanctuary Island so she could be there to run the Cliffside Inn for breakfast and check-out.

Scott took Lena to Jean's only a couple of hours later, because he actually drove the ferry to and from Sanctuary Island, starting at seven a.m. Jean then took Lena to the supermarket by ten. They were all home by three or four at the latest, and Clara couldn't complain about this turn.

She couldn't believe she was happy here in Five Island Cove, but she was. Happier than she'd been in a while. Scott was happier. Lena was thriving.

The things that had been rebuilt in Clara's life surprised

her, as she hadn't thought her friendships needed work. She hadn't thought she'd be able to accept that Lena needed other influences besides her and Scott. She hadn't ever thought that she could come back to this place which she'd disliked so much growing up.

All of those were true, though, and Clara knew she still had walls to break down, and new rooms to build. She had plenty to work on, but the real joy came from the fact that she *was* working on it.

"Can I talk to you for a minute?" Robin stood in front of her now, and Clara blinked.

"Sure," she said.

Robin moved several steps away, and Clara followed her. The tension between them rose to a level Clara could feel in her stomach, and she wasn't sure what would come out of Robin's mouth.

"Is everything okay?" Clara asked, for Robin just stood there, silent.

"I know my mother came to you with an investment... option," she said. "I want to know what it was."

Clara's first instinct was to shut down. Deny everything. Tell Robin she didn't know what she was talking about. She'd told no one but Scott about Jennifer's offer, and only Scott and Tessa knew the money had been turned down.

Clara needed more time to figure out what to say, and she opened her mouth and then closed it again.

Robin folded her arms and cocked her head. "Clara," she challenged.

"Nothing came of it," Clara said.

"I still want to know what it was," Robin said.

Alice drifted closer, and she stood next to Robin. "Everything okay?"

"She won't tell me either." She glared at Clara, and the "either" made Clara want to clam up even more.

She swallowed and searched for the right thing to do. "Your mother didn't want me to tell anyone." She glanced over to her mother, who stood watching. Everyone was watching.

The world narrowed to her looking at all of them, and she knew whatever she said or did next would determine if she could still be part of them or not.

She wanted to be part of them.

She needed to keep her home as well, and she rented from Jennifer.

She wished Scott stood at her side and could help her know what to say or do.

"Guys," Eloise said. "I have an announcement while we're all here."

Clara's eyes widened as she looked Eloise. "El," she said.

"Clara is my new morning manager." She took a few steps toward the trio Clara was a part of and bridged the gap to the others near the waiting area. "She has been for a few weeks now, and she's amazing at it."

"Wait," Kelli said. "You're not rebuilding Friendship Inn?"

All eyes came to Clara, and she didn't like the weight of them. "No," she said somewhat harshly. "It was too much. A pipe dream." She couldn't believe she ever thought she could renovate something as huge as Friendship Inn. "We couldn't do it. We decided to list it for sale, and our realtor is doing word-of-mouth advertising right now before listing it publicly." Sam knew so many people in the commercial industry, and he had three people interested in the inn already.

AJ stood too. "Why didn't you tell us?"

"Because Clara is better than us," Robin said sarcastically.

"No," Clara said, and she wasn't the only voice. Eloise had spoken too.

"Robin, that's not fair." She gave Robin a look that Clara appreciated. It told her Eloise was on her side, though still curious as to why Clara couldn't open up.

"Why is she on our group text if she's not going to share?" Robin demanded.

Clara's pulse hammered through her whole body. "I wanted to make sure everyone had adjusted okay," she said. Her voice came out much smaller than it had previously.

"Not everyone is as comfortable as you are with sharing," Alice said.

Robin glared at her. "So I'm wrong here, in wanting to

know what's going on with one of our friends. Someone we *trust* to share all of our news with." She looked around at everyone.

"*You're* sharing with her, and she's *not* reciprocating. That doesn't bother anyone but me?" She put her hands on her hips. "I don't believe that." She turned and faced Clara. "That's not how to get and keep friends. I have to feel like I trust every single person on the group text thread, and I don't trust you."

Clara swallowed. "Robin," she said as everyone looked at her again. They likely felt the same way, and Clara realized that she needed to do better.

"It took Laurel a while to contribute too," Alice said. "We're all different."

"Does she even care about us?" Robin asked. "Doesn't she want us to celebrate with her, or to support her when she has a hard day?" She looked over to Kristen. "She probably texts Kristen and Jean, which is great. She can have a group thread with them."

Everyone hovered in the wake of all Robin had said. Clara met her mother's eyes, and Mom practically begged her to say something. Clara didn't know what, and she supposed the next step on her journey of rebuilding herself would be to speak before she was ready. Just say what was in her heart, whether she'd had time to weigh it all out, test it on her tongue, or consider how it would sound.

"I don't want to be on a group text with my mom and

Jean," she said. "I don't." She looked at Robin. "I'm sorry, really. I'm..." She took a deep breath for Clara's heart beat at her to admit a weakness.

She never did that. She concealed those from everyone and everything until she didn't have to think about them anymore or until she was alone.

"I'm bad at letting people in on the bad things," she said. "I only want to share good news."

"Selling the inn is good news," Eloise said. "I've been telling you that for a couple of weeks now."

"I think so too," Clara said. "But I wasn't sure anyone else would think so. I thought they might judge me for giving up."

More silence, and Clara couldn't decipher all of the expressions fast enough. Finally, AJ said, "Honey, if they were going to do that, they'd do it to me. Lord knows I'm the screw-up in the group."

"You are not," Kelli said.

AJ only gave her a one-shouldered shrug. Robin's expression softened, but it went nowhere near a smile. Alice offered Clara a small one and said, "We've all made mistakes. We're all uncertain about things. That's why we tell each other."

"Then we can reason through confusing things with different minds," Jean said.

Clara heard them, really *heard* them, and her regrets doubled. "I'm sorry," she said again. "I've been trying to hide my inadequacies for so long...I don't know how to simply admit that I'm struggling, that I don't know what the right thing is, or that I need help."

"We'll help you with that," Eloise said. She too smiled, but in Clara's book, Eloise was the nicest person in the world.

All of these women were. They knew her story. They knew why she and Scott had moved to the cove. They *knew*, and there Robin stood, angry because Clara hadn't been sharing.

Somehow, she knew it was more than that, and she focused on the woman again. "I'm sorry, Robin. Maybe if I'd opened up sooner, I could've talked to you about your mother."

She hardened again, the transformation almost instant. She didn't have to repeat her question for it to be shouted into the room.

"Your mom called me one day," she said. "A few months ago. Beginning of July, maybe. She said she might want to invest in the inn."

Alice exchanged a glance with Robin. "But I saw you at The Glass Dolphin in August."

"I put her off," Clara said. "I was getting companies to donate to the inn, and I was busy, and I didn't meet with her until August. She told me I couldn't tell anyone." Clara drew in a breath. "I told Scott, though, and Tessa, so they came to the meeting with me."

"She offered you money." Robin didn't phrase it as a question.

Clara nodded. "A lot of money."

The answer only seemed to add gasoline to Robin's already burning fire.

"She said she'd be a silent investor. She'd own forty percent of the inn, and once it started turning a profit, that forty percent of it would go to her." Clara's throat hurt, because she hadn't revealed this many personal things in a long time, at least not in such a short time. She spoke to guests all morning, but this was ten times worse.

"I needed the money, but giving her that much of the profit would've left very little for me and Scott. We were still going to do it..." She let the words hang there.

"Until you decided to give up," AJ said.

Clara nodded, not sure why she couldn't say out loud that she'd "quit" the inn. Or that she'd given up. Because of her father, those things were shameful. They'd been slammed into her over and over and over.

We never, ever, ever give up. That one, her mom had once displayed on a wood block in the kitchen.

I'm not going down without a fight. Clara couldn't even tell how many times her dad had said that. At least five hundred. Probably more.

He did fight too. All the time. He actually thrived on arguing, and Clara had played into his hand far too many times. She'd quit when she'd left the cove and refused to return. She hated the feeling of quitting something.

"Until the inn," she said out loud.

"I don't believe in continuing to do something that makes us unhappy and unfulfilled," Mom said. "Simply to say we didn't give up. Sometimes what we *need* to do is quit."

"Everyone," Eloise said. "Quitting can be refreshing."

"It can be necessary," Alice said. "Like when I quit lying to myself and finally left Frank."

Clara's eyes filled with tears. "I quit the inn. I told Jennifer no. Scott and I walked away, and we've been really struggling for the past several months, but we've come together a lot this summer." She swiped at her eyes, frustrated with herself for getting emotional—another thing that she believed showed weakness—and for telling these women about her private life with Scott. She never did that.

Clara took a breath, trying to find reason in her frenzied, emotional mind. She felt no remorse for quitting, and she told herself she didn't need to be embarrassed in front of these women.

Eloise came toward her and hugged her. "You're doing amazing," she said. "On all levels." Alice joined her, and then Jean. AJ and Kelli and Mom came over from the waiting area.

"Robin," Alice said, and the other woman sighed.

"Fine," Robin said. "I can see this isn't Clara's fault."

"Not even close," Kelli said.

Robin joined the group hug, and only then did Clara close her eyes and sink into the hug.

"Who wants to go back?" Paul asked, effectively breaking up the group. He held his son in his arms, and the infant looked minuscule next to his father's chest and biceps.

"Ooh, he brought the baby out," Eloise cooed, and she danced over to Paul.

"Tell us what the doctor said." Alice also approached Paul and Jamison, and he passed the infant to Eloise.

"Mom."

Clara turned toward Lena and quickly wiped her eyes. "Yes, dear?"

"Why are you sad?"

"I'm not, honey." She hugged her daughter and added, "Let's take James his new elephant, okay?"

They went over to Eloise, who eagerly showed them the baby. He slept, but he was so beautiful with his pink face and shock of dark hair.

"She's doing well," Paul said, and Clara listened in on Laurel's health report too. She couldn't imagine Scott coming out to a waiting room full of women and giving them an update on her private health matters.

"They want to keep her for another day, so we won't go home tomorrow either. He said something about releasing

Jamison before Laurel, and I nearly lost my mind." He chuckled and looked over to Eloise.

She'd taken Lena over to the loveseat so she could hold Jamison. Clara's heart warmed at how tender Eloise was with Lena, and she knew she'd been doing her daughter a disservice by keeping her so close.

"I can't feed him. I can barely hold him without breaking him."

"You'd be okay," Alice said.

"Your mother-in-law is here," AJ added.

"And your sister," Jean said, and Clara hadn't known that. She did want to be involved with these women, and she vowed she'd do better in paying attention to their messages and participating with them too.

"And all of us," her mother said, and Clara found she wanted to be involved in that number too.

"Thank you," Paul said. "He said they'd keep James too, thankfully. I guess we'll see what tomorrow brings." He looked past the huddle of women in front of him, and his face brightened. "Chief."

Clara turned to find Aaron Sherman approaching, and he seemed a bit shocked to find everyone there too. "Hey, Paul. I'm looking for my wife..." He came straight toward the group like he'd enter the fray of women easily, but they parted like the Red Sea.

"She's over there," Robin said, indicating Eloise on the couch.

Aaron grinned, shook Paul's hand, and went over to Eloise.

Clara glanced over to Jean, and her sister-in-law linked her arm through hers. "Come on," she said. "We'll go back while Paul is out here."

Clara nodded, and she let Jean lead her through the doors and to Laurel's room. She sat up in bed, her face a little paler than Clara thought it should be. Concern spiked inside her, which was another indicator of how much she cared about the women here in Five Island Cove.

"Laurel," she said, and she hurried over to the bed and hugged her. "He's beautiful."

Laurel simply hugged her back, no words needed.

A few days later, Clara pulled up to the lighthouse, her heartbeat once again beating, beating, beating against the back of her throat.

Usually it was because she disliked this place so much. Or she'd have to have a hard conversation with her mother about why she didn't want to stay for long. Since Jean and Reuben had taken over the lighthouse, Clara hadn't minded coming as much. She still saw and heard her father in every room, through every window, and lurking in every wall, but he was quieter now.

"Here's fine," she said, and the RideShare driver

stopped. She jumped out and ran for the navy blue door just as it opened.

Jean and Reuben exited the lighthouse, and Clara's step slowed. "Jean," she said.

Her sister-in-law had been crying, that much was clear. She smiled anyway and said, "We'll send so many pictures."

"You better." Clara stepped into both of them and hugged them, then pulled away. "Now go, before you miss your flight."

Jean headed for their car, but Reuben stayed with Clara. "Thanks for coming," he said. "You sure you're okay to miss work for a few days?"

"Yes," she said firmly. She'd warned Eloise she'd be on lighthouse duty when Jean and Reuben went to get their new daughter. "Lena's done at two-thirty, and we'll be fine here. We'll make sure everything is ready for you and Heidi." She smiled at him, then grabbed onto him again. "I love you, big brother."

"I love you, too, Clara."

He left, and Clara waved until their car disappeared. Alone now, she faced the lighthouse. She'd listened to her mother's Seafaring Girls' stories, and she knew how they viewed the lighthouse.

Safety.

Acceptance.

Love.

Those were words they used to describe how they felt

there. Clara wouldn't have used any of them, and as she took the first step toward the door and then up the steps to the control room, she decided it was time to banish all of her childhood demons.

It would just be part of her internal, personal renovation.

Chapter Thirty

Jean's hands would not stop shaking. Her whole body had been trembling since Miranda had called and said the baby was on her way, and Becky wanted her and Reuben to come.

"Surely she's been born by now," she said, not for the first time.

"Maybe," Reuben said. That was all he'd said every time Jean had suspected the baby had been born already.

They currently rode in a cab to the hospital, and Jean swore they'd hit every red light in the city. They finally arrived, her last nerve fraying rapidly, and she was glad she wasn't the only one with rushed footsteps. She could barely keep up with her husband as he led them toward the elevators, and then Miranda met them in the waiting area.

Jean's heartbeat positively stopped, but Miranda shone

like a diamond, and she said, "She was born literally three minutes ago." She reached for Jean's hand. "They're giving her a bath, and then she'll want her mother."

"Me?" Jean asked, already getting towed along beside Miranda. Her feet felt so clumsy, and she wasn't sure why she'd chosen now to forget how to walk.

"You," Miranda said. "Becky doesn't want to see the baby. So it's up to you and Reuben to make sure she knows how very loved she is."

Jean's throat went dry, though she loved the little girl she hadn't met yet with her whole heart.

Miranda took her through doors Jean was sure she wouldn't have been able to go through without her, and then they arrived in the nursery. In the corner, two nurses stood at the sink, and Miranda nodded Reuben and Jean toward them.

Reuben took Jean's hand now, and they went over to the baby. Both nurses looked over to them. "You must be the mom and dad."

"Yes," Jean and Reuben said together, and the nurses parted to reveal the most beautiful baby Jean had ever laid eyes on. Tears filled her vision, blurring everything, and she quickly blinked them away and brushed them back. She didn't want to miss anything her new daughter did.

Right now, she was being held by two very capable hands while the other nurse carefully spread warm water over her scalp.

"Look," she said as if Reuben wasn't. "She's bald."

The baby opened her mouth and started to fuss, and the nurses wrapped up the bathing. Her body seemed abnormally small compared to the size of her head, which only made Jean grin wider and wider.

The nurses handled her with care and strength at the same time, and before Jean knew it, they had the baby swaddled and calmed. One of them held her while the other tugged a cap down over her head, adjusting the pale pink band so it sat just above the girl's closed eyes.

"Here you go, Mama." The woman smiled and passed the baby to Jean without hesitation. Jean had held plenty of babies in her lifetime, but this one was different.

This one was hers.

She smiled down at the precious little girl, tears coming to her eyes again. She let them this time, because she'd never thought she'd be standing in a hospital, holding a baby she'd get to take home with her.

"Look at her, Reuben," she said again, this time in a whisper.

In true Reuben fashion, he put one big hand on Jean's lower back and one on their baby's chest, right over her heart. He practically covered her whole body, and she grunted with his touch. She turned her head toward Jean, and she tucked her in tightly, and whispered, "We're here, baby. We love you so much."

"Do you have a name for her?" A different nurse stood there, and Reuben cleared his throat.

"Yes," he said. "Heidi Lynn Shields."

The nurse's pen scratched, and she kept asking questions for the birth certificate and legal documents for the adoption. They wouldn't be able to put their names on the birth certificate until the court hearing in six months, but Jean's heart didn't care about any of that.

She loved Heidi with everything inside her, and she couldn't wait to introduce her to everyone important in her life.

Once Reuben finished with the paperwork, Jean went with him to a separate nursery room. He sat, and Jean passed him their baby. "Smile," she said, and she tugged her phone out of her dress pocket.

Reuben wore sunshine and heaven in his eyes as he grinned first at Heidi and then Jean. She tapped and snapped several pictures, then he bent his head to kiss the baby tenderly on the head. She captured a picture of that too, and looked at the sweetness shining from the photo.

"Let's do a selfie," she said. He shifted the baby to the side so Jean could sit on his lap too. She held her arm out as far as she could, and he moved Heidi up to his shoulder so she'd be in the picture too.

Jean smiled, seeing the rays of light coming from her own eyes, and took the picture. She didn't immediately send it to her mother, though she knew she was waiting for news.

Everyone was, but Jean just wanted another few moments with her, Heidi, and Reuben. She leaned against his shoulder and sighed as they both looked down at their baby.

"She's so pretty," Jean said.

"She looks like you," Reuben whispered.

The baby did have slightly olive skin and dark hair, and Jean pictured her birth mom in her mind. Becky had been darker too, and while she'd given no details about the father, it looked like he'd had dark features as well.

Reuben did too, and Jean couldn't help thinking that God had brought them a baby that fit precisely with them.

"YOUR MOTHER IS AT THE LIGHTHOUSE ALREADY," Jean said a few days later. Her hair bobbed against the back of her neck, as she'd secured it in a ponytail and then looped it through itself so the bottom was curled under.

She hadn't slept much the night before, and the culprit currently cried for her next bottle. Jean had just started heating it, and Reuben bounced and shushed the girl to no avail.

"She is?" Reuben asked. "She knows we don't take off for another four hours, right?"

Jean smiled. "She knows. They all know." She opened

the microwave and shook the bottle. "You know they're all going to be there when we get there."

All of her friends and his family. Jean wasn't upset by it, but she did want to be back in her own home, with just her, Heidi, and Reuben. They needed to start establishing their own patterns and routines, and Jean needed to be home to do that.

"It's ready," she said.

"They won't stay long," he said. "I'll text my mother and tell her they get a couple of hours." He was as tired as Jean. Thrilled, yes. Happy beyond belief. But tired.

She hadn't brought AJ's first-week-survival kit with her to the mainland, and she wished she would have. She'd texted Laurel, and she'd given her a list of the items.

Jean's mother had painkillers and Epsom salts, but she didn't have an eye mask, and Jean didn't have access to her own pillows and blankets. Heidi hadn't slept in her own bed yet.

Even the bottles Jean and Reuben used would stay here. Jean had everything they needed at home, and her mother had bought a few things so they could stay for a few days after Heidi's birth.

Reuben settled into the recliner in her parents' living room, and Jean handed him the bottle. "I'm going to go shower." She leaned down and pressed a kiss to his head as he finally got Heidi to start eating. The noise level went down, and Jean turned to leave.

She met her mother coming out of the hallway, and she eased into a hug. "Thanks, Mama," she whispered.

"We've loved having you," she said back. "Your daddy and I are planning to come to the cove in a couple of weeks too."

Jean stepped back and nodded. "I'd like that. Reuben can show you the lighthouse, and we can go boating before it gets too cold." She grinned and then remembered how much she needed to pack before they left. "I love you, Mom."

"Love you too, Jean. I'm so happy you finally got your baby."

Jean ducked her head and continued into the bathroom. Inside and alone, Jean looked at herself in the mirror and smiled. "I finally got my baby." She pressed her eyes closed, and added, "Please let me be a good mother, Lord. Please, and thank you for the journey to this point."

She could recall such low days, and she truly thought she'd finally learned the lesson of accepting the good with the bad and learning and knowing the difference between the two.

"They're here," someone said, and as Jean was trying not to trip down the uneven lighthouse stairs, she couldn't place the voice.

Heidi had been asleep since the car ride to the airport in New York, for which Jean was grateful. But that also meant she'd wake soon and want to eat.

She pushed aside her worry; someone could feed the baby. They *wanted* to do that, and Jean didn't need to hog her. They'd all be gone soon, and then Jean would have to shoulder everything herself.

"We're here, Heidi," she said, stepping through the door Reuben held open for her. The bottom level of the lighthouse held her kitchen and living room, two bedrooms and a bathroom. It felt like every inch of the space had been filled with people—and love.

The first face she saw was Kristen, and Jean's chest filled with life. Her mother-in-law had often been Jean's lifeline and anchor at the same time, and she loved her dearly.

"Here she is," Jean said. "Heidi Lynn." She passed the baby to Kristen, who smiled and breathed in the baby as if fusing her to her soul through oxygen.

"Oh, she's so beautiful," Kristen whispered. "Yes, you are, Heidi. So beautiful."

Jean moved out of the way, and Robin crowded in with Kristen.

Eloise took Jean into a hug, and she got passed through the crowd. She kept saying, "Thanks," and "Thank you for coming," and "You didn't have to do that."

It was incredible to see all the love which had gathered here in the lighthouse...for her. For Reuben. For Heidi.

At last, she stood beside Clara and sipped a Shirley Temple. "How are things with you and...everyone?" Jean didn't want to name Robin specifically, though the conflict had definitely originated there.

Robin could be scary, and Jean had taken some months to get used to her louder personality. She cared so deeply, and that came out in different ways than it did for Jean.

"Okay." Clara took her own sip of her drink. Scott laughed loudly from across the room. "I texted her and suggested we go to lunch together, just the two of us."

Jean swung her attention to her sister-in-law. "Oh? What did she say?"

"It took her four seconds to say yes." Clara smiled. "She came up to me before you got here, and we're going to try a new place on Rocky Ridge next week, on my day off."

"The White Whale?" Jean asked.

"Yeah, that's it."

"She's been wanting to go there for a couple of weeks." Jean didn't say that no one wanted to ride the ferry for forty-five minutes when they had a plethora of restaurants and café right here on Diamond Island.

No, not all of the women in this room lived on Diamond Island, but a lot of them. Jean didn't see going out to lunch in her immediate future right now, and that was absolutely okay with her. She could have people here, and once she knew how to handle a baby in public for more than a few minutes, she'd resume going to the luncheons.

"All right," Reuben called, and the chatter in the tiny room of the lighthouse quieted. "Thank you all for coming. My mother has made more food than all of us can eat, but we should try." He grinned out at everyone and met Jean's eye. She went toward him though he didn't ask her to. She just knew he wanted her at his side.

She took his hand and beamed at him.

"We're so glad Heidi is loved by so many," Reuben said. "It's taken Jean and I twenty years to get her, and we hope and pray we can be the parents she deserves." He paused, his throat working as he swallowed a few times.

"We love you," Jean said, her voice strong and sure. "And we're glad you love us." She looked over to Kristen. "Did you want to say grace?"

"Yes," Kristen said, her hand firmly in Theo's. "I'll say grace, and then I'll pass Heidi to someone else."

Jean thought if Kristen didn't give her to Robin, they'd have a mutiny on their hands, but she stifled her giggle and bowed her head for the prayer.

Chapter Thirty-One

Clara looked into her daughter's eyes and knew she wasn't going to win this conflict. "All right," she said. Giving up wasn't the end of the world. It didn't sting the way it once had. Besides, Clara knew now that she could give up and still be a good person.

She could quit and open doors to a better future.

There were some things she was glad she hadn't given up on: her marriage with Scott, her relationship with her daughter, her own mental health and well-being.

"Mama has to go to an appointment after lunch," she told Lena. "You'll have to sit by yourself on the couch for an hour." She raised her eyebrows. "Can you do that?"

"Can I bring the tablet?"

"Is it charged?"

Lena turned away from Clara, who'd accidentally let it

slip that she was going to lunch with Robin that day. Lena loved Robin, and she'd instantly gripped onto the idea of skipping work in favor of riding the ferry—twice—to eat with Robin.

Clara had tried to get her to choose work instead, using the ferries and the fact that Lena didn't like riding them, as well as how her boss needed her at the supermarket.

Nothing had worked, and Clara honestly didn't mind if Lena came to lunch too. She didn't think Robin would either.

"It's not charged," Lena said.

"I need to ask Robin if you can come," Clara said.

"I don't want to sit by myself," Lena said. She looked like she might throw the uncharged tablet. Her eyebrows dropped into an angry V. "Can we go to lunch with Robin another day?"

"Yes," Clara said easily. "You can call her and see when she's available." She lifted her eyebrows, silently asking Lena if she wanted to go to lunch badly enough to make a phone call.

"Okay." She tossed the tablet onto the built-in-desk.

"You better go get ready for work, then," Clara said.

Lena's face screwed up, and Clara waited for the scream. It didn't come. She growled loudly and then stomped down the hall to her bedroom.

Clara exhaled slowly, refusing to classify the sound as a

sigh. Lena could throw a tantrum, and it wouldn't be a weight on Clara's conscience. Not anymore.

She sipped coffee and flipped through her social media while Lena got ready. When it was time to get going, she called for her daughter. She came out of the bathroom, her long hair secured back into a ponytail. She'd slicked it tight and sprayed it with hairspray.

Clara smiled at her. Jamie, Robin's daughter, had taught Clara how to do her hair like that, and she did it that way every day now. It lasted through her whole shift, and Clara often commented on it when she picked up Lena after work.

"You look great," she said.

Lena wore black pants and the blue polo for the Cove Market, the bottom of the swooping C going underneath the whole logo.

"Thanks." Lena didn't smile, but she'd gotten ready on time, and Clara did think her daughter looked amazing.

"Maybe Carter will be working today," she said as she turned to pick up her purse.

"Mom." Lena sounded completely disgusted. "Gross."

"Gross?" She faced her daughter again and grinned. "I thought you liked Carter."

"Last week," Lena said, rolling her eyes. "There's this new boy in the deli."

Clara's eyebrows went up, but she didn't feel shaky like

she had the first time Lena had started talking about boys at the supermarket that she liked.

"How old is he, Lena?"

"I don't know." She led the way toward the garage. "His name is Kurt."

Clara said nothing, but she did smile as she followed her daughter into the garage. She drove her to work in the car she'd borrowed from her mother for today.

She dropped Lena at the market and continued toward the ferry station. Her mother had an annual parking pass, so the gate lifted for Clara without any effort on her part. A lot of her life in Five Island Cove had felt like a total struggle, but not the past five months. Things had gotten considerably easier once she and Scott had chosen to stop rebuilding Friendship Inn, and Clara could honestly say she was happier now than she'd been in a long time. Happier than she'd ever been in the cove before, that was for sure.

She boarded the ferry and went left when all the other passengers turned right. She went to a door marked "personnel only" and knocked smartly a couple of times.

Scott opened the door a few moments later, checked behind her, and stepped out of the way. "Hey."

She smiled at him as she squeezed into the tiny room with him. She didn't always stow away in his control room, but she had a few times now, and it was exciting. It felt forbidden, especially when he checked the walkway like he had.

"Are you driving this shift?" she asked.

"I'm on braking," he said. "They'll radio when I need to be on."

The remains of his lunch sat on the tiny desk, and Clara nodded as she picked up the empty bag of chips and put them in the brown bag. "So about a half-hour."

"Yep." He took the bag from her and tossed it in the trashcan by the door. They faced one another, and Clara smiled at him as she reached for his collar. He kissed her, and Clara fought him for the first few strokes.

She then sank into him and let him lead. With the door locked from the inside and the only key in Scott's pocket, a thrill moved down her spine at making love to him here in this tiny, private space.

They'd only done it one other time, but Clara had told him how much she'd liked it, and when she'd told him she was going to lunch with Robin today, he'd said to come to his "office" and he'd hopefully be on braking.

If he'd been driving, he wouldn't have been alone, and he'd have said something completely different. She wouldn't have come in at all.

He lifted her onto the desk she'd cleared, and she held her legs out so he could remove her panties. "Clara, you're the sexiest woman I've ever met."

He lowered his mouth to hers again, and Clara arched her back, feeling very much like the woman he said she was. She didn't mind if it wasn't true for every man in the world.

She just wanted it to be true for Scott, and by the way he kissed her, she knew it was.

After they'd finished, she quickly dressed while he tucked himself back together. Not a minute later, his radio beeped and a male voice said, "Approaching the dock at Sanctuary. We're going into gate four. Switching controls and visuals in thirty seconds."

Scott turned to the controls, already re-dressed. Their love life had increased and improved dramatically in the past year, and when she was a simple passenger, it seemed to take so long to get the ferry lined up and docked. When she was Scott's secret lover in the control room, trying to redress so she could disembark with everyone else, it took mere seconds.

She slid on her second sandal just as he said. "We're flush and in," into the radio.

A chime sounded, and that meant they'd open the exits soon.

Scott turned to her and she stepped into his chest and kissed him. "I love you," she whispered to him.

He crushed his mouth to hers again, and when he pulled away, it was almost painful. "We're signing the papers tomorrow afternoon."

"Yes." She hadn't heard a question, so she cocked her eyebrows at him.

He gathered her into his arms and slow danced with her. "I put in for the whole day off, the same as you."

Clara wrapped her arms around him. "So I should ask Jean if Lena can sleep over at the lighthouse."

"Nope." He grinned at her. "I already asked your mother." He kissed her again, and Clara really could get lost in the touch of this man.

As she slipped out of the control room and hurried down the narrow walkway, she felt for the wedding band on her left ring finger. It sat there, hard and hot and letting her know that she was Scott's, and he was hers.

It felt really good, and Clara smiled to herself as she flowed into the crowd getting off the ferry.

Now, she just needed to make sure everything was good with Robin, and she might be able to truly enjoy life here on the cove—with her family and all of her new friends.

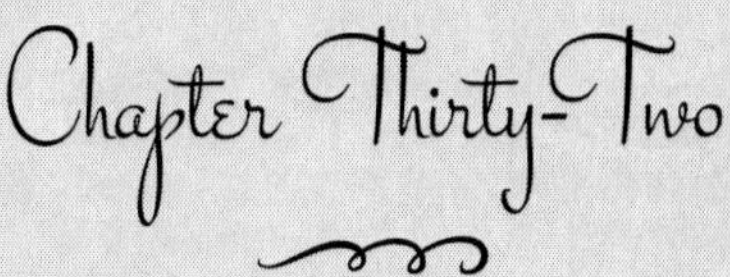

Chapter Thirty-Two

Robin rose from the bench outside The White Whale as the tall, curvy form of Clara Shields got out of the car that had just pulled up to the curb. She smiled at the driver and then faced the restaurant.

She saw Robin, and her smile grew bigger and brighter. "Hey," she said, coming toward her. "I hope you haven't been waiting long. I caught an early ferry and had to stop by Eloise's mother's to grab something and take it up to the inn."

"Five minutes," Robin said. "I wondered when I didn't see you on the ferry."

Clara only smiled, and Robin told herself she wasn't hiding anything. "Should we go in?"

"Sure." Clara stepped toward the door and opened it.

Robin let her say they had two people for lunch, and she let her follow the hostess first.

They sat down and Robin said, "I'll have water with lemon, please."

Clara took another few moments, flipping the menu to find the drinks. She asked questions about the teas and the lemonades, and then she ordered a London fog. Robin marveled at her level of confidence, and she wished in a lot of ways that she was more like Clara when it came to getting what she wanted.

"Is Mandie coming home for Thanksgiving?" Clara put her arms on the table and folded her hands over one another.

Robin's smile appeared instantly. "Yes. We're picking her up on Wednesday morning."

"Are you coming to Appetizer Hour at Alice's?"

"Yes. You?"

"Wouldn't miss it."

Robin nodded, secretly pleased. She'd suggested Appetizer Hour to Alice, and she'd run with it. Robin didn't mind, because she didn't want to host everyone at her house and then put on a big Thanksgiving feast too.

Her mother had gone to Maryland to celebrate the holiday with Robin's brother, and Robin wanted a simple, festive meal with her core family before she had to send Mandie back to college.

All of her texts and calls had been filled with experiences and learning opportunities. She'd had a great semester, and while she'd been complaining that she'd gained ten pounds, she was happy. She had all As in her classes right now, but she'd started stressing over finals weeks ago.

Robin had never been more proud of her daughter than she'd experienced the past few months.

"She's still dating Charlie," Robin said. "They seem to really like one another."

"You sound okay with that." Clara smiled at Robin, and Robin couldn't argue with her.

"I am. Charlie's a good boy."

The conversation stalled, but Robin didn't want it to. "I talked to my mother again." She shook her head. "She's impossible, and I apologize that I immediately jumped to you consorting with her."

Clara gazed at her with such familiar eyes. Eyes that had seen pain. Eyes that knew sorrow. Eyes that had loved, and understood happiness, and that yearned to make things right.

"I'm sorry," she said. "My mother is everyone's hero, so I don't dare say I understand how frustrating they can be sometimes." A kind smile curled her lips, and Robin felt it deep in her soul.

"I know your mother has her faults," Robin said.

"Do you?" Clara challenged. One eyebrow went up. "Is it that she only makes deviled eggs for Lena, because she finds them disgusting? She won't make them for me or anyone else, but Lena? All the deviled eggs she wants."

Robin grinned, because if someone's biggest fault was that they made deviled eggs for their granddaughter, they had to be pretty dang near perfect.

"She accepts people too easily," Robin said. "She's still learning how to protect herself and not trust instantly."

"That can be a gift," Clara said without missing a beat.

Robin found she really liked Clara. She challenged Robin without fear, and only her friends in the Seafaring Girls had really ever done that. She grinned at her. "You know what, Clara? You're right. It can be a gift or a curse."

They laughed then, and as the waitress approached with their drinks, Robin scurried to pick up her menu. "Shoot," she said. "I haven't even looked yet."

"Me either." Clara wasn't worried, and Robin took her cues from her. If they needed a few more minutes, so be it. The waitress wouldn't care.

The conversation didn't stall again, and Clara ordered four things simply to "try them all." Robin loved that, and she vowed the next time she and Duke went out, she'd get a few things to sample. If she only took one bite, then she'd have leftovers.

She left with Clara and her big bag of leftover food, and the two of them hailed a RideShare back to the ferry station.

"Thanks for coming out here," Robin said. "I couldn't get anyone to come with me."

"I would've come," a woman said, and both she and Clara turned toward the voice.

"Maddy." Robin's surprise didn't keep her from propelling herself into the woman and hugging her. "What's new with you?"

"Not much." She smiled as she pulled back from Robin. She retook her place at Ben's side. "We're just heading to Bell Island. We heard there's a great new café."

"And you're willing to travel from island to island."

Maddy grinned and looked up at Ben. "We definitely are. Ben was born to be on a boat, so he doesn't mind the ride."

"Good to see you again, Ben," Robin said diplomatically. They shook hands, but his smile was fleeting. Both he and Maddy looked at Clara.

"This is Clara," Robin said at the same time Clara said, "I'm Clara."

"I remember meeting you," Maddy said. "But it's been a while." They shook too, and then the line started moving to get on the ferry.

The four of them got on together, and Robin found a spot at the railing. She faced into the spray and the wind and looked over the water.

She'd always loved the cove, and that hadn't changed. The people who'd come in and out of her life over the past few years had, and as the ferry started moving, taking her back to her beloved Diamond Island, Robin knew she needed to work a little harder on her relationship with her mother.

It'll be hard, she thought. Because her mom didn't seem to want to work on the relationship in the same way. But that didn't mean Robin should give up.

So she wouldn't. She'd find a way to move past her bitter feelings, and then she'd try again. That was all anyone could do, right?

She once again saw Clara as an example. The woman's husband had been involved in a terrible extortion scheme. They'd lost everything. She'd returned to the cove, a place Robin knew she'd once hated.

Clara had never left Scott's side. Things might have been strained between them for a while, but she hadn't given up. She'd stayed. She'd worked on the challenges between them, and Robin couldn't even begin to fathom what they'd been.

She didn't know what lay ahead for her and her mother either. She'd find out, because she wasn't going to abandon the path she and her mother had started on forty-six years ago.

"We're here," Eloise said as she bustled into Alice's kitchen. Behind her, Aaron carried an extremely hot casserole dish of bacon-wrapped water chestnuts. The glaze on which wouldn't be good for another thirty minutes.

She couldn't dwell on it. Being here was better than having the perfect appetizer. No matter what she did, hers wouldn't be the best anyway, and she'd never spent much time caring if her dish got praised the most.

"You made it," her mother said, and Eloise stepped into her and gave her a kiss. She noted the cat hair on her mother's sweater, and a pang of nostalgia for a simpler time hit Eloise unexpectedly.

At the same time, she wouldn't trade her current life, not for one with her and her two cats and any students she'd managed to scrounge up sharing a small Thanksgiving meal out of her Boston brownstone.

Now, she had an amazing, doting, caring, loving husband. She was the mother to two amazing girls. The dog they had could challenge the most patient person on the planet, and she said, "Prince couldn't resist the bacon this morning."

Her mother laughed, and Eloise rolled her eyes. "I had to start over on the water chestnuts, and they haven't had time to sit."

"Don't worry." Her mom swept her hand toward the house, where people stood in groups, laughing and talking. Some sat at one of the tables Alice had set up. Some lounged on the furniture in the living room. "You're not even the last one to arrive."

"No?" Eloise scanned the area. Alice and Arthur stood with Duke and Robin. Their kids sat in the living room, laughing at something on Ginny's phone. Billie and Grace had gone that way, and not far from them, Lena stood with Jean, Kristen, Theo, and Scott.

She didn't see Clara, but then the woman came down the hall from the front door with Kelli and Parker on her heels. AJ sat at the dining room table with Matt and Asher, the little boy already strapped into a high chair there.

"Who's not here yet?"

"Reuben had to reprogram the fog signal," her mom said. "Alice's father and step-mother missed the ferry from Rocky Ridge. She said we wouldn't have to wait for them, but Robin said it wasn't a problem."

Eloise and Aaron weren't serving their Thanksgiving dinner until closer to evening, and it wasn't noon yet.

Aaron had dressed and bagged the bird, sliding the hen into the oven only a few moments after Eloise had taken out the second batch of water chestnuts.

"Laurel and Paul said James had a bad night, and they're running late," Eloise's mother said. "So they're not here yet either."

Eloise nodded, feeling some measure of relief that she and her family weren't the last ones to arrive. It wouldn't matter if they were, as Eloise wouldn't think anything of whoever arrived last.

Alice caught sight of her and came over. "El." She

hugged her, her powdery, rosy perfume striking Eloise as so Alice. She wore a dark brown pair of wide-leg pants that flowed easily with her lithe frame, and Eloise looked down at them.

"I'm never wearing jeans again," she said. "Don't you love the wide-leg pant?" She grinned at Alice, who agreed that she loved them. Her blouse bore autumn leaves that had clearly just been gusted by some invisible wind, and two or three of them matched the brown in Alice's pants perfectly.

"Aaron." She moved over to him and hugged him. He told her about the water chestnut mishap, and Alice simply laughed.

"I think there's enough food. Plus, we're not starting for a few more minutes anyway."

The Thanksgiving Appetizer Hour idea had been a big winner with everyone on the group text, Eloise included.

She'd been able to get Billie and Grace up and looking presentable with the promise of delicious foods and fun, older friends, and she looked over to the girls in the living room.

Billie had braided her own hair back on the sides, and then she'd done Grace's. They both perched on armrests, Billie looking over Mandie's shoulder while Grace pointed at something on Lena's tablet.

Aaron slid his arm around her waist and leaned into her. "So no stress."

"Yeah, sorry," she said. Sometimes, she still couldn't believe how different her life was with him in it. She couldn't believe he was in her life, and that he continued to want to be there.

"Stress isn't good for baby-making," he murmured, and then he moved away from her as Arthur said his name.

Eloise leaned into the counter just as Madeline Lancaster and Julia Harper came into the living room. Her mouth instantly watered, because both of them were excellent cooks. Maddy worked at The Glass Dolphin, for crying out loud, and it had quickly been hailed as Five Island Cove's newest premier restaurant.

"In the kitchen," Alice said, pointing. "El will help you."

The women came toward her, Tessa Simmons right behind them. They each carried a tray of something delectable, and Eloise wanted to try the stuffed dates Maddy had, as well as the cheese and spinach mushroom caps in Julia's hands.

Tessa cleared a spot for Abe, her boyfriend, to put down the largest meat and cheese platter El had ever seen. "My goodness," she said.

"He's almost retired from the deli," Tessa said with a beaming smile at him. "Then he's going to move here."

"That's amazing." Eloise smiled at the two of them. "Are you two going to—?" She cut herself off, because it wasn't any of her business if they got married or not. Not everyone wanted to be legally bound to their partner, and she wished she could take the words back.

"She's going to have to fight me for Robin," Maddy said. "If someone would ever ask me to marry him." She gave Ben a pointed look, and he simply smiled at her.

"Hey, I'm not engaged either," Tessa said. Julia met Eloise's eyes, and she'd heard her lament her fifth-wheel status plenty over the past few months since they'd started working together.

She'd had a boyfriend for Maddy's son's wedding, but once she'd moved to the cove, they'd split up. Eloise liked Julia a lot, and she'd invited her to the luncheons and events over the months that she did with her friends.

Julia had attended here and there, but nothing consistent. Eloise hadn't asked her why she hadn't come; she simply kept inviting.

Alice's house groaned with the addition of Laurel and Paul, but they came in with a couple of bags of groceries that Paul unloaded loudly as he explained that James was "being a beast" and refusing to eat, then screaming loudly that he was hungry.

He laughed about it, but Laurel looked a little worn around the edges. She'd already given her baby to Alice, and Eloise would be able to get him from her. If Robin got that baby, El would have to beg to be able to hold him.

She met Aaron's eyes, and he looked over to the beautiful, dark-haired boy in Alice's arms. Eloise couldn't help the pinch of want in her belly, and she simply smiled at Aaron when he looked at her again.

She migrated over to his side, taking Julia with her.

They'd been trying for a baby for a couple of months now, which Eloise knew was no time at all. She wasn't even sure she could have a baby. Her doctor had said there wasn't a reason other than age, and Eloise had told Aaron she wanted to try.

They both knew how and when babies were made, and she hooked her arm through his. He leaned his head down, and she swept her lips across his cheek, and whispered, "I'm going to be stress-free all day."

He grinned at the code between them, and then nodded to Julia. "Hey, there, Jules," he said to her. Then he nodded over to someone Eloise hadn't seen come in. "Look who Paul brought."

Beside her, Julia pulled in a breath. Probably silent to Aaron, but Eloise stood closer and had excellent hearing.

Eloise brightened and switched her arm from Aaron's to Julia's. "Oh, Liam, I'm so glad you're here."

"El," Julia hissed, but El moved by her and then took her with her.

"I wanted you to meet a good friend of mine. I think Paul's mentioned her." She realized she'd drawn the attention of Alice and Robin, as well as AJ, Kelli, and Kristen. She met Billie's eyes too, and the girl looked absolutely horrified. She got to her feet and everything.

All of it screamed at her to *stop*, and yet she was already in motion. Couldn't be stopped.

Liam's smiled slipped as Eloise rounded the table. He looked from her to Julia, and then to a teenage boy who came to his side.

Eloise did stop there, her mind short-circuiting. "Liam, this is Julia. Julia, this is one of Aaron's cops."

Liam Coldwater grinned at her, that lopsided grin that probably drove women like Julia crazy. "Oh, come on, El. You usually say I'm one of his *better* cops."

Eloise smiled too, recovering quickly. "You're right." She looped her arm through Julia's and brought her to her side, ignoring Billie as she waved one hand above her head. Aaron saw that, his frown catching in El's peripheral vision.

"This is Julia Harper, one of my *better* managers at the inn."

Liam had slid a mask into place, and he shook Julia's hand. Eloise could see the spark of interest in his eyes, but Julia looked one breath away from passing out.

"This is my son," Liam said. He clapped the teen on the back, grinning and obviously proud of his boy. "Ian."

El knew that name, and she cocked her head at the handsome blonde boy. She couldn't quite place it, and she looked past the pair of them to Billie again.

Her face flamed red, and Ian turned and looked too. He sucked in a breath and said, "Billie?"

"Hey, Ian," she said just as Aaron arrived at her side.

Silence had fallen over everyone in the house, and Eloise's stomach flipped.

Definitely not stress-free.

"It's time to eat," Alice said into the quiet, obviously trying to cover it up. "My parents are almost here, so let's get this party started." She stepped past Liam and his son and said, "El, could you?" right before she slipped James into her arms.

Robin started talking too, as did Maddy. Smaller conversations broke out, and Eloise went into the formal living room with the baby. She could eat later. Billie joined her, and El said nothing as the girl sat across from her, her foot bouncing a mile a minute.

"What's wrong?" she finally asked.

Billie shook her head, her face definitely more pale than usual. Eloise didn't like the clear agitation in the girl, but Aaron came into the smaller, quieter front room before she could think of what to say.

"Food for you, sweets." He set down a plate filled with all of the things Eloise would've picked for herself and then looked over to Billie. "What's eating you?" he asked.

Billie looked up at her father, and Aaron moved over to her and crouched in front of her. "Bills, talk to me. I don't like how white you're getting."

"That's—" She swallowed and tried again. "That's Ian Coldwater. He's the one that Addie really likes, and then he asked *me* to the Christmas Ball."

"Okay," Aaron said, but this was the first Eloise had heard of the Christmas Ball.

"I told him you wouldn't let me go." Billie hung her head. "He said he'd talk to you, because he really wants to go with me, and I never responded after that."

Aaron said nothing, and Eloise rocked with baby James in her arms. "When was this, Billie?" she asked.

"A couple of days ago," she said. "I didn't want to hurt Addie." She looked from El to her father. "He's going to talk to you, Daddy." She hung her head again. "Probably tonight. As soon as he can."

Aaron looked over to Eloise, which she appreciated. She raised her eyebrows as if to tell him *she's your daughter*. If they had a baby together, she wouldn't be able to do that.

"Hon." He straightened. "I can't crouch like that." He shook his head and offered Billie his hand. He pulled her to a stand too and put his arm around her. "What do you want me to say? That you can go, or that you can't?"

"I didn't mean to lie to him."

"Would I have let you go with him?" Aaron asked. "Wait. I know the answer to this one. He's the son of one of my 'better cops.'" He grinned at Eloise. "Who me and El keep trying to set up. So my guess is, I wouldn't have objected to this particular boy."

Billie shook her head. "Probably not."

"Billie," Eloise said gently. "You can't let your father

take the heat on this one. He's willing to do it for you when it matters, right, sweetheart?"

"Yes, always," Aaron said, but Eloise was trying to get Billie to take some heat this time.

"I think you should talk to him," she said. "Right now, before he has a chance to talk to your dad. Then he won't embarrass himself, and your father won't have to lie for you."

Billie started nodding. "Okay. I can do that." She drew in a deep breath. "I can."

"I'll send him in here," Aaron said. "El? Do you want to sit in?"

Billie turned to stone, and Eloise smiled at her. With a bit of difficulty, she got to her feet with the baby in her arms. "Nope. Grab my food, baby, and let's go find a place in there with our friends."

He led the way, and Eloise gave Billie a kind smile. "You can do this, honey. Just be nice to him—and be honest."

"Nice," Billie said. "Honest. Okay."

Eloise nodded, and she left the room. She passed Ian at the mouth of the hall, and he wore questions in his eyes. "She's this way?"

"Yes." Eloise blocked him from continuing. "She is an amazing girl. Try to remember that."

The teenager swallowed, and Eloise liked the air about him as he nodded. "Yes, ma'am."

She nodded, and they went by one another. She re-entered the kitchen and living room area, and Robin flagged her down. "Over here, El." She'd saved her a seat, and Aaron had already put her food there.

She squeezed behind Kelli and Shad to her spot, and she positioned the baby on her lap so she could eat with one hand. "Thanks, Robin."

"Nice try with Julia and Liam."

Eloise took a bite of a water chestnut and looked for them. They'd found spots on nearly opposite ends of the house, and her heart fell to her shoes.

"Well, I tried."

"Keep trying," Maddy said from across the table.

"She likes him," Tessa said. "She just won't admit it."

"No, something happened," Clara said. "She was talking about this blind date she had with a cop." She looked over to Julia as well, who'd taken a seat at the folding table with Laurel and Alice. "I think it was him."

Liam stood in the kitchen, laughing with Arthur, but Eloise saw him cast a look over to Julia, and it sure felt full of longing to her.

"A toast," Alice yelled into the fray of bodies and voices. "To friends."

"To friends!" the crowd repeated, and Eloise hurried to grab the closest cup to her. She wasn't sure if it was something Aaron had gotten for her or someone else's entirely.

"To family," Alice said.

"To family," everyone chorused, Eloise included this

time, her plastic cup held high. A smile filled her whole body, and she looked up at Aaron slid into the seat beside her.

"And to friends who become family," Alice said, smiling with grace and beauty. "Arthur and I are so happy and grateful to have you in our home today. Stay as long as you want. Leave when you want. Eat what you want." She nodded, marking the end of her speech, and sat back down.

"Friends who become family," Eloise repeated. She looked over to Aaron. His cops felt like that to him, she knew. Her friends were definitely part of her family.

She looked over to AJ and reached past Robin to squeeze her hand. Then she did the same with Robin. "I love you guys."

"I do think of you like family," Robin said. "I think that's why the thing with Clara hurt so much."

Eloise switched her gaze to Clara, who smiled at Robin. "I'm just now opening that door," she said. "It's nice, just so you know. To be cared about, and to have more than just a couple of people to care about."

Eloise was glad to hear that, and she put her hand out in the middle of the table, the way sports teams did to cheer the other team. "Friends that become family," she said.

Others put their hands in, including Aaron, Matt, Shad, and Duke, and soon enough, the entire dining room table of people were chanting the phrase.

They all lifted their hands into the air at the same time

and laughed, and Eloise was so glad she had a place at this table. She knew she could go to any of her friends at any time. Stay as long as she wanted, and eat what she wanted. They'd welcome her—and she'd do the same for them—and that was a very comfortable place to be.

Read on for the first couple chapters of **THE GLASS DOLPHIN, the next book in the Five Island Cove series.**

Sneak Peek! The Glass Dolphin

Chapter One:

Julia Harper couldn't stop herself from glancing over to Liam Coldwater every few seconds. She told herself to stop at least a dozen times before Laurel leaned over and whispered, "What is with you and him?"

Julia couldn't answer, so she stuffed another piece of bruschetta into her mouth. She'd eat the whole platter if she had to. She wasn't going to answer any questions about Liam tonight. It would be great if she could stop looking at him.

She focused on a conversation Alice was having with Kristen, but she knew few of the players in the conversation, and it didn't hold her interest. She felt the weight of a gaze on her face, and she once again looked across the living room, through the dining room table, and into the kitchen, where Liam stood.

He'd been talking to Arthur Rice and Duke Grover, but they'd both dispersed. Liam stood there alone, and their eyes met. The entire Appetizer Hour fell away, and while Julia felt certain someone very nearby was talking to her, she couldn't hear them. She couldn't look away from the handsome Liam Coldwater.

At the same time, shame burned through her chest, and the embarrassment of their encounter late last week forced her to drop her head and break the connection.

The conversations surrounding her continued, and she looked up as Alice's son joined the table. They all started adjusting to make room for the extra chair, and Julia smiled at the young man. He was a good-looking kid, and he reminded Julia so much of her own sons.

"May I speak to you for a moment?" The man's voice in her ear hummed, lighting Julia with a fire that burst into a white-hot inferno. She didn't have to turn to see who it was, but her chin dropped in Liam's direction. The scent of his breath—like raspberry jam and mint—and the warmth of his skin filled her from head to toe in a single inhale.

She took the napkin from her lap and put it on her plate, though she'd only eaten half of her food. "I'll be right back," she managed to say.

"I'll save your spot," Laurel said. Julia bore the weight of several pairs of eyes as she faced first the kitchen. Liam stood in the direction of the front door, and he made the choice for them by taking her hand and tugging her in that direction.

She sucked in a breath at the electricity flowing from his arm and into hers, and she wasn't sure if she wanted him to feel that too or not. Her track record with dating the past couple of years hadn't been good, and she'd come to terms with healing herself before bringing someone new into her life. If she ever did.

Liam said nothing, and the party continued behind them as they went outside. It had been raining when Julia had arrived with Tessa and Maddy, and a steady drizzle still covered Five Island Cove.

He released her hand as the door closed behind them, and Julia wrapped her arms around herself. She wanted him to speak first, because he'd said nothing since she'd caught him in his lie.

Liam continued down the four steps to the sidewalk, but Julia stayed on the porch, under the eaves and out of the rain. He paced to the end of the sidewalk before he turned back to her. "I'm sorry," he called across the distance to her.

Part of her wanted him to lower his voice. Alice's neighbors would surely come investigate the source of the disturbance in the street. She glanced around, a sense of romanticism entering her bloodstream. What woman didn't want a man to proclaim his love for her to the world?

He's not doing that, she told herself. They'd been on one date—a fantastic, amazing date. Julia had even given herself permission to kiss him should he make the move when he dropped her off.

He hadn't, but they'd had another evening planned for a few days later.

"He's my son," Liam yelled now. "His name is Ian, and he's the best thing in my life. I don't tell women about him until things are more serious, because it's a lot." He threw his arms out to the side. "*I'm* a lot for them to take in. The job. The badge. The insane hours!" He yelled into the storm now, his head tipped back to the angry, gray sky.

Julia found him downright adorable. Strong, tall, sexy, and utterly charming. All adjectives she'd use for Liam Coldwater.

He looked at her, the ends of his longer, curly, blond hair dripping with the drizzle now. He looked absolutely tormented, and Julia wanted to erase all of that for him.

"So I didn't say anything. When you ran into us in the market, I froze. I didn't mean to lie, and I've hated myself every hour since." His arms dropped to his side, and that was almost the permission Julia needed to move. Like he was an air traffic controller, holding her at bay with his arms up, and now that they'd gone down, she could go to him.

She went down the steps deliberately, not looking at them. Only him. She walked toward him slowly, the way she'd approach a scared dog she desperately wanted to soothe. He let her come all the way to him, the silence between them only punctuated by rain.

Julia took his face in her hands, the warmth of his skin infusing into her chilled fingers. "I would've kissed you after our first date," she said.

Liam searched her face, those bright blue eyes filled with hope and sorrow at the same time. "I wanted to," he said, his voice scratching in his throat now. Probably because of the way he yelled everything else. "I was scared."

Julia pressed into him, and he finally put his hands on her waist, one of them moving up her back. "You?" she teased. "The tough, gruff police officer?" She studied his collar for a few moments before looking up into his face again. "I didn't think men like you got scared."

"Only of gorgeous women," he said. "After an amazing date which I never wanted to end."

"I have three sons," she said. "You could've told me."

He nodded as he held her close, close, close. Alice's neighbors sure were getting a show this morning. "I keep him close to the vest," he said. "He's an amazing kid, but I don't want him getting hurt again."

Julia noted the "again," and she'd like that story. Maybe not in the rain, with the whole neighborhood watching, but sometime. "Take me to dinner this weekend? Or are you working?"

"I'm off on Sunday until three," he said, his schedule right there in his mind. Julia had liked his intelligence when they'd first met, and again on their first date.

"So not dinner." She smoothed his collar down flat.

"Breakfast? Brunch? Lunch?" He listed them off, and Julia liked that it seemed like he wanted to see her. "All three?"

A smile touched her mouth, and Liam finally cracked too. He allowed a tame grin to spread his lips, and Julia fantasized about kissing him. Straightening that smile and really being able to taste the mint and raspberry jam on his lips.

"You can keep him to yourself for a while," Julia said. "Okay? I won't ask you to introduce me to him formally until you're ready." She regretted how quickly she'd reacted to the lies he'd told. She had a reason for that—a good reason—but he didn't know it. She hadn't told him about her cheating ex or the way she felt unworthy of the pure, undivided attention from others.

"Okay," he murmured. "Can I kiss you now?"

Julia put a couple of inches between them and looked him right in the eyes. "Out here? On the street in front of my friend's house?" She shook her head. "Mm, I don't think so, Liam."

He smiled again. "Not good enough for you?"

Julia had no doubt it would be the best kiss of her life. She didn't want to say that, though, so she shook her head. "I want to enjoy it," she whispered. "And I can't do that if I think everyone's watching us."

He looked over her shoulder to the house. "I think the curtains just fluttered, so you're probably right."

Julia backed up again, the idea of her friends watching her stand in this man's arms overwhelming for her. They separated, and she said, "I didn't block your number." Enough rain had accumulated in her hair that it ran down the side of her face. She brushed the droplet away, gave him a smile, and turned back to the house.

She ran on her tiptoes to the porch and out of the rain. Upon re-entering Alice's house, she saw Maddy herding several others back into the living room and dining room areas, and she'd definitely caught them spying on her.

A smile caught in her chest, and she decided she didn't care. She still wasn't going to answer any questions about Liam Coldwater tonight.

She paused at the end of the hall, trying to decide if she should simply return to her seat in the living room or try to get a little dryer in the bathroom. The living room had carpet, and Julia wiped another drop of water from her face as she took in the crowd there.

Alice wasn't in the living room anymore, and she came around the corner and into the kitchen. She held up a pale blue towel, effectively eliminating another decision Julia had to make. She went toward her, and Alice bustled her into the master bedroom.

"Thank you," Julia said. She took the towel and buried her face in it. Alice didn't ask any questions, but Maddy would. Tessa would. Eloise would.

She wiped her hair back and met Alice's eyes. "Did everyone run into your office?"

"Pretty much, yeah," she said with a smile. "Maddy yelled at all of them when you started backing up." She wore pure curiosity in her eyes, and Julia wanted to tell her. Maybe if she could get some other opinions, she'd know what to do about Liam.

At the same time, she knew what to do about Liam—keep seeing him. She didn't know if they'd work out, because her last relationship had ended when she'd left Nantucket. She wasn't like Tessa and Abe, who'd stayed together and then made plans to both settle in the cove. Maddy and Ben had done the same thing.

Julia hadn't been so lucky.

She actually did count herself as lucky, because she didn't want a man who wouldn't move heaven and earth to be with her. Liam had texted her seventeen times since their encounter in the food mart. He'd called three times, until she'd finally texted to tell him she didn't want to see him again.

Her phone buzzed now, and Julia finished drying her hair before she checked it. *Breakfast on Sunday. Nine o'clock. Too early? I think we could try this place*. He'd included a link to the cutest little bistro she'd ever seen, and she smiled as she looked at the image that had populated with the text.

"Have you been here?" She showed Alice the phone,

and she didn't mind that the woman took a few extra moments to obviously read the previous texts.

"Yeah." She grinned at Julia. "They have amazing breakfast. Fast too. Tell him to get a reservation if you're going on Sunday. They're busy on the weekends." She took Julia's towel and left her alone in the bedroom to confirm her date with Liam Coldwater.

MADELINE LANCASTER NOTED THE RED SUV IN her driveway the moment the RideShare car made the turn to join it. "Who's that?" she asked, swinging her attention to Ben.

"Don't know," he said. He usually wore a serious expression, and that didn't change. He smiled the most when with her, and sometimes she felt like she had to work hard to get that mouth to curl upward.

"Thanks." She tapped to pay the driver and got out of the car. Ben met her at the front of the car and took her hand. They went by the car, and she eyed it suspiciously. She wasn't expecting visitors, and her house on Rocky Ridge wasn't exactly on any tourist loops.

"It's a rental," Ben said. "Chelsea? Kyle?"

"They didn't say they'd be coming," Maddy said. Excitement leapt through her, because she'd love to see her kids today. She'd ordered Thanksgiving dinner from a specialty market here on Rocky Ridge, and it would be perfect for a quiet meal at home for two. Before the red SUV in the driveway, that was what her Thanksgiving was going to be. Just her and Ben.

She went into the garage as Ben held the door for her, the scent of sugar floating on the air. "Someone's definitely here," she said.

Ben darted in front of her and said, "Let me check it out." He went up the few steps to the landing outside the house and then opened the door. The sugar turned to frosting, and Maddy moved slowly as her boyfriend went inside the house fully.

The spring-loaded door slammed shut, sealing Maddy in the dark garage. She expected Ben to open it again immediately and tell her everything was okay, but he didn't. She couldn't hear any yelling or laughing beyond the door either, and she wasn't sure if she should go in or stay hidden in the garage.

She hadn't heard of much violent crime in Five Island Cove, especially out here on this furthest north island, but it was a holiday, and this less-populated part of the cove could be a good target for thieves for all she knew.

Maddy hadn't quite committed to entering the house yet when the door opened again. Her daughter stuck her head out and said, "Mom, get in here and see what I made for you."

Joy exploded through Maddy, and she said, "Chelsea," before hurrying toward her. "What are you doing here?"

Her daughter laughed as Maddy flew into her arms, and they entered the house together. She hugged her tightly in the mudroom again, and then hung her purse over a hook while Chelsea went into the kitchen, chattering about how she was glad Maddy had a few staples here at the house.

Maddy followed her, coming to a complete stop when she saw Kyle and Bea there too. They stood in front of the countertop, both of them holding a sugar cookie the size of their hands. Chelsea skipped over to them and picked one up as well. She faced Maddy, whose heartbeat had started jumping like water droplets in a screaming hot pan.

The sugar cookies weren't shaped like turkeys or pumpkin pies, the way Maddy expected them to be. Fall leaves, maybe. Something with brown frosting, or oranges and yellows.

Kyle and Bea held pure white frosted cookies that Maddy suspected were wedding bells.

Chelsea lifted a treat that was frosted in fall colors—gold. It was a diamond ring, with blue lines for the facets of the gem on top of the gold ring, which had been cut out expertly.

"What is going on?" she asked. Ben entered the kitchen from around the corner that led into the living room, and he carried a black box.

Her breath caught in her throat.

"Madeline," he said, oh-so-serious as usual. "I'm in love with you. I'm crazy about you. I want to spend my life with you." He spoke in that sexy, *I'm-in-control-here* voice he often used, almost like he wasn't nervous at all. Maddy knew the man in ways others didn't, and she watched his pulse flutter in his throat.

He was nervous, and that only made Maddy's anxiety increase.

Ben arrived in front of her and got down on both knees. He slowly opened the black velvet box in his hand to show her the ring. He looked at it, and then up to her, and Maddy beamed down at him. "Will you marry me?"

Maddy looked over to her children and back at him. "Did you ask my kids to come here just for this?"

"Yes," he said. "I needed the help, and I figured you'd like to have them here for Thanksgiving. So I asked them to come."

Tears filled her eyes. "You're amazing." She loved him, and they'd been talking about marriage and weddings and an engagement for months now. She loved having him in her life, and in her children's lives.

"Is this Maddy-code for yes?" he asked. Those gorgeous blue eyes searched hers, and Maddy decided she didn't need to torture him.

"No," she said. "That's not Maddy-code for yes." She took his face in her hands and leaned down, almost touching her lips to his. "Yes, I'll marry you. No code necessary."

He kissed her, and Maddy kissed him back while her kids cheered. So many emotions ran through her, she couldn't categorize them all. She pulled away from Ben and held out her hand so he could slide the diamond onto her finger.

She'd never thought she'd wear another wedding band. She'd never thought she could love another man as much as she loved Ben. She'd never thought her journey in life would lead her here.

Ben stood and took her into his arms. "I love you, baby."

"I love you too," she whispered just before her squealing daughter arrived. Maddy hugged her again, laughing with her. Then she gripped Kyle in her arms, tears filling her eyes the way they had when he'd come to her for help when he and Bea's wedding venue had flaked on them.

She hugged Bea last, saying, "Thank you so much for coming."

"Of course," she said, grinning. "Kyle and I love the cove."

"Where's my grandbaby?" Maddy asked, just now realizing that Knox wasn't anywhere to be seen.

"Asleep in his crib," Kyle said. "Come on, Mom. Try the cookies and tell us which ones you like best." He cast a look over to Chelsea, and Maddy sensed a competition between them. She took a bite of the wedding bell, and it was flaky and moist at the same time. There was a bit too much frosting for her liking, but she grinned at her son.

She took a bite of the diamond, and this frosting was too weak. She would never say so, and she said, "They're both amazing."

"Told you she wouldn't pick," Chelsea said. She rolled her eyes, and Maddy looked around for her fiancé.

"Where'd Ben go?" she asked.

He came into the kitchen then, another specialty market box marked with a Thanksgiving dinner, and she couldn't believe his level of detail. She wanted to kiss him again, this time without the audience, but she helped him get it unpacked and get the turkey breast into the oven to get heated.

"I'll do it," Bea said, coming to Maddy's side to take over. "Kyle, Knox is fussing. Will you go grab him for your mother?"

"Oh, this is Daddy," Chelsea said, lifting her phone as it rang. She bustled into the front of the house to take the call, and Maddy took the opportunity to grab Ben's hand and duck into her bedroom with him.

"You'll move in here permanently, right?" she asked as she closed the door behind him. He stayed with her sometimes now, but she wanted him here to live here.

"Yes," he said. He took her into his arms again and lowered his head to kiss her. It started sweet and slow, but as things tended to do with Ben, it turned heated and passionate rather quickly. She tipped her head back, and he slid his mouth along the column of her throat.

"Thank you for getting my kids here," she said breathlessly.

"I'm regretting it a little," he admitted.

She grinned at him, feeling flirtatious and far younger than she actually was. "You want me to yourself."

He growled, his eyes meeting hers. "I want you to myself," he admitted before he claimed her mouth again.

When he pulled away, Maddy looked at him, not wanting to tease him anymore. She wanted him to *know*. "I want you to myself too," she said.

"When do you want to get married?" he asked, simply holding her now.

"Spring," she said. "Right here in the cove. I'll talk to Robin about the weather, but maybe April?" She looked at him. "Did you tell your parents?"

He nodded. "Showed them the ring last week." Another rare smile came to his face. "She's going to drive you crazy at Christmastime."

Maddy groaned, but it was all in good fun. His parents were great, but his mother did like to shower Maddy in gifts, as if she needed another skin care kit. His brother worked for a huge skin care corporation, and his mother was simply regifting things.

"Mom," Kyle called, and Maddy pushed away from the door.

"Coming," she called. She looked at Ben again. "I'm so in love with you. You know that, right?" She needed him to *know*. She spoke her feelings quite often, actually. It was Ben who showed her how he felt.

"I know," he whispered. "I love you too."

She nodded and turned to go see her grandson. Then she'd call Robin and see about booking her to plan the spring wedding Maddy was going to have. She'd also need to talk to her boss, make sure she could have time off in the spring, and balance everything with The Glass Dolphin.

If Ben can get away from the Coast Guard, she told herself as she went out into the kitchen and saw her beautiful grandson. He kicked and squealed, and she laughed as she took him from her son.

Then you can make a spring wedding work with your job.

Sneak Peek! The Glass Dolphin Chapter Two:

When the doorbell rang, Kristen Shields dusted her hands against her apron and hurried out of her cramped kitchen. The only people who'd ring the doorbell were exactly the people she'd been baking for, and her pulse knocked against the back of her throat.

"Coming," she called. She very nearly tripped over the rug she'd put down between the kitchen and the doorway, but she managed to stay on her feet.

She opened the door to find Theo standing there with a man who looked very much like him.

His son.

Kristen hadn't met any of his children yet, and she wished she wasn't so nervous about doing so. Theo had made it clear his feelings for her wouldn't change based on his children's opinions, but Kristen still wanted to make a good impression.

"Terry, this is Kristen," Theo said. "Kristen, my oldest, Terry." He stepped back and indicated the woman there. "His wife, Cleo, and their kids, Marty and Violet." He beamed at his grandkids, who were both in their teens. Mid-teens, if Kristen had to guess.

"Hello," she said. "Come in, come in." She stepped back, pulling the door open further to make more room for them.

"It smells good," Terry said, and he smiled at Kristen as he entered first. "Dad said you were making cookies."

"So many cookies," Kristen said. "There's a whole bunch of them on the table. Help yourself."

The kids smiled at her politely as she entered, and once everyone was in, Theo put one hand on her hip and swept a kiss across her lips. "Did you make those snickerdoodles?"

"Yes, sir," she said, working hard not to giggle. The man loved cinnamon and sugar, and Kristen made snickerdoodles at least once a week, just for him.

Her cat, whom she'd named Sweetie, came down the hall to see what the fuss was about. Violet pulled in a breath and said, "Mom. Look at that cat."

Her mother turned and looked, and Kristen watched as she then exchanged a glance with her husband. "Is she allergic?" Kristen asked. "I can put her in her carrier in the bedroom." That wouldn't rid the apartment of cat hair, but

Kristen had vacuumed meticulously last night and then again this morning.

She wanted everything to be perfect for today. She wasn't even sure why, only that she wanted Theo's kids to like her.

"It's fine," Cleo said. "Violet thinks she needs a cat."

The girl rushed toward Sweetie, who sat down as her eyes widened. She scooped the cat into her arms, and Kristen thought they'd be best friends before anyone else arrived. "She's so cute," Violet cooed.

"She might scratch your face off," Marty said.

"Martin," Terry said. "Don't antagonize your sister. Look." He pointed to one of the plates of cookies. "Kristen made thumbprints. Come get one, and then take these oatmeal raisin ones to your grandfather."

Marty, who was clearly older than Violet, did as his father said. Kristen's chest vibrated as he then bit into one of her thumbprint cookies. She'd made the raspberry jam and the apricot jam from scratch, and pure satisfaction poured through her when Marty leaned his head back and groaned. "This is so good," he said around a mouthful of cookie and crumbs and filling.

"They look so beautiful," Cleo said. "I love the thumbprint for Christmas." She picked up a cookie too, and she smiled as she took a bite of it. "Mm." Her eyes widened, and after she swallowed—she had more manners than her son, and Kristen liked them both immensely—she said, "Kristen, these are delicious."

"Thank you," she said. "I got the recipe from a fellow lighthouse wife." She rounded the counter as the timer on the oven went off. She bent and took out the last sheet of sugar cookies. By the time everyone arrived, they should be cool enough to decorate.

Theo had seven grandchildren, and Kristen had thought planning an activity for all of them to do made the most sense. Then she could finish dinner while they did that, and as snow had come to the cove for Christmas, herding them all outside wasn't an option.

To prove her point, Mother Nature drove a gust of wind into Kristen's windows, and they shook slightly.

"Rowena is here," Theo said. He started to get up, but his son told him to stay on the couch. He went to the door before anyone knocked or rang the bell and opened it. He went outside, and it didn't take long for the cold to leak in.

Terry started to laugh, his voice as big and as boisterous as his father's. He said some things Kristen couldn't decipher, and then he entered her condo again, this time with another woman.

They definitely belonged to each other, and to Theo, and Kristen put down her oven mitts and went to greet her. "Hello," she said, smiling with everything she had once more. "I'm—"

"Kristen Shields," Theo said, appearing at her side. His

hand moved along her waist, and Kristen couldn't resist leaning into him. "This is my daughter Rowena. She's divorced, but she brought her daughter, Miley. Where is she?"

"Sulking for a moment," Rowena said with a heavy dose of eyerolling. "I swear, I don't know how anyone survives seventeen-year-olds." She gave Kristen a smile that didn't seem as warm as Terry's or Cleo's, but Kristen could've imagined it. Or, Rowena could've been dealing with her own family situation and simply not felt like smiling at her father's new girlfriend.

Kristen told herself she and Theo weren't that new. They'd been dating for six months, and honestly, she couldn't believe it herself.

"What goes around, comes around," Theo said.

"Dad." Rowena scoffed and rolled her eyes again. "I don't need a lecture." She started to shed her coat, the awkwardness and tension in the room suddenly expanding to the rafters. Kristen looked over to Theo, and he didn't seem ruffled at all.

"She'll know where to come to?" Kristen asked.

"I'll go get her," Marty said. "I'll take these mint chip cookies, and she won't be able to resist them." He smiled at Kristen, the whole plate of double-chocolate chip cookies—yes, some of them were mint—in his hand. He ducked out of the condo, and Kristen sincerely hoped he'd come back with some cookies...and his cousin.

Rowena joined Cleo on the cusp of the kitchen and surveyed that spread. "Wow," she said, genuinely sounding surprised. "You said there would be cookies, but this is a *lot* of cookies." She didn't look at Kristen at all, but her brother and sister-in-law.

Kristen had made little labels for each kind by folding a small card in half and writing the variety of cookie on it. Some of them had themed plates that went with them, and she admired her cookie bar. Robin would be thrilled, and Kristen had snapped a few pictures before anyone had arrived.

"They're amazing," Cleo said. She pushed the last bite of a cowboy cookie—coconut, oatmeal, pecans, and chocolate chips—into her mouth. She didn't try to speak around it, but when she finished, she said, "I've eaten four already." She giggled, but Rowena didn't join in.

"Dad has the oatmeal raisin," Terry said.

Kristen hadn't joined them, and looking at them from across the room, she knew she didn't fit with them yet. They'd had their whole lives to mesh, to learn about one another, to become a family. She was the outsider here, though Theo still stood at her side.

Rowena lived in Connecticut, and her divorce had been finalized in the fall. Kristen knew women like her; some of them were her own Seafaring Girls, and she knew Rowena likely needed time to heal. Having Kristen and Theo's relationship shoved in her face wasn't something she wanted.

Kristen stepped away from Theo and went around the people standing at the end of her peninsula. She started getting out the frostings she'd made and colored that morning and putting them on the dining room table. She'd already put the leaf in it, and it still wouldn't hold them all for their dinner tonight.

Theo would probably have his sons set up the folding table that currently waited in Kristen's hallway, and they'd butt it up against the table to make one big long one.

"So," Rowena said as Kristen returned to the kitchen. "Are you and Daddy going to get married?" She took a bite of her shortbread cookie, which Kristen had decorated like a wreath, and looked at Kristen fully for the first time.

Panic shot through her chest, sending barbs into her ribs and fleshy organs.

"Row," Terry admonished. "Don't."

"What?" Rowena asked. "It's a valid question."

"One Dad said not to bring up." Terry gave his sister a pointed look and then Kristen a warm smile. "Don't mind her. She's—" The rest of his words got drowned out by a hearty shout from the direction of the doorway.

Kristen looked over to it and found Theo's final child entering. Nelson carried more weight than his older brother, and he had far less hair. He'd shaved his head completely, but he wore a full beard. He laughed and practically yelled, "We're here!" as he held the door open for his four children to parade through.

Two boys and two girls entered, each of them wearing a bright red or green sweater. They were a festive bunch, and they were followed by their mother, who wore a red, white, and green plaid dress with a pair of four-inch, bright red heels.

Kristen had never met anyone like her before. Her blonde hair had been swept up into a ponytail high on her head, and she surveyed the condo like she could single-handedly transform it into a penthouse suite if given a few hours and a roll of duct tape.

"Nelson!" Terry boomed, and he went to hug his brother. Lots of greetings got exchanged, one where Nelson picked up Rowena and hugged her in a bouncing way while she loudly protested.

Kristen stood out of the way and watched Theo interact with his kids and grandkids. He glowed, as he obviously loved them all. He'd told her they hadn't gotten together like this in a few years, and he'd really been looking forward to having the holidays with his family back together again.

She swallowed as he finally looked at her. He held out his hand, and Kristen forced herself to move to stand beside him. The door opened again, and Marty and another teenage girl entered.

"Ah, Miley," he said. "Rowena's daughter. My son, Nelson, and his wife Victoria. Their kids, Raven, Fiona, Denver, and Dallas. The last two are twins." He beamed at the boys in matching red sweaters like they were the cutest things on the planet. They had good genes, and they were good-looking boys.

Kristen smiled at all of them, and said, “Welcome. Thanks for coming.” She gestured to the cookie bar behind her. “It’s great to meet you all, and I have dessert first today. We can decorate the sugar cookies when everyone’s ready too.”

All four of Victoria’s children looked at her for permission to eat a cookie, and she gave it with a quick nod of her head. They then converged on the counter, nearly knocking Kristen out of the way.

She laughed as she moved into the safer recesses of the living room, Theo at her side. The noise from the kitchen only reached its current level when she held the luncheon for her girls here at the condo. She’d only done so once, because it was easier to meet at a restaurant. Then someone else cooked and cleaned up.

“They’re great,” she said.

Theo took her hand in his. “I think so too. Even Rowena. She’ll come around.”

Words gathered in Kristen’s mouth, and she tried to order them properly before they came out. She finally landed on, “You told them not to ask about our relationship?” She looked at him, searching those brilliant navy blue eyes.

He suddenly looked nervous, and Theo never looked like that. “I didn’t want it to be awkward for you.”

"Why would it be awkward for me?"

"Because we haven't talked about it." He waved to one of the twins, who lifted a sandwich cookie Kristen had made from a boxed cake mix.

"Maybe we should," Kristen said, her voice dry and brittle.

Theo looked at her. "You want to get married?" He seemed genuinely surprised, and that sent a barb of uncertainty into Kristen's heart.

"Maybe," she hedged. "Do you?"

"To be honest," he said. "I—"

"Grandpa," Miley yelled to him. "Get over here and look at this stained glass cookie. It's amazing!"

Kristen edged away from him, the echo of his words in her ears. *To be honest. I—*

"Just a minute," he said to his granddaughter. But that only spurred her to groan and insist he come now, before Marty ate the artwork.

What came after that I? He what? He never wanted to get married again? He never thought he would? He liked things how they were?

Theo sighed amidst more insistence that he come join them at the cookie bar, and he said, "Be right back," and walked away.

Kristen stayed over by her electric fireplace, watching. Part of her mind whispered at her to *go join them. You can't be part of them if you stand over here.*

The other part really wanted to know what Theo was going to say. *Needed* to know.

Cleo met her eyes and gave her the tiniest gesture to get over there. Kristen would have to shelve her disappointment and rein in her imagination for now. Once Theo's children left, she'd ask him again. Oh, yes, she would, because she needed to know what the past six months had been, if anything, if it hadn't been building to a permanent, long-lasting relationship.

Scan this QR code to grab THE GLASS DOLPHIN from Amazon.

OR grab it from the Feel-Good Fiction Book Shop!

JESSIE NEWTON

Books in the Five Island Cove series

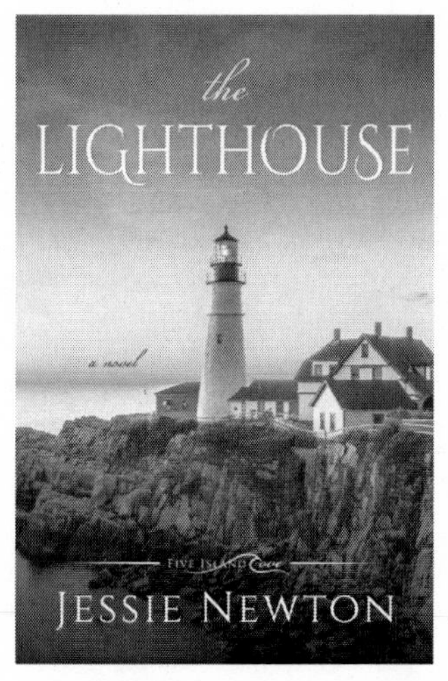

The Lighthouse, Book 1: As these 5 best friends work together to find the truth, they learn to let go of what doesn't matter and cling to what does: faith, family, and most of all, friendship.

Secrets, safety, and sisterhood...it all happens at the lighthouse on Five Island Cove.

The Summer Sand Pact, Book 2: These five best friends made a Summer Sand Pact as teens and have only kept it once or twice—until they reunite decades later and renew their agreement to meet in Five Island Cove every summer.

Books in the Five Island Cove series

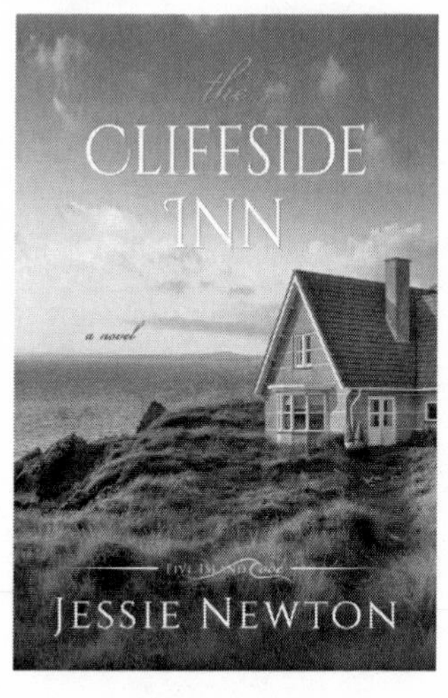

The Cliffside Inn, Book 3: Spend another month in Five Island Cove and experience an amazing adventure between five best friends, the challenges they face, the secrets threatening to come between them, and their undying support of each other.

Christmas at the Cove, Book 4: Secrets are never discovered during the holidays, right? That's what these five best friends are banking on as they gather once again to Five Island Cove for what they hope will be a Christmas to remember.

Books in the Five Island Cove series

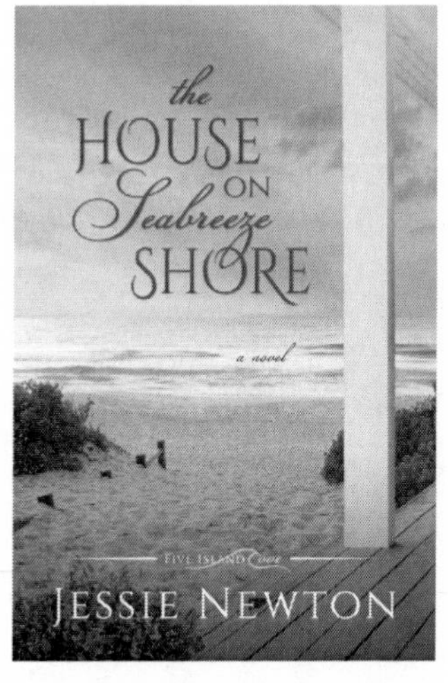

The House on Seabreeze Shore, Book 5: Your next trip to Five Island Cove...this time to face a fresh future and leave all the secrets and fears in the past. Join best friends, old and new, as they learn about themselves, strengthen their bonds of friendship, and learn what it truly means to thrive.

Four Weddings and a Baby, Book 6:

When disaster strikes, whose wedding will be postponed? Whose dreams will be underwater?

And there's a baby coming too... Best friends, old and new, must learn to work together to clean up after a natural disaster that leaves bouquets and altars, bassinets and baby blankets, in a soggy heap.

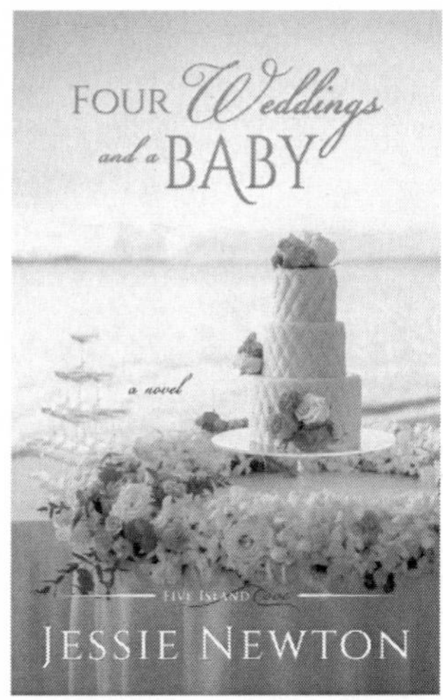

Books in the Five Island Cove series

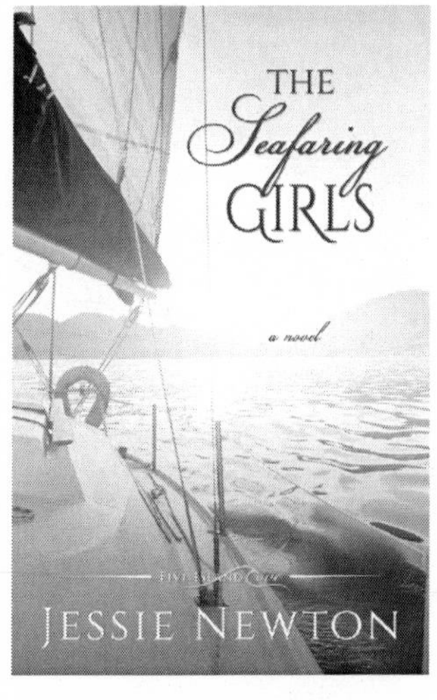

The Seafaring Girls, Book 7: Journey to Five Island Cove for a roaring good time with friends old and new, their sons and daughters, and all their new husbands as they navigate the heartaches and celebrations of life and love.

But when someone returns to the Cove that no one ever expected to see again, old wounds open just as they'd started to heal. This group of women will be tested again, both on land and at sea, just as they once were as teens.

Rebuilding Friendship Inn, Book 8: Clara Tanner has lost it all. Her husband is accused in one of the biggest heists on the East Coast, and she relocates her family to Five Island Cove–the hometown she hates.

Clara needs all of their help and support in order to rebuild Friendship Inn, and as all the women pitch in, there's so much more getting fixed up, put in place, and restored.

Then a single phone call changes everything.

Will these women in Five Island Cove rally around one

another as they've been doing? Or will this finally be the thing that breaks them?

Books in the Five Island Cove series

The Glass Dolphin, Book 9: With new friends in Five Island Cove, has the group grown too big? Is there room for all the different personalities, their problems, and their expanding population?

The Bicycle Book Club, Book 10: Summer is upon Five Island Cove, and that means beach days with friends and family, an explosion of tourism, and summer reading programs! When Tessa decides to look into the past to help shape the future, what she finds in the Five Island Cove library archives could bring them closer together…or splinter them forever.

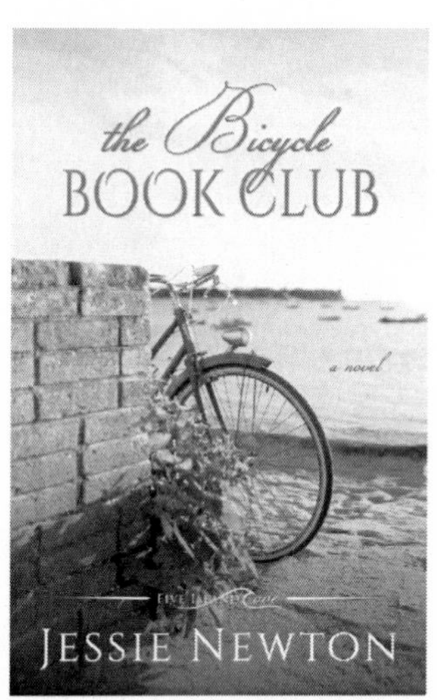

About Jessie

Jessie Newton is a saleswoman during the day and escapes into romance and women's fiction in the evening, usually with a cat and a cup of tea nearby. She is a Top 30 KU All-Star Author and a USA Today Bestselling Author. She also writes as Elana Johnson and Liz Isaacson as well, with over 200 books to all of her names. Find out more at www.feelgoodfictionbooks.com.

Made in United States
North Haven, CT
25 July 2024